CHAPTER ONE

1940

On a chilly autumn Sunday, Rosie, in a world of her own, gazed at the glowing coals in the tiny Victorian fireplace, isolated from the warm chit-chat between her brother and mother sitting at the small square table playing cards. At the age of five, she had already learned not to try to be part of a scene she had not readily been drawn into.

'I'm not tarring you with the same brush, Tommy,' reasoned Iris, studying her cards, 'but others will, if they haven't already.'

'Let 'em think what they like. We know different.'

'*You* don't have to go to the baths! Cows. Steam or not, I see their smirky sideways glances. Not that they don't want me to know who they're whispering about.'

'Why don't you say something then? Tell 'em I wasn't there.' Tommy raised his eyes and looked into Iris's hardened face. 'You're saving queens, you crafty cow.' He looked from her to Rosie, curled in the fireside chair. It was true she was plain but she could dance like Shirley Temple. She spent enough time in her bedroom practising.

'What d'yer reckon, Sis? You think Mum's got a good 'and?'

She glanced up at Iris and shrugged. 'Dunno.'

'One-word Rosie.' Iris raised an eyebrow. 'You'd think she'd 'ave a grain of intelligence to compensate for that long face.'

1

'She's all right. Turn into a swan, won't yer?'

Sliding her fingers across her face to hide her flushing cheeks, Rosie swallowed, pressed her lips together and turned back to the fire.

'Come on then, Tom boy,' said Iris, 'lay the queen you don't want and see if you're as smart as you think.'

'If I'm wrong, Ro . . . I'll be a tanner lighter. If I'm right, I'll treat us both to a toffee apple.' The fourteen-year-old looked at the clock on the mantelshelf. 'Bandy Candy'll be around in five minutes. Get your coat on. You can come with me, get some fresh air.'

'What if she *is* saving queens?' murmured Rosie, peering at the tiny gap between the floorboards and the edge of the lino from where she thought she could hear the sound of scratching. If her mouse were to appear while her mother was in the room, she had no reason to believe that it would not be killed with the poker. Discreetly pushing her foot across the fender, she scraped the floor with the heel of her boot to warn the pet she had tamed with breadcrumbs not to come out.

'*She*,' said Iris, emphasizing the word, 'will put the sixpence towards coal for the copper to soak your sheets and blankets.' Shaking her head slowly she sighed. 'Wet the bed again last night. Lazy bitch.'

'Ah, don't call 'er that, Mum. She can't help it.'

'I wouldn't bet on it. You gonna lay a card or what?'

'All in good time, Mother . . . all in good time.' Tommy winked, attempting to lighten her mood and take the attention off his sister. Slowly turning a card between two fingers, he placed it on the

2

KEEP ON DANCING

Rosie Curtis is devastated when her brother Tommy is viciously murdered after dabbling in the criminal underworld. Not only is her carefree existence suddenly over but, without Tommy's support, her dreams of becoming a dancer are shattered. Powerless to avenge her brother's death, Rosie throws herself into saving a local music hall from closure and planning a musical spectacular, despite the misgivings of her family. But when Rosie comes face to face with her brother's slayer, she realises she must stop at nothing to see the criminals punished. While she fights to stage her show and put Tommy's killers away for good, her brother's smiling face appears in her thoughts, telling her to keep on dancing . . . can she find the strength without him?

KEEP ON DANCING

Sally Worboyes

CHIVERS PRESS
BATH

First published 1997
by
Headline Book Publishing
This Large Print edition published by
Chivers Press
by arrangement with
Headline Book Publishing
1999

ISBN 0 7540 1272 7

Copyright © 1997 Sally Worboyes

The right of Sally Worboyes to be identified as the
Author of the Work has been asserted by her in
accordance with the Copyright, Designs and
Patents Act 1988.

British Library Cataloguing in Publication Data available

Printed and bound in Great Britain by
REDWOOD BOOKS, Trowbridge, Wiltshire

table and chuckled. It was the king of hearts.

'Thank you very much. Just the job.' Iris grinned broadly, lifted the worn playing card off the green cloth and laid down her hand—three kings and a run.

The laughter and teasing banter continued, interspersed with innuendoes that if Tommy was involved with the gang who had been stealing lead from rooftops, it would be more than a silver sixpence he stood to lose.

Pouring herself and her son a cup of freshly brewed tea, Iris pulled his leg about his card-playing. Sometimes they would laugh loudly and sometimes speak in low voices, when they talked about Tommy's lesser petty thieving to which his mother did turn a blind eye.

Reminding each other with gestures that 'little ears' were listening, they began to deal another hand and all talk of Tommy's misdemeanours were dropped.

It made no difference to Rosie. She wasn't listening. Her mind was somewhere else—with the mice under the floorboards, where it was warm and a glow from the fire could be seen between the cracks.

Iris had rejected Rosie at birth and if it hadn't been for Granny Harriet, she would have been put up for adoption. There had been a furious row at the time when the subject was broached, and Iris had reluctantly given in and kept the scrap of a baby she did not want.

Five years on and still she blamed Rosie for her husband leaving her. She had not carried well that second time, and Bill had been deprived of sex during the first few months of her pregnancy. The

3

child, with her light blue eyes and curly brown hair, was a constant reminder of the selfish bastard who ran off when Iris was six months pregnant.

*   *   *

Staring at the back of Rosie's head at her long, unkempt hair, she chided herself for not going for a backstreet abortion when she had missed that second period.

Rosie felt her mother's eyes on her, and turned and offered a cautious smile, but Iris's stony expression warned her to leave the room, to get out of her sight, to go into her bedroom and count the flowers on the wallpaper. It was something she had been told to do many times before. Since she could only count up to ten, she had marked in pencil twenty sections of ten flowers.

'And keep off the banisters! I don't wanna hear you falling down the staircase!'

Turning slowly the child said, 'In case I hurt meself?'

'No ... I'd be the one to have to mop up the blood.' This time Iris did not look at her, in case pangs of guilt spoiled her comfortable mood. She heard a sigh from Tommy but ignored it.

With tears welling behind her eyes, Rosie slid her back against the passage wall and sidestepped towards the staircase, repeating to herself over and over *I must not cry. I will not cry.* She knew only too well that if she did howl, as she wanted to, a good sharp smack on the buttocks would follow—a punishment for being a cry-baby. With her foot on the first stair, Rosie slipped into one of her make-believe worlds, far away in a country house, where

4

she was a wanted child and loved by everyone.

Sitting on the stairs, halfway up, she was smiling, a glazed look in her eyes as she imagined herself wearing fine clothes instead of oddments from the rag man which were always washed and pressed before anyone else had a chance to see them. Running her finger up the long grey boy's sock on her thin leg, she pushed her finger into a moth-hole and twirled it.

Using the excuse of getting some coppers from his jacket pocket, Tommy arrived to check that his sister was OK. 'What you sitting on the stairs for, Ro? You'll catch a cold from the draught.'

'I'm all right.'

The sudden warning sound of the air-raid siren caused each of them to freeze until Tommy grabbed their coats off the hooks on the passage wall and then scooped up his frightened sister. Running with her through the passage and out on to the streets of Wapping, Rosie could feel her body jerk with every thudding stride he took.

Looking over Tommy's shoulder, she could see her mother in the turmoil as families rushed out of their homes. She was yelling up at Granny Harriet, who was at the window of her flat in Riverside Mansions, telling her to move herself, and Gran was advising her daughter to calm down and take her time.

Squeezing her eyes tightly shut, Rosie tried to blank out the scene of panic. 'Please God don't let Mummy fall over and please don't let the Germans bomb Riverside Mansions because of Grandad and Granny Harriet and please don't let mouse be frightened and keep him safe till I get back.'

'All right, Rosie?' Tommy shouted above the

sounds of the siren, the shouting and the running feet, as the inhabitants of Garnet Street made their way towards the railway arches and air-raid shelters.

'I'm OK, Tommy! Put me down if I'm too heavy for yer!'

'No chance!' he yelled, trying to keep the fear out of his voice. After all was said and done, her brother was only fourteen and not exactly Mr Universe. 'Love the searchlights, blossom!' he yelled.

'I love 'em Tommy! I love 'em!' Close to tears, Rosie gripped his shoulders tighter and buried her face in his neck and quietly cried, 'Nearly there now, eh, Tom? Not far now, is it?'

'That's right darlin',' he said, breathless, 'soon be safe.'

1958

Rosie's bedroom had always been her favourite place and now, with the flowery wallpaper replaced by the modern black, red and grey wheel tracks, she spent most of her spare time in there, when she wasn't out with her friends at the dance halls or picture palaces. With her cupboard door open and serving as a jiving partner, her long wavy hair bouncing, she danced to her new and prized record, Eddie Cochran's 'Sittin' In The Balcony'.

'Mum wants you to turn the record down ...' Tommy stood in the doorway grinning, 'but Gran wants you to turn it up. To use her exact words, "She knows that's one of me favourites—and she knows I'm bleedin'-well going deaf!"'

Chuckling, Rosie practised her new dance steps.

6

'She's 'aving a go at Mum. Stirring it up. Well I'm not gonna be in the middle this time. Tell Gran to come up.'

'You and Shirley Martin goin' to the Lyceum tonight?'

'She's too young for you Tommy—I keep tellin' yer.' The record finished, she switched off her record player and pushed her left foot forward. 'Like me red shoes then?'

'She fancies me, you know.' Tommy smoothed his immaculate Slim Jim tie, fastened one of the three buttons on his single-breasted bum-freezer jacket and waited for a compliment. This was the first time he'd worn his latest made-to-measure Italian suit.

'Real patent these are. All I need now is me brother to treat me to a dress I've got me eye on . . .'

'Get me a date with Shirley and I'll think about it.' He checked his freshly manicured nails.

'Treat me to the frock and I'll think about it.'

Quietly laughing at her cheek, Tommy went downstairs. It warmed his heart to see his sister looking so happy. She was a good-looking kid with a lovely smile. There was a time when he had wished she would laugh—now she hardly ever looked glum. He couldn't remember exactly when she had perked up. When he had asked what had put the roses in her cheeks she had grinned and said, 'I don't care any more, Tommy. I don't care, 'cos I'm gonna be a dancer.'

That was when Rosie was nine years old and now, at twenty-two, she still had her heart set on the stage. Making boxes at the local factory was fine for now, with overtime she earned enough to

7

keep up with the rest of her pals when it came to buying clothes and socializing.

The love she had for her mother, Iris, had dried up somewhere along the way and with it had gone the pain. Once she had stopped looking for a motherly hug or a show of affection, her life took a turn for the better. Spending more time outside of the terraced Victorian house, she found that neighbours, strangers even, looked at her and spoke to her as if she were a person and not something the cat had dragged in. The secret hidings had stopped too—the dragging from one room to another by the hair when Iris was in one of her spiteful moods became a thing of the past. So long as she kept out of her mother's way there was peace.

Rosie was heartbroken when her grandfather Arthur had died but happy when she heard that Granny Harriet was to move in with them. She loved her gran and was pleased when her mother had said, in a derogatory fashion, that Rosie was a chip off the old block. She had seen a faded photograph, taken when Harriet was eleven years old, and the resemblance between them was uncanny. The only difference was the colour of their hair. Granny Harriet, according to what Rosie had been told, had had as a child masses of ginger hair, whereas her own was honey-brown.

All things considered, Rosie had come through with flying colours. Those first ten years had almost faded from her mind and now, enjoying life to the full, she had no time for misery.

'You should see the way Shirley looks at me, Ro.' Tommy was back in the doorway, his hair combed to form a perfect quiff and smelling of Brylcreem.

8

'You should see the way some of your mates look at me.' She pushed her face closer to the mirror of her dressing table and brushed on blue eyeshadow with the tip of a finger. 'That's surprised you, innit?'

'Don't even think about it.' His tone grave, his expression serious, he waved a finger at her. 'They're not your kind.'

''Ow do you know?' I might like villains.'

Inhaling slowly, he pursed his lips and shook his head. 'Don't take liberties, Rosie. And keep your mouth shut when you're out there. Unless you want to see me locked up again.'

'Oh, you think I'd tell everyone what you do?' She tossed her unruly hair back and shrugged. 'They think you're a bank manager as it 'appens; just, 'cos I said you was in banking.' She grinned at him and stopped herself giggling, something that Tommy hated. 'You gonna treat me to a new dress to go with these shoes or not?'

'Here.' He threw two five-pound notes at her. 'If that's not enough, too bad.' He pointed a finger again. 'You'll end up a spoiled brat if I'm not careful.'

'Tommy. I'm twenty-two for—!'

'You swear and I'll 'ave them notes back, and I mean it. You've been effing and blinding too much. It's not funny and it's not very feminine.'

'Gran says fuck every other word. I 'aven't noticed you have a go at her. I learned it all from Gran.'

'That's different. We 'ave to respect old Harriet, for all her coarse ways. But that's not to say you 'ave to follow suit. I hear you swear again and you won't get another penny out of me.'

Leaning forward, sporting an expression of indifference, she kissed him on the cheek. 'It don't worry me if I swear or not.'

'Good. Don't forget to put a word in with Shirley.' He smiled, winked at his sister and swaggered out in his new Maxie Cohen suit to do a bit of business.

Smiling to herself, Rosie couldn't wait to tell Shirley what Tommy had said—she had been stuck on him since she was fourteen and this was the first time he had shown any sign of interest. She looked at the five-pound notes in her hand and clenched her fingers around them. Now she could buy that dress! That shocking pink, boat-necked dream. With its full-circle skirt, tiny waist and matching belt, it was perfect. She imagined herself jiving under the revolving mirrored globe at the Lyceum, shining lights reflecting like stars on her dress as she danced with one of her boyfriends, spinning her around the dance floor.

'Who told you to turn that off? His bloody lordship I s'pose!' The arrival of her gran interrupted her dream. 'Too bleeding scared to say boo to the old goose. Well sod 'er! Turn it back on and turn it up. I'll be six foot under soon. A bit of my own way before I peg out's not much to ask. Where'd you get that from?' Harriet peered at the notes in her granddaughter's hand.

'Tommy treated me.'

'Pity he don't bung his old gran a few bob.' She sniffed and eased her small frame into the yellow-painted bedroom chair. 'What have you got on your bloody feet?'

'Winkle-pickers.' Rosie tap-danced her way over to the record player. 'Before you say it, *no*—I'm

10

not gonna take 'em back!'

'Be a waste of time. What was it, a clearance sale? Saw you coming!' She slowly shook her head and chuckled. 'What shopkeeper in 'is right mind would take them things back?'

'Get up Gran.'

'What for? I've only just sat down!'

'I wanna try out my new dance steps.'

'Well you can want on. Use the door 'andle.'

Harriet locked her hands, sat forward and waited. 'Well, go on then, get on with it! I need a laugh. Crumpet-face'll be goin' out soon. I'll miss 'er.'

'She'll 'ave you put away if you keep on tormenting; and I won't come and visit yer! It'll serve you right. I wouldn't 'ave you living with me. I'd put you on a train and send you to bloody Land's End, to an old people's 'ome. Far away as possible. A one-way ticket.'

'You changed your knickers today?' Harriet pursed her lips and narrowed her eyes.

With her hands on her hips, Rosie glowered at the mischievous eighty-year-old. 'If you dare say that in front of any of my mates again . . .'

'Yeah . . . go on. What will you do?' Harriet slapped her knee and laughed. 'Should 'ave seen your face that one time when I did say it! It was a picture!'

'You know I change 'em every day—'

'Be in trouble if you didn't, my girl. Now turn on that gramophone and bring a bit of life into this place. Let me reap *some* reward for them dancing lessons I paid out for when you was at school.'

'Record player! And don't take the mickey. I want your opinion, not your sarcasm.'

11

'Oh, switch the blooming thing on! Sarcasm? I don't know what you're talking about half the time. Opinion. Sarcasm. Must 'ave dipped a page of the dictionary in your tea instead of a biscuit.'

Placing the pick-up at the beginning of the track, Rosie smiled inwardly. She couldn't imagine life without Harriet. Her long wiry hair was still thick and had a will of its own, sprouting out beneath the numerous tortoiseshell combs she used in an attempt to make it behave. Even when she pulled it up into a bun, long wavy strands escaped and gave her the appearance of someone who'd been dragged through a hedge backwards.

Today, though, Harriet had chosen to let her wild hair do as it would be done by. She hadn't brushed it, nor used grips or combs, because today Harriet was in one of those moods, as her daughter Iris would put it. Life on Saturdays could be very boring and today was no exception. Iris had decided to boil everything white in sight. She was in a bleach mood. The scullery, the cupboard doors, the window sills—all would be washed down with boiling water and soda. Then, no doubt, she would start on the floors. When this industrious mood was on, Harriet was expected to sit, as if paralysed, in her chair by the fire in the living room, while Iris scrubbed everything around her.

'Your mother's in the backyard showing off her whites on the clothes line ... your brother's gone parading down the Waste, showing off his new suit—'

'Well let's hope he stops by Paul's record stall then, eh?'

'No one gives a fuck about me. I might as well be dead.' Harriet gazed at the window. 'What a lovely treat it would be if one of you took me to Joe Lyon's for tea. Still—there you are; I don't s'pose it's the fashion to be seen with an old woman like me.'

'Too bleeding right.'

'Cruel, that's what you young are, wicked and cruel. My Arthur'd turn in his—'

'Grave!'

'And so he would.'

'Gran . . . how many times 'ave we asked you if you wanna go for a walk down Whitechapel? Go on, how many? See? You couldn't count the times.'

The loud urgent banging on the front door stopped them dead. 'Who the 'ell's that? Bloody cheek! What d'they think this is, a knockin' shop?' Rosie stormed out of her bedroom and went downstairs ready for a battle of words. The door knocker went again. Three loud bangs. 'All right! Give us a sodding chance!'

'*Rosie!*' Iris's urgent voice stopped her in her tracks. Her tone was full of concern. 'Don't answer it.'

Turning to face her mother, Rosie saw something in her eyes which she had not seen in a very long time: a look of concern, not just for herself, not just for her darling son, but for all of them. 'Don't open it.'

'Why not?'

She looked from her daughter to the front door and back to Rosie again. 'It might not be one of us.'

Nodding slowly, Rosie indicated that she would listen at the street door. As she crept along the passage the knocker resounded again, causing her to cower back.

'*Open the door!*' It was Tommy, his voice

strangled with pain.

Rosie was there in a flash, pulling at the brass catch, pulling at the door which so often jammed. When it came open, Tommy fell, bleeding, into the passageway. 'The Maltese . . . close the—'

Slamming the door shut, she fell to her knees at Tommy's side and stared blankly at his blood-soaked clothes. Shocked by what she saw, she could not believe that a rival gang of immigrants from Malta had actually knifed her brother. She knew about gang violence, of course she did, in that part of London it was not so unusual. But her brother? Her Tommy?

'Get Mum,' was all he could manage to say.

Kneeling beside him, Iris cupped his head in her hands and looked into his ghostly face. 'I'm here, Tommy. What happened?'

'In the back, Mum. They got me in the back. Three times.' His glazed eyes looked as if they were sinking into dark wells. 'Short blades. They used short blades.'

'Well that's all right then, love . . . no damage to your heart or lungs, eh? That's good, you know it is.' She put out her trembling hand and touched the side of his head. 'You'll be all right.'

As Rosie watched Iris slip one arm under Tommy's shoulder, she winced for him. Short-bladed knives were not murder weapons, so her brother would live, but she had heard why they were used; the blades would have been twisted once in the flesh, to cause as much damage as possible—damage and pain.

Leaning against the passage wall, she looked across at the fading floral wallpaper, aware of the fear which engulfed that small space. Gang fights

14

were one thing, but gang attacks singling out one victim was something else. Her brother was in trouble and as likely as not the boys, as he called them, would disappear into the alleyways of Wapping until the dispute had been sorted. Her brother was not a prominent figure in the underworld; he was one of many pawns, but, unlike the others, Tommy was ambitious and daring. He had talked of soon becoming a Knight. When Rosie asked what he meant he had just winked and smiled, saying, 'It's all a game of chess, babe. A silly war game.'

'Shall I send Rosie to fetch someone?' murmured Iris.

'No!' Tommy winced with pain as he turned to his sister. 'Don't go out there.' The serious tone of his voice and look of concern caused Rosie to shudder.

Arriving, Harriet shook her head and sighed. 'A lot of good leaving 'im on the floor'll do. Fetch him in the living room before he bleeds to death.'

'Gimme a minute, Gran.' Tommy cast a glance at Harriet and rested his head against his mother's arm.

'Did they chase you after or before they put the knife in?' Harriet demanded.

'They didn't chase me. They jumped me. George Rider was about, he tried to 'elp me out . . .'

'And?'

'They slashed 'is face. Then some other people stopped to see what was goin' on. The Maltese legged it.'

'You'd best come away from that door then. I shouldn't think they were far behind.'

'Talk sense, Gran!' snapped Rosie. 'They're not

15

gonna come after 'im again!'

Bringing his arm up and showing the flat of his hand, Tommy motioned for them to be quiet and then pointed to the door. Not daring to move a muscle, the four of them listened to the shuffling outside and low murmur of voices. Men's voices. Foreign accents.

'Lock yourselves in the bedroom,' whispered Tommy.

'Can you walk?'

'Forget about me, Mum . . .' gritting his teeth, he pushed his mother away. 'I'm all right where I am. Just go!'

'You're coming with us! Now get up!' Harriet punched Rosie's arm. 'Move yourself!'

With the help of Iris and Rosie, Tommy eased himself up on to his feet and struggled against the pain. As they stepped into the sitting room, once again the loud, chilling sound of the door knocker echoed through the house. Harriet, her anger rising, told them to barricade themselves in.

Once she could hear the sound of furniture being scraped across the floor as they pushed it against the door, she stretched to her full height, ready for battle. Rolling up her sleeves, she drew her sharp cutting scissors from her apron pocket.

Taking a deep breath she counted to three, opened the street door and stepped outside, shutting it behind her. Glaring into the face of the tallest, broadest Maltese, who wasn't that much taller than herself, she pushed the pointed scissors close to his face and opened them.

'Get back to Commercial Road before I scream fucking blue murder!'

Startled by the unexpected, the three men,

16

dressed immaculately in mohair suits and heavy gold jewellery, eyed the scissors, speechless.

'Crazy!' The smallest of the three slapped the side of his head and glared at his cronies. 'You gonna just stand there? Let this old bag wave scissors in your face?'

'That's all right, Mrs Dean!' Harriet shouted to one of the passers-by who, like others milling around, had half an eye on what was going on. It was rare to see Maltese flash boys in that part of Wapping. 'They've knocked on the wrong door! They're leaving!'

'Come on. We've finished our business.' The tallest member turned smartly away and strode along the street, ignoring the suspicious looks and asides from the Wapping people out to do their Saturday shopping and betting on the races. Protesting in their own language, the other two followed, cursing Harriet in English.

Once the men had turned the corner of the narrow street, she took her door key from her pocket and let herself in. Trembling, she made her way to the staircase and sat down. 'They've gone! Come out and make me a cup of tea for fuck's sake!'

When the door opened and Rosie's petrified face appeared, she smiled for the sake of her granddaughter. 'They won't be back. Tommy OK?'

'He should go to hospital, Gran.'

'I don't doubt it.' She pulled herself up and went in to take a look at her grandson. 'Is it just the flesh wounds, or more?'

'*Just* the flesh wounds? Jesus!' He rolled his eyes to heaven and winced with pain.

Perching herself on the edge of the settee where

he was lying face down, Harriet examined the grotesque wounds.

'Well I'm not gonna stand here and watch 'im bleed to death!' snapped Rosie. 'I'm going for the doctor. Like it or lump it!'

'Go and get the green jar of liniment from the medicine cupboard in my room!' Harriet's voice was grave, and her expression as she looked up said it all. There was no room for tantrums or rows. 'Call in a doctor and the law won't be far behind. Go and get the ointment.'

Rosie looked from her gran to Iris for a reaction. 'Do as Gran says . . .'

'Don't you use that horse's ointment on me!' Tommy pulled back, a terrified look on his face.

'If it was good enough for your grandfather, it's good enough for you. Lie back down.'

Returning with clean lint and the jar of ointment, Rosie stroked Tommy's hair as he buried his face in the cushion and dug his fingers into the sofa.

'Well don't just stand there, the pair of you! Go and put the kettle on and fetch a drop of brandy from my room.'

Smearing the pieces of pristine white lint with thick brown ointment, Harriet pressed them on to the gaping wounds. 'If you kept your nose clean you wouldn't get into fights, would yer? Silly bastard. Maltese gangs, Italians, Irish . . . you want your brains examined!' She ripped paper off a bandage. 'Ease your chest up so I can pass this under.'

'Gimme a minute, for God's sake. Where's Rosie with that brandy?'

Pausing, Harriet shook her head. 'This is gonna

18

have to stop, Tommy. You must 'ave crossed the line.'

'Don't talk silly. Me and Freddy Vale offered to look after a little snooker club in Aldgate, that's all. 'Ow was we to know the Maltese were covering it?'

'Don't give me all that! If you're that green they wouldn't 'ave come after you. If you've bin involved in their business, Tommy . . .' She paused, looking him straight in the eye. 'Commercial Street?'

'Oh, leave off Gran . . . I am in pain y'know.'

'You must be getting your cash from somewhere. There's nothing 'appening down the docks, that I do know.'

'I do all right. Thieving's my game, not whores.'

'You're lying. I can read you like a book.'

His eyes wide, bulging as if to burst, his face red, he opened his mouth ready to bully her with his loud voice.

'Don't you dare! Don't you dare use that old ploy on me, you little fucker! You've bin poncing off whores!'

'Looking after 'em!' he bellowed back. 'Managing 'em! There's a difference! Where d'yer think the money's come from to look after you three!'

Rosie's arrival stopped the dispute in an instant. 'Don't look so worried; he'll be all right. Been taught a lesson, that's all. I 'ope he learns from it.' Harriet took the glass from her and drank some before placing it between his lips. 'Just 'ope you don't get an infection, that's all. I can fix your wounds; I can give you something for the pain; but penicillin 'as to come from the doctor, and we both know you can't go down that route. The Old Bill love it when something like this 'appens.

'God help the poor bastards who won't talk to 'em—and let Him 'ave mercy on those that do.'

'Go away, Gran. Give me five minutes' peace, for Christ's sake.'

Standing by the door, the tea tray shaking in her hand, Iris opened her mouth to say something but all that escaped was a garbled sound as the trembling worsened and everything on the tray shook.

'They're . . . in . . . the . . . back . . . yard. I told you . . . to fix that bolt . . . Tommy. I said . . . that . . . one day—' The crashing sound of the back door being kicked in stopped her. The room became silent as each one of them listened, too terrified to breathe as they heard rapid footsteps in the passage. The door to the living room flew open.

'You! You! And you! Upstairs!' One of the gang pressed the point of his knife against Rosie's stomach. 'Move.'

'Do as he says, Rosie. And you Mum, Gran.' Tommy eased himself up and spoke to one of the men. 'Don't you hurt them.'

Throwing Tommy a look of contempt, the Maltese pushed Iris out of the door and then Harriet. With a long-bladed knife poised menacingly he gripped Rosie by the arm and yanked her out of the room. Pulling away, she kicked his shin and went back into the sitting room. 'Haven't you done enough, you bastards! Leave him be!'

'Rosie!' Swinging his legs off the settee, Tommy looked into his sister's face and closed his eyes tight. 'Go upstairs, darling.'

'What they gonna do, Tommy? Why did they come back?' She took a step towards her brother,

20

only to be hauled back by one of the men. Struggling as he dragged her to the doorway kicking and punching, she shouted at them not to hurt him any more.

'Come on, slut . . . you'll still get work. You can come and whore for us instead of your brother.' He showed her his tongue and smiled before slamming the door in her face.

*　　　*　　　*

'So what was you doing in Commercial Road, then?'

Tommy looked up at the three men and shrugged. 'I was taking my girlfriend for a drink.'

'But you was seen taking money off her.'

'I was skint. She was 'elping me out.'

'She's a whore and you were in our territory. Who you working with?'

'No . . . you've got it wrong. I'm not a pimp. I thieve . . . a bit 'ere, a bit there. I've 'ad a bit of bad luck lately . . . that's why my girlfriend—'

'Bollocks. You were working Commercial Street. You've been seen before. Who're you with? Names!'

'Nar . . . not me. I'm telling you . . . you've got the wrong bloke.'

A flick knife was produced. 'How many whores 'ave you got?'

'Look . . .' Tommy could see there was no point in denying why he was in Commercial Street. He would try another tactic. Plead ignorance,

'She was just a tart. From the North. I felt sorry for 'er. She's got a kid to keep. Ain't got a clue about the East End. I showed 'er where to go.

21

What do I know about that side of things?'

'Too much for your own good.' The smiling one showed his pearly-white teeth.

By the time the door burst open and the gang pushed past the women, they were shaking and crying, holding on to each other and praying that talking was all the Maltese had in mind.

The last of the departing trio turned and poked Iris in the chest, pushing his face up close to hers. 'We were never here. He arrived back like that.' He gave Rosie a little slap on the face and winked, 'Come and whore for us.'

Once the last of them had gone, the women stared at the doorway to the living room and then at each other. It was too quiet, too still. 'Wait here—both of you.' Iris walked slowly into the room and across to where Tommy was slumped, half on, half off the settee, blood pouring from the fresh stab wound.

A mournful cry from Iris broke the silence and then her screams of shock and grief filled the house. Lowering herself on to the staircase, Rosie sat next to her gran. Neither said a word as they stared blankly at nothing, too stunned to react.

Appearing in the doorway, her face expressionless, her eyes dead, Iris looked at Rosie as if she were expecting something. Waiting for someone to tell her it hadn't happened. That the past fifteen minutes had not really been. That her son was at that moment strolling along the Waste in his new suit. 'They've killed my Tommy,' she murmured; 'my Tommy's not breathing any more.'

Again the sound of knocking at the door cut through the silence. 'I'll go,' whispered Rosie, strangely composed. 'Shut the living-room door.'

Allowing a few seconds to pass, she stood up and walked slowly along the passage, with no idea of who it might be this time. Certain that the cowardly bastards would not show their faces again, she unlocked the door.

'All right, Rosie?' Tommy's friend Reggie towered above her as he stood with three others on the doorstep. 'We 'eard that Tommy had a bit of bother; just wanted to make sure he's all right.'

Pulling the door open wide, Rosie lowered her head and waited as the men filed in. Then she shut the door and, leaning against it, gazed watery-eyed into their stony faces. 'They came 'ere, Reggie.' She swallowed and wiped her tears with the back of her hand. 'Tommy's dead.'

'Fuck me ...' murmured Reggie, gritting his teeth, and then quickly resumed his cool, controlled godfather-like image. It was obvious that the four of them were gutted. Gutted and angry. 'Where is he?' Reggie asked, his emotions only just contained.

'In there.'

As the men looked at each other, too shocked to speak, Rosie took Reggie aside. 'They said I was a whore. Then they went in and murdered Tommy. Gran says I can't go to the police. My Tommy's dead and ...' She broke down and covered her face, with her hands, sobbing. 'My Tommy ... what am I gonna do without him, Reggie?' Her chest heaved as she tried to stop crying. She splayed her hands. 'This house ... without my brother ... ?'

'All right, babe ... all right ...' Reggie pinched his lips together. 'We'll get 'em, don't you worry about that. We'll have the bastards.' He squeezed her arm and managed a weak smile. 'You know what Tommy would 'ave said, don't yer . . . keep on dancing.'

Nodding slowly, Rosie leaned against the passage wall and closed her eyes while the men showed their respect to Iris and Harriet. White-faced and obviously in shock, Harriet tugged his sleeve, took him aside and whispered in his ear.

'If it gets out that he was working the street girls—'

'Don't be silly, Harriet . . .' Reggie frowned. 'We're not into all that.'

'Reggie . . .' She raised an eyebrow and shrugged. 'Tommy, not you. That's why they came for 'im. I don't want Rosie to find out—ever.'

'All right. I'll see to it.' He inhaled slowly, hitched back his shoulders and went into the living room, telling her not to worry.

CHAPTER TWO

The day of the funeral started early for Rosie. She woke at first light and watched the dawn through the window as she lay in her bed listening to the early morning street noises. Wondering if she would ever get over her loss, she reached for the small framed snapshot taken when she, Tommy, Harriet and Iris had gone to Southend for the day. She trailed her finger across the group photograph and stopped at her mother's face, scratching at the surface, telling herself that if Iris hadn't been giving the living room that unnecessary going-over on the day Tommy had been murdered, maybe he wouldn't have gone out; maybe Rosie wouldn't

24

have been in her room practising her dance steps but downstairs with her brother and gran, watching the racing, cheering on their fancied bets.

She looked from Tommy's smiling face to her own and wondered if she would ever laugh again. She couldn't imagine it. Tommy's mates had done their best to lighten things during their numerous visits, telling stories of the hilarious situations that they and Tommy had found themselves in when a job had gone wrong. Harriet had done her bit— telling the men what a little rascal he was when he was knee-high to a grasshopper.

Checking her bedside clock, Rosie counted the hours of sleep she had managed to get that night. It had just gone five o'clock. Four hours. Four hours of nightmares. The forever recurring dream had slipped in somewhere between the others ... her brother alone in an empty room, on the top floor of a block of flats which had no staircase; the same puzzled expression on his face as he looked down at her. His eyes always asking the same question— *Why won't you come up, Ro? Where is everyone?* In her dreams she had screamed at the top of her voice but all he did was to stare down at her, pale-faced and looking older than his years, his hair thin and greying instead of thick and dark brown.

'No stairs Tommy,' she sighed, 'and no lifts ... no way up or down.' Pressing both hands into her face, she stopped herself from crying. Today she would be strong. Today she would laugh at the jokes, for Tommy's sake. For all she knew her gran could be right and his spirit might still be around. He wouldn't want to see her looking downcast. Harriet had insisted that she had smelled his Brylcreem in the air and sensed his presence. She

25

had said that it would be only natural for Tommy to want to be there, seeing all his mates coming and going. As far as Harriet was concerned, her grandson would not miss his own funeral—not in a million years. Let the devil try to stop him! Those had been her words, and she had meant what she had said—believed it.

'Once today's over,' Rosie told herself, 'I'll be all right. I'll pack all your things into a suitcase and I'll give them away. They won't go to waste.' She thought about him wearing his new suit on that Saturday and began to cry. 'Everyone dies sooner or later . . . every single one of us. So I'll see you again, Tommy . . . I'll see you up there.' She closed her eyes tight and asked God to help her through this one day—just this one day—then she would cope by herself.

Pulling at the top sheet, she pressed it against her face and allowed it to soak up her tears. 'I'll make your prediction come right, that's a promise. I'll make it on to the West End stage, even if I have to flirt with the director. I'll close my eyes and think of Wapping,' she repeated one of Tommy's sayings. Whenever there was an unpleasant task to be done, be it scrubbing and whitening the doorstep on Iris's orders or having to take something to the pawn shop, he would wink and smile and cut short the sentence—*Wapping, Rosie, Wapping*. There was no real meaning to it, but it had become their own way of hanging on to some self-respect.

Family income had been spasmodic to say the least. They were either skint or in the money, depending on the success or failure of a planned robbery. Tommy's wages from the docks had been,

26

in so far as he was concerned, bread and butter and no more. When an illicit job was successful, the larder was full, the cocktail bar in the living room replenished and new clothes bought all round. For Tommy it was down the Waste to Sabel's or Davis's for a suit, and Albert's for silk shirts and ties. For shoes it would be Dolcis, Medway's or Bresloff's. The shopping always had to be local: his ill-gotten gains went no further than the East End— Tommy's way of spreading his booty around his neighbourhood.

Remembering the good times, shopping with her gran came to Rosie's mind. Shopping in Merlyn's and Pearl's, ladies' fashion. Harriet would go from one store to the other, trying on every dress and coat on the rail and trying to beat them down, using the competitive shops as levers. Iris never went with them; she preferred to go by herself to Vanity Fair, next to the Empire Picture Place, to shop in peace. For that Harriet had thanked Christ, in her usual way. She didn't want her stony-faced daughter spoiling her fun.

Sighing, Rosie plumped her pillow and lay back again, wondering how the family would manage now. She loved her job at the box factory, it was a good laugh, but the pay was low compared to other factories. Charrington's brewery paid better, but she had never fancied working on a conveyor belt. There were other ways of making money, of course there were. She could find herself a couple of sugar daddies, like her schoolfriend Sandra who loved strolling around Wapping in her classy West End clothes, giving off airs and graces. Or she could go to work for the Butler brothers in their private gambling club in Bethnal Green. She'd been

27

offered a job there once, working the roulette tables, but Tommy had given it the thumbs down, telling her that some of the men there were evil.

The living nightmare returned; the vision of him slumped across the settee; the three men with their black, slicked-back hair and sneering, jeering faces twisted inside like the knife which had killed him. She regretted not having grabbed it and stuck it into one of them.

That's right darlin'—make it a good one. Tommy's imaginary voice caused her to look up at the rising sun as it shone through her window. An unexpected smile appeared on her face; she began to glow, and in her mind's eye she could see her brother smiling and winking at her.

'Gran was right, then. You do want to come to your own funeral.'

That's right, darlin'—make it a good one. Go and help Mum to make the sandwiches and that. She's in the kitchen. And 'ave a couple of whiskies for me. Whipping back her bedclothes, she leaped off the bed. Vivid imagination or not, it made no difference to Rosie. If she could pretend he was in the room with her, that was better than nothing. She stood barefoot on the rag mat made by her gran and slowly turned around, half expecting to see a vision of her brother. 'Are you here, Tommy, or is it all in my mind?'

The room was silent and still but she felt in her heart that he was there.

Smiling, she went in search of her gran. Sending Harriet's bedroom door crashing against the wall, she fell into the room to see Harriet in bed, propped up against four pillows, sipping a glass of brandy.

28

'What the 'ell d'you want at this ungodly hour?'

'Gran, will you take me to see Lou Ambrose?'

'What for?'

'You know what for. I wanna go to a seance.'

Harriet narrowed her eyes and sniffed. 'I thought you didn't believe in all that bollocks?'

'I've changed my mind.'

'Oh, 'ave you now?' She peered at Rosie's face. 'Something's brought the colour back into your cheeks . . . What you bin up to?'

'You gonna take me or not?'

'We'll see.'

'Stop sodding about. Yes or no?'

'I'll tell you after the funeral. See 'ow you behave yourself. I was gonna go for a little seance next week, as it so happens. If you get all morbid and miserable again the answer's no, you can't come. Bloody face on you all this week's enough to make us wanna slit our wrists.'

Rosie pointed a finger at her gran. 'Right. I'm keeping you to that.'

'Keeping me to what?'

'If I don't cry . . . if I laugh at his mates' jokes and stories, we go to see the medium, right?'

'Medium, is it?' Harriet chuckled. 'I'll tell Lou she's been upgraded.' She drained the last drop of brandy from her glass. 'She'll wanna tell your fortune.'

'Good.'

'But I stop in the room and earwig. That's the deal. Like it or lump it.'

'Got no bleedin' choice then, 'ave I?' Flicking her hair back, Rosie left the room, believing she had just won a round. In truth, Harriet had often considered taking Rosie with her but had always

29

decided against it. Lou was a good spiritualist—if she couldn't see into the future, no one could, and Rosie was too sensitive for all that. Harriet remembered Lou once telling her that she would lose someone close when they were too young to die. Tommy had only just turned thirty-one. No doubt her impetuous granddaughter would forget all about it. If not, Harriet would find a way round not going. She could out-talk most people.

*   *   *

Stepping into the aisle of the packed church, George Rider looked across at Rosie, Iris and Harriet and smiled. 'There are three women here today who meant more to Tommy than anyone could. I think we all know who those women are. And if he had been given half a chance to say something before he died, he would have apologized for giving his family all this grief. That was Tommy. And that's why I chose this song which I'm gonna sing for 'im.'

Standing by the coffin, facing the mourners, George, tall and broad, immaculately dressed, cleared his throat, braced himself and then filled the church with his heartrending voice.

'I'm sorry for . . . the things I've done,
I know that I'm the fool-ish one . . .'

'Bang on,' whispered Harriet, the tears rolling down her cheeks. She had heard her grandson play that song many times and remembered telling him to mark the words. Without thinking she took hold of Iris's hand.

30

Pushing her chin out defiantly, Iris willed herself not to cry and clasped her other hand around Rosie's. 'We'll be all right,' she said, straining the muscles in her throat, 'we'll be fine.'

*   *   *

Once Tommy had been laid to rest and the three women were seated in the funeral car, Iris, still dry-eyed, spoke in a deadpan voice. 'Rosie ... I'm sorry. OK? I'm sorry. I blamed you for your father. That's all there is to say.'

Rosie looked away, out of the window, wishing that her dad would suddenly appear, out of breath from running, saying that he had gone to the wrong cemetery; showing that he did care enough to turn up for his only son's funeral.

'It's taken me all these years ...' Iris slowly shook her head, 'all this time ... and his murder ... to see the light. Your father was—and still is—a very self-centred man.'

'And you were too obstinate to listen to a bit of common sense,' said Harriet bitterly. 'Sorry? After the way you've neglected her? Think yourself lucky she's not bitter as well.' She turned her face away, feigning interest in something outside.

'Like me, you mean?'

'If the cap fits, Iris ...'

An empty silence followed as the driver slowly pulled away and they privately said their last farewells to Tommy. 'I thought that was really lovely of George to sing,' murmured Rosie. 'I didn't know he had a voice like that.'

'The acoustics helped,' Harriet said, ending that line of conversation. She didn't want to think about

31

that song now that the funeral was over; didn't want to think about him having to say sorry for anything. He had done more for the three of them than anyone could have asked. 'George thought the world of Tommy . . . and he's got a scar to prove it. Thanks to those vicious bastards.'

'It's gonna be strange around the house without him,' said Iris, caught up in her thoughts.

'We'll all 'ave to make an effort then, won't we? Make up for 'im not being there. Talk *to* each other instead of *at* each other.' Harriet gave her daughter a sidelong glance, adding, 'Show a bit of feeling.'

'Think you can take that, do you?' There was a touch of humour in Iris's voice, which surprised Rosie. She had only joked when she was scoring points with her son.

'You'll get a bloody clip round the ear if you get too lippy, my girl. I should 'ave given you a right 'ander when Bill buggered off. Letting your man go like that! Never known anything so bloody stupid.'

'What was I s'posed to do, beg?'

'Fight! Like most other women! You 'ave to fight to keep your man with all them bloody tarts out there waiting to get their 'ooks in.'

'Over my dead body. Me, fight for a man? Never!'

'Nor me,' Rosie said, surprised at her gran's sweeping statement. 'Did you 'ave to fight over Grandad, then?'

'No I bloody well didn't! He was too petrified to even look at another woman . . . which is how it should be.'

'If you say so, Gran.' Rosie smiled, catching her mother's eye. 'If that's what they did in your day, in Victorian times . . .'

'And you can get that tone out of your voice! My mother would turn in 'er grave if she could hear her own great-grandchild—'

'I didn't think you knew your mum, Gran?'

'She can still turn in 'er grave, can't she? Besides . . . I did know 'er up until I was ten, when I ran away.'

Rosie looked at Iris and shrugged. Harriet hardly ever spoke of her early life. 'Why did you do that then? She wasn't cruel to you, was she?'

''Course she wasn't cruel! I knew where my bread was buttered, that's all.' Harriet looked out of the car window again and quietly chuckled. 'I could tell you a thing or two. Tommy thought it was hilarious. Had to know all the ins and outs, of course. It was your grandfather who told 'im. I suspect the two of them are up there now, enjoying the joke.'

'Well, come on then! Tell us. Get it off your chest. Get the skeleton out the cupboard.'

'It'll keep.'

Rosie turned to Iris. 'Do you know what she's going on about?'

'No idea. What she's just told you is about as much as she's told me . . . a hundred times. She's making it up for a bit of attention.'

'Madam bleedin' know-all . . .' Harriet shook her head and chuckled. 'It's bin driving 'er mad for years. I know something that she don't. And what a something, eh? What a something!' She slapped her knee and laughed. 'One of these days I might tell yer . . . depends.'

'We're not interested.' Iris spoke as if she were bored hearing it. 'Old people's 'ome . . . that's where we'll put you if you're not careful.'

'You and the world'd 'ave to drag me there. Good God, we're back home already!' Harriet straightened her black straw hat and brushed the creases out of her skirt. 'Let's 'ope that Shirley Martin's mother's got the kettle on.'

'She will have,' said Rosie. 'And don't you forget to thank her! She's doing us a favour getting everything ready.'

'I did it all before we left.' Harriet let herself out of the car before the funeral director had a chance to open the door for her.

'She's in one of her mischievous moods,' muttered Rosie impatiently.

'It's her way of coping. She'll be different once we're inside with everyone milling around her, filling her with brandy.' Iris turned to face her daughter. 'I meant what I said; I am sorry. I never hated you. I just . . . I don't know . . . I can't explain what I felt.'

'Try to forget it. I have.' Try as she might, Rosie could not show her mother the love that she was searching for. There was nothing there. 'Come on. Let's get inside before all the others arrive.' She got out of the black car, surprised by the resentment rising from the pit of her stomach. She didn't want to be reminded of her past, of all those empty years when she was a child and desperate to feel Iris's arms around her.

*   *   *

The passage, stairs and living room of the house were packed with friends and relatives within minutes of the women's return, and the sound of Harriet's laughter rose above the chatter. If

34

nothing else, she was determined that the send-off drink would not be a morbid affair. If she had had her way, the record player would have gone on, too.

'It was a nice service, Rosie,' Reggie the ex-boxer said, his voice full of compassion.

'It was lovely, Reggie. The vicar kept it short and honest. I liked the way he slipped in that bit about it being tough for young people growing up in the East End . . . not that he was talking to anyone who didn't already know that, but at least it showed he knew and cared.' Rosie, half smiling, commended herself for being able to talk about the funeral service without getting emotional. She felt a strange relief. 'George surprised me. I never knew he could sing like that. I was really touched.'

'Can't 'elp it, can he,' grinned Reggie. 'Given half a chance he'd sing at everyone's funeral. The boy's a performer looking for an audience.'

Laughing at his sense of humour, Rosie looked across the room at George. 'Scar don't show all that much, do it?'

'No-ooo . . . 'course not. It was just a scratch . . .' Reggie drank some of his beer and chuckled. 'Bit of a cry-baby is George.'

'Don't be mean.'

'I'm pulling your leg, Rosie. Gotta look after your welfare . . . otherwise Tommy'll be waiting for me when I get up there.'

'My welfare . . . ? I don't get it.'

'George. He's a womanizer. Got a girl in every dance hall.'

Taken aback, she peered at him. 'What's that to me?'

'You mustn't go falling for 'im . . .'

35

'I was admiring his voice! What's wrong with that?'

'And 'is face. You must 'ave been looking at it, Rosie, to 'ave noticed the scar.'

'Leave off.' She looked across at George. 'As it 'appens, he is a looker.' And so he was: dark-blond hair, blue eyes and a nice tan. 'I reckon Tommy's clothes would fit 'im. They've got the same taste. D'yer reckon I should ask if he wants them?'

'No . . .' Reggie pressed his lips together and turned his head to one side, choked. Those few loaded words were more gut-wrenching than anything the vicar had said during the service.

'The flash boys 'ave been sorted out, by the way . . .' he said, changing the subject. 'By their own people. They caused a lot of trouble taking a liberty like that. Killing one of ours for no reason.'

'What, the Maltese hit three of their own people?'

'To keep the peace. Gave 'em a good hiding and sent them away on a long journey. I wouldn't like to 'ave been in their shoes.'

'Them sausage rolls are lovely!' George said, arriving with a plate of food in one hand and a pint in the other. 'You've done your Tommy proud.'

'Thanks.' Rosie felt herself blush. 'And thanks for singing in the church. You should be on the stage, George. Earn a fortune.'

'Oh, don't tell 'im that . . . we'll never 'ear the last of it.'

'Reggie's always bin a bit jealous of my talent.' He smiled and winked at Rosie. 'And my looks. I'm better looking than 'im and he knows it.'

'Not now you ain't. Not with that fucking scar.' Laughing, Reggie made a hasty retreat towards the beer table.

'Now then Rosie,' said George, his face serious, 'how about you and me going out for a drink tonight and then on for a steak supper at Ziggy's?'

'Talk sense. We've only just buried my brother.' She felt her cheeks glow.

'So?'

'What would people think?'

'Who cares? If they think you're a diamond . . . what difference would it make to your life? None. Right?'

'Right . . .'

'So?'

'No. Thanks anyway, but I couldn't. It's bad enough that Gran's blackmailed me into not crying today, let alone going on a pub crawl with you.'

'Tomorrow then. For Tommy's sake. He'd want me to look after you.'

'Oh, and that's why you're asking, is it?' Rosie said, mildly flirting with him.

'No. I think you're a little cracker. Always 'ave done. Tommy always said I was too old for you. Wouldn't let me ask you out.' He shrugged, trying to win her over. 'I'm only twenty-eight and what are you, twenty-three . . . four . . . ?'

'It wouldn't 'ave bin the age difference, George. It's because you're a Jack the Lad. You thieve for a living.'

''Course I don't! I'm a docker.'

'Yeah . . . and the rest.'

'A week from today, then?'

'I'd rather go to the pictures.'

'Fair enough. Pictures first and then a steak. Right?'

She sipped her sherry and looked back into his

eyes instead of avoiding them. 'No funny business.'

'Wouldn't dream of it,' he laughed, turning away and easing himself through the crowded room. Admiring his broad shoulders, Rosie felt a tingling inside. Catching sight of herself in the long mirror in the passage, she was pleased. Her new black two-piece with its fitted jacket and mid-calf skirt showed off her figure to a treat. She admired her legs, ankles and suede stiletto shoes. Her face was pale from the lack of sleep and her hair, although freshly washed and gleaming, hung down in unruly curls and waves, reminding her of Harriet. Still, she didn't look too bad. A match for George, anyway.

Watching as he joined Reggie and the rest of the boys, she began to feel angry again. Tommy should have been there, laughing and joking with them. This gathering should have been one of the many parties held at one or the other's houses over the years—not a funeral.

Remembering the way he had looked at her when he knew that his life was in danger, she shuddered. He was scared. Terrified. So much so that he couldn't cover it up the way he would have wanted. From as far back as she could remember, her brother had protected her from all life's cares and woes. He had a smile that had said *Don't worry, it's all in hand*.

Of course she wished that day away in its entirety; but her worst memory was that look on his face which she could only hope would fade with time and take away the bitter ache inside: the resentment, the hate. The one thing that still puzzled her was the one-liner from the Maltese who had slapped her face: *You can whore for us instead of your brother*. Surely the boys weren't involved in that seedy side of life?

Working her way through the crowded room, smiling and nodding at well-meant words of comfort, she made towards Reggie and squeezed his arm for attention, whispering that she wanted a word in private.

Leading him upstairs to the only part of the house devoid of guests, she went into her bedroom and sat on her bedside chair and lowered her head. 'I've got something to ask you, Reggie—and I don't want a load of lies.'

'Go on then.' He cleared his throat and waited.

'Are you and the boys ... were you running a whores' ring?' She raised her eyes and stared him out. 'I'll find out from somewhere else if you won't tell me.'

''Course we wasn't. The Maltese had the 'ump with us 'cos they couldn't muscle in on our patch. The police turn a blind eye to the clubs we look after; they're well run and there's never any bother. If we pull a little job, we make sure we bung a bit their way ...' He laughed quietly and shook his head. 'Tommy wouldn't get involved with whores, Rosie, you should know that.'

'So that's it then? They get away with a bit of roughing up after murdering him. Killing 'im just because they had the 'ump?'

'It's more complicated than that, babe ... Anyway you'll be pleased to know that there are four less of their clubs in Commercial Street.' He raised an eyebrow. 'Petrol bombs.'

'You didn't ...' Rosie found herself smiling.

'Not us ... some well-wishers. No one was really harmed ... just a bit bruised 'ere and there. He didn't go as quietly as you think.'

39

Nodding, Rosie clenched her hands and stared down at the colourful rag mat. 'I just wish he didn't 'ave to go like that. If you'd 'ave seen 'is face when they waved that knife . . . he was as white as a ghost and shaking. He wouldn't have wanted you to know that.'

Releasing a long-pent-up sigh of grief, Reggie passed a hand across his face, forcing back the tears, searching for something to say to lighten things. 'I've slipped a briefcase under Iris's bed. The boys had a whip-round . . .'

'Thanks,' Rosie said quietly, finding it difficult to cope with his emotions. To see hardened men who moved in a world that was sometimes violent close to tears, was not easy. 'Tell 'em thanks . . .'

'Forget whores. There's a good girl. You're getting yourself upset for nothing. It's what the Maltese wanted—to smear our reputation. It's the oldest trick in the book.'

Leaving Rosie to herself Reggie went downstairs, cursing Tommy for splintering off and trying to get a slice of something he knew nothing about. At least Rosie was convinced. That was the main thing.

'Rosie all right?' George had seen the two of them go upstairs and he was waiting in the passage. 'Looked a bit down.'

''Course she's a bit down. What do you expect?' He pulled George into a quiet corner. 'I've just told 'er that Tommy wasn't dabbling in Commercial Street. All right?'

'Right.' George bit into a sandwich and nodded. 'I'm taking 'er out next week; that's OK, innit?'

'Yeah. Keep 'er away from the clubs though, George. Take 'er to see a nice show up West, or a

40

drive out to a little pub in Kent. You know 'ow precious he was about 'er. Didn't want her mixing with us lot.'

'I know ... I know. She'll be all right. I'll look after 'er.' He closed one eye and focused the other on Reggie's face. 'You ain't got a soft spot for 'er, 'ave you?'

'Leave off. I'm twenty years older than she is, old enough to be 'er father.' He pulled back his broad shoulders. 'Forty-two next month. Don't look it, do I?'

'Nar ... take some vitamin pills,' he said, laughing and backing off. 'That'll get rid of them premature lines on your face.'

'Won't do much for that line on yours though, will they? Dozy bastard ... lettin' 'em get a blade near your face.' Reggie pulled himself up to his full height and smiled. 'I can't teach you, can I? You won't listen to your Uncle Reggie.'

'Bollocks.' George went off in search of jellied eels and sausage rolls.

'George!' Reggie called across the crowded room, 'Behave yourself next week!' There was no need to mention Rosie's name; George knew exactly what he meant.

*   *   *

By seven o'clock everyone except for five of the boys had gone. Leaving Harriet and Iris, who were more than tipsy, to listen to drunken funny stories Rosie stayed in the scullery, content with her own company, washing and drying up the stack of plates, cups and saucers. The day had gone as well as it could have under the circumstances and she

41

was looking forward to dropping into her bed. Now that the funeral was over they could get on with their lives again. She had already made up her mind, after speaking to one of the women about Charrington's brewery and work. A word was going to be put in for her and she was to go in the next day to have a word with the foreman. It wasn't what she wanted, but the insurance money and cash from the whip-round would soon run out now that there was only her wage and Harriet's pension coming in.

'Do you wanna hand, babe?' George stood at the scullery door, his eyes glazed, his body swaying. Even in that state he was attractive.

As he casually walked across the scullery towards her, she could smell his aftershave, faint though it was. 'I would rather give these crocks back to the neighbours in one piece.' She raised an eyebrow and smiled at him. 'I think you should go and lie on Harriet's bed and sleep it off.'

'I'm all right. You should come upstairs. Right laugh it is. Terry the Shoulder is well away . . . wiv 'is hardship stories.'

'I've heard it all before, George.'

'Yeah, but it's still funny. He changes it a bit every time and he's pissed as a newt. It's doing your mother the world of good; rocking with laughter she is.' He leaned on the butlers' sink and looked into her face, admiring her light-blue eyes.

'I s'pose Gran's putting in her pennyworth?' She turned away, embarrassed at his front. He was making it clear with just one look that he hadn't come down to the scullery to dry the plates. Wiping her hands on the tea towel, she hung it on the wooden towel rail. 'Swearing with the best of 'em, if

I know Gran.'

'No . . .' he said, touching the ends of her hair and twirling it in his fingers. Still his eyes were on her face. 'As it happens, she's been telling us about the Ripper stories. She reckons they're way off line.'

'Again? She's 'aving you all on. She was only ten, what would she remember?' She just managed to stop the habitual tossing back of her hair. She loved the way he was pushing his fingers through it and lifting strands, brushing his fingertips across the back of her neck. 'She's telling pork pies.'

'Can't we go for a drink before next week?' He eased his body a bit closer, keeping a light grip on her hair. 'I've waited long enough to pluck up the courage to ask you out.' He shrugged and tried to look boyish. It was a waste of time. His high cheekbones and straight nose reminded her of Paul Newman playing tough.

'Stop blaming Tommy. If you'd 'ave asked him properly he wouldn't have minded.'

George threw his head back and laughed. 'You must be joking. I'm telling you . . .' He stopped as he caught her eye. 'Anyway, he was right. You are special. There's something . . .'

'A box-maker girl? What's special about that?' She allowed him to pull her closer, until her breasts were pressed against him and he was gently kissing her neck. 'Someone might come in . . .'

'We're not doing anything wrong.' His breath hot on her neck, he brushed more kisses across her cheek and then touched his lips against hers. Aware that there was whisky on his breath, he lifted his mouth from hers and cupped her face. 'Sorry . . . booze and cigarettes . . . can't be very

43

nice . . .'

Embarrassed that he might hear the pounding inside her chest or feel her pulsating veins, she stepped back. 'We'd best go upstairs and join the others.'

'All right, but before we go, I just want to say— and it's not the drink talking—I really do like you . . . I'm not out for what I can get.'

'Just as well then—'cos I'm not a tart.'

'You think I don't know that?'

'I think you do know that. Come on.'

Once she was back in the living room with the others, Rosie found herself laughing at Terry who was telling his laborious but funny stories. Sitting on the floor, leaning against an armchair, nudging her head against her gran's knee, she caught her mother's eye. 'All right, Rose?'

'Yeah . . . I'm OK.' She lowered her eyes to the floor and wished that Iris would stop trying to be nice to her. It was too late for all that. Much too late.

CHAPTER THREE

The days that followed the funeral turned out to be the worst days of Rosie's life, and try as she would she could not blank out the reality—that Tommy was never going to walk in through the door again; that she would never hear the familiar sound of his whistling when he was spruced up ready to go out for the evening. The finality of it all and the silence that filled the house made her want to sleep until the spring came round, when she could wake to a new day and face life without her brother being there for her.

Since the day of the killing, up until the day he was buried, there had been a nonstop stream of visitors to the house. If it wasn't family friends at the door it was the police, intent on drawing information from them. The coroner's report had stated that the fatal knife wound had been inflicted seconds before death, and the detective inspector handling the case was a persistent man. He had badgered and bullied Rosie, Iris and Harriet one by one and, one by one, they had insisted that Tommy came home on that Saturday in the state they found him, each of them murmuring the same practised words over and over—street-gang warfare.

Reggie had briefed them on what they were to say before he had allowed them to call in the police, adamant that justice through the legal channels would only mean more shedding of family blood. After tears, tantrums and straight talking, Rosie and Iris had finally given in, agreeing that Reggie was right and that Tommy wouldn't have wanted a hair on any of their heads to be harmed, especially since the trouble had been caused by himself and the darker side of the life he had led. They could see the sense in Reggie's reasoning and had agreed to go along with him, spending precious time collaborating their stories, going over and over his arrival home that day down to every last detail, every step, until it was etched in their brains as if it had really happened that way.

One saving grace for Rosie had been George. She had had her doubts about him from the day of the funeral when he made his first move. She had

45

thought at the time that the flattery and compliments he had thrown her way had been shallow. That he had seen an opening, now that Tommy was no longer there to shield her from flirts, and had been quick to move in with his technique for getting the girl. But she had been wrong. Their first date, when he took her out for a candlelit dinner, had been wonderful and George had proved to be not only a perfect gentleman but a shy one. The restaurant he had chosen, Salvo Jure in Brushfield Street on the edge of Spitalfields fruit market, with its low lighting and soft blues music, was the ideal setting in which they could get to know each other properly. After the meal and wine, when they were enjoying good Italian coffee, George had confessed that he really had had a soft spot for her for a very long time.

When he finally said goodnight to Rosie, she was relieved that, instead of waiting to be asked in, in the hopes of sharing the sofa with her in the best room, he had kissed her lightly on the cheek before asking if he could see her again. It was Rosie who took things a little further by kissing him on the lips, and she had no regrets. That first kiss had been magic and had said more than a thousand words could have done.

*   *   *

Watching her gran as she sat in front of the electric fire in her room, Rosie cleared her throat to make her presence known without making the old woman jump. She had been very edgy of late. Harriet raised her eyes from the photograph at which she had been gazing, and stared into the imitation orange flames that flickered in the darkened room. She had been going through her cardboard box of old snapshots, looking for any which had been taken when her grandson was a boy. Swallowing against the lump in her throat, she mumbled quietly to herself, unaware that Rosie was standing in the doorway.

'Gran? Why're you sitting in the dark?'

Rubbing her eyes with her fingertips, Harriet turned slowly and peered up at her. 'It's not dark, is it?'

''Course it is!' She switched on the light. 'It's crept up on yer. It's a wonder you could see anything.' She leaned over her gran and looked at the photograph in her hand. 'I 'aven't seen that one before. Who is it?'

'Sod electricity,' Harriet grumbled, slipping the faded picture back inside her box and shielding her eyes from the sudden glare. 'How'd you get on then? Bit frosty were they—the women?' She carefully fitted the cardboard lid back on and lowered her box to the floor. 'First day anywhere's not all it should be. The brewery's no different. Give you stick, did they?'

'It was OK. Bit different from the box factory. Not many laughs. Well . . . not for me, anyway.' She sat in the fireside chair opposite her gran. 'Didn't know a soul. I kept expecting one of my mates to appear with a bit of factory gossip.'

Quietly laughing, Harriet assured her that in a fortnight or so she would be coming into that same room with stories to make a straw curl. 'Work it out for yourself,' she said, spreading her bony hands in front of the glowing bars and rubbing them together. 'How many do Charrington's employ

47

compared to the box factory?'

'A lot,' sighed Rosie, stretching out a leg and unfastening her stockings.

'A lot? That's putting it mildly. Hundreds if not a thousand troop into that brewery every day. I know, I've seen 'em. You'll soon 'ave more friends than you've had 'ot dinners. Speaking of which . . . what's your mother got on the stove? I'm bloody starving.'

'Rabbit stew.'

'Has she now? Wonder what she's after? Can't be my money 'cos I ain't got none.'

'Lying cow. You've got it stashed somewhere, I know. Your purse smells of mothballs. You'll be sorry if you die before you tell me where it's hidden. Not that it'll be much use. I bet it's all in old white five-pound notes.'

'Yeah,' Harriet smiled and sniffed. 'I'm not all that sharp when it comes to the readies.'

'Not much you ain't.'

'Never crossed me mind to hand them into the bank when they changed over to blue notes . . . or was it green? Too late now. Still, I shan't need 'em: not much to spend all that money on, not at my age.'

Throwing her head back, Rosie burst out laughing. 'You're such a liar! You was up that bank like a shot as soon as you 'eard. First in the bloody queue.' She peeled off her nylons and wriggled her toes. 'You're a right four-be-two on the quiet.'

'Not me, no. Pity . . . .' Harriet shook her head and sighed deliberately. 'All them bundles of white fivers . . . and you won't be able to spend 'em when I've gone. Still. That's life for yer.' She eyed her granddaughter craftily. 'Don't see what there is to

48

smile about.'

'No? I do. I've wormed it out of you at last. You have still got it stashed away.'

'Wormed it out of me! Ha! That'll be the day, girl. I only tell you what I want you to know. Now then . . . either you go down there and fetch me up my rabbit stew . . . or you tell me how the day went. Stop fritt'rin' away me time—Gawd knows I've not got many more years left to waste away listening to you prattling on.'

Lowering her eyes, the smile faded from Rosie's face. She hated it when her gran spoke like that. She didn't want to think about what it would be like without her. 'I had to wear clogs,' she said sulkily. 'Wooden clogs with a strip of material across the front. And a hat. And a bleeding khaki wrap-over.'

Ignoring her gran's irritating chuckle, she went on. 'You 'ave to wear cotton gloves an' all. Otherwise your hands get ripped to pieces by the bottle tops. You 'ave to work non-stop at the conveyor belt, snatching bottles and dropping 'em into the crates. Skivvies—that's all we are.'

'Skivvies? Get your wages, won't yer? And a darn sight more than you got at the other place. That's the trouble with you young, you want it all on a plate. An easy life.' Harriet narrowed her eyes and peered at Rosie. 'You wasn't on crate-filling all day long, was you?'

'No. You do a turnaround every hour. Anyway, I don't wanna talk about it no more. I'll go and see if dinner's ready.'

Just as she was about to leave the room, Harriet spoke again, a soft tone to her voice. 'Rosie . . . your mother's trying to make amends. Don't be too

49

hard on her.'

'Why? What's she said?'

'She hasn't said anything. I'm just saying you might . . . well, you might try talking to 'er, that's all. She's lost without our Tommy and she's still mourning for 'im. Always will be. It wasn't all that easy for her . . . what with your father going off. She needs a bit of loving.' Harriet stared at nothing, caught in her own thoughts. 'She never did take another man into 'er bed—that was the trouble. Life without a bit of the other's not good for a woman who's been married. A good shag would 'ave done 'er the world of good—still would. Me and your grandfather was like a pair of rabbits at 'er age. Fifty? There are plenty of men round 'ere who'd—'

'Gran!'

Pulling herself back to the present, Harriet realized that she had been thinking aloud again. 'Oh, stop acting like the Virgin Mary. I dare say they've bin sniffing round you by now.'

Taking a step back to put a bigger gap between them, Rosie kept a straight face as she said, 'Just 'cos you used to go over the railway yard with every Tom, Dick and 'Arry.'

'You cheeky little cow! I'll strap your arse!' Half rising from her seat, Harriet was pleased to see the back of her granddaughter as she made a quick exit. It wouldn't do to be seen smiling . . . and Harriet was smiling. Couldn't help it. She was remembering all the Toms, Dicks and Harrys.

'Ah . . . but I never strayed once my Arthur declared 'is love for me. Didn't have to.' Now she was remembering *his* dick, his pride and joy, glistening in the moonlight which used to stream

50

into their bedroom through the gap in the curtains. All lovely and clean and stretched to the limits. Always washing was Arthur, always taking good care of his most prized possession. She sighed at the thought of it and felt an old familiar tingle deep inside. She wondered if the old boy next door was up to it. She'd often seen him going out in the evenings without his dog and dressed up to the nines. Maybe she would rub a bit of Pond's cold cream on her face later and pinch Iris's red lipstick. After all, old man Ben had chased her in the past, so why not turn the tables?

She rested her head back and tried to imagine it. The thought of all the effort and fumbling killed her desire within seconds. Tired, she closed her eyes, content to relive old memories of her and Arthur.

'You'll never guess what.' Rosie was back in the doorway. 'She's put a white cloth on and laid up for three. She said to see if you fancy having your dinner downstairs with us for a change.'

'Silly cow. She knows I like my own comp'ny when I eat. She'd be the first to complain if I had to take me teeth out.'

'No she wouldn't—I would. Well?'

'I can usually manage to chew rabbit . . . I'll give 'er that; she makes it nice and tender with her overcooking of it. White tablecloth, eh?' She pushed her lips together and went thoughtful. 'She must want a bit of company. All right. Tell her I'll be down in a few minutes.'

'I'm gonna start mine now. I'm starving and . . . I'm going out. Going to see about joining the theatre workshop at Stratford.'

'What's that when it's at home?'

51

'A drama class run by the theatre. What d'yer think it is?' Rosie waited for a rebuke but her gran just looked at her, waiting for more. 'They might let me dance in a show once they see what I can do.' Still Harriet gazed at her, a show of interest on her face.

'Someone told me about it at the brewery. Said they teach acting and singing as well. Her cousin goes of a Monday ... or was it Friday?' Rosie deliberately played for time. She wanted a reaction.

'What is it you want, mog—to be a chorus girl?' Harriet was being sincere and her voice held a note of worry. 'I mean ... Ginger Rogers wouldn't get work now and she was the best. It's gone out of fashion, surely? No one'd wanna go to a show and watch you on the stage rocking and rolling, would they?'

''Course they wouldn't! Jiving is for the dance halls. I'm talking about a different sort of dancing. Modern dance as opposed to, say, ballet or tap. You've seen films of musicals, Gran; you know what I mean. Stop sodding about.'

'I've seen Ginger Rogers and Fred Astaire right enough but ... oh, I don't know—it's another bloody world, the Fifties. Motorbikes and fast cars! What next, I ask myself, what next?'

'A table for three. Get yourself downstairs.'

'Oi!' Harriet called after her.

'What?'

'Just because your brother's not here to chastise yer ... don't think you're gonna start swearing again, 'cos you're not! You've got me to answer to now. I'll skin you alive if I ever hear you use those words again. And don't think I won't! I'd do it for my Tommy.'

52

'What words are those, Gran?' Rosie grinned in mock innocence.

'Sod off downstairs, you tormenting cow.'

Ever amused by her gran Rosie left her to herself, having marked her words; she quietly promised herself that she would not slip back into her old ways. She would do her best to be a lady—against all the odds of being bred in the London slums. The word jarred—*slums*. Like most of her neighbours, she was not ashamed of where she had been born, even though outsiders thought differently. The kerbsweepers took pride in their work as did the gardeners at the parks. The hamlet wasn't such a bad place to live. Why else had theatrical people from other parts of England found reason to settle there?

Excited by the thought of meeting one or two of them, she sat down to her supper, remembering Harriet's request for her to try a bit harder with Iris. 'This is lovely,' she said, keeping her eyes down, complimenting her mother for the first time in years. 'Gran should enjoy this.'

Surprised by the unexpected, Iris simply nodded and pushed a small forkful of food into her mouth. The silence in which they ate was strangely comfortable; a small but important step had just been made and it hadn't taken much to induce a change of atmosphere in that small room where the fireplace still glowed with coke. Her mother had stood up to Tommy when he tried to get her to agree to sealing it behind hardboard, and replacing it with a modern electric fire similar to the one Harriet had in her room.

Pleased that Iris had got her way, Rosie wondered if she would ever sit around the open fire chatting quietly to her mother the way she often chatted to her gran upstairs. The rain pattering on the window pane created a familiar cosy feeling in the room and brought back unhappy memories. Maybe they would fade with time, Rosie told herself. Maybe it wasn't as bad as she remembered. Maybe it had been her fault?

'Let's hope that's as good as it smells.' Harriet sat at the table as if it were still a lifelong habit. As if she wasn't trying to rally the small family around.

'You've brushed your hair, Gran,' Rosie chirped, 'and pushed your combs in. You look quite presentable.'

'She's not too old for a clip, you know,' Harriet said to Iris. 'It's all these fancy ideas she's got. Wants to be on the stage.'

'Wouldn't surprise me if she made it, as well. She always was a bit of a dreamer. Going off into her "other worlds".'

'She don't like it at the brewery.'

'I never said that,' protested Rosie. 'I'm not used to it, that's all. It's good money so I'll stick it out.'

Iris put down her knife and fork and looked into Rosie's face. 'You don't have to worry about us not managing. He had a bit put by. I found it under his mattress ... and the whip-round that Reggie arranged will see us through for a good few months. We won't go without. Anyway ...' She picked up her cutlery and began eating again, 'I'm gonna get myself a job. Now that Tommy's gone there's less for me to do around here. I was thinking maybe Charrington's ...' She eyed Rosie carefully.

So that was it. This was the reason her mother was in a different mood. She wanted something.

54

She wanted Rosie to put in a word for her. 'I'll ask tomorrow at the office if—'

'There won't be any need for that. Mr Kent's still there from what I hear,' Iris said.

'Who's he when he's at home?'

'Manager of the wages department. Sits in the office at the top of the building. I always got on well with 'im . . . and I know there's a vacancy—'

'What d'yer mean—you always got on with him? You never worked for Charrington's, did you?'

Iris caught Harriet's eye and shrugged off her warning look of caution. 'I was assistant wages clerk and girl Friday. Did a bit of everything. That was before the war. Long before the war, after I'd taken a course at Pitman's college.'

Stunned, Rosie peered at Iris, waiting for more. She could hardly believe her ears. She had had no idea that her mother had taken a secretarial course. It had never been so much as hinted at. It was fast dawning on her that she hardly knew anything about the woman who had brought her into the world.

'I had to leave when I was seven months pregnant with Tommy. I never managed to go back again. Your father would have none of that. As far as he was concerned, a woman's place was in the home. Pity he didn't take a lesson out of the same book when I was pregnant with you. If a woman's place is in the home where is a man's place, I'd like to know. Not in the tavern with a fancy woman, that's for sure.'

'I don't get it. How comes you never said any of this when I went for my interview? If you worked there, why didn't you say so?'

Harriet sighed loudly, hoping to turn the

conversation. 'This rabbit's lovely. I can feel it lining me stomach.'

'Because I listened to your gran, that's why. We both knew that the only work you'd get there was on the conveyor belt; you've never had a head for figures.'

'Yeah? So?'

'So she didn't want me to make you feel as if . . .' Iris shrugged, 'As if I was cleverer than you—'

'You mean you didn't want to tell me you both think I'm as thick as two planks and factory work is all I'm good for! That I 'aven't got my mother's brain! Well sod you two!' She threw down her cutlery and stood up, pressing the palms of her hands on the table, looking from one woman to the other. 'I've got brains. Good brains. You think you don't need 'em to learn how to dance properly? Learn all the steps? Well you're wrong!' She tapped the side of her head. 'It's not full of sawdust!'

'Stop showing off, mog, it's not clever.' Harriet's voice was quiet.

'You knew all along, didn't you? You both knew she was gonna apply for a job in the office but you waited till now to tell me. As if I would care! You dozy pair! Of course I wouldn't have cared, I would have been proud!' She pushed her chair away from her, sending it crashing to the floor, and stormed out.

'Well done, Iris—as bloody tactful as ever.' Harriet shoved a piece of meat into her mouth, slowly shaking her head. 'Next thing we'll hear is the slamming of the front door.' She was right.

'She had to be told sooner or later. I start next Monday.'

'Eager, ain't yer? Can't wait to get away from me?'

'We'll need the money. I lied about what was under the mattress. It wasn't money, it was a list of the call-girls he was managing. That and a wad of betting slips. Tommy was broke. That's why he got himself into Commercial Street, no doubt. It's true about the whip-round, though. I've got three hundred and thirty-five pounds in my drawer but without his weekly wage coming in . . . well, it won't last a lifetime, will it? Besides, I want to get out of the house. I'm lonely.'

The two-word confession touched Harriet. 'I told you before that you should go out more,' she said quietly.

'Yeah, well, before it was different. I was happy enough looking after the place and ironing his shirts . . . polishing his shoes . . . cooking his favourite dinners.' Overtaken by grief, she covered her face with her hands and began to cry. 'I miss him. I want my son back but I can't have him. I want my son! I *want* him!' She raised her haunted eyes, tears streaming down her face. Hardly able to speak she forced out the words. 'I've never known such pain, Mum. I can hardly bear it!'

Sliding her hand across the small square dining table, Harriet patted her daughter's hand and then squeezed it. 'You've got Rosie, be thankful for that. Try to love her, Iris. She's out of the same mould.'

'I *do* love her! Of course I do. I couldn't . . . I just couldn't . . . I don't know.' She shook her head and pressed her lips together. 'I just could never show it!' She slammed her fist down on the table, causing the plates to jump.

Gazing at the drawn, pale face that had once

been the envy of the local women, Harriet drew her fingers through Iris's unwashed, short wavy hair and pushed a few lank strands back off her forehead. Her almond-shaped eyes were bloodshot and puffy. 'You've got to pull yourself together. No one else'll do it for you. People back away from grief and failure and that's the message you're giving out. You're telling the world you're a has-been. Don't do it, love . . . you'll just sink lower and lower and there's no one down there who can cheer you up and as for sympathy, it means fuck all.'

Hiding her own pain, Harriet managed to smile at her daughter, an encouraging smile, while all the time she herself was in dire need of a strong shoulder. Eighty years old and having to be strong! This wasn't what she had planned. God knows she had had more than her fair share of heartaches. Her expression grave, her voice low, she asked Iris to be an angel and go and make her a cup of strong tea.

Alone with her thoughts, Harriet brought to mind the lovely face of Mary Birchfield, who had taken her in when, at the age of ten, she had been reduced to sleeping rough under a tarpaulin in Spitalfields Market. Mary Birchfield, Arthur's older sister, who had been a lovely innocent matchbox girl at the local Bryant and May factory before she went on to become a lady of the night.

She thought about the big house in Bow where Harriet, Mary and Arthur had spent many happy years before all the troubles began. Before the painful expulsion of herself and Arthur from Mary's life.

CHAPTER FOUR

Gazing absently through the window of the bus as it slowed down in the traffic, Rosie admired the mosaic figure of the woman on the wall of the Yardley building, the 'Yardley Lady', as she was commonly known. Of course she had seen it before, when she had taken a bus to Forest Gate on her way to the skating rink, but this time she seemed to be looking at it through different eyes. She had been thinking about the Theatre Royal and imagining herself on stage in a musical, in a show, but when she had tried to picture the leading lady she had drawn a blank. She had had a clear picture in her mind of the supporting cast of dancers in costume; she could even hear the music they were dancing to. As the bus moved forward again, she closed her eyes and smiled. She had just found her imaginary star.

'Lavender Lady?' she murmured, quietly chuckling. She had given the famous effigy a new name without thinking. Well, in her unreal and very private terrain, that's what she would be called.

Allowing herself the pleasure of fantasizing, she held the vision of herself on stage with the rest of the cast, looking out on an audience as they stood cheering and clapping as the cast took a bow. It was the sound of the conductor's voice and the intruding 'ding' of the stop bell which brought her back very sharply from that realm. She had arrived in Stratford, E15.

As she stepped down on to the pavement, sudden waves of trepidation rose up in her.

Thinking about this venture, as she had been for days, was a lot simpler than seeing it through. She wished now that she'd asked Shirley to come with her, and was in two minds as to whether to turn back. She thought about Tommy and what he would say. His words leaped into her mind—*close your eyes and think of Wapping*. She found herself doing just that, replacing the word Wapping with 'the stage'.

When she arrived at the Theatre Royal she was somewhat relieved to find that, except for the small stage door, the place was in darkness and every other door was shut. She would no longer have to ignore that tiny but persistent feeling in her gut telling her to run. The burning desire to put her words into action had been curtailed by fate. She could return home with the same pride with which she had left.

Not believing that the stage door would be unlocked, she gave it a casual push with her foot and was surprised to find that she had been wrong. She was even more surprised to see an old man in the small, dimly lit area to the side of the stage. He was replacing a large set of keys on one of the many hooks on a square wooden board fixed to the wall. Glancing suspiciously at her, he sniffed and removed a different set of keys. 'If you've come to collect something you left behind, you're unlucky. I'm just leaving. You'll have to wait till your next session.'

'Who said I was 'ere to collect anything?' Rosie took an instant liking to the old caretaker. He was play-acting. She had met droll Jewish men like him before.

'So what do you want?' He looked at her with

half-closed eyes. 'If it's a handout, you've come to the wrong place. We're the beggars, not the angels.'

She was right. He was one of a dying breed. 'What kind of a theatre is this, anyway? It's as dead as a bloody doornail.'

'Tell me something I don't know.' He ordered her away from the door with a wave of his hand. 'I would like to lock up and go home for my supper, if that's all right?' He slipped his overcoat off a hanger, gripped the sleeve-end of his jacket and pushed his arm into the soft, worn lining.

'Do what yer like, it's nothing to me. I came to see the organ-grinder, not the monkey. I want to join the classes. I'm a dancer. Mind you, now that I've seen the place ... not that brilliant, is it? I'm not so sure I'd wanna come 'ere and learn how to dance professionally.'

He raised one eyebrow higher than Rosie had ever seen anyone do before—it was his party trick, or one of them. She tried to suppress her laughter but he was on to her, and raised both eyebrows and then spun his eyeballs. 'So you want to be a star? Well you've come on the wrong night. Fridays is when that lot are here, worse luck.'

'Mad.' She tried again not to show her amusement but her chuckle gave her away. 'You've got bats in the belfry,' she grinned, using another of her gran's sayings.

'I'm very good on faces,' he said offhandedly. 'If this place gets burgled tonight, I'll turn you in. What's your name?'

'What's your'n?'

'Mr Simons.' He pushed his expressionless face forward and waited.

'Rosie.' She looked at his shirt under his jacket

61

and overcoat. 'That's a bit bright, innit? Orange?'

'One hundred per cent silk. One of the actors left it behind. A poof. Come on, I'll walk you back to the main road. I wasn't gonna go that way but . . .' He shrugged. 'You've put me on the spot. I wouldn't sleep knowing that you might have had your throat slit.'

'What way was you gonna go then?'

'Through the backstreets. To the old music hall. The Grand Star.' He bent his arm and silently instructed her to take it, as if he had known her for years.

'Never heard of it,' she said, slipping her arm into his. 'Must be a dump.'

'Did I say it wasn't? Mind you . . . it was a beautiful place years back. My parents used to take me there as a boy. So I'm going back quite a few years.' Trying to walk in time with his long, slow gait, Rosie looked down at his large feet that were clad in very old but polished shoes. Casting a discreet eye over him, she could see that he was a man who took pride in his appearance, and it reminded her of Harriet whose motto had been and still was, 'Make the best of what you have'. With her gran it was brass and wood that had to be cared for and polished until it shone. With Mr Simons it was his attire—his outmoded suit was clean and well pressed and his overcoat had obviously been well cared for over many years.

'They finally shut down the Star in nineteen thirty-nine, more's the pity. We had variety acts, jugglers, ventriloquists, wonderful singers . . . and we put on some very good plays. They came from all over London, places you wouldn't believe. People with plenty of money . . . and those who didn't have a sixpenny bit left at the end of a working week. They all came to the Star. The Star of David, as it's known to some of us.'

'Well, I'll come with you then. See if it's as good as you say it is.'

'If you don't mind flea bites . . . I think I've got the rats under control now, so your feet should be OK. We have to go up this way.' He guided her to the right, in the manner of a true gentleman.

'Bit dark, innit?'

'I didn't ask you to come.'

'I never said you did. Why you going there, anyway?'

'Because I am the caretaker of that place, too. I've been looking after it since the day my father died. He was a wonderful caretaker. The best. How could I let it go to rack and ruin after all the trouble he took? The place reeks of cat's piss, it's true. I don't know how the little bastards get in. But I'll tell you something . . . the boiler in the Star is better than the one in the Royal. I'm telling you—I've kept it as my father left it. There's not a dead light bulb in the place. Empty sockets, sure . . . but not so many.' The old man's voice was full of pride.

'And I'll tell you something else, the Tannoy still works like a dream, and there are two separate toilets for the gents and the ladies. Two dressing rooms and a telephone—antiquated, true—but it still works.'

'Mr Simons . . . do you ever stop talking?'

'Excuse me for breathing.' He half smiled at her insolence. 'How come you're interested in the theatre? I would have thought the dance halls were more your age group.'

63

'I'm not *that* int'rested.'

'No? So you often wander around the backstreets at night then?' He brushed a finger across her black armband. 'Who is this for?'

'My brother.'

'I'm very sorry to hear that. How old?'

'Thirty-one.'

'Children?'

'No. He wasn't married. Engaged twice, but didn't wanna leave us. Had to in the end, though, didn't he,' she said, her voice fading to silence.

'When?'

'How comes they never cut the phone off, then?' she said, ending that line of conversation.

'You have to know people in the right places.' He tapped the side of his hooked nose. 'I've friends at the electricity board and the telephone exchange. It's the next turning on the left. Star Passage.'

Turning into the cobbled passageway, Rosie felt as if she had stepped back in time. 'Pity you 'aven't got a friendly road sweeper an' all. Look at it.' She kicked away a small empty milk carton from a vending machine.

'Not many come down here now.' He splayed a hand and waved it at the boarded windows of the terraced houses. 'They've been like that for years. It's a disgrace.' He took her by the arm and steered her across the narrow street. 'OK. Close your eyes. You can grab my jacket to steady yourself. Just a few more paces and we're there.'

'I must be bloody mad,' she said, chuckling. 'Lamb to the slaughter or what? You could be a Jack the Ripper.'

'You ready?'

'Yeah, go on, get on with it.'

'OK. Now you can look.'

With her eyes open, Rosie slowly raised her head, hardly able to believe the spectacle before her. There, wedged between an umbrella factory and a ladies' fashion wholesalers, stood the Grand Star Theatre, filthy with years of dirt that covered its Victorian façade. Allowing her eyes to roam from the marble step up to the wrought-iron brackets just below the rooftop, she took a deep breath, feeling as if she really had slipped back into the last century.

'That old lamppost used to be gas, you know. But . . . like all the others they converted, that too will go, you'll see. Replaced with a bloody concrete eyesore.' Rosie could hear the old boy rambling on about progress and stupidity, but her mind was elsewhere as she gazed at the old-fashioned street lamp, dirty paper swirling around it. She was visualizing the ghosts of the past. Courting couples meeting under the lamplight before going in to see a show.

'The Grand Star,' he murmured, 'one of our best theatres in the East End.'

Rosie looked up at the awning between the wrought-iron brackets and took in the faded, artistic hand-painted sign—*Grand Star Yiddish Theatre*.

'Was it always a Jewish music hall, Mr Simons?'

'The name's Larry. From nineteen eleven until nineteen thirty-nine. Before that, it was a heap of shit. The Hagars and Ishmaels took it on and did a wonderful restoration job. Of course,' he shrugged matter-of-factly, 'the blackshirts put an end to all of that.'

65

'And it's been closed all this time?'

'More or less.'

'What d'yer mean, more or less? Either it 'as or it 'asn't?'

Larry raised an eyebrow at her. 'What difference does it make?'

'None.' Rosie used the same droll tone that he did.

'I suppose you want to see inside?'

'Of course I wanna see inside. What d'you expect?'

'I don't even know why I asked,' he said, taking her arm. 'I've got a granddaughter ... and if you weren't such a goy, I would have said my son had been casting his seeds. Sarah is just as bossy as you are. Bossy and a bloody know-all—with a big mouth.'

'My gran's always saying I must 'ave a bit of Jewish blood in me. Reckons they found me in the street, in a cardboard box that the Germans dropped just before the war; they couldn't tell the difference between a bomb and a baby.'

'Your gran sounds like a very charming woman.' He pushed the key into the lock of a small door next to the main entrance into the theatre. 'Don't expect red velvet and gold paint. It's there ... but covered in dust and grime and full of moth-holes and mouse droppings.'

Stepping into the narrow entrance, Rosie felt her heart quicken; a surge of excitement rushed through her and she wasn't sure why. It was, after all, a run-down, disused fleapit. 'Bloody hell, Larry—it's pitch-dark.'

'Of course it's pitch-dark. Wait there and don't move until I tell you to.' He pulled a small torch from his pocket and shone a light at a set of switches, flicking two of them down and bringing alive a solitary light bulb above her head. 'OK, come through and wait for me by the stairs. I have to bolt the door.'

'Phe-ew! You were right about the smell. It'd take gallons of disinfectant to get rid of that. I don't think it's just cat's wee either.'

'You wanted to see it—don't drive me mad. Go on; up you go.'

'Not much room, is there? Couldn't swing a soddin' bird, never mind a cat.' She walked cautiously up the stone steps, making certain that only the soles of her shoes touched anything. 'If this was the stage door . . . the actors must 'ave 'ad to be skinny. I wouldn't put up with this!'

'Then you have a lot to learn about the theatre and what you *will* have to put up with,' he laughed. It was a throaty, contagious laugh. 'Quite a lot to learn, I should think.'

He rambled on as they climbed the stone stairway, their footsteps echoing eerily. His flow of words drifted through her head as he kept up his running commentary on the place. He was telling her that the costumes which had been wrapped and kept in a large tin trunk ought really to be in a museum. That the bits of furniture in the props room would fetch a fair penny and that the house lights were in good working order. He told her there were very small bars, one in the main entrance and one in the gallery . . .

'The old tickets from the twenties are still in the box office . . .' she heard him say, 'tickets and programmes packed into every cupboard and on every shelf.'

'That's enough, Larry.' She stopped and leaned against the grimy wall, her head bowed.

'What did I say?' His voice was tinged with hurt and concern.

'You have to give me time to take all this in.'

'Why should you be upset? You're not frightened, are you? This place isn't haunted. I wouldn't come in here myself if it was.' He stroked her hair and placed his hand under her chin. 'What's wrong?'

'I don't know.' She smiled and wiped away a tear. 'Something's happening.' She pressed her lips together and took a deep breath. 'Right 'ere. Right now . . . and I don't know what it is.'

'It's this place. It has the same effect on me. On all of us.'

'All of you?' she cleared her throat and composed herself.

'Sure—on all of us. Us, in our club. Come on, I'll show you something.' He took her by the hand and led her up another short flight of steps and unlocked a green door marked Office. As he very slowly opened the door for her to see all, Rosie could hardly believe her eyes. It looked like any cosy, comfortable living room that you would find in a family home. The red patterned carpet was not only clean but hardly worn, and the eight deep-red armchairs looked luxuriously inviting. There was a central round coffee table of polished mahogany, and a wooden bookshelf full of theatre memorabilia.

'Now . . .' said Larry, smiling, pleased and very proud, 'would you like a cup of tea in a china cup?'

'What's goin' on, Larry? I don't get it.'

'You weren't meant to. I'll get shot for this.

Don't get too excited,' he said, filling the kettle, 'only this room looks like this, except for the toilet just outside the door; everything else is falling apart.' He waved a finger at her. 'But not the building. No, the building is sound and in good order. We make sure of that. Of course we would have liked to have done the whole place up, who wouldn't, but it would cost a fortune. So . . . we are happy, more than happy, to come here once a week and talk about the theatre . . . the shows that went on in the past, and . . . best of all . . . have play-readings. Sugar?'

'Two. What are play-readings?'

'You don't know what a play-reading is, and you want to be an actress?'

'Dancer.'

'Ah. Well . . . we become actors for an evening, except we don't have to learn our lines, just get into character and read our parts in the comfort of this room. It started when we found some old scripts here, plays which had been put on in this theatre. We enjoyed ourselves, so much so that now we buy published plays. We've built up quite a library,' he nodded towards the bookcase, 'as you can see.'

'Why don't you put one of 'em on, then? You've got a bloody theatre for Christ's sake!'

'For one, we don't have a licence and for two, wait until you've seen the rest of the place and you'll know why.' He poured boiling water into the teapot and glanced at her. 'It would cost a fortune to bring it back to something just half as good as its former glory.' He opened a tiny fridge and took out a half-empty bottle of milk.

'I thought you could get grants for that kind of thing. From the Arts Company.'

'Arts *Council*. A stone that I would not wish to try to get blood out of. If they won't give it to the Royal, why would they give it to the Star? They're a bunch of bureaucrats who know little about the workings of a theatre.' He handed her a cup of tea and sank into a chair. 'If this theatre is ever to be restored, the funds would have to come from businessmen ... who will only be interested in returns.' He sipped his tea and then slowly shook his head. 'With the best will in the world you could never make this place pay its way, never mind profit. Except for one way—and it won't be too long before that happens.'

'Turn it into a supermarket?'

'Close. A bingo hall.'

'They wouldn't do that.'

'Why not? It's the way others have gone. Cinemas will be next, you'll see. People would rather sit at home in front of a bloody box and watch old second-rate films.'

'Not if they had a good reason for coming out, they wouldn't. I'm hardly ever in. We go dancing or to the pictures or parties ...'

'Do you go to the theatre?'

'Leave off! Who wants to spend good money to sit and listen to some boring old play?' She started to chuckle. 'I can just see my new chap putting up with that. He prefers lively places, pubs and clubs and dance halls. Now if it was a really good musical—that'd be different. He'd be up for that. So would his mates. You should turn this place back into a music hall, using songs from the hit parade. My bloke can sing. He sang at my brother's funeral service. There wasn't a dry eye in the church.'

70

'And does your chap sing for a living?'

'You must be joking. No he ... he's a docker, among other things.'

'Ah ... a villain.'

'No, he ain't! Bloody cheek! He's good wood; Robin Hood, if you know your slang.'

'Touché. Well ... if he and his cronies want to pass something on to the poor and do a very good turn ...' he waved a hand to indicate the theatre.

'Don't you think that didn't go through my 'ead?' She stared down at the floor, thoughtful. 'The second I opened my eyes outside and saw this place, a family friend came to mind. They'd want a return though, so we'd 'ave to come up with a bloody good plan of action. Put on a musical first— one that'd appeal to them—and you'd soon fill this place up. How many seats are there?'

'Four hundred and seventy.'

'Sounds all right. Come on, I can't wait to see the stage. Has it got them lovely box seats you see on the telly when they put a show on?'

'Of course.' He looked at his wristwatch. 'But you're going to have to wait until next Monday. I'm an old man who needs his sleep. Come to the side door of the Royal an hour earlier next time, six o'clock, and I'll fetch you back here for a grand tour. Mondays are always quiet, it's everyone's day off ... except mine, of course. I'm only a casual worker but I put in more hours than anyone. All or nothing, once you've reached retirement age. They think they're doing me a favour, giving me something to do to fill in the hours. Ha!'

'Oh come on. It won't take a minute.'

'No. I like to do things properly and not in a rush. Next Monday.'

71

'Can't I come before then? To meet your cronies? I might join the club.'

'Where's the fire?' He half closed his eyes and slipped into his droll tone again.

'When d'yer meet up?'

'On Sundays.'

'That's six days away!'

'Like I said, what's the rush? It'll take me weeks to drop hints about fresh blood joining the group—and a goy at that.'

'I never said I would join it, I said I might. I'm talking about fetching some life back into this place. Turn it back into a music hall,' she said, half jokingly.

'Which is what we have been doing for nigh on fifteen years—talking about it. It's not exactly a new idea. They're not gonna anoint your feet with oils.'

'They will if I can bring some pound notes in.'

Larry stood up and held out his hand for her empty cup. 'Wait until you've seen the state of this place. I think you might change your tune.'

'Tunes can be changed, can't they?' She smiled and winked at him. 'Arts Council? They'd be begging to chuck money this way if you decided to reopen this place. I bet yer.'

'I wouldn't bank on it. I hear everything back there at the Royal. If you had any idea of how hard those *meshuggener* work trying to resurrect that building from being a sad, third-rate music hall . . .' He shook his head and shrugged. 'They put on classics as well as new plays. It could be wonderful. It's a beautiful building—and potentially a source of great pride to the borough. And yet, I don't think there's a hope in hell of the Arts Council giving them any money for redecoration. So what chance would we have here?

'I'm telling you—it's a hopeless dream. Go to the Royal and get some training ... become a professional dancer or an actress ...' He waved a hand. 'Stick to the hope of becoming a performer—that in itself will be a struggle. Come on. I've got hunger pains.'

'You're losing your ambitious drive, Larry,' Rosie said, standing up and stretching.

'What makes you think I had any?'

''Cos some of it's still there.' She poked him on the shoulder, 'And you know it.'

'Ah ... what difference does it make? You're young—you have your dreams, why not? They won't harm you.' He pulled the door open. 'Just don't build your hopes too high.'

His voice held little conviction and she was not convinced by his protestations. She hadn't been there for fifteen minutes, and already there was something exciting stirring inside. The place was screaming out to be reopened. If she had picked up on it in that short time, what must he feel? Really feel, deep down?

'Larry ...' She stood her ground, not wanting to leave. 'I know this'll sound daft, but ...'

He waited, feigning a look of impatience. 'Well?'

'Ever since I was little ... I've dreamed of dancing in a show. One of the ones I've made up.' She tapped her head with a finger. 'I've got four or five shows in there. Every story's different. I can even hear the music sometimes.'

'Others have been locked away for talking like that. Next you'll be telling me you hear voices.'

'I do. They all talk to each other. If you was to

73

reopen this place, I could put one of my shows on.'

He flapped a hand at her. 'I've heard enough, thank you. It's time to go.'

'What if I rallied people round to help restore it?'

He looked at his watch and raised an eyebrow, sporting an expression of intolerance. But Rosie had seen a glint in his eye and knew that she had piqued his enthusiasm. She also knew that she had gone as far as she dare for the time being. She would have to leave it there and give him time to sleep on it.

Once outside, alone in the street, she crossed the narrow road and gazed at the lovely old building. Something had brought her there. It already seemed as if it were part of her world. She had not seen it before and yet it was familiar. 'I'm not gonna let them turn you into a bingo hall,' she said, fully aware now of her growing excitement. 'You're gonna be alive with the sound of music, filling every corner.'

'I'll walk you as far as the main road,' said Larry as he came out of the stage door.

'You don't 'ave to do that. I was brought up a street urchin. I know how to look out for myself.'

'I'm sure you do. Come on.'

Making no attempt to move, she went on, 'And I'll tell you something else. I know a lot people, friends and neighbours, who'd help clean up this place.'

'There would be no point. It would just get dirty again.'

'D'yer reckon?' She began to chuckle. 'Not once we've put on a musical. People would want more. Let me do it, Larry! Let me put on a show and dedicate it to my brother, my Tommy. Right back, since I can remember, he always said I'd end up on the stage. You know what he used to say to me, whether I was up or down? "Keep on dancing, babe."'

Holding out a hand, Larry recognized the hurt in her voice. It had been in his own when his wife had passed away. He hadn't meant to dampen this girl's spirits, but he was not going to raise her hopes, either.

They walked arm in arm along the dark turning, neither of them saying a word, each deep in thought. For that he was thankful. She did know when to shut up. This vibrant young lady who had walked into his life had managed to stir emotions he thought had died with the passing of the years. With her contagious smile and cheek-of-the-devil attitude, she was just the spur that he and his friends needed; just what the group had been waiting for.

*   *   *

Once Larry had seen his newly acquired ward on to a bus he made his way through the backstreets, caught up in his own thoughts. The girl had, for some strange reason, brought back memories of when he and his wife Moira had enjoyed evenings at the Grand Star. Lita Rosa had sung her heart out there as a young woman, backed by Ray Ellington and his band.

Turning into Star Street, he questioned the company that Rosie was keeping. He knew enough about the East End boys to write a book. They were lads who, if they could not make a living one

75

way, made it another. He hoped her boyfriend had learned something from villains of the old style, men like Timmy Hayes, Dodger Mullins and Wassle Newman, who never hurt women, children or old people and only did damage to their own kind. Rogues that they were, at least they had had a code—honour among thieves and neighbours.

As he pushed the key into the lock of the theatre door, he remembered one or two he had gone to school with, when most of the lads, himself included, would collect newspapers and sell them to the paper factory. Even then, at the age of twelve, thirteen, there was a minority who had marked out their territories, threatening anyone who collected old papers from their patch.

Larry used his torch to see his way up the staircase and into the club room, and then switched on the light, secure in the knowledge that no one from outside could see that he was in there—a window would have been very nice but a dead give-away.

Pushing the plug from the two-bar electric fire into the socket, he rubbed his hands to warm them. Tonight he would be having chicken soup, made the day previous. Chicken soup and a fresh roll.

As he pulled the white basin from the fridge, he wished there was someone to share it with, someone to talk to. Rosie, for instance. But to have allowed her into this clandestine side of his life would have been foolish. She was young and spoke before she thought. Besides which, he knew nothing about the people she mixed with. That she was a natural and honest girl, he had no doubt, but that was not enough. For three years he had managed to keep his makeshift home a secret from the general public. His trusted friends knew, of course they did: it was they who had suggested he move into the theatre when he was told to leave his three-up, two-down and offered a one-bedroom council flat.

There was only one real threat which caused him to wake in the night . . . If Bob, the fire officer were to be drafted into another area, he would be faced with someone who might not turn a blind eye to his sleeping arrangements, and he would be turned out and the building officially closed down.

Once the soup was simmering on the small hob, Larry opened the stock cupboard, took out his bedclothes and pulled down his put-U-up settee. The extra walking at the end of a long and tiring day had worn him out. Once he had eaten, he would be more than pleased to settle himself down for a good night's sleep. He had a feeling it would be a good night, too. Rosie might have left him feeling nostalgic for things past but she had also injected a bit of life into him. Life and hope.

Even if her wild dreams were to come to fruition, he would not be without a home. The theatre was full of rooms, and if the one he had settled into was needed for any reason, he could easily find another nook or cranny where he could hide away and sleep in peace.

In a comfortable mood, he sat at the small Formica table and ate his supper, listening to the silence of the old music hall and remembering one of his favourite songs; 'The Boy I Love Is Up In The Gallery'.

CHAPTER FIVE

Walking through the streets of Wapping at that time of night was something Rosie usually avoided.

With her mind full of the Grand Star and how it might be brought back to life, she had passed the place she most feared without even realizing it: the gasworks. Now, approaching the Prospect of Whitby just before closing time, she could hear the medical students belting out the penultimate verse of one of their bawdy songs, one she had heard many times before.

'Oh, Sir Bastion do not . . . ! Oh, Sir Bastion do not . . . ! Oh, Sir Bastion do not . . . !

'As she lay between the lily-white sheets with nothing on at all . . . !'

She immediately stepped up her pace, remembering when she and Shirley had gone in there one Friday night and had been made to feel as if they did not belong. Most of the medical students were from a different walk of life, and they had made it clear that locals were not welcome in the Prospect. Scrubbers, was the word bandied around when she was in there. Little scrubbers. If Rosie had passed that on to her brother or to any of his friends, the snobs would have been ousted, bruised, eyes blacked and looking for another East End pub to take over.

Expecting the usual insulting remarks from the few who were outside the noisy riverside pub, she decided that this time she would not cross over to the other side of the street. If they tried to put her down she would give them a mouthful; a mouthful of the abuse she had longed to throw their way in the past but hadn't had the nerve to. Now she had enough grit for an army of women. Tommy's murder had seen to that. Let anyone try to slur her good name and she would give vent to the pent-up anger and hatred that had been with her since the Maltese pushed a knife into his heart.

'Business not so good tonight, luvvy?' came the mock-cockney cliché from a red-faced, glassy-eyed young man. 'Punters away at sea, are they?'

Stopping in her tracks, Rosie pushed her face up to his and smiled, murmuring the word 'bollocks'.

'Ye-es . . . and they're staying right where they are, whore. In my underpants . . . with my John Thomas,' he slurred, laughing and spraying beer over the student next to him.

'Well let's hope that someone's slipped a scalpel in there then, eh?'

'Salt of the bloody earth!' another young drunk chimed in. 'Marvellous sense of humour! Bloody marvellous!' He slapped a chum on the shoulder. 'Bring her inside, Bertie—our brainy slags might learn a thing or two, what?'

Affronted, Rosie sneered at him. 'Go in there? With you lot? I wouldn't soil my shoes. Been sick yet, 'ave they? The spotty-faced boy wonders?'

'She's got balls, I'll give her that,' came a very camp reply from another.

'Well now, that would be something to see . . .' retorted Bertie. 'I mean to say chaps, a lovely harlot like this . . .' he veered a graceful hand through the air and brought it under her chin. 'Have you got balls under your pretty skirt?'

Constraining herself, she smiled at him, giving no hint of her intention to wipe the smug grin off his face. With her right hand by her side and clenched into a fist, she gave a wonderful performance of a girl impressed by his wit as she gazed into his bleary eyes. Flirting, her expression was full of promise that he could examine her body whenever he wanted. Mesmerizing the drunken fool like a snake, she waited until she had him on the hook, and smiled just a little more seductively before bringing up her fist, ready to throw an almighty punch the way her brother had shown her. But the cocky student made a mistake that he was to regret; the mistake of showing Rosie the tip of his tongue—and back flashed the vision of the Maltese. Her smile gone, she drew her head back, winked at him and then lurched forward, landing a cracking head-butt on his perfectly straight nose. A trick Tommy had told her to keep for emergencies—but fury had overcome dignity.

Flabbergasted, the others watched as Bertie howled and reeled under the blow, stumbling to the floor. Then, one by one, the intoxicated group burst out laughing, throwing the odd compliment her way.

'He's had that coming for a long time,' came the serious voice of another student who had just arrived in the open doorway. 'Well done you.'

Ignoring remarks from the others, Rosie felt herself go cold: the voice she had just heard, apart from the clipped accent, could have come from the mouth of her brother. Slowly turning to face the young man she allowed her lips to part, unable to hide her expression of shock. Not only had he sounded like Tommy but he looked like him too; the same dark hair and thick eyebrows, the same dark-blue eyes.

'I think you owe the girl an apology, Bertie.'

The injured man looked daggers at his peer, and then stared at the blood on his fingers which had come from his broken nose. He was shocked and in too much pain to speak.

'Come on,' The medical student, clad in faded green corduroy and brogues, stepped forward and guided Rosie away without a word of protest from her. 'They're in high spirits tonight—it's someone's birthday. Any excuse . . .'

'Our boys would never talk to a girl the way they do,' murmured Rosie, finding her voice.

'No?' He smiled, and she could sense him looking at her face. 'You should be there when they pop in the Prospect for a drink. They make fun of the girls. Call them a bunch of lesbians. What's your name?'

'Rosie.'

'Mine's Richard. Do you have far to go?'

'No. You can leave me at this corner.'

'That's OK—I'll see you all the way home.'

'You won't.' She regretted her sharp retort the moment it was out. 'I don't need a bodyguard,' she added more softly.

'Your parents don't mind then . . . your being out this late by yourself?'

He was probing, and for some reason she didn't mind. 'I'm not on the game, if that's what you're wondering. I've just come from the Theatre Royal—my dance classes,' she lied. 'I'm training to be an actress, as well.'

'Ah . . . so we do have something in common. I've directed several of our student plays. I thought I wanted to be an actor at first, but my very first and last performance put an end to that idea. I was

81

dreadful. Forgot my lines, fell over my own feet and hated every moment of it. If I had the choice, I would be a director.'

'If you wanna be a director, why are you at the medical college?'

'Because it's what my parents want and they call the shots. The mere mention of my working in the theatre and they'd threaten to cut me off without a penny. I am not prepared to starve for my art.'

Rosie stopped at the lamppost and offered him her hand. 'It was nice meeting you . . . though I can't say the same about the company you keep.'

Bemused at her attempt at good manners, he gently shook her hand and asked if he might telephone her sometime . . . maybe they could have a quiet drink and talk theatre. 'All that lot ever talk about is medicine and sex,' he said, waving a hand in the direction of the Prospect of Whitby.

'We're not on the phone.' She smiled and backed away.

'Rosie.' His tone ordered her to stop. 'Let me give you my phone number.'

'What for?'

'Well . . . so that we can fix an evening . . . ?'

She slowly shook her head. 'My bloke'd go spare. My gran wouldn't go much on it neither. We're from different worlds.'

Watching her walk away, Richard Montague was nonplussed. With his good looks and stature, he always managed to get the girl. His gut reaction was to put it down to her being out of her depth, but he knew that that was not the case—she wasn't interested, it was as simple as that. He stood there for a while, questioning himself. Was it just his pride which had been bruised, or something more than that? She was a lovely looking girl—but they were ten a penny. She had a natural personality but that wasn't so unusual. So what was it about her that made him want to see her again? What was it that had swept aside the class barrier in seconds?

Walking back to the Prospect, he was comfortable in the knowledge that she was certain to take that route again and that she didn't live far away. He made a mental note of the time and day. If she was telling the truth as to where she had been, he would see her the following Monday, on her way home from the theatre.

*   *   *

'Where the 'ell have you been?' Harriet stood defiantly in the passage, her hands on her hips. 'We've bin worried sick—you little cow. Your mother's bin pacing the floor, wearing out the carpet! Marching out like that and slamming the door without saying a word about where you was going!'

'I told you where I was going so you couldn't 'ave been listening, could you? I went to see about joining the drama class. And don't give me all that about pacing the floor! She never worried about me when I couldn't take care of myself, so why should she bother now?'

Harriet stepped forward and gave her granddaughter a good hard slap on the arm. 'Don't be so bloody mean!'

'Why not? It's a bloody mean world, innit? Least that's what you've always said.'

'Cheeky moo . . . and don't give me all that fanny about the theatre! It wouldn't 'ave taken you this

83

long to book lessons, I know!'

'Leave her be, Mum,' said Iris, stepping out of the sitting room and making her way towards the kitchen. 'Go and warm yourself by the fire, Rosie. I'll fetch you a hot milky drink.'

'See? She's only too pleased to see you back safe and sound!'

'All right, all right. You've made your soddin' point!'

Grumbling to herself, Harriet returned to the living room with Rosie following. 'If you think you can do what you want now, you've got another think coming.'

Happy to be back in her own surroundings, Rosie kicked off her shoes and lay back. 'I don't suppose George called round, did he?'

'Yes he did, and he left more miserable than when he arrived. Done up to the nines, he was. I doubt if he'll call again on the off chance.' She peered at Rosie. 'I take it it was on the off chance? He was surprised not to find you in; tried to 'ide it, mind.'

'But nothing gets past you, eh, Gran?'

'He's a lovely fella. Don't you go breaking 'is heart.'

'You don't have to tell me what he's like. I already know. I wish he'd 'ave waited for me to come in.' Ignoring her gran's mocking sounds of remonstration, Rosie gazed into the fire. 'I only saw 'im two nights ago and I miss him already. I've never felt like this about anyone before.' She was talking more to herself than to her gran. 'I've always wondered what it felt like to be in love. If this is it, I'm not over keen. If I miss him after two days . . . what will I be like when he packs me in?'

'Daft ha'p'orth! Who said he'll pack you in? Stop wallowing in self-pity.'

'He's bound to. With his looks ... he can 'ave the pick of the best.'

'Maybe he don't want the best. Maybe he's satisfied with an ugly, miserable doss-pot like you.'

'Thanks.'

'Don't give me that look. You know full bloody well that you're a looker. George's daft about you. Anyone can see that.' Harriet sniffed and sank further into her old armchair. 'Did you meet up with anyone then? At the theatre?'

'Yeah. I met a lovely old man called Larry, if you must know.'

'Did you now?'

'I've just been drawn back into the last century ...'

'Ah ... so that's where you've bin while we've been looking at the clock every ten minutes, visiting the past! Your mother was just about to go out and look for you. I wouldn't mind, if it was main road all the way. I s'pose you took the short cut past the gasworks.'

'Yeah ... it was all right though, not all that dark. It's a shame they converted the gas lamps ...'

'Don't you believe it! It put an end to people getting up to no good, I'll tell yer. The streets are twice as bright now; which is just as well, since you've taken to walking about at night.'

'Did you go to the music halls much, Gran, in the olden days?'

'Stop trying to change the subject.'

'I'm not. I got caught up with something important. If you was to stop nagging I would 'ave a chance to tell you where I've been!'

'You could at least have said you were sorry to your mother.'

'I will—if you let me get a word in edgeways!'

'Good. Now then . . . what was you asking me?' Satisfied that her granddaughter wouldn't be making a habit of staying out late, Harriet calmed down. 'Music halls, weren't it? Yeah, we went all right, as regular as clockwork. It was a lot cheaper than picture palaces, I'll tell yer . . . Live entertainment—you couldn't beat it.'

'What about the Grand Star?'

'What about it?'

'Did you go there?'

'Moons ago I did. I think they turned it into a Yiddish theatre before it was closed down. The Pavilion in Shoreditch was my favourite. Me and your grandfather used to love that place. Best music hall there was. Lusby's on the Mile End Road was all right for a good laugh. We saw Charlie Chaplin there a couple of times. It was a bit gaudy—a music hall-cum-gin palace. 'Course, you know it as the ABC. It was the Empire before that . . .' A distant look swept over Harriet's eyes. 'There's nothing so romantic as going with your sweetheart to see a live performance. All dressed up . . .'

Arriving with Rosie's drink, Iris raised an eyebrow at Harriet. 'Not back in the old days again, is she?'

Rosie didn't answer; she let them rattle on while she slipped into her own private world. She was imagining her and George, all dressed up and going into the Grand Star when the streets were lit by gas lamps. She pictured him opening a tiny box lined with black velvet, and nestling inside it a diamond ring . . .

'I reckon it was the wireless what killed the music halls. No one wanted to go out at night. Not when they could sit round the fire and listen to a bit of free entertainment. Then came the telly, of course . . .'

'Which you love!' Iris again.

With Rosie sipping her drink and Iris studying her knitting pattern, Harriet enjoyed the pictures which came flooding back to her. It was better than watching a film. The horse-drawn carriages, the omnibus, the long, bustled dresses and the men dressed as smart as their pockets would allow. Even in the Jago, the back of beyond of Bethnal Green, which had been one of the deprived areas of the East End, the inhabitants had had their pride, whether they slept on the pavements or in squalid rooms. She remembered herself as a child, staring into the bootmaker's window wishing she didn't always have to wear old, worn boots from the second-hand stall. All that had changed once she had been taken in by Mary Birchfield. Once they had been ensconced in the house in Bow, courtesy of Mary's rich benefactor, she and Arthur had enjoyed a high standard of living for five or six years.

'I know you're thinking about the old days, Gran, and for a change I'm not gonna discourage you, but before you start, I've got one question to ask—and I want a straight, truthful answer, right?'

'If you're gonna ask why me and your grandfather 'ad to leave Bow for Wapping, you're out of luck.'

Pulling herself up from the chair, Harriet yawned. 'It's past my bedtime. Don't stomp about

87

in the morning when you're getting yourself ready for work, Rosie. I need me beauty sleep. Goodnight.' Smiling, Harriet left the two of them to ponder and made her way up to her bedroom, pleased that she had at last piqued their curiosity with her hints of the past.

'I wasn't gonna ask her about leaving Bow. I wanted to ask if she'd go to an old music hall if it was reopened.' Seeing no reaction from her mother, Rosie decided not to pursue that line of conversation.

'What's this family secret she won't tell us about then?' Rosie said, vaguely interested.

'Something to do with her and your grandad. I've never asked because I really don't think she can talk about it.'

Rosie left the table and sat in the armchair, her mind working overtime. 'This Mary Birchfield who took her in was grandad's sister, right? Your aunt. And she 'ad a couple of kids, according to Gran, who would be your cousins . . . yet you've never seen 'ide nor 'air of 'em.'

'No. Well . . . maybe when I was very small. I can remember vaguely that a rich Aunt Mary came to visit us once. I don't know, though, it might have been a dream. More importantly, to me anyway, is your gran's family. They were split up; her mum and younger sister went to live with a relative over the water, in south London. I don't know why they didn't take Gran with them.'

'Too many mouths to feed, or not enough space. Or . . . maybe Gran was the unloved daughter?'

Whether Rosie had meant to or not, with those words she had struck Iris a blow. 'You'll be hard-pressed to find a mother who doesn't love *all* her

88

children, Rosie. Sometimes they find it difficult to show their feelings ... maybe.' She sighed and gazed at the thin band of gold on her finger. 'For one reason or another.'

'Gran didn't stop long in the workhouse though, did she?'

'No, she didn't stop long,' Iris sighed. 'She ran away after a few days from what I can make of it all. Lived rough on the streets until this Mary came along and rescued her. Ten years old and nowhere to live, no mum, no dad, and missing her little sister. It must have been very hard to take. No wonder she doesn't want to talk about that side of her life.'

'I'm not so sure.' Snapping herself out of her melancholy mood, Rosie cleared the table. 'I'll take her a mug of cocoa up. Do you want one?'

'No; I think I might treat myself to a little drop of sherry. Cheer myself up. Then you can tell me about the theatre lessons and how that went. George came round, by the way. Said he was passing, so he popped in to see us all. I think he's got it bad, Rosie.'

'He might not be the only one,' she said, tossing her hair back and returning the smile. 'Did he leave a message?'

'He's gonna meet you from work tomorrow. I said you finish at five o'clock, so don't put in for overtime. He'll be passing the brewery at that time ... or so he said.'

*   *   *

Unsure whether her gran was still awake, Rosie tapped quietly on her bedroom door and waited.

89

'What're you knocking for? Royalty now, am I?'

Turning the brass knob while balancing a small tray and a mug of cocoa, Rosie pushed open the door and smiled at the sight of her gran sitting up in bed, a book in one hand, a magnifying glass in the other, dwarfed by four big fat pillows. 'Thought you might fancy a hot drink.'

Harriet peered at the round tin tray. 'No fig biscuits?'

'No, but if you really want one . . .'

'Depends 'ow many sugars you put in. I fancy something sweet.'

'Three.' Rosie sat on the edge of her gran's bed and feigned exhaustion. In truth she felt as if she had enough energy for two, but didn't fancy going back downstairs again.

'That'll do.' Harriet took the mug, cupped it in her hands and sipped the milky drink. 'What d'yer want?'

'I don't want anything! Just trying to make amends, that's all. I thought you might like to know what's happened to the Grand Star music hall, but—' she shrugged, 'if you're not interested . . .'

'You'll tell me anyway. Go on.' She took another sip of her drink, keeping her eyes on Rosie's face. 'Something's brought the roses into your cheeks. I thought you might 'ave bumped into George and found out what the bit between your legs was for.'

'You're so dirty at times,' chuckled Rosie, 'you wouldn't dare say that in front of Mum.'

'I dare say she knows what hers is for . . . at least she will once she starts back at the brewery. Them men'll be round 'er like flies in a butcher's shop. It'll put a smile on her face, which'll be a blessing. Miserable cow.'

'You've changed your tune. Couldn't praise 'er enough, lately.'

'Yeah, well . . . can't have two of us having a go at her. It'd spoil my fun.' Harriet sniffed and narrowed her eyes. 'Well? What you got to tell me, then?'

'The old boy I mentioned earlier, Larry, he was locking up the Royal. He offered to walk me to the main street and we got talking. The Grand Star went dark in nineteen thirty-nine and 'asn't bin open since. The building's in good nick but wants a few bob spent on it. Larry's been looking after it. It's a bit of a hobby for 'im. Although the pour soul would love to see it open again . . . one day.' She glanced at her gran to see if she was taking it all in.

'Yeah . . . so? What's intriguing about that? All the bloody music halls went dark—I told you that; more than once.' She rolled her eyes, disappointed.

'It would be lovely to see it open though, wouldn't it? Bring back a bit of the past. Your past. Lovely memories.'

'Don't talk stupid. Costs a fortune to upkeep one of them buildings. Why d'yer think they were boarded up in the first place?'

'Because people wanted to stay in and listen to the wireless . . . at least they thought that's what they wanted. If they'd have known that it would mean the death of local music halls, they might 'ave thought twice about it.' She walked over to the window and pulled the curtain back a little to look out. 'It's dead out there. Once upon a time you would have heard people talking and laughing, on their way home after a good night's entertainment. It don't make sense. Not when places like the Grand Star are sitting there waiting to be used

91

again.

'I wish Tommy was alive. He'd get excited about it. His dream was to buy the old Forster picture palace, you know?' She turned and looked at Harriet. 'Did he ever say anything to you or Mum about that?'

'No, he never.'

Rosie could tell by Harriet's agitated tone that, deep down, she did want to see things changed back to the way they used to be. She didn't want to part with any of her savings, that was all. That, more than anything, bothered her. She was a saver. Always had been, always would be. 'He was always bunking in to the pictures. He loved films. You've got to admit that Gran. You know what he was like. Bloody albums full of film stars and bits cut out from the papers that had anything to do with films. He was—'

'Yeah, all right. You've made your point. Tommy never got the chance to do what he dreamed of, so let's make sure you do. Right?'

'No! I was just reminding you, that's all. Reminding you of what he wanted for himself . . . and what he wanted for me.'

'So where's the money gonna come from?' Harriet said.

'I could go to a loan club.'

'You will not. Sodding sharks.'

'Anyway . . . it might not need all that much spent on it. It's filthy but I thought if me, Mum, Shirley, Shirley's mum and a few other neighbours were to go in with scrubbing brushes—'

Harriet's high-pitched burst of laughter stopped her dead. The cocoa spilling out of the mug in her bony hands and on to the bedclothes made Rosie

92

even more angry. It was her turn to go to the launderette, and if she had to take the thick cotton throw-over and the week's wash, she would have to take two machines and there were hardly ever two available at once.

'Look what you're doing! Spilling cocoa everywhere!'

'That's all right . . .' Harriet chuckled, wiping a tear off her cheek, 'we'll get the neighbours to boil it up. They might even clean our windows an' all!'

'You think you're so funny. You'll smile on the other side of your face if I do borrow the money and do it up! I'll make a nice little packet out of it. Outsiders can't resist coming to the East End . . . especially the tourists . . . and especially Americans. Once they got to 'ear about it, we'd make a bomb.'

'Neighbours . . .' said Harriet, softening her tone. 'As if they ain't got enough to do.' She shook her head and sighed. 'Things you come out with! Stick to your dreams of being a dancer and give us all a rest.'

Rosie cast her eyes down and tried another tactic—sounding hurt and despondent. 'I just thought that if we all went down there in a van with as many vacuum cleaners as we could borrow and as many pails and scrubbing brushes . . . they love rallying round for a cause, you know they do. You included.'

'Stop acting. You're not on the stage yet. I'll ask you the same thing as I asked when you walked in with this cocoa—what d'yer want?'

Rosie slowly raised her eyes. 'Money for carbolic, an' that.'

Harriet placed her mug on her bedside table, splayed one hand and pointed a finger with the

93

other. 'You'll need ... One:' she held out her thumb, 'Windowlene. Two:' she held out a finger, 'soda.' Then the next finger. 'Bleach.' Then the next. 'Block of soap for the floors and paintwork; polish; flea powder; rat poison; mousetraps; and no doubt new stage curtains and new theatre seats. Never mind all the paint and varnish. You're potty to even think about it. Go and get me a figgy biscuit.'

'Mr Davies—five doors up—don't he work in a paint factory?' said Rosie, knowingly.

Harriet let out a prolonged sigh. 'You don't listen, do you?'

'Yes I do,' she smiled, 'you just said you'd pay out for the cleaning stuff and that ... if it fell off the back of a lorry.'

'Good God ...' Harriet was for once genuinely taken aback, and unable to hide it. 'You really can see right through me ... see more'n I can meself. Get there before I do.' She shuddered. 'You've made me go all goose-pimply.'

'We're two peas from the same pod, don't forget. Everyone says so. Now then, do you really want me to go all the way downstairs just to get you one fig roll?'

Harriet shook her head, too absorbed with her present mood to think about eating. Rosie had struck a chord with her casual use of an old saying. When she and Arthur had played together, after they had first met, the same remark had been made by his sister, Mary, more than once. *You're like two peas in a pod.* Later in life, when all the trouble was brewing, Mary had repeated the saying in front of her own two children, the ones she had had by her wealthy lover, Sir Robert; giggling, one of them,

94

the arrogant girl, had remarked that maybe the same maggot, in the pod, had crawled over both of them.

The hollow in Harriet's chest worsened as she recalled how Mary's children had had an upbringing she could never have dreamed of; there was plenty of money, nannies, a governess. Sir Robert saw that his children were brought up to live belonging to the upper classes—and have the same snobbish attitudes as he had towards her and Arthur. Mary had tried her best, but those children would never look upon them as anything more than ignorant peasants. She wondered for a moment what had happened to those spoiled, pampered kids, and if they ever knew that their mother had been a kept woman and that they were, in fact, bastards.

'Why do you really want to get the music hall up and running again?' she asked in a quiet, sombre voice, pushing away all thoughts of her past.

'I don't know Gran ... not really. It'd be easier for me to go back to the theatre another night, when the drama teacher's in the building ... but now that I've seen the Star and met Larry, the old boy ...'

'I doubt he can be bothered with it all,' she said, all-knowing.

'Now that's where you are wrong. He loves that place. You should see 'ow he keeps one of the rooms! It's as if he lives there. Tommy loved the picture palaces ... Larry loves old music halls. Each to their own.'

'We'll talk about it tomorrow. I'm worn out listening to yer.' Harriet yawned, rearranged her pillows and inched herself down into her bed.

'Switch my light off on your way out, there's a good girl.'

''Course I will.' Rosie leaned over and kissed her gran on the cheek. 'Night-night—don't let the bedbugs bite.

'Oh, I nearly forgot to tell you . . . I nutted one of the cocky sods from the Prospect of Whitby. He really insulted me. He'll think twice next time.'

Lifting her head a couple of inches off her pillow, Harriet peered at her granddaughter. 'I hope that's a joke?'

'No. Why should it be? Toffee-nosed sod deserved it. You should 'ave heard the crack,' she chuckled.

Concerned by Rosie's matter-of-fact confession, she lowered her head back down into the feather pillow and murmured, 'Turn over if you have a nightmare.' Something which she had repeated several times when Rosie was a child and had cried out in the night. She had a feeling, though, that it might be herself who would be having bad dreams. Her granddaughter had brushed up against violence twice in a very short space of time and if, as she had always believed, events came in threes, what might come next?

With her hand on the light switch, Rosie stood in the doorway looking at the small bundle under the bedclothes. 'See you in the morning, Gran,' she said quietly, switching off the light and closing the door behind her.

CHAPTER SIX

With the March wind blowing into her face, Rosie gripped Iris's arm as they stepped out of the brewery gates on to Mile End Road after what had proved to be an important day in both of their lives. Working together in the same factory had created a bond between them which neither had expected. Synchronizing their schedule that morning, Iris's first day back at the brewery had proved to be less chaotic than they had envisaged. Harriet had helped with her role-playing, behaving as if they were small children being sent to school with lunch boxes and polished shoes.

'I was wondering . . .' Rosie said hesitantly, 'if I should 'ave driving lessons instead of us selling Tommy's car. What d'yer think?'

'I've already thought about it. We'll sell it through the *Advertiser*. You couldn't afford to run it, Rosie. Tax, insurance, petrol—never mind the cost of driving lessons. Anyway, it's not all that reliable; think back to how many times your brother had to have Mike the mechanic round to get it going. It's been nothing but trouble from the day he got it. He should never have sold that old shooting brake . . . but there you are, he had to show off and have the biggest car in the street.'

Taken aback by the reprobation, Rosie glanced at Iris. It was the first time she had heard her mother criticize her beloved son.

'I s'pose George's a bit flash as well . . .' Rosie offered, testing her mother. 'The way he dresses and that.'

'I don't think so. He's a bit swanky, that's all. Keeps up with the style. Your brother wasn't flash, Rosie, he—'

'I know that.' She withdrew her arm and pushed her hands into her coat pockets. 'It was you who said he was a show-off.'

Turning the conversation, Iris asked Rosie if she was seeing George that night, adding that she thought he was very polite, that she liked him. 'I do worry a bit about the difference in your ages though, Rosie.' She stretched an arm across her daughter to stop her stepping on to the main road. 'The lights are changing.'

'Why should that worry you?'

'Well . . . you can bet your bottom dollar he's cruised up the Nile. He might expect more from you than he should.'

'I'm twenty-three Mum—not a teenager! I know all I need to know about sex, if that's what you're building up to. I've courted a couple of boys . . . I think I know what they expect and what they don't expect.'

'There is a difference. George's twenty-seven; he's not a boy.'

'That's what makes him so special. And no . . . to answer your question. I'm not seeing him tonight. It's Monday. I'm going to the Theatre Royal, remember? You're getting as bad as Gran for not listening.'

'Why can't George go with you? Save walking through Wapping by yourself at that time of night.'

'I 'aven't even told him I'm going.' She tossed her long curly hair off her face and smiled. 'I don't want him to know yet. Him and his mates have got certain opinions about people in the theatre. They

98

reckon the men are all poofs and the women upper-class sluts.'

'Tch . . .' Iris shook her head and sighed. 'Things you come out with.'

'I'm only repeating what I've 'eard. Anyway, I doubt I'll be that late back. I'm goin' there to black my nose, that's all.' She didn't want to say that she was going to the Theatre Royal to meet up with Larry for a tour of the Grand Star. She had told her gran where she was going, but had asked her to keep it to herself for the time being. Her mother might put a damper on things.

'Anyway; enough about me. How'd your first day go?'

'I told you at lunchtime. It was fine.'

'I wasn't born yesterday. You 'ated every minute of it.'

'Only at first . . . during the morning. I soon found my feet. It's been a very long time since I was in an office; an age. It took me back . . . and it brought me to. What have I done with my life? Fifty next birthday. Fifty.' She shook her head despairingly. 'What a waste of time . . . washing and polishing things that didn't need it—passing the time of day until—'

'Tommy got in from work,' Rosie cut in.

'And you came home from school . . . and then from the box factory. All those years spent indoors when I could have been out here, earning and being my old self.'

'Now you really do sound like Gran.'

'Yeah, all right, I'll admit she had a point. But right or wrong, how often do any of us listen to our mothers?' The remark was meant to be double-edged, but Iris had not yet earned the privilege of

99

preaching to her daughter and she knew it—they both knew it. Rosie could not remember a time when she had been offered her advice. At least the comment held promise.

Pushing open their front door, the two women caught a whiff of something nice and savoury coming from the kitchen. 'Smells like Lancashire hotpot,' murmured Iris, 'she's going all out, bless 'er.'

'I only 'ope I'm as active as she is when I'm eighty. Not that I'd want her to hear that. She'll be shoving cod liver oil down my throat, putting crushed garlic in my slippers and spouting old remedies non-stop.'

Surprised to see George perched on a kitchen chair enjoying a cup of tea, Rosie smiled. 'What are you doin' 'ere?' He looked more attractive than ever in his donkey jacket, jeans and leather boots.

'I've come to give you the good news. I'm getting out of the docks. I've had a little windfall.'

'Got the sack more like,' Harriet snapped, while turning the gas down low under the bubbling saucepan of brussels. 'Silly bugger sees it as a dividend.'

'She's wrong,' he grinned, winking at Rosie. 'A bit of business worked out very nicely. I always fancied myself as a businessman. There's a shop for let in Watney Street. The man wants to sell his stock and goodwill ... a tobacconists, with a nice little flat above. I thought we might go out for a steak tonight, babe, to celebrate.'

'You bloody won't.' Harriet again. 'Took me all day to shop, prepare and cook for their dinner. Take 'er out tomorrow. Me and Iris'll 'ave fish and chips, save me cooking. Slaving over a soddin' stove

100

all day.'

Rosie and Iris looked at each other and smiled. This was the first time Harriet had cooked a meal in ages, and she was loving the chance to brag and complain.

'We'll go out for a drink then—*after* she's had her dinner.'

'I can't, George, not tonight. I'm going somewhere.'

'Oh yeah?' He sniffed and peered into her face. 'Who with?'

'Shirley Martin,' Rosie lied, thinking it might not be such a bad idea to take her friend with her.

Suspicion swept over his face as he looked from her to Harriet who, by her expression, was making it clear that she had no intention of getting involved. 'Well that's funny 'cos Shirley left 'ere ten minutes ago full of the joys of spring. She came to show you her solitaire. Big diamond.'

'Shirley's got engaged?' Rosie beamed, fully aware that her cover was blown. 'When?'

'Today. They're taking both sets of parents out for a meal . . . tonight. The engagement party's this Saturday.' He pulled a cigarette from his packet and avoided her eyes. 'She must have forgot she was going out with you.' He shook his head slowly. 'Never mentioned a word of it. No message of a change of plans; nothing.'

Rosie was hearing him, but other sentiments were touching a nerve: envy and disappointment. 'She's my best friend. How come she never told me she was getting engaged?'

'Because her fella wanted to keep it between themselves till the day. Best friends have to take second place sometimes,' he added pointedly, with

101

a touch of disappointment in his own voice. 'That was a lovely cup of tea, Harry, girl!' He stood up and pushed his shoulders back. 'I'll leave you to eat in peace. See you, Iris.' Making his way to the kitchen door he paused, looked at Rosie, went to say something, and then changed his mind. 'Mind how you go, babe.'

The kitchen filled with silence as they waited for the sound of the street door closing behind him. 'Now you've done it,' Harriet murmured, testing a brussel with a fork. 'The webs we weave . . .'

'You're not two-timing him, are you?' Iris's self-righteous, accusing voice rankled. What right had she to behave like a mother all of a sudden?

'Yeah, I'm seeing a lovely fella tonight; Larry. How long's dinner gonna be, Gran?'

'Five minutes. Pour these spuds into the colander for me, Iris. My wrist can't take the weight of that saucepan.'

'Right. I'll have a quick wash then, and put a bit of lipstick on.' Hiding the touch of regret at having lied unnecessarily to George, Rosie went to the bathroom.

'So that's why she was so late home last Monday. She's seeing someone else.' Iris pulled off her coat and mumbled, 'Like father, like daughter.'

Pointing the potato masher at Iris's face, Harriet looked far from pleased. 'Don't be so bloody judgemental! She's not seeing anyone else, right? Now leave it at that and give me a hand.'

'I doubt that George'll believe *that*. She'll lose a good one there; silly mare.'

'You reckon?' Harriet turned away, smiling and shaking her head. 'He'll feel a right lemon when she does finally tell him who she's seeing tonight. A right bloody lemon!' She laughed at the thought of it. 'And so will you if you don't keep your gob shut and leave her be.'

*   *   *

As she approached the Prospect of Whitby, on her way to catch a bus, Rosie wished she had acted more lovingly towards George. All she had had to do was speak to him privately, outside the street door, and explain why she had not told him the truth as to where she was really going. That she wanted to keep it quiet until she had either joined the theatre workshop or got round Larry to open up the old music hall. He would have laughed at her for sure, but that would have been better than letting him go off believing she was two-timing him.

Rosie quietly cursed herself for being stupid, and stepped up her pace. If she was back early enough she would go round George's house and surprise him. Then she would sort things out properly. Happier and lighter inside, she braced herself for another possible round of abuse from the young men drinking beer outside the Prospect.

She glanced sideways at them, relieved to see that the one she had shamed wasn't there, although someone else was; the one who had reminded her of Tommy. Passing the small group, she smiled at him, nodded hello, crossed over the narrow road and turned left into the badly lit street.

Preoccupied with the student who had befriended her the previous week, she was regretting not having said something to him. He was worthy of more than a polite nod. She wondered why he had reminded her so much of her brother. Maybe, unconsciously, she was searching for a substitute, just like her gran had when she lost her soulmate. She and Grandad Arthur had been the best of friends as well as husband and wife.

Remembering the way Tommy had always had her welfare at heart, she was unaware of the group of students approaching the gasworks from the opposite direction, on their way to the pub.

'Just off to the boxing ring, are you?' came one smart remark.

'Or is it down to the gym for a bit of wrestling?' chortled another.

Rosie hastened on, looking straight ahead and ignoring them, relieved that they had not slowed down and offered no threat. This particular stretch of road was not welcoming, and there was a damp foggy atmosphere reminiscent of midwinter instead of late March and the promise of spring. She instinctively looked over her shoulder to check that they really had carried on walking. She scolded herself for being so jittery; allowing her gran's warning about the gasworks to get to her.

'Hello, whore.' The sneering, hushed voice startled Rosie. She stopped dead, gripped with fear.

Stepping out of the shadows, the student she had injured the week before stood in front of her and grinned. 'I thought it was you.' His eyes darted everywhere, checking his surroundings. It was very quiet on the street, not one footstep to be heard. 'Wicked night, isn't it?'

Swallowing the rush of saliva to moisten her dry throat, she tried to hide her terror. 'I've arranged to meet my boyfriend here.'

'Have you really?' Bertie sneered. 'Do you

know . . . they had a *very* difficult time resetting my nose.' His hand flew to her throat and clutched the long woollen scarf, twisting and turning it until it was tight around her neck. 'Not quite as cocky now, are we?' He pushed his face close to Rosie's, breathing into hers. 'Scum of the earth.' With his left hand gripping her scarf, his knuckles pressed into her windpipe, he drew back the other hand and hit her in the face. 'Slag!'

Trembling and too stunned to scream, Rosie flinched, contracting every muscle in her body as his hand came at her again, this time slapping her cheek with the flat of his palm. The third and most excruciating pain came when he rammed his knee between her legs. A penetrating, stinging sensation surged through her body; a rushing stir of burning, icy-cold hurt.

With one hand spread across her face, the nails digging in, he used the other to grip and squeeze one breast until he heard an agonized cry. He then gave her a right-hand slap which sent her sprawling to the ground.

'Slag!' He drew phlegm, spat at her feet and strode away, heading for his digs, glad that it had started to rain. Glad that the slut would lie there in the wet. She had made him the butt of all the jokes at the medical college, besides inflicting excruciating pain and disfiguring his face. His pride was still smarting, and no doubt would be for a while yet. The common tart had not seen the last of him. The beating he had given her had not satisfied him, and he had no intention of remaining the victim. He would turn it around somehow. He would have his peers slapping him on the back and congratulating him for putting the ignorant bitch in her place.

*   *   *

With the light drizzle moistening her face, Rosie slowly came to her senses and tried to focus on her surroundings, but the sound of quick, echoing footsteps sent a renewed rush of terror through her.

'Rosie! It's me, Richard Montague.' Kneeling by her side, the student looked into her face, which was beginning to swell under the streaks of blood and dirt. Shamed by what he saw, he brushed her damp, bedraggled hair from her face. 'I'll see the coward go down for this . . . I swear it.'

'I want to be sick . . .' she whispered.

He placed his hands on her shoulders. 'Bend your head forward and down.'

Doing as she was told, Rosie felt a throbbing in her face and temples as the blood rushed to her head and the need to throw up ebbed away. 'What's happening?'

'Can you stand up?'

'I don't want to.' She raised her glazed eyes to his. 'I don't know what's happening.'

'The coward had been lying in wait for you. If you can manage to walk a few steps, you'll feel better. Then I'll help you home. I'll carry you if you like.'

'No . . . get me a taxi . . . there's a phone box along the turning.'

'I want to see you on your feet first. Once I can see you're OK, you can sit down again and rest while I've gone. I'll be a few minutes, that's all. Grip my arm and ease yourself up.'

106

'Is she OK?' One of the other students appeared, out of breath from running.

'Hardly, Simon. Look what he's done to her! They were right, he was out for revenge. You couldn't fetch your car, could you? We should get her home . . . where we can look at her properly.'

'Put . . . put me in a taxi,' Rosie murmured, dropping her aching head to one side and leaning on Richard's shoulder. 'I want to go home.'

'It'll be quicker if Simon drives.'

Drained and too overwhelmed to argue, Rosie slowly nodded. 'OK . . . but drop me off at the corner of my turning.' She closed her eyes and took a long, slow breath. 'Drop me off at the corner. I'll walk the rest of the way.' Having used the last of her resources to get her message across, she licked her dry lips and slipped back into oblivion, limp in Richard's supporting arms.

By the time Simon had collected his car and returned, Rosie had recovered enough to stand with a little assistance. Composing herself and trying to stop the trembling, she thanked Simon for coming back.

'If you could drop me off outside my house . . .' she said, trying to stop her teeth chattering.

'Don't worry, we won't let your parents see us,' Richard smiled, helping her into the front passenger seat. 'I know we're not the most popular people around here.'

'I don't want them to know who did this. There'll be trouble.'

'Well . . . your parents have every right to fetch in the police.' He closed her door and got into the back of the car.

'That's not our way,' Rosie managed to say,

wishing they would just get on with it.

As he pulled away, Simon looked at her sideways. 'I suppose what you're saying is that they'd give the guy who did this to you a bloody good hiding.'

She lay her head back and nodded slowly. 'Something like that.'

'Well, that might be a good thing, mightn't it?'

'No.' She placed her hands on her face. 'My eye's throbbing.'

Once they had reached the street where she lived, she asked them to pull up. Thanking them, she got out of the car, desperate to be in the comfort of her own home where she would be safe.

'Let me at least walk you to your door.' Richard's concern made her feel worse.

'No ... honestly, I'll be all right. You can stop there till I've gone in if that makes you feel better.' She walked slowly away, taking each step as if it might be the last.

'Rosie!' Richard called after her. 'Here's my address.' He handed her a neatly folded piece of paper. 'I've written down the telephone number. Just ask for me or leave a contact number.' He looked directly into her face and smiled. 'I really do want to see you again. Away from the Prospect.'

'Thanks. You've been great.' She slipped the note into her pocket and waved a hand, forcing back her tears. The last thing she needed was to be cross-examined by Harriet and Iris.

With throbbing pains pounding, Rosie leaned on the front door and pressed the bell. Her hands were shaking too much for her to use her door key.

When Iris opened the door, her reaction of surprise changed instantly to one of dread. Her eyes filled with fear and questioning; she stood immobilized, voiceless and tight-lipped.

'It's not as bad as it seems', is what Rosie tried to say, but the words wouldn't come. Instead a weird sound escaped. A pitiful wail which grew, faded, and grew again, as the tears ran down her face. 'Mum ...' she heard herself cry. 'Mum ... he hit me ... kept hitting me ... I don't want to be hit any more. I don't want anyone to hit me any more.'

She fell into her mother's arms and they held on to each other, hugging tightly. 'No one's gonna hurt you again, Rosie, no one.'

'Now what's 'appened?' Harriet was in the sitting-room doorway. 'Letting all the heat out and the cold air in!'

Guiding her daughter into the warm room, Iris sat her down on the settee, by the fire. 'D'you want a milky drink or a drop of something stronger?'

'Stronger.' She wiped her face with the back of her hand. 'I was knocked down by a car, Gran. Hit and run. He must 'ave been drunk. The car was all over the place and—'

Harriet placed a finger under Rosie's chin and gently lifted her face. It wasn't the swollen eye, the weals on her face, the blood smeared with dirt, the fat lip or Rosie's bedraggled hair which caused her to stiffen. It was the look in her granddaughter's eyes. The look of someone who had been assaulted. 'Did he rape you?' She remained stony-faced.

'No, Gran. He just ...' her face twisted again as she shook her head and wiped her runny nose with her hand and began to weep. 'I thought he was gonna kill me.' She raised her eyes to meet Harriet's. 'I don't know where my handkerchief is.'

109

'I'll fetch you a clean one. Lie back and I'll fetch you something to drink as well. A draught. And something to put on your face.'

'Not brown ointment,' she whispered, too fragile to argue her case against it. Lifting her feet, she sank down into the feather cushions and closed her eyes.

'Just a spirit wash, Rosie, that's all. It'll help keep the bruising down and cool your skin. I'll soak a nice soft bit of lint and you can lie there with it on your face.'

'And that's it?' she said, her eyes half open.

'That and my own recipe draught for shock.'

She accepted the freshly ironed handkerchief from Iris and managed a smile. 'Just let me lie quiet for a while though, eh?'

Iris stroked her daughter's hair while Harriet went into the kitchen to prepare her remedies. 'When you're ready . . . we'll just sit and listen.' She took Rosie's hand and gently squeezed it. 'I'll stop Gran if she starts to ask questions.'

'She won't ask. She knows what 'appened. I brought it on myself.'

Surprising Iris, Rosie, having dropped the pretence of a hit and run, quietly recounted everything that had happened from the moment she had first run into her attacker on her way back from the Grand Star, to the following week when Richard and Simon had come to her rescue, pausing only when her gran put the draught to her lips, and again when she laid the cool wet lint on her face. Through it all, neither Iris nor Harriet said a word.

'I should 'ave known better. It was stupid.' She pressed her hands against the lint and then handed

110

it back to Harriet. 'I'll put it on again in a minute.'

Harriet examined Rosie's face, keeping her fury in check. 'I think Vaseline's gonna be the best thing for that lip. Can you bear to smear a bit on?'

'Yeah . . . anything to stop it throbbing.'

As she turned to go, the ringing doorbell stopped her. She stood very still, praying that history was not about to repeat itself.

'It's all right, Gran,' Rosie said, 'it won't be him. He doesn't know where I live.'

'Stay here, Mum. I'll go.' The tone of Iris's voice marked her mood. She was a mother affronted.

'It might be George. Don't say anything. Not a word about what happened. Tell him I was knocked down and—'

'All *right*, Rosie!' Annoyed that she would have to hold her tongue, Iris left the room.

'Larry'll wonder where you've got to,' murmured Harriet, reflectively.

'Nothing wrong with your memory, is there. Fancy you remembering his name.'

'I've always been one for names. Not faces, though . . . I'm not all that good on faces.'

'That's a new one on me,' said Rosie weakly. 'I've never heard you say that before . . .'

'Give your tongue and brain a rest, for Gawd's sake. You always was a terrible patient. Would never lie down and sleep; even when you was in pain with the mumps.'

'So you told me . . . a hundred times. Anyway . . . I'll go and see the old boy tomorrow.'

'Not on your own you won't.'

George, frowning and looking even more handsome than ever, his blue eyes bright with anger, arrived in the doorway. 'Did you get his licence number?'

'No she never—and she don't wanna talk about it!' Harriet glared at him, charging him to drop it.

George kept his eyes on Rosie. 'You all right, babe?'

''Course I am.' Rosie smiled and relaxed, comforted by his protective ways. 'They're making a fuss over nothing.' His unexpected arrival was the best healing she could have wished for. 'Come and sit down.' She dragged her legs under her, hiding the pain which became sharper as she eased her bottom into a more comfortable position. 'I've got something to tell you.' She would use the Grand Star as a diversion.

'Go on then.' He sat down and glanced at her, dubious. 'You're gonna have a right shiner in the morning.'

'Gran's thinking about investing some of her savings into a project of mine.'

'That's news. Since when?' Harriet asked.

'D'yer fancy coming in as well? There'll be returns, but not for a couple of years.' She ignored her gran's soundless gesture of remonstration.

'Depends what I'm in *for*,' he said, slipping a hand around her stockinged foot and squeezing it.

'Enough of that. No handling the goods till you own 'em,' said Harriet, giving her very first hint of what she would like to see happen between Rosie and George. As far as she was concerned, he was just the man for her tempestuous granddaughter.

'You'd have to go a long way to find anyone who could own Rosie. She's 'er own person.' George winked at his girlfriend, squeezed her toes and removed his hand. 'So,' he said, leaning back and trying not to look at her wounded face. He knew the injuries had not been caused by a passing car. Promising himself that he would get to the bottom of what had really happened, he ignored the rage in the pit of his stomach and waited to hear what she had on her mind.

Placing the wet lint on her brow, Rosie rested her head back again. 'I want to reopen an old music hall in Stratford.' She spoke in a quiet monotone. 'Get a team of women down there to scrub the place from top to bottom. Put on a musical, even. You've got a smashing voice, George . . . it's not right to waste it. You only sing with the band at family and friends' weddings.'

'You want to . . . reopen a disused theatre *and* put on a show?' George did his utmost to keep a straight face.

'That's right,' Rosie murmured, easing her head on to the pillow that Iris had slipped under her. Closing her eyes, she said, 'I've worked out the story already. I've been slowly building it up in my head for years. I even dream it.'

'You didn't bang your head did you, babe, when that car hit you?' Half joking, half worried, George eyed her with uncertainty.

'It's where I was meant to go tonight.'

George shrugged and splayed his hands, looking to the other women for support. 'I'm out of my depth,' he said honestly. 'Help me out, ladies. Is she serious, or what?'

Quietening him with a wave of her hand, Harriet peered into her granddaughter's pale face. 'Don't you think we should get you into bed, Rosie?'

Not wishing to dampen her daughter's spirits or make her sound like a simpleton, Iris spoke softly: 'Someone must own the building. The rent'll be a

113

fortune.'

'I'll tell you all about it tomorrow ...' Rosie's voice trailed off into a yawn. 'What did you put in that potion, Gran? A sleeping pill?'

'Harriet's right. You should be in bed,' said George, a positive tone to his voice. 'We'll talk about it when you're over this.'

'I'll be all right after a sleep ... you can all discuss it meanwhile. It won't cost the earth.'

Smiling into his girlfriend's face, George pushed his arms under Rosie and lifted her, holding her close and brushing a kiss across her cheek. 'Let's get you between them sheets.' Ignoring Harriet and her loud throat-clearing he added, 'Then I'll be on my way. You need a rest.' He would find out what had really happened to her in a day or so.

*   *   *

With Rosie tucked up and George gone, Harriet had time to consider all that had happened—Rosie's beating uppermost in her mind. Iris had made it clear that she wanted to tell George what had taken place by the gasworks, and Harriet had been adamant that they should respect Rosie's wishes which, in her opinion, were right. She had been feckless but more importantly, her granddaughter had learned a hard lesson about life and about people.

The business of the theatre had amused Harriet at first, but now a strange sensation was warming her, a radiating glow overcoming all her doubts. The money she had put by, apart from her own savings, now had a purpose. When her grandson and the boys had waylaid a cargo of whisky en

114

route to Dover a few years back, she had been given a wad of notes for safe keeping. It was soon after this that she had been taken aside by a trusted friend and told of Tommy's habit; that he was a compulsive gambler.

At first he had denied it, over and over, until his fury at his gran for not disclosing where she had hidden his money overtook his ardent respect for her. That was when the rows started, but no matter how much he hollered she had stood firm, determined that until he proved the money was to be spent on something worthwhile and not frittered away in the gambling clubs, she would not give it back. Sometime afterwards, once he realized that she would not budge, he had agreed that she should hold it for him until he needed it to pay for either his or Rosie's wedding.

Had Tommy lived to see that day, Harriet would have returned it to him, but half-heartedly. A white wedding, as far as she was concerned, was an expensive way of getting married when all that was required was the simple signing of a marriage certificate and a knees-up.

'I s'pose we'd best go with her,' said Iris, pensive, 'next time she goes to that theatre.'

'She won't want that. Not yet.' Harriet looked from the floor to Iris. 'Best leave 'er be for now; let her get on with it. She'll soon give us an earbashing once she's sorted 'erself; done her sums and that.' She chuckled and shook her head. 'Who would 'ave thought it, eh? Our little Rose wants put to on a show in the Grand Star.'

'I know,' Iris smiled, 'and she's worked it all out for herself. She's grown up quite a bit these past weeks.'

115

'And that pleases you, does it?'

'Yes and no. She can't go on behaving like a teenager all her life. I only wish I'd have ...' She looked back at Harriet and shrugged. 'I missed out when she was growing up, didn't I? She spent more time with you than she did with me.'

'You've got to put all that behind you, Iris. Don't try to make up for it in one clean sweep. Give it time. I've seen a big difference in the pair of you since Tommy went.' She stood up and stretched. 'Now then. I don't know about you, but after the shock of seeing her like that ... I'm ready for a shot of whisky.'

'Me too.'

Harriet sat down again. 'Well, go and get it then! Show a bit of compassion. I've bin on my feet all bloody day!' In truth, Harriet wanted a few minutes to herself, to think things over. If she or Iris did tell George what had been going on at the Prospect, more blood would be spilled with another fight. If they chose to keep quiet, say nothing, Rosie would still be in danger of attack from a man who obviously had no scruples about beating up women.

'You know what I think ...' said Iris, returning with their drinks, 'I think we should give Madam a good dressing down once she's feeling better and she's over this shock.'

'Oh, so you've been doing some thinking as well.' Harriet sighed, pleased that she was not alone in worrying over Rosie.

'Of course I have.' She handed her mother a drink and sat down. 'I think we should keep this attack to ourselves for now. Gradually draw more information out of Rosie ... find out who the bastard is who did that to her ... and pay him a

116

visit ourselves. Give *him* a dressing down and a warning—that if he so much as looks at her again, we'll tell Reggie and the others what's happened.'

'Sounds sensible. What about George? You don't think we should tell him instead of Reggie?'

'No. Absolutely not. He'll murder 'im. There'll be no thinking it through first, no plan of action—he'll be straight round there. We're talking about his girl, don't forget.'

'All right. Yeah ...' Harriet found herself smiling. 'I can't wait to pull that little bastard to one side.'

*   *   *

In the privacy of her room, Rosie soaked the lint which her gran had given her and laid it across her groin, pressing her hand against it to try and dull the painful throbbing. She was sitting up in bed with her legs outstretched, leaning against propped-up pillows. Grateful for the quiet, she ran the events of the evening through her mind. It had been feckless of her to go anywhere near the Prospect, and she had no one to blame but herself. It was obvious, now, with hindsight, that *his* type of person would want to retaliate.

Her thoughts ran on to the Grand Star and Larry. If she was up to it, she would pay him a visit the next evening, avoiding the gasworks. She would tell him of her plans to reopen the theatre before she lost her nerve. Why she had gone from wanting to be a small player in the world of theatre to someone ready to take the lead, she had no idea. One thing she did know: she stood to lose more than her pride if no one came to the old music hall, once it was in business again.

Sliding down under the bedclothes, she closed her eyes and tried to ignore the worry inside; the uneasy feeling that she was about to leave behind the old Rosie and let a more mature woman come up for air. If she gave up now, at this early stage, she would have to live with herself knowing she hadn't had the grit to finish what she had started.

* * *

'I've never 'eard anything so stupid!' Harriet slammed around the kitchen, furious with Rosie for insisting that she was going to go into work. 'Look at your face! The swelling might be going down, but your face is still black and blue!'

'Don't exaggerate,' Rosie said as she peered at the small mirror above the sink. 'It's nowhere near as bad as I thought it was gonna be.'

'I know why you're doing it. Just so's you can go to that bloody fleapit tonight. If you're fit for work, you're fit for pleasure—that's the way your mind's working.'

'No, it's not. I don't want to sit around dwelling on what 'appened. I thought you'd be pleased.'

Seeing Iris arrive at the kitchen door, she directed her frustration at her. 'Can't you talk some sense into your daughter?'

'She's old enough to think for herself. It's time we were leaving.'

Rosie kissed her gran on the cheek. 'Stop worrying—I'm stronger than we thought. See you later.'

'If I'm still here! I might just go round that pub and find out a bit more about that bastard. P'raps

118

I'll get my face slapped as well!'

With a shake of the head and a sigh, Rosie left the kitchen and followed Iris out of the house, hoping her gran would have calmed down by the time they got home.

As she closed the street door behind them, Rosie returned Iris's faint smile and shrugged. 'There's no appeasing Gran when her temper's up.'

'Are you really gonna go tonight?'

'Yep. I owe the old boy an apology. Poor sod—there's not much going on in 'is life. He could do without me letting him down.'

'And you still want to go on with this new project?'

'More than ever. I'll be able to tell you more once I've talked to Larry and had a good look at the place. If it's out of the question . . . it's out of the question. I won't cut my wrists over it.'

*   *   *

Having to get through the day on the conveyor belt, explain away her bruised face and take the many quips thrown at her, Rosie was very pleased when she heard the five o'clock hooter resounding through the brewery. The hiding she had received had affected her more than she had let on. By two o'clock that afternoon, she had felt ready for bed and had toyed with the idea of asking her manageress if she could leave early. The only thing which had kept her going was the thought of seeing the theatre again.

On their way home, Rosie's and Iris's conversation had been mostly about the latest gossip at Charrington's.

119

'It must be the smell of beer,' joked Rosie. 'The place reeks of it. We're probably all a bit pissed after a day's work.'

'You're getting more like your gran every day.'

'Am I?' she said, not hearing her. She was peering at a yellow Ford Zodiac waiting at the traffic lights. Stopping in her tracks, she lowered her head and checked the driver's face. Looking sideways at her, he grinned and winked; a sickly grin—an offensive wink. Was her mind playing tricks? He looked so much like one of the men who had killed Tommy. His smooth, tanned face was clean, unmarked.

Feeling sick, she watched the car pull away. 'Did you see who was driving that car, Mum?'

'No. Why?'

She slowly turned and looked into Iris's face and knew in an instant that she had no right to bring back the nightmare. 'I thought the driver looked like someone famous . . . an actor . . .'

'You've got actors on the brain,' Iris chuckled, pulling her daughter by the arm. 'Come on, dreamer.'

Silent for the rest of the journey through the backstreets, Rosie could not get the sighting out of her mind. If it was one of the murderous swines, he certainly hadn't been punished by his own people, or anyone else. Her faith in Reggie evaporated. Had he and his pack let the bastards get away with murder for the sake of keeping the peace on their patch? And if so, had George known all along? Had her brother been so insignificant in this world that his unnecessary death meant nothing?

'What's wrong, Rosie? You've gone all quiet and pale. Was today too much, after all?'

'Yeah. That's probably it.' She linked arms with her mother and snuggled up close, quickening her pace. She must have been mistaken. She was hardly in a fit state to think straight so soon after her own assault. She began to lose confidence in herself. Was this the beginning of paranoia? Were there worse moments to come? She shook her head to clear its dark thoughts.

'I'll be all right once I've got Gran's speciality in front of me. She's making bangers and mash with fried onions for tea.'

'That should put the smile back on your face, then.'

''Course it will.' She couldn't imagine anything making her smile, not until the sickening doubts had gone from her mind.

Thankful that her mother was content to be quiet, Rosie mapped out her evening. She would have to go to the Prospect and make peace with the young man who beat her up. After all, she had broken his nose and for no reason other than a bit of taunting. The very thought of talking to him made her stomach turn, but having to worry about him being an enemy as well as the Maltese was too much for her to cope with.

Intent on bringing some light back into her life, she determined there and then that she would do everything in her power to make it possible for her to put on her show—come what may.

*   *   *

'*Well* ...' declared Bertie, his eyes flicking over Rosie's battered face, 'you *have* surprised me. The hiding I gave you obviously had an effect.' He took

Rosie's arm and led her away from the door of the Prospect. 'It couldn't have been easy for you, walking in there, knowing you would be surrounded by your betters.'

Jerking her arm from his grip, she pointed a finger at his face, ready to give him a mouthful. 'Now, now, now . . .' he crooned, 'we don't want the spectators to think we've not *really* made up, do we?' He closed his hand around her finger and squeezed it seductively.

'I didn't do it for show. I just wanted to clear the air.'

'Well you *have* . . .' he sailed a hand through the damp atmosphere, 'You've caused all bad feelings to . . . evaporate.'

'Good. That's all I wanted.'

'The chaps have got me over a barrel, really. Should I lay a finger on you, I'll be reported for appalling conduct. Sweet, isn't it? So you needn't worry your pretty head. I *shan't* lay a finger on you. Not one. I can't . . . *promise* not to be there, mind you; in the shadows . . . or marking your footsteps . . . after all, it's such a small world in which we move. Bye, bye . . . whore.' Quietly laughing, he walked back to his friends who had been watching with interest.

As she walked slowly away, their peals of laughter crushed her confidence. She hoped that Richard would not come after her this time. The expression on his face when she had gone into the pub and apologized to the swine had shown compassion; but had that been real? Why should he be any different from the rest?

'Sod the lot of them!' She strode past the gas-works, defying threat or risk. This was home

122

ground and she *would* walk freely, dark and gloomy or not! This was where she had played as a child. This was where she and her friends had stretched a long rope across the road, skipping and chanting familiar rhymes. These narrow backstreets were her roots and *no one* was going to warn her off. Not even that vicious bastard!

She would go to the Star whenever she felt like it, and continue to take the route past the Prospect, ignoring the upper-class twits who threw a bad light on the other students of similar background. Students like Richard and Simon, and probably most of those who frequented the pub. More importantly, she would tell her gran and mother a white lie. She would say that Bertie had apologized and that they had agreed it was time to call a truce.

CHAPTER SEVEN

When she arrived at the Theatre Royal, Rosie received a frosty reception from Larry, which she had not been expecting.

'I'm very sorry to disappoint you,' said the old man while searching in the drawer of an old wooden desk, 'but I have work to do. There is a new play in rehearsal—*A Taste of Honey*. I'm wanted elsewhere. You were lucky to find me here. I came down to fetch something.' Not looking at her, he jerked and thumped the ill-fitting drawer shut.

'It wasn't my fault that I didn't turn up, Larry,' grouched Rosie, disappointed by her new friend's attitude.

'It never is,' he said, turning to the stairway. 'It's never anyone's fault . . .'

'If you took the trouble to look at my face,' she snapped, 'you'd give me a minute to explain!'

'I don't have a minute. And I've seen your face. It suits you. Now if you will excuse me . . .' He placed his hand on the handle of the door which led into the theatre, his back to her.

'I was assaulted near the gasworks,' said Rosie morosely.

'I beg your pardon?' Larry slowly turned and studied her face. 'Come out of the shadow.'

Rosie stepped forward and turned her bruised, swollen cheekbone to the light. 'No quips about my fat lip, Larry. I've had to listen to that all day at work.'

He placed his hand under her chin and turned her face to one side, examining the damage. 'Who did this?'

'A young drunk.'

'Why?'

'I'll tell you later . . . when we go to the Grand Star.'

'Which will have to be much later. Rehearsals are not going well. I shall be here for a good couple of hours yet.' He tut-tutted at her injuries and slowly shook his head. 'I trust you have reported the thug?'

'No. Give me the keys and I'll go now. It'll give me a chance to—'

'Out of the question. Come on, I'll smuggle you in. It'll be good for you to see the hard work which goes into producing a show. If anyone should see you . . . you're my niece. You can use the phone upstairs to call your parents.'

124

'We're not on the phone . . . and it's parent, not parents.'

'Well then maybe you should go home. Come back on Sunday when there're no rehearsals. Your mother will be worried.'

'No, I want to see it tonight. I said I would be late. I'll get a cab back.'

He shrugged. 'I'm pleased you can afford it. Come on.'

Once seated at the rear of the stalls, Rosie sat back and watched, thankful that something had come out of her nightmare experience the night before. She wouldn't have wanted to miss this fluke opportunity. Her pulse racing, she soaked up the atmosphere, taking in every instruction given to the actors. The director was wonderful: confident, positive and direct, with the players minding every point, no matter how hotly delivered. She was obviously the no-nonsense type who could be charming one minute and a taskmaster the next, her voice changing constantly from subdued to high-pitched within seconds.

'Have you seen all you want?' Larry spoke quietly into Rosie's ear. 'You've been stuck there for two hours. That should have been time enough for you to see what you could be letting yourself in for.' He sat down next to her. 'Not quite the same as on the night,' he chuckled.

'She's brilliant.' Rosie gazed at the taskmaster, who was having a private conversation with one of the young actors. By the expression on his face she could see that he was hanging on her every word. 'Is that it? Rehearsal over?'

'I should think so. They've been working since ten o'clock this morning. Come on. You can wait in the side lobby. I have to check a couple of things before I go.'

'Don't you have to wait until they've all gone? They must have homes to go to?'

'Possibly . . . but not tonight.'

'You mean they're gonna work through till morning?'

'No. I mean that a few of them may well sleep here. It's not the Ritz exactly, but what do they care? This is their world. Five minutes.' He pulled himself up and left Rosie wishing she had the nerve to go up to the director and ask if she could join the group. Next time, she told herself. Next time, once my face is back to normal.

*　　　*　　　*

'I can't believe they'd wannna sleep on the premises,' Rosie murmured as she walked beside Larry on the way to the Grand Star.

'Why not? A room in there is as good as their digs. And they can work until they drop. What did you think of the play?'

'I thought it was good. Real. Real people in a real world. I didn't expect that. I was expecting something else . . . something boring . . . Shakespeare . . .'

'Shakespeare's plays are not boring! You have much to learn. The play you saw in rehearsal is a modern realistic piece. *A Taste of Honey*. I think it will do well. The writer is a young lady around your age, I should think. This is the first thing she has written. That's why the rehearsals are long and exhausting. They are having to pull it together; make changes without losing the freshness.

126

'Do you want to talk about your assault or not?'

'Not. Do you want to talk about us reopening the Star, or not?'

'Us?'

'You, me, my gran, my mum and my boyfriend.'

Chuckling in his usual way, Larry opened the side door of the Grand Star. 'And where are the funds coming from?'

'My gran, Mum and my boyfriend.'

'So where do I fit in?'

'You must know the landlord.'

'And if I do?' He turned on his torch and flashed it at the light switches.

'Work on 'im. Find out 'ow little he's prepared to take for rent. Then there's the business of getting permission to open it again. You must know how to go about that. We'll need a licence to sell alcohol as well.'

Instead of taking her into the small club room, his bedsit, he led her to the front of the house, which was now lit. 'There it is,' he said. 'This is the theatre you expect people to pay to come into. Look at the seats.'

'We could do the repairs ourselves.' She pressed her hand on one of the seats. 'The springs 'aven't gone.'

'Do you have an upholsterer in the family?'

'No, but I've got friends and neighbours. Someone's bound to know someone.' She looked from the rows of seats to Larry. 'I'm being serious, you know.'

'I don't doubt it.'

'Apart from the seats, curtains and redecoration . . . what other expenses would there be? And don't sod about. Be earnest.'

127

'I'll speak with two or three club members who may fancy the idea. You won't be able to boss them around, mind.'

Smiling, Rosie punched his arm. 'That's more like it. Now then, how do I get up on to that platform?'

'Through there.' He nodded towards a single door on the right-hand side of the stage.

'Come on then. I wanna see what it looks like from up there.'

'Have you told your family about the play-reading group?'

''Course I 'aven't. You told me not to.'

'I did?'

'In so many words. I'm not daft, Larry. I know when to hold my tongue, believe it or not.'

He shifted his head to one side and scrutinized her face. 'Was it your tongue which provoked the attack?'

Silent for a moment, Rosie deliberated and then answered honestly, 'I suppose it was.'

'I thought as much. You should think a little more before you open your mouth.'

She nodded and shrugged. He was right. She had told herself the same thing several times—after the event. She was going to have to take a leaf out of Larry's book. When provoked, she would bring his face to mind, his lingering expression, the practised ploy which allowed him time to consider.

Stepping on to the stage and hearing the echo of her footsteps on the boards was a new experience, a first time. 'This is it,' she murmured, as if she were alone and talking to herself. All thoughts of changing her impulsive ways gone, she tap-danced across the stage and slipped into a world of her

128

own until she had completed her favourite dance routine.

'Where did you learn to do that?' asked Larry, impressed.

'At school. My singing and dancing lessons,' she said, finishing with a high kick. 'You can see why I need to come to the workshop.'

'I'm not so sure. You're a natural. Count your blessings.' He waved a hand at the auditorium. 'Well . . . there it is, in all its glory.'

'It's nowhere near as bad as you made out. It smells worse than it looks. You 'aven't been growing mushrooms, 'ave yer?'

'The place is damp. It hasn't been aired in a very long time.'

'Just imagine it . . . once we've cleaned, decorated and added the finishing touches. I reckon we should keep everything the same; all red, gold and blue.' Her eyes moved to the balcony wall lights. 'Were they gaslit, once?'

'Before they were oil-burning and after they held candles, yes. Come on. I'm gasping for a cup of tea.'

Following him to the club room, Rosie fell quiet, her mind racing. The clearer the vision became of the music hall in its heyday, the less daunting the idea seemed.

'And you think you'll raise enough cash for what is needed?' Larry said, opening the club-room door. He too had been visualizing the possibility of things to come.

'By hook or by crook.' She sank into a chair. 'The biggest problem is gonna be rent. I 'aven't got a clue what that would be. I s'pose you know who owns the place?'

'Of course,' he said, filling the kettle.

'How much d'yer think it would be?'

'Stop racing. We have to work out how much it's going to cost to strip down and reupholster the seating. Redecorating will cost a fortune but by the sounds of it, that's one item you've sorted out.'

'That won't be a problem. I can get the materials cheap and the labour free. I know a few men who owe me a favour.' She was referring to Reggie and the boys. 'D'yer think the carpet'll be all right if we give it a good clean?'

'Maybe. It's not so much worn as dank. Once we heat the place—which is another big expense—it's coal-fired ... or rather, coke-fired. Fuel is not cheap,' he muttered, wondering why there should be men who owed her a service.

'So you think the carpet'd be OK, then?' She ignored his remarks about fuel. It was something that she had already considered.

'It's possible. I shall have to look at it properly, when I have time.'

While he went about his business of making them tea, Rosie found herself thinking about the Maltese again. No matter how hard she had tried, she could not get that sighting out of her mind. The more she thought about it, the more the knot inside her tightened. Going to the police and shopping them when she wasn't even sure if the man in the car had been one of the gang would be senseless, and it would certainly annoy Reggie and the boys. Part of her was saying keep it to yourself Rosie, while another was urging her to tell George of her doubts; that the murderers had not been punished. Forcing it from her mind, she concentrated her attention on her new project.

'So what d'yer think then, Larry? Am I living in cloud-cuckoo-land?'

'All things are possible if you have your heart set on it, but . . .' he handed her a cup of tea, 'it will take more than passion. You will have to be resolute and have the capacity to take all the rubbish that will be thrown at you—and believe me, at you it will be thrown. You will be the scapegoat for every miscalculation and mistake.' He leaned back in his chair and sipped his tea. 'You won't be allowed to walk away when things go wrong.

'You will have to wave farewell to dance halls and parties, sweethearts and family obligations. You will be committed to the cause. At the end of the day, you may find yourself disillusioned and feeling like a dog's dinner. There is a good chance that the word "failure" will be etched across your brain and your heart.

'Should you get as far as actually producing a show, then you will have to stomach what the critics have to say. You will no longer live in comfortable obscurity. Rosie the playful mouse will become Rosie the butt of all complaints . . . and, worse still, the butt of all jokes. Do you think you could take all of that?' he asked finally.

'You've given me the upside . . . now tell me what could go wrong.'

He scratched his ear and smiled. 'Where would you like to start?'

'By 'aving a good clear-out. Pull them bloody stage curtains down and get scrubbing. I'll fetch a team down 'ere as soon as you give me the nod.'

He shrugged and shook his head. 'I must be bloody mad. Fetch them next Saturday. Meanwhile

131

I'll apply for a licence. But,' he pointed a finger at her, 'you don't mention a word about *this* room—to *anyone.*'

'So we can't come in 'ere for a tea break, then?'

'You could get me into trouble.'

'Fair enough. If it's that important. I can't see what's so terrible about—'

'It's none of your business,' he sniffed and finished his tea. 'I'll walk you to the main road.'

'You don't have to. I was brought up in Wapping, don't forget. I'm used to looking over my shoulder. Nothing's gonna 'appen to me.'

'No?' He deliberately peered at the bruises on her face. 'So how come that happened?'

'None of your business.' She winked and stood up. 'Let's go and get that cab.'

As they strolled towards the main road, Rosie summarized the show she had been creating in her mind for years and had now begun to put down on paper. Knowing that Larry was more a talker than a listener, she explained concisely and was relieved to see that he nodded thoughtfully rather than shake his head. 'I'm not really sure what the ending will be. There are three ways it could go . . .'

'I don't like the title,' he said, cutting her off, having heard enough. '*The Lavender Lady*? Sounds like someone who goes from door to door selling bars of soap.'

'It's only a handle, Larry. Something to refer to. I was gonna think of something else . . .'

'Your leading lady is from the East End, correct?'

'What's wrong with that?'

'Nothing. The reason she goes to Norfolk to work on the lavender fields is because a love affair

132

is over, right?'

'It's more than that, but yeah, that's the main reason.'

'So she's running away to Norfolk which is flat, bleak, windy and in the back of beyond. She must be punishing herself.'

'*No*. She's going because she *wants* to.'

'Once she arrives . . .' he said, carried away, 'she thinks differently. Once she sees the blanket of lavender stretching across the fields she thinks it's not such a dreary place and that she might even find love there.'

'The women don't accept 'er. She's too miserable to find love.'

'Exactly. Then she comes a cropper with the boss—who just so happens to be tall, dark and handsome and has every female at his feet.'

'Yeah, all right, Larry. You've made your point. It stinks.'

'It doesn't stink. Her boss may well be tall—but dark and handsome? A man from a farming family? A Norfolk farming family? I would have thought he'd be rugged and earthy.'

'What's all this got to do with the title?'

'Everything. It's your sales pitch. You want people to come in; *pay* to come in; then you must seduce them with something more powerful. What about . . . *Death by Lavender*? Something like that?'

'No one dies in the show.' She hated the title, but didn't want to hurt his feelings.

'Then kill off one of your characters. The boss, for instance. Maybe his jealous ex could attack him with a scythe.'

'I haven't got a jealous lover in the plot.'

'So get one.'

'And where's my happy ending gonna come from?'

'Don't have one. It'll be more true to life. You could give the promise of better things to come.'

'What, with the man she loves six foot under?'

'No funerals. End it before that. Maybe the Lavender Lady's lover from London turns up in the penultimate scene, before the boss is killed. Have him come in search of her.'

'He's meant to be a horrible character—not a hero.'

'Then change your story a touch. You can do what you want at this stage. If you—'

'I recognize that car.' Rosie stopped dead. 'That one . . .'

Watching the car reverse towards them, Larry gripped her arm. 'If there's going to be trouble, we can head back to the Royal.'

'No, it's all right. These are my friends.'

'Rosie!' Richard called from the open window of the car. 'We thought we'd missed you. We waited outside the theatre but no one came out and the doors are locked. We thought you might like a lift home.'

'See?' she grinned at Larry. 'I'm not without sources. I've got a taxi service already. See you on Saturday, round about ten in the morning. We'll bring flasks of tea with us.'

'Good. And don't forget: keep your mouth shut. Tell only those whose help you need.'

'Stop worrying.' She opened the back door of the car and got in. 'This is good of you, Simon; save me forking out for a taxi.'

'It was Richard's idea, I have to say.' Simon adjusted his rear-view mirror and drove off.

134

'It's your bloomin' car. Why should Richard get the thanks?'

'Who's the old boy?' Richard asked, making eye contact.

'A very good friend of mine. What made you come out and pick me up? Not that I mind, but . . .'

'We were on our way back to our digs. I wanted to have another look at the Theatre Royal in any case so—'

'What did Bertie the Beast have to say?' Simon chipped in.

'That he'd been warned off . . . by my knight in shining armour.'

'No threats?'

'None that bothered me. One word and I could arrange for 'is kneecaps to be shot.'

'Very funny,' Simon murmured, uneasy. 'I'll drop you off at the pub, if that's OK? I might be in time for last orders. You can meet me back there once you've walked Rosie home, Richard.'

'What a good idea.' Richard smiled and winked at Rosie. 'Doesn't sound a bit like a well-worked-out plan, does it?'

'Don't give up easily, do yer?'

'It would seem not.'

'I told you, I've got a fella, so don't go saying I led you on.'

'Wouldn't dream of it.'

'I don't two-time. I'm not that sort of a girl.'

'Tell that to your fella when you kiss him goodbye.'

Laughing, Simon pulled up outside the Prospect. 'Don't be long.'

'Can you drive on a bit, Simon?' murmured Rosie, having seen Bertie leaning on the pub wall,

135

drinking beer from a bottle. 'Drop us off further down the road, away from that lot.'

'No. That's the whole point,' Richard cut in. 'We want to show the toad that we're your friends. Hold your head high and your temper down if he makes a quip.'

'I'll smack him in the face if he does.'

'OK, Simon . . . drive on. I think she means it.'

'I *do* bleedin' well mean it! I offered an olive branch and he slapped *that* in my face.'

'So he did threaten you again?' said Richard, getting out of the car and opening the back door.

'Thanks again, Simon. You're a brick.' She closed the door and blew him a kiss as he pulled slowly away.

Standing awkwardly by the front door, Rosie's mind raced. Agreeing that Richard could see her home could be interpreted as her accepting that something more than a casual friendship was in the air. The only way out was to invite him in for a coffee. Harriet would soon make it clear that a romance was out of the question, and would no doubt mention George a dozen times.

'My gran's probably at the curtains and wondering who the hell you are. You'd best come in.' She pushed her key into the lock, hoping he would turn down the offer.

'Your father doesn't own a shotgun, does he?'

'My dad doesn't live with us. It's just me, my mum and my gran.' She pushed open the door and switched on the passage light. 'Don't expect Buckingham Palace.'

Relieved that George was not in the living room, had not deigned to pop in again, she returned Harriet's inquiring look with a smile. 'Any tea in the pot, then?'

Harriet looked from Rosie to Richard and back to her granddaughter, waiting.

'I'll make a fresh pot,' said Iris, standing. 'I'm pleased to see you had the sense not to come back from the Royal by yourself this time.'

'Richard's friend gave me a lift. Who does he remind you of, then?' Rosie said, hoping to win her gran round.

'Tommy,' smiled Iris, glancing at Richard. 'Why don't you sit down, love? We don't stand on ceremony here.'

'Thank you.'

'Tommy's my elder brother,' Rosie explained, ' . . . or was. He died a few weeks ago.' She lifted her arm to show the black band.

'I'm sorry to hear that. I didn't like to ask who you were mourning.'

'Richard who—the Lionheart?' Harriet again.

'Montague.'

'And you're one of this theatrical lot, are you?'

'Gran . . . stop interrogating him. He's a medical student.'

'I knew you wasn't from these parts, the minute you stepped in that doorway, before you opened your mouth. You're a bit on the posh side, but I won't 'old it against yer, so long as you're not after the other.'

'Gran!' Rosie felt her cheeks burning. This was not the first time Harriet had managed to embarrass her.

Chuckling, Richard lowered his head. 'We hardly know each other.'

'I'm not surprised. She's courting, you know. George wouldn't be too pleased to know you're

137

sniffing round 'er. He's a big fella, too. Where d'yer come from?'

Bemused by her straightforward manner, Richard tried to keep a straight face. 'My parents live in Belgravia for most of the time, but the family home is in Berkshire.'

'So you've got no family link with the East End then?' Harriet turned to the fire, away from those eyes; those dark-blue eyes which reminded her of Tommy—of Tommy, and Mary Birchfield. It had not escaped her that one day someone from her other life might appear out of the blue. The touch of dread in the pit of her stomach was worsening by the second; the disquiet which he brought with him was growing greater. He was a Montague, with a plummy accent similar to Mary's lover and a tell-tale smile which added to her worst fears.

Wrapped in thought, she was oblivious to Iris's return and the quiet conversation between the three of them. The more they chatted, the more she withdrew into her past, reviving old memories of Mary and her lover, Sir Robert Montague.

'Well, there you are then,' she heard Iris say light-heartedly, 'you might well share the same roots as us. Did you hear that, Mum? Richard has an aunt whose maiden name was Birchfield.'

Recoiling at the sound of the name being spoken out loud, Harriet raised her eyes to meet the young man's, and in that split second knew that the past had presented itself. 'But your father's a Montague,' she said, affirming the nightmare.

'Yes. It was Birchfield, apparently, but he had it changed by deed poll. My aunt wouldn't have any of that. She kept the name until she married; even then she retained her maiden name . . . within her

138

profession.'

'And what was that?' Harriet asked. It was clear now. Richard's father and aunt were Mary Birchfield's children by her wealthy lover: the same spoiled, pampered brats she had known in her youth. Richard was Mary's grandson—and by extension her own great-nephew by marriage. She could hardly believe that destiny had brought this young man walking through her door and waking the memories of how his father and aunt had done their best to ruin her life . . . and nearly succeeded. Curious as to what the bitch had done with her life, she looked up at Richard. 'Within what profession?'

'She's an actress—or was. Bit past all of that, now. She's still involved with the theatre. It's her life. She's working with the new musical, *My Fair Lady*.'

'How comes you never told me that?' Rosie's animated voice went above Harriet's head. She held her hands in front of the fire to warm them. The icy shiver she had felt on hearing the name Montague had returned. Blanking everything from her mind, she was taken over by a tightness in her chest.

'I didn't think it that important. Is it?'

'Richard? *My Fair Lady*? Not important? Even if I could get a tiny part . . . Fancy telling me *now*; now that I've taken on the Star! Why didn't you say something earlier on?'

'Rosie . . .' Iris broke in, chiding her. 'You shouldn't ask favours like that.' She turned to Richard. 'You must get asked that kind of thing all the time.'

'It's not outrageous . . . Everyone does it.'

139

'Yeah, well . . .' shrugged Rosie, 'too late for me now. Anyway . . . I'd rather be in my *own* show and 'ave no one to thank for it. You can get me an audition once *Lavender*'s gone on, though—*if* you think it's important enough.'

'Don't talk rubbish!' snapped Harriet, keeping her back to them, her frame bent over the fireplace, hands outstretched. 'Who d'yer think your are? Miss High and Mighty? First you're gonna open a theatre and now you think you're good enough for the West End!'

Surprised by Harriet's acrimonious response, Rosie felt her cheeks flush with embarrassment. 'I got carried away,' she said, keeping her eyes fixed on the floor. 'Maybe I should just settle for asking if she'd give me some advice on how I should go about running my show instead.'

'I'm sure she'd love to do that. Sees herself as a guru, does my aunt.' Draining his cup, Richard sensed it was time for him to go, before a proper row broke out between Rosie and her grandmother. He would find out more about the opening of the theatre another time. His intuition, after seeing her with the old man returning from somewhere other than the Theatre Royal, had been right. She was involved in something interesting; something he quite fancied being a part of. Taking on the role of director was never far from his thoughts. He turned to Iris and smiled. 'Thank you for the tea, Mrs . . .'

'Curtis. Thanks for seeing Rosie home. We had a bit of a shock when she got in last night. But I expect you know all about that.'

'Yes, I do. The swine responsible has been sent to Coventry. He won't be any more trouble.' He

140

placed a hand on the back of Harriet's shoulder. 'Goodnight.'

'I'll see you to the door,' Harriet said, rising from her chair.

'No you won't, Gran, I will.'

'Put a bit more coke on that fire, Rosie, it's burning low.' Stepping past Iris, Harriet opened the living-room door and waited. She would have her way.

Obliged to go along with her, Richard raised an eyebrow at Rosie. 'Would it be all right if I called round—'

'I'll phone you,' Rosie said, ending it. She was angry with her gran and still embarrassed. 'I kept your phone number.'

Once her gran and Richard were out of earshot, Iris let out a frustrated sigh. 'She goes too far at times.'

'Why did she do it? Did something happen to put her in this black mood?' Rosie wondered.

'I don't think so. She was fine. Maybe seeing you with someone else got her goat. We heard you come in and she assumed you were with George. We both did.'

'But Richard's just a—'

'Shush! She's on her way . . .'

Harriet came back in, fuming. 'I don't know *what* you were thinking! Bringing his sort back 'ere! You're a right nuisance at times.'

''Er . . . excuse me? But this is my home as well, you know. I'm entitled to bring friends back without getting your permission first! And what d'yer mean—"his sort"? What's wrong with 'im?'

'Use your brain.' Harriet eased herself down into her favourite fireside chair. 'He's from a different

141

class of people. His lot would crush you on sight, whether you opened your mouth and dropped your aitches or not.'

'You crushed *him* on sight! You're a bleedin' hypocrite!'

'What about when he takes you home to meet his *family*? They'll eat you for dinner and laugh while they're doin' it.'

'Laugh?'

'Yes, laugh! And don't tell me I don't know what I'm talking about, because I do! They did it to me and your grandfather. They'll do it to you as well.' Trembling, Harriet wrung her hands. 'Treated us like wild 'orses that needed to be broken—and by God they made a good job of it. They broke us all right. Tried to destroy our self-respect as well.' With tears rolling down her face, Harriet continued, slowly rocking herself to and fro. 'We were degraded. They were clever with it—even managed to get our own people to believe their filthy lies.

'I've said it before and I'll say it again—half-truths are the blackest of lies—and they knew it. Oh, by Christ, they knew it.'

Choked at seeing her gran so upset, Rosie knelt beside her and squeezed her hands. 'Come on, it's all over . . . whatever they did, it's over.'

'Is it? I don't think so,' she cried. 'I knew it would come back again, one day . . .' She lifted her apron and dried her eyes. 'You mustn't see that young man again, Rosie.'

'Why not?'

'You mustn't, that's all. Let's leave it at that. For my sake as well as your'n.'

'No, Mum,' Iris sat facing her mother. 'That's

not fair. Half a story's worse than none.' She took a deep breath and silently counted to three. 'Has this got something to do with you sharing the same name as his aunt?'

'That's it, Iris . . . set the ball rolling.'

'It's been rolling for years, you know it has. Come on . . .'

Lips pursed, slowly nodding, Harriet prepared herself. 'She might fall for 'im. And it's obvious he's keen.' She shook her head again and looked down at Rosie.

'That young man . . . Rosie.' She swallowed and then drew a breath. 'He's your cousin once removed, God 'elp us. His grandmother and your grandfather were brother and sister. That's why he looks like Tommy. Have you got it now? Have I spelled it out enough for you?'

'I don't understand.' Mortified, Iris gazed at Harriet. 'What are you saying?'

'Mary Birchfield, the young lady who took me in, was your dad's sister, right? Mary got involved with a wealthy married man who set her up in a house in Bow. Robert Montague, *Sir* Robert Montague, whose wife was ill. He couldn't leave her. Mary bore two of his children, first a son and then a daughter.'

'You're not making this up, Mum, are you? Because if you are, it's not fair—we've been through enough.'

Harriet lay back, adjusted a cushion and closed her eyes. 'Go and get me a brandy, Iris—you won't miss nothing. I'll wait.'

With her mother out of the room Rosie sat quiet, half expecting her gran to tell her something she hadn't wanted Iris to hear; that the brandy was

143

a ploy to get rid of her.

'You all right, Gran?'

'I will be, after I've had a drop.'

'You don't have to tell us any more if—'

'I know that.'

'I've brought three glasses. I think we all need some of this.' Iris poured the brandy and then put the almost empty half-bottle on the table. Placing a glass in Harriet's hand, she smiled into her face. 'You can finish your story tomorrow if you like.'

'What's the matter? Can't the pair of you take it? You were full of questions in the past—now you can hear the truth whether you like it or not.' She sipped her drink. 'I knew it would have to come out one day. Can't remember where I was now.'

'Mary had two children . . .' Rosie prompted.

'Brats more like. Spoiled brats. As soon as they were old enough to talk they took the piss out of me and Arthur; made fun of our cockney accents. Things went downhill when they caught me and your grandfather having a kiss and cuddle. Up until then they had been brought up to believe that their mother was my sister as well as Arthur's. It's what Robert wanted. Our neighbours in Bow were led to believe the same. It suited me at the time, we were a family. But once me and my Arthur realized we were in love . . . all hell was let loose.

'No one believed us when we said we weren't related. No one. They called us all manner of names, spat at our feet and said that we would go to hell. There wasn't much that Mary could do to stop it, not once it started.

'So we were banished from Bow as if we were heathens; as if we were spawned from Satan and out of hell. We had been marked for life, or so they

144

thought. Give me Wappin'ers any time. Bow? Ha. Back then, in the eighteen-nineties, the Bow people were the elite all right . . . and where did it get 'em? Look at it now.'

'There were poor parts as well, Gran. Anyway . . . you must 'ave had a birth certificate?'

Harriet found that very amusing. 'Even if I had and we set about proving ourselves; where would that have left Mary? If one of those vicious gossips probed further, found out that the man she called her husband didn't go away on business but back to his own wife, they would have spurned the lot of us. Mary was a decent young woman, God rest her soul.

'Once we left, she was forced to cut all ties. It was hard for her and for us; especially for your grandad. They were very close. She had been more like a mother to him once they were orphaned. He never saw her again.'

'But how can you be sure that Richard's part of that family, Gran? Just 'cos he's a Montague? There must be 'undreds of people with that name.'

'Yeah, but he was a Birchfield first, don't forget. At least, his mother was. No . . . there's no mistaking it, Mog. He's a cross between our Tommy, Mary and Sir Robert. A mixture of Birchfield and Montague, no question. And Sir Robert had a house in Belgravia as well. The properties have been kept in the family, that's obvious. How the rich look after their own, eh?'

'What a story,' Rosie flopped back in her chair. 'Wait till I tell 'im we might be cousins.'

'You'll do no such thing.'

'Gran . . . what difference will it make?'

Sighing, Harriet shook her head. 'His father—

145

and his aunt—are bastards. Robert met Mary in a house of assignation, in Stepney Green; an upmarket whorehouse. She was a courtesan and he was her first "gentleman caller". Poor cow had to earn more than they paid 'er at the match factory if she was to keep her and Arthur out of the workhouse.'

'Good God . . .' was all that Iris could say.

'Bloody hell,' was Rosie's response. 'Mind you . . . if his dad changed his name by deed poll, they must have found out, surely?'

'Probably. But they wouldn't have told their kids the family secret. Richard's grandfather was titled, don't forget. He was a bigwig in Parliament—or so we were told. Could 'ave been royalty for all I know. He 'ad the breeding.

'So . . . like me, Rosie, you've got to keep it to yourself. Well, not any more *I* 'aven't.' She pulled herself up, smiling. 'G'night girls. Sweet dreams.' She left the room, relieved to have shifted some of the anger inside. Pleased that at last she had been able to speak about the worst time of her life.

'She's made all that up!'

'I don't think so, Rosie. No one could come up with a story like that; not even your gran. I think you're gonna have to stop seeing that young man.'

'I've not been "seeing" him. Not in the sense you mean, anyway. He's a nice bloke and I feel sorry for 'im.' She avoided her mother's questioning look by turning away. 'It strikes me he's pining for 'is family. Maybe he missed out on something when he was small as well.'

CHAPTER EIGHT

Cajoling neighbours and friends into spending a Saturday cleaning up a disused theatre had proved to be less of a problem than Rosie supposed. Shirley's mother, Mrs Martin, had been the first person she approached, and her reaction had not only pleased but surprised her. She had loved the idea from the start, offering to rally round a few of her workmates from the box factory. Shirley herself had rejected the idea at first, but once Rosie had related in detail what her ultimate plans were, she was fired up and ready to go.

George, with his measured ways, had wanted to know all the ins and outs regarding cost, promising that he would enter into the spirit of things once she itemized and priced everything. His lack of confidence in her ability to think things through properly had simply strengthened Rosie's resolve to prove herself.

When she turned up at the Theatre Royal on the Thursday evening before her team of cleaners was due to go in, Rosie was fully expecting Larry to be impatient with her for pestering him. She was wrong. He saw her conduct as dedication to the cause, and got permission to leave early in order to take her to the Star.

With Larry's help and the use of stepladders, she managed to take down the rotting stage curtains without damaging the old brass fittings and was measuring them for the curtain-maker, when Larry casually announced that she would not have to pay rent for the first twelve months.

'That can't be right,' she said, staring up at him. 'You must 'ave heard wrong. No rent?'

'I'm telling you! You have a year's grace. Although ... there will be rates to pay. That you *will* have to take into account when you're doing your sums. I can't remember how much that will be, but I have the figure written down somewhere.'

'Who is this landlord? The owner of Harrods?'

'Hardly. He's a poor Jewish man who had this place left to him by his father. He's very happy that life is going to be brought back into it and ...' he shrugged, 'if you do well, he'll do well—eventually. He's not a saint. He's a shrewd businessman.'

'Well, shrewd businessman or not, I wanna thank him. Where does he live?'

'That's none of your business. Are you going to measure those curtains or not? I'm getting cold standing here.'

Abstracted by this latest development, she tried to concentrate on the job in hand. Taking the final measurement, she jotted it down on her notepad.

'Right, that's that done. Now then—carpet. Let's take a look at that, and see if it'll do once it's been cleaned.'

'It will. I've already checked. It may need patching up by the doorways. Other than that, it's fine. Next?'

Rosie looked from the walls to the ceiling. 'Paintwork. Will it need stripping down to the bare wood, or will a lick of paint do?'

'The paper on the walls is OK. All we have to do is get a decorator to give it a wash and a fresh coat of paint. The gloss will have to be cleaned with sugar soap, and then given another coat of the same colour. Keep everything to the original and

148

it'll be less expensive and less work. Next?'

'Lighting?'

'The electrics are fine but you'll need to buy bulbs, lots of them: bulbs and new shades.'

'Any idea what that'd cost?'

'No, but if you hurry yourself and leave me in peace, I'll do an inventory and see exactly what we need. Tomorrow I'll check with the wholesalers and get the best price.'

'Fuel for the heating?'

'I'll check in the files and make a note of how much we paid last time. It will have gone up, but that's life.'

'Repairs?'

'I beg your pardon?' He cocked his head to one side and lowered his eyelids a fraction.

'Repairs? You know ... door handles, hinges ...'

'I've kept the place in good repair. I thought I told you that already. I thought you might have noticed.'

'I'm a woman, Larry. I don't look at things like that. What about the seats? Am I allowed enough time to check each one? Or are you gonna throw me out?'

'Throw you out. I've had a look at the seats. Eighteen need a complete re-cover, ten need to be replaced, the others will do once they've been cleaned. When you're ready I have an American friend in the trade who will bring his steam machine in. He'll be cheap.'

'What about the carpet then—will he do that as well?'

'*If* you vacuum thoroughly, he will.'

'You haven't seen my mother at work. She's like

a tornado.'

'I suppose you've asked your boyfriend to meet you again?'

'If you mean Richard, he's not my boyfriend. My fella's name is George. Richard's a distant relative. Georgie's the one who's gonna put some money up, so he'll wanna come and see what I'm up to.'

'Fine.' He looked at his wristwatch.

'All right, all right, I'm going! You will 'ave the figures ready for me on Saturday, won't you? George wants to see 'em before he agrees to dish out the dosh.'

'You sound more like the boss every time I see you.'

'Good. So do you. Two chiefs are better than one. Between us, we'll keep the Indians on their toes.'

'You think so?'

'I know so.'

*   *   *

With so much to think about, Rosie decided not to take a taxi home. She was in the mood for a good long walk, with no one in her ear telling her what she might be letting herself in for. Fully aware that it would be pointless arguing, since she had had no experience, she would have to take all the well-meant advice as if she was hearing it for the first time. As far as she could tell, so long as the cash was available, the task of getting a show together, providing she found talented singer-dancers, would be a challenge she'd relish. If it failed, at least she would have brought an old theatre out of the dark, however briefly.

Passing the Yardley building, she looked up at the Yardley Lady who had sparked off a story she was to weave around dance routines she had yet to create. Conveying her ideas to other dancers would be testing. If she couldn't get her concepts across, then she would have to call in someone with experience. Someone who, like others in the show, would have to work knowing there would be no salary but a share-out from money taken on the door.

Rosie's mind was racing, and she arrived at the street leading to the Prospect of Whitby before she realised it. Having no choice but to pass the pub, she decided to keep to the opposite side of the road, to avoid an undesirable confrontation. As she passed the gasworks, Rosie felt herself shudder as the nightmare of her ordeal returned. She quickened her pace, checking the shadows on either side of the street.

By the time she reached the lights of the pub her heart was pounding and she could feel the perspiration soaking into her blouse and sweater. With her hands plunged into her coat pockets, she instinctively pulled her coat close to her body.

The few people outside the pub, laughing and drinking, were too engaged even to notice her. Telling herself not to be weak, she crossed the road, heading for the corner of her turning. She would have to make that journey several times in the future, and if she was to arrive home calm and collected, she was going to have to overcome her fear.

Hearing footsteps behind, she glanced over her shoulder. With his head held high, as cocky as ever, Bertie the intimidator strode along. 'Hello whore,'

151

he said, passing her.

Whether or not it was by chance that he had happened to be there, he had managed to unnerve her: his nearness, his smell, his voice. Turning into her street, she shivered and felt sick. By the time she reached her front door, her hands were shaking and she had trouble getting the key into the lock. Throwing the door open, she shot inside and slammed it shut.

'Is that you, Rosie?' called Iris from the living room.

''Course it's me—who else?' She did her best to sound light-hearted.

'You've got a visitor!'

Walking slowly along the passage, she hoped it wouldn't be George: he would see immediately that she was traumatized and would want to know why.

'Hello, babe—all right?' George sat there, smiling, delighted to see her.

'Yeah ... exhausted, but all right.' She leaned over him and brushed a kiss on his lips. 'I'm gonna have a quick bath. I'm filthy. Been touching fifty-year-old dirt.'

He looked doubtful. 'Sure you're OK?'

'I said I was, didn't I? I won't be more than ten minutes.'

'If I'd treated my Arthur the way you treat 'im ...' chided Harriet in her usual way. 'Not enough he's bin waiting for you for over an hour!'

'Leave her be, Harry, girl. She's been working all day at the brewery as well as the music hall. Give 'er a break.'

'See?' Rosie poked out her tongue and made a quick exit.

'I think you're gonna 'ave to keep tabs on that

young lady, George. If you're as keen as you make out.'

'Oh Gawd . . . here we go.' Iris stood up, yawning. 'I'm whacked. I'll put the dishes away, Mum, and then I'm off to bed. G'night George.'

'Night, Iris.'

Once she was out of the way, George leaned forward in his chair and eyed Harriet. 'Come on, then. Get it off your chest. What's Rosie up to?'

'I'd be a clever woman if I knew that. She's 'ardly ever in.' Harriet sucked her lips and waited. He had taken the bait.

'So what are you saying, then?'

Harriet shrugged and pulled a face. 'Keep your eye on 'er . . . that's all.'

Falling back into the chair, Georgie laughed quietly. 'And the rest. Got someone else, 'as she?'

'I never said that. But she 'as started to mix with a different set of people. Toffs. She'll be getting all uppety next. One of 'em was in a couple of nights ago. He walked 'er 'ome . . . late at night. Good-looking chap. A medical student. She met 'im in the Prospect. One of that lot. He's got it bad, I should think. The way he looks at 'er—all moony-eyed.'

'I don't think you should be telling me this, Harriet. Rosie won't be too happy about it. Telling tales out of school.'

'Ha! Since when did I ever go to school? Still . . . if you wanna bury your 'ead in the sand—' she pulled herself up from the chair, 'I won't lose any sleep over it. He looks as if he's got a few bob.'

'And you reckon Rosie's fell for him, do you?'

'I never said that. You're putting words into my mouth. Goodnight, son.' She slunk out of the

153

room, leaving him to mull it over.

'That's nice,' Rosie said, arriving in her long, light-blue dressing gown, 'they've left us to ourselves for a change. Fancy a mug of Ovaltine?'

'No. You have one though ... I've waited this long I can wait a bit more.' He looked at his watch and raised his eyebrows. 'Not much longer, though. I've got to be up early.'

Pushing her fingers through her hair to free the tangles, she slipped on to his lap and kissed him on the cheek. 'What's up?'

'Nothing. Why?'

'Don't give me all that,' she grinned, 'you're sulking.' She stroked and squeezed the back of his neck. 'I didn't know you was coming round tonight, otherwise I would 'ave got back earlier.'

'Sure about that, are you?'

''Course I'm sure! What is it with you? Look at your face, straight as a poker! If you wasn't so handsome I'd chuck you out now.'

'You won't have to because I'm going anyway.' He removed her hand from his neck, ready to leave.

'No you're not,' she said, gripping his sleeve, 'we've got the room to ourselves and ... I want a cuddle.' She kissed him on the lips, to no response. Pulling her face away, again she asked what was wrong.

'Who's this other bloke you're seeing?'

'Larry?'

'No, not fucking Larry! You know what I'm talking about. Stop acting like a silly schoolkid.'

'Oh, pardon me for breathing.'

'What's going on, Rosie?'

'*Nothing* is going on, George. I'm not seeing

154

anyone else. Keep this up though, and I might do.'

'What, the medical student's made you an offer, has he? Waiting in the wings in case I misbehave?' He pushed his face a little closer to hers. 'Well, fuck you.'

'What *now*,' she said, straight-faced, 'with Gran and Mum upstairs? Or do you wanna creep into my bedroom and then creep out again before the crack of dawn? 'Cos that's what people like me do, ain' it? In one bed . . . out the other; quick bath in between . . . if I can be bothered . . .'

'That's enough!' He raised his finger to her face. 'You're not funny.'

'Neither are you. Calling me a two-timer.'

'So you're not, then?'

'No! Not if you count Larry. He makes three.'

'All right . . . so Harriet overdid it. I'm sorry.'

'Gran! You've been listening to 'er rambling on. You should know her by now, George. She's not happy if she's not stirring it up.'

'But someone did walk you home the other night?'

'Yeah . . . and he's good-looking and a really nice bloke. But in case you hadn't noticed, I'm already going out with someone. Someone who I can't imagine not being here for me. Someone who I miss if I don't see him for a couple of nights. Someone who—'

He cupped her face, holding a finger over her lips. 'All right, babe . . . I said I was sorry. Do I get a pardon?'

She returned his earnest gaze. 'Let's make each other a promise. If either one of us falls out of love we won't string it along; we'll be honest. That way we can stay friends.'

155

'So we're in love, are we?' His big smile lit up his face.

'Oh, you know what I mean. I don't know what else to call it. We love being together . . .'

'It's all right, babe, I'm not complaining.' He pulled her face to his, showing her in the only way he knew how that he did love her, deeply. His arousing kiss sent delicious waves through her as she responded to his craving for more. His hand, sliding beneath her dressing gown and over her silky nightie, squeezed and caressed as their breathing grew hot and urgent.

'Take everything off Rose . . . please. I want you naked. I want to see you.' His voice was deep and gruff, his face shone with perspiration. 'Naked, Rosie . . .'

'No,' she whispered hoarsely, 'in case they come down.'

'They won't come down, babe . . . please . . . please, Rosie.' He pulled at her knotted belt and freed it.

'I'll leave it on . . .' she murmured between trembling breaths, 'just in case.' She pulled open the robe to reveal her flimsy nightdress and then slid her hand down the silky material to the hem and slowly drew it up her thighs and above her waist, showing herself to him for the first time.

'Jesus . . . you're beautiful . . .' Lowering his face to her breast he drew down a strap and filled his mouth, sucking as he pulled her gently to the floor.

Filled with a delicious longing, she opened herself to him. She was like a ripe plum, her juices just under the surface. Urging him on, she whispered in his ear, 'Now, darling, now!' She wanted him inside her before this sudden arousal

156

peaked. Smothering his face with kisses, she felt him push his way in, deeper and deeper as she drew her legs up and wrapped them around his body, thrusting her buttocks to and fro, in perfect time with him. Arching her head backwards she let go, allowing the throbbing inside to escalate to fever pitch. Losing herself, she felt herself break deep inside, releasing her liquid on to his erection as they came together.

Holding on to each other, they waited for their breathing to slow down, enjoying the last of the measured throbbing sensation as it faded to a warm, loving feeling. Allowing her legs to slip from him as she relaxed her grip, Rosie lay back, every tiny muscle in her body relaxed.

'I love you, Rosie.' George's quiet, husky voice made her want to cry. 'I think about you all the time.'

She looked into George's face and smiled. 'Well, that's a relief 'cos ...' she swallowed against the lump in her throat, 'because I keep waking up with you on my mind.'

'I wonder what that must mean?' he said, pulling her close again.

'It means ... that I love you, too.' She kissed the tip of his nose. 'But ... I'm not ready to ... well, to ...'

'Tie yourself down?'

'I can't, George. Not yet. Not until the show's over.'

'I know that, I'm not daft.'

She smiled again and kissed him on the mouth. 'Promise me one thing. If I get so involved that it looks as if I've lost interest in us—you will say something?'

'You can bank on it, babe.'

'Good. I'm gonna make a milky drink. D'yer want one?'

'No, but if you could sneak me a dram of Harriet's medicine . . .'

''Course I can. There's still a drop in the bottle.'

Tying the belt of her robe, she inhaled slowly and said, 'Thanks, babe.'

'For what?' There was a tinge of hurt pride in his voice. Why should she thank him? He wasn't a stud.

'For being you, and for loving me.' Moved by her own honesty, she left the room and shed a tear in the kitchen while she boiled the milk. Things were going so well she could hardly believe it. Her life had changed drastically in a matter of a month or two. She had had a kind of freedom pushed on to her when Tommy died. A freedom from something she would not have given up—not in a thousand years. Her brother had been her keeper and guardian angel, looking after her every need and being there whenever she needed to talk. Since he had gone she had had to think for herself—and she liked the new experience. It was as if she had been born again.

'It's quiet upstairs. They must be soundo.' Georgie was in the doorway, gazing at her.

'Gran was really tired, Mum as well.'

'I thought you were bushed when you came home: now I'm not so sure,' he smiled.

'I was. Something must have stirred me,' she suppressed a grin. 'Sure you don't want a hot drink?'

'Positive. What's up?'

'Nothing.' She raised her eyes to his. 'Why?'

158

'You've got that faraway look.'

'Have I *really*?' She shook her head. 'You and Gran make a right pair. A couple of mind-readers.'

'So there is something?'

'Well . . .' She poured the hot milk into a mug. 'There is something I wanna ask you.'

Stirring her drink, aware that he was waiting, she brought Larry to mind: *Think before you open your mouth*. If she didn't ask the question uppermost in her mind, she would have to carry it around with her; a sickening doubt which she could do without. 'Are you certain that Tommy's murderer got what he deserved? You sure he's not been left to carry on as if nothing's happened?'

'No, I can't be sure. But I've got Reggie's word on it and that's good enough for me. Why?'

'I thought I saw 'im in a car.'

'I doubt it.' He chuckled quietly. 'Why don't you let it go, Rose?' He cupped her face with his hand. 'Tommy's gone, and no amount of hate for those guys is gonna bring 'im back. They're not worth it. And I hate to think they're still haunting that lovely mind of yours.'

Satisfied that he was telling her the truth, she managed a smile. 'I s'pose you're right. But if we found out that they weren't sorted, you wouldn't blame me for getting justice my way? The way I wanted to in the first place? Through the law?'

'No, I wouldn't blame you. I'd back you, all the way.'

'What about Reggie?'

'So would he, silly! He's your friend, not your enemy. He'd do anything for you.'

'Yeah. You're right. I shouldn't think it was 'im, anyway. I'll push it out of my 'ead.'

'Good.'

Slipping his arm around her waist, George kissed the back of her neck. 'Now then, I've got a question for you.'

She slowly turned to face him. 'What's that?'

'This friend of yours—you going to introduce me, or what?'

'You wanna check him out?' she smiled, flattered.

'No ... I just want to take a look at the competition.'

'In that case, no.' She pointed a finger in his face. 'You've got to learn to trust me.'

'Fair enough. But why're you mixing with him? What's in it for you?'

'He's a medical student, but ... he also directs the student plays, right? I'm gonna need 'im once I've got the music hall in shape ... to help me with the show.'

'Makes sense.' He lit a cigarette and looked into her eyes. 'So who did that to your face, then? And don't tell me it was a car. I'm no medical student, but I'm not daft either.'

Resigned to his ways, she drew a breath. 'Someone who'd had too much to drink. But don't worry—he got worse than I did. I broke his nose with me 'ead. Tommy would 'ave been proud of me.' She carried their drinks into the sitting room, smiling at the memory.

'So that's it, then? I've got to let him get away with smacking my girl in the face?'

'Yep. Anyway ... he's gone. He was only 'ere on a visit. One of his friends is a medical student. He won't be back. Now can we forget it?' She crossed her fingers behind her back and recited, under her

160

breath, one of her gran's favourite sayings: *A white lie is an angel's lie.*

'I'm being serious, George. I don't want you to bring it up again. I've forgotten it—so you can do the same. And as for Richard, my new friend, you can stop harping on about him as well. When I've got a bit more time, and when I'm not so tired, I'll tell you something to do with 'im. But it's a family secret, so you'll have to keep it to yourself and not let on to Gran that I've told you.'

He narrowed his eyes and looked thoughtful. 'Ah . . . so that's why Harriet stirred it up! She doesn't want you to mix with him either. Your old man's chickens 'aven't come home to roost, have they?'

'No, but Gran's 'ave . . . and it's upset her. It's a long story but I will tell you . . . soon. I promised Harriet not to say anything yet. She's only just learned it for 'erself.'

'Sounds intriguing.'

'It is, but we're all right. Me, Gran and Mum—a little threesome with no complications. And that's all I want, George—an easy life.'

'Oh yeah? That's why you're taking on this mountain of a task, is it? You *could* settle for training to be a dancer.'

'I could, yeah—and you could settle for stopping in the docks instead of taking on a tobacconist's.'

'Point scored,' he said, stretching his legs and yawning.

'Don't get too comfortable. I'm chucking you out now.'

'So I've got nothing to fear from this other bloke, then?'

'Depends. If you don't change your ways you

161

might have. I was quite 'appy with Tommy ruling me, but now I've had a taste of being able to think for myself and make my own decisions . . . and I like it. Don't think you're gonna take over from where he left off, 'cos you're not.'

He winked at her, smiling. 'We'll see.'

CHAPTER NINE

Arriving on the dot of ten on Saturday morning, in a van borrowed from one of George's friends, Rosie and her team of helpers were in fine fettle. When first approached, they had seen her request as a cry for help, and knowing what Rosie and her family had been through of late, they were more than willing to volunteer. Once they were in the van, joking and laughing, they behaved as if they were on a beano; a girls' day out.

Harriet, sitting in the front seat beside George, wiped the steamy window with the back of her hand and peered out. 'Good God, look at the state of it! It was never like that when I came 'ere.'

'How long ago was that, Harriet?' Shirley Martin asked.

'Too bleedin' long. When I was thirteen or so. It wasn't much more than a penny gaff then . . . but it looked better than it does now. Don't bother to turn your engine off, Georgie. We ain't stopping.'

'You might not be, but we're ready for the challenge, eh, girls?' Rosie said, doing her utmost to keep up the kindred spirit.

'We cleaned up enough after the Germans during the war,' answered Iris. 'This'll be a piece of cake compared to that.'

The women agreed wholeheartedly, yelling at George to get a move on and open the back doors of the van. 'You'll love it, Harriet, mate,' another neighbour chipped in, 'we're gonna put you on scrubbing.'

'You reckon?' She chuckled. 'I shan't do manual work. I'm the foreman. Gonna sit in the director's chair—so mind you do everything properly.'

Laughing, the women climbed down from the back of the van, each carrying their own personal equipment: vacuum cleaners, buckets and brooms. Helping the last one out, George slammed the door shut and stood with the women as they studied the exterior of the Grand Star.

'That'll come up a treat,' said one.

'It'll look smashing,' claimed another.

'Right ...' George looked at his watch. 'I'll pick you up at five o'clock. Be ready.'

'George ... ?' Rosie looked at him, her bottom lip beginning to curl under. 'Don't you wanna come in and see the inside?'

'When you've cleaned it up, yeah.' He looked from her to the theatre and shuddered. 'I bet it smells.'

'You don't think much of it, then?' Rosie felt her heart sink. She had expected a better reaction than this.

''Course, I do, babe. It's ... great. I love it. But I'll love it more once it's shining like a new pin.'

'He's like all the men, Rosie!' Mrs Martin laughed. 'Frightened of spiders and beetles.'

'Too right.' George kissed Rosie on the cheek. 'Don't wear yourself out.'

A loud thumping on the front passenger door

163

stopped him. 'Open this fucking door!'

A roar of laughter echoed in the narrow, deserted street as the women realized that they had forgotten about Harriet. 'Get in the van, George, and drive to the end of the road with 'er.'

'She'll have my guts for garters, Shirley.'

'Go on . . .' Iris egged him on, 'we'll pretend we can't hear her and go in the music hall.'

Sighing, Georgie shook his head. 'Go on then. The air in the van'll be blue but . . . anything to please.'

With their heads lowered and hiding their muffled laughter, the women crossed the narrow cobbled road, ignoring Harriet's rapping on the van window.

Once Georgie had turned the vehicle around and driven a couple of yards down the road, they doubled up with laughter and waited for him to stop and let her out. With a face like thunder and swearing in the wind, she strode towards them. 'Silly bleeding mares! Waste of time my coming if all you're gonna do is sod me about! Get inside, the lot of you!' She shoved Iris through the door. 'You ought to know better! Lot of bloody good you bunch'd be without a foreman. Eighty years old and that's the respect I get!'

'*This* . . . is your grandmother?' Larry spoke in his usual slow manner.

'Who're you?' Harriet peered into his face, half smiling.

'The caretaker.'

'Well you 'aven't made a very good job of it, 'ave yer? You'd best give me a tour so's I can see what my girls 'ave taken on.'

'*Your* girls?'

164

'This is Larry, Gran, the gentleman I was telling you about. My gran's gonna supervise us.'

'Where d'you brew up?' Harriet asked.

'That's my business. If it's a cup of tea you're after ... there's a café just around the corner. Would you like me to take you there while the workers get down to it? I'll tell you all that needs doing and you can make a list.'

'That sounds more like it.' Harriet turned to Iris who was inspecting their immediate surroundings. 'See, Iris ... respect. And it has to come from the caretaker instead of my own daughter! Come on, if you're coming. I'm gasping. It's all this dust and dirt, it's got down my throat.'

Following Harriet out of the lobby, he looked sideways at Rosie and grimaced.

'Thanks Larry,' she whispered. A look of understanding passed between them.

'OK ladies! Follow me!' Rosie went upstairs, struggling with a cumbersome vacuum cleaner. 'Let's get organized before she comes back.'

*　　　*　　　*

'She's a very nice girl,' said Larry, joining Harriet at the table for two at the small family-run café. 'You did say two sugars?'

Harriet nodded and took the cup of tea he was offering. 'Thanks Larry. You're a brick.'

'But not a diamond?'

'If you'd 'ave done what I asked—and *only* what I asked, I would 'ave said you were a diamond ... a rough one, mind.'

'With your granddaughter—I had a choice? If I hadn't agreed to help, she would have gone ahead in any case, and poked her nose in where it wasn't wanted. She reminds me of you.'

'I wouldn't mind betting she's clocked that you're living there by now. She's like an aeroplane . . . gives us lot down 'ere the impression that she's a slow mover—when all the time she's breaking the bloody sound barrier.'

She sipped her tea, eyeing him. 'If I'd 'ave known what would 'ave come of my visit, I would never 'ave got on that bus that day.' She looked into his brown, doleful eyes. 'Why did you 'ave to show her the Star? Why couldn't you have just done what you promised and put a word in for Rosie at the Royal? You're a soddin' nuisance, Larry; always was.'

'You think I don't rue the day you sent her to me?'

'No. I think you're enjoying a second delinquency.'

'Maybe. Anyway . . . to answer your question, I don't know how it came about. One minute she was there, outside the Royal, the next I was taking her to see the Star. The rest is history. She moved so fast I couldn't feel my feet. I'm seventy, not seventeen! I like a slower pace.'

'Have you ever been any different?'

'Who knows? I'm too old to remember.'

'But you're not too old to remember what 'appened to me and Arthur, in Bow?'

'How could I not? Those stuck-up bastards stayed around for a while once you had left, don't forget. Every time I saw that sister-in-law of yours I felt like wringing her neck for not standing up to Sir's family, and those spoiled brats of hers. It was a disgrace.'

166

'My sister-in-law had no choice, take my word for it. Anyway . . . they may well get their come-uppance. Rosie's made friends with a medical student, by the name of Montague.'

'Not *the* . . .'

'The boy's her second cousin and he's got the 'ots for 'er. She's not interested though. Not in that way. His aunt, Mary's brat, is something to do with Drury Lane where they're getting ready to put on a new show. I wouldn't mind betting they'll come face-to-face one day.' Harriet chuckled, amused with the picture in her mind. 'Rosie wants an introduction so she can get a dancing part.'

'Montague is not *such* an unusual name. You're letting your imagination run away with you.'

'You reckon? Her name's Birchfield. According to Rosie's new friend Richard, his father changed his name by deed poll. From Birchfield to Montague. Now tell me I'm dreaming.'

'Sounds like a bloody nightmare.'

'Well, you know what they say—we reap what we sow.'

'How did Rosie find out that this young man is a relative?'

'I told 'er.'

'Ask a silly question,' he sighed. 'I suppose you were as tactful as ever?'

'I told 'er not to let him get inside her knickers because he was her cousin. I thought it best to be delicate. She's a sensitive kid. Who owns the Grand Star?'

'That's none of your business.'

'Just as I thought. Your father bought it way back.' She raised a finger and smiled. 'Nothing passed me by in them days. Old Man Simons might

167

have thought it was a well-kept secret. So . . . you own it but you can't afford to pay the rates. Rosie's doing you a favour.'

'I could sell and get a good price. Someone wants it for a bingo hall. Bingo hall up front, gambling club out the back.'

'Well, why don't you then?'

'I might. If you drive me mad every time I see you.'

'So you're scratching each other's back.'

'That's *one* way of looking at it—yours.'

'What other way is there?'

'I could sell and be a wealthy man. Living in luxury instead of in a bloody box room.'

'Ah . . .' Harriet beamed. 'But that's not what you want, is it? You want to live in your little music hall. Put you in a posh house and you'd die within a week.'

'A day, more like. I suppose you want another cup of tea?'

'I do.'

He held out his hand and waited. 'I'm a poor man, living on a pension.'

'I never asked you to pay,' Harriet said, taking her purse from her handbag. 'I've never scrounged in me life.' She slapped a shilling into his palm.

'Liar,' he murmured, and went to the counter. 'I'm having a cheesecake—do you want one?'

'That's very generous. Thank you, I will.' He looked from her to the shilling in the palm of his hand. 'I'm paying?'

Turning her head so he wouldn't see her look of triumph, she quietly thanked providence. Rosie's interest in the theatre had prompted her to go and see Larry. A very good and old friend of hers and

168

Arthur's who she hadn't seen in ages. She couldn't have wished to have been reunited with a lovelier man.

'Do you know how much they charge for a cheesecake today?'

'No,' she sniffed, 'I can't afford luxuries. Have to make do with an arrowroot biscuit when I want a treat.'

'I'm sure.'

Once they had satisfied their stomachs, Harriet and Larry made their way back to the theatre, talking ten to the dozen about old times and new times and things to come. When they arrived at the entrance to Star Passage, Larry stopped. 'Do we really want to go in there with that lot?'

'What else do you suggest?'

'We could go and see how my niece is getting on with the curtains.' Harriet eyed him suspiciously. 'The stage curtains?'

'Yes—the stage curtains. Why that look?'

'You didn't by any chance pinch the measurements that Rosie took down on Wednesday?'

'I borrowed them.'

'Well thanks to you she 'ad me turning the place upside down looking for 'em. Swore blind she'd put them down somewhere. Nearly cried with rage.'

'It was for a good cause. With a bit of luck they'll be ready to go up in a week or so. Tilly is like a woman possessed once she gets in front of a sewing machine. I bought an end of roll from the textile factory in Brick Lane. It was cheap ... and it is blue; royal blue, as it should be. Left to herself, Rosie would have put red velvet up there.'

'I thought you was a poor man, Larry?'

169

'I am now. Do you want to go in there or come with me to my niece's house? It's just five minutes away.'

Pursing her lips, Harriet looked thoughtful. 'We'll go in and make an appearance—keep 'em on their toes. Then we'll go. I wanna have a look at this cheap remnant you've bought.'

Walking side by side, Larry took Harriet's arm. 'You're very good for your age, you know that?'

'I'm bloody marvellous. What are you after?'

'Why should I be after anything? I was paying you a compliment. I don't want you in my bed, thank you. A couple of hours of your company now and then is more than enough.' He opened the door for her. 'Go on up, I'll wait down here for you. I'm fed up with going up and down the backstairs.'

'You'll come up and like it. They'll shove a broom in my 'and as soon as look at me. You're my escape.' Grabbing the handrail, she dragged herself up the staircase, moaning about it being too steep; about her energy being wasted on the place. 'You'd best not mention why we're going to your Tilly's. Rosie'll want to come with us to check what curtains you've 'ad the nerve to choose.'

'I had no intention of telling her. Wait until they're finished, then I'll *show* her. She'll be pleased. She'll get the gold trim that she went on about.'

'Yeah . . .' Harriet said tormentingly, 'but she'll be stuck with royal blue whether she likes it or not.'

'I'm telling you, she'll love them.'

*   *   *

'You took your time, didn't yer!' Rosie got in before her gran, off the mark with her bossiness. The girls were working like Trojans and she didn't want them needled. 'Larry ... what colour d'yer think this lino between the rows of seats is?'

'I have no idea—but I *do* know that that lino is tar-based and good for several years. Why?'

'It's red! Come and see for yourself. See the difference in the bit I've scrubbed and the rest. It's changed from grimy brown to red. How come you let it get in this state?'

'What difference does it make? The red was under the dirt. It wasn't going to go away. Have you found any mice yet?'

'No, but we've put traps everywhere. Listen ... we can't work with stone-cold water. Light the boiler.'

'There's no fuel.' He turned to Harriet. 'Have you heard enough?'

'Yeah. Come on, let's get out of 'ere.'

Smiling, Rosie watched them leave. She knew how to handle her gran and she was beginning to see how to handle Larry. They were from the same mould, almost. 'They've gone, girls! We can stop for a cuppa!'

Just as Larry put his hand on the lock of the door to open it, he felt Harriet tug at his sleeve. 'Here.' She pulled a roll of five-pound notes from her coat pocket. 'This is for fuel. Make sure they've got hot water by the time they come back next Saturday.'

'I can't take that.'

'It's from one of her sponsors. From Tommy. Ask no questions, hear no lies. Take it.'

'How much is here?'

'Enough to light the boiler for a year.'

He looked at the wad of notes. 'With a bit left over to buy a few arrowroot biscuits so I don't starve?'

'Put it away, you silly bugger, before we're coshed and robbed.'

Stuffing it into his inside pocket, he took her arm again. 'You'll never change, will you? Always hiding that heart of gold of yours. I bet you had this put by in case you became a family burden.'

'I always fancied a room by the sea—in an old people's home, as it happens. But that's not what that was for. It was for my Rosie's big day. Now she tells me she don't want a white wedding—so there you are.'

*   *   *

By the time they arrived at Tilly's tiny two-up, two-down end-of-terrace house, the pair of them were ready for easy chairs. 'I hope to God she's in,' Larry murmured, his finger on the doorbell.

'Uncle Larry! How lovely, come in. I was just thinking about you.'

'This is the old friend I was telling you about. Harriet.'

'Come in, Harriet, I've been dying to meet you. Uncle Larry told me all about you and about your niece too. Fancy her wanting to open up the Grand Star again! Isn't it wonderful?' She stood aside to allow them in.

Guiding Harriet into the front room, Larry smiled inwardly. It would be interesting for him to see how these two women got on together. His life had been very dull of late, until Rosie walked into

172

it and renewed his spirits. The old mischievous Larry was coming back. 'Let me have your coat, I'll hang it up,' he said.

'Hang it up? Why? We're not gonna be 'ere all bloody day, are we? I've got to keep an eye on them girls.'

'She won't let you dump it on the back of a chair. Houseproud? The word doesn't cover what my niece is like.' He took Harriet's coat and winked at her.

'I can't help it,' said Tilly, plumping the floral cushions on the sofa. 'There's nothing worse than an untidy room. I should have married money. Had servants to do for me.'

'Shouldn't we all . . .' said Harriet, sinking into an armchair. 'This is a nice room, Tilly.' She focused on an oval-framed portrait photograph of a child with long wavy golden hair and green eyes. 'Is that you?'

'Sure. Even then I took pride in my appearance. You know what they used to call me round this way? The Jewish Princess. It was their little joke, Harriet, but . . . I loved it.' She flicked her hand in the air and shrugged. 'I felt like one, do you know that? From as far back as I can remember I behaved as if I was out of the royal family. So I like to keep my home like a palace. How bad? It drives my old man crazy. He leaves in the morning, and these walls are white with a pink patterned border; he comes home in the evening and it's primrose with a green edging. I papered this room myself a month ago. I doubt I'll change it for a few months yet. Don't you think it looks lovely, Harriet, all these roses? We haven't got much of a garden out the back so I thought we'd have flowers on the

173

walls instead. I made the loose covers for the three-piece myself ... and the curtains. If I'm not decorating I'm sewing. So, I'm a nest-builder. How terrible.' Stopping for breath, Tilly sat on a chair at the highly polished oak dining table. 'I've nearly finished the drapes, Larry. They'll look wonderful. Wait till you see what I've got in mind for the valance.

'Don't you think it's wonderful what they're doing?' She waved a hand at Harriet. 'When he told me ... I nearly broke down. Doing up the old Star.' She shifted her head from side to side. 'My mother would have cried in her sleep, God bless her soul.'

'I'll put the kettle on then, shall I?' Larry exaggerated his usual half-awake expression.

'Sure, but don't splash water all over the place, Uncle Larry. And get out the china cups and saucers. Don't put your fingers all over the glass.'

'Anything else?'

'I don't think so ... unless Harriet would like a biscuit?'

'No thanks. I've just had a cheesecake.'

'Am *I* allowed a biscuit?'

Tilly drew down the corners of her mouth and sighed. 'Must you? You get crumbs everywhere Uncle Larry, you know you do. Have an apple.'

'You want me to dip an apple in my tea?'

She looked from Larry to Harriet. 'He's the only person I know that can never manage to get a tea finger from the drink to his mouth without it sagging over and dropping on to his cardigan, or the floor. He's worse than a baby.'

Larry rolled his eyes and left her with Harriet. 'I think the world of that man. He's been more like a father than an uncle.' She leaned forward and mouthed the words: 'He worships the ground I walk on. Never shows it though, but that's men for you. My old man's the same. Every morning before he goes out of that front door I have to ask him the same question, "Sammy ... do you love me?" It never crosses his mind to ask me. Men.' She swatted the air again. 'They don't know how lucky they are. So tell me about yourself, Harriet.'

'Nothing to tell,' grouched Harriet, wishing she'd stayed at the Star. Tilly was already irritating her beyond belief.

'Tch. You've led a sheltered life, then? What we sacrifice for our families, eh? They'll know it once we're dead. So where do you live?'

'Wapping.'

'Do you ... ?' Her face showed commiseration. 'Ah well ... we can't always choose where we lay our head, can we? And you live alone?'

'No. I live with my daughter and granddaughter.'

'No?'

'Yes.' Harriet was beginning to lose her rag.

'Well, I think that's wonderful. I expect you do all their washing and ironing?'

'No.'

'You *don't*?'

'Let's 'ave a butchers at these curtains then.' Harriet fell into her broadest cockney accent. 'Royal blue, ain't they?'

'With a gold trim,' she said, proudly. 'Once we've had our tea I'll show you round the house. The drapes are in my sewing room. Upstairs. At the front of the house. The second bedroom.' She could see she wasn't making any impression.

'Did you 'ave children?' Harriet asked, hoping to

175

change the subject, taking the chance that Tilly might not go on for hours about them if she had given birth.

'Of course! Two. Boy first and then a girl. Now they're married with families.' A glazed look came over her eyes as she gazed down at the floor. 'They moved out of the East End, of course . . . gone to Golders Green. They come to see us, sure they do, but not that often. They're not keen on these backstreets. I brought them up to appreciate the finer things in life.'

And now you're deeply regretting it, thought Harriet, feeling sorrier by the second for this unhappy mother who had unwittingly alienated herself from her children with her snobbery.

'You should come over and pay us a visit in Wapping, Tilly. You and my Iris'd get on like a house on fire. She's always fussing the place up as well. Cleaning and polishing everything in sight.'

'I would love that, Harriet, I really would.'

Returning to the room, having drunk his tea in the comfort and quiet of the kitchen, Larry said, 'What would you love?'

'Harriet's invited me over for tea.'

'Rosie, Harriet, Rosie's mother and *you*, all in the house at the same time?'

'Well, Tilly . . . I like your company but I mustn't stop. I've left a team of women at the Star and if I'm not there to keep an eye on 'em, nothing'll get done.'

'I don't suppose you need another pair of hands,' said Tilly, looking as if she were asking a favour.

'Many hands make light work.' Harriet pulled herself up from the comfortable chair. 'We'll be back there next Saturday. You're more than

176

welcome, but I warn you, it's filthy.'

'I suppose it must be.' Her eyes lit up. 'Wonderful. I like nothing better than to be able to see the result of my work. I'll be there.'

'Are you mad? You walk in that place and you'll have a heart attack. You should wait until it's clean and then start cleaning.'

'If that's not arse about face, I don't know what is!'

Disgruntled, Larry shook his head. 'Why did I let myself in for this?'

'We'll need gallons of bleach ...' murmured Tilly, miles away, 'and a few good scrubbing brushes. Good *tools* make light work ...'

'Thanks for the tea, cock. See you next week.' Harriet rushed out before Tilly got too carried away.

Once the street door was between them, Harriet drew breath. 'Give us one of them fivers back. I'm getting a taxi 'ome. She's exhausted me with all that energy of 'ers. Is she always like that?'

'No ... she usually talks between the pauses. Here.' He handed over the note. 'So I've got to put up with that lot by myself now?'

'I'm sure,' she smiled slyly at him, 'you'll lock yourself in that room of yours if I'm not mistaken.'

'You're not mistaken.' His hand suddenly shot up as he caught sight of a black cab. 'Taxi!'

'God. Once a loudmouth ...'

'If I hadn't shouted, you would have missed him. Think yourself lucky he only lives round the corner and is just on his way out.' He stepped up his pace and spoke to the cabbie through the window. 'Look after this one for me, Ted; see she lets herself in with her key before you pull away.'

177

'What you two whispering about?' Harriet opened the back door and sank into the seat. 'Wapping please, mate. Turner Street, just off—'

'By the Prospect?'

'That's it, cabbie. Number seventeen.' She gave Larry a wave, leaned back and closed her eyes. 'Nudge me once we're there, driver,' she said, yawning. She wasn't tired but she did want some quiet. She wanted to think about the old days when life was slower. She wanted to think about Mary Birchfield walking out in her long silk and satin dress and matching feathered bonnet, strolling along the Whitechapel Road, causing men from all walks of life to turn their heads and their women to burn with jealousy. She was a beautiful young woman who, to escape the poverty and the workhouse, had chosen the career to which she was best suited—high-class prostitution.

Smiling inwardly, Harriet remembered how it had not been a vocation without prospects. Mary hadn't been in the profession for more than a couple of weeks before she was swept up and whisked away by her wealthy client, Sir Robert.

Meeting up with Larry again after several years, and then listening to Tilly who was obviously unhappy because her children had gone off to pastures new, Harriet realized just how much things were changing. The future of the East End of London had, as far she was concerned, a big question mark over it. If the building of tower blocks continued and all the old character houses were pulled down, the area could so easily become an extension of the City. The old East End was fast fading. The young were getting out and the old were hanging on for dear life. With that thought in

178

mind, she became even more determined to help her Rosie who, in her own way, was going against the trend.

'This do you, love?' The cabbie's soft voice broke into her reflective mood.

'Yeah . . . this'll do.' She offered him the five-pound note and waited for the change.

'Looks like you've got a visitor,' he said, nodding towards her front door.

Peering through the cab window, Harriet sighed. 'One of our Rosie's admirers.'

'Want me to see him off?' The driver passed her the change through the open sliding-glass partition. 'Looks 'armless enough, mind.'

'He's all right.' She gave him a threepenny-bit tip. 'That was a comfortable ride, cabbie. Lovely.'

*   *   *

Arriving at Richard Montague's side, she eyed him cautiously, wondering whether to ask him in and draw from him his intentions with regard to her granddaughter. 'Rosie won't be back for hours yet.'

'Ah. It hadn't occurred to me that she worked on Saturdays,' he said, trying to cover his embarrassment at being there. 'I was passing—'

'I'm sure.' Harriet pushed her key into the lock. 'Now that you're 'ere you may as well come in for a cuppa. That's if you don't mind the company of an old woman?' She had made a snap decision to take the opportunity of ten minutes alone with this young man.

'Absolutely not. I mean . . . I'd be really happy to join you. Tea. Marvellous.'

She switched on the passage light and then

looked him straight in the eye. 'You can drop all that polite stuff. Talk to me the way you talk to your own family and mates.'

'I er ... I ... believe I was, Mrs Birchfield. Really.' His sincerity touched Harriet, and the expression in his eyes reminded her of his grandmother, Mary. Her sister-in-law certainly had passed on her good looks to this young man, especially the dark-blue eyes.

'Well if that's 'ow you go on all the time, you must waste a lot of breath on words you don't need.' She nodded towards the fireside chair in the sitting room. 'If you could stoke that fire up a bit for me ... I'll go and fill the kettle. I take it tea's all right. We've got a drop of Camp coffee if you—'

'Tea's fine.' He stopped himself from saying thank you and smiled instead.

Once alone in the kitchen, Harriet's brain raced. This was a perfect opportunity to see this young man off by way of the truth. If he were to learn that he and Rosie were related, he would likely disappear lickety-spit. On the other hand, if she were to tell it another way, gently-gently rather than shock the life out of him, maybe he would reconcile himself to remaining good friends, and help her with this new venture she had set her heart on.

Wondering how he would take the news, she carried the tea tray into the sitting room and placed it on the table. 'I didn't fetch any biscuits 'cos it's nearly your dinner time and I'm not gonna be responsible for spoiling your appetite.' She offered him his tea and then sat down with hers. 'I never eat much during the day. Make up for it at teatime with me dinner. One meal a day does me.'

'I usually skip lunch too. Big breakfast, and then a good dinner . . . in the evening,' Richard said, beginning to relax.

'So what is it you want with my Rosie, then?' Harriet spoke in her usual direct manner.

'Confidentially?' Richard raised his eyes to meet Harriet's, and in that instant she knew what was coming.

'You're not gonna tell me you're in love with 'er.' She hoped her dismissive tone might put him off.

His cheeks flushed and his eyes sparkled as he grinned like a lovesick schoolboy. 'I've been bumping into lampposts ever since I first saw her. She's . . . wonderful. Full of life; has a sense of humour; artistic . . . and . . . she's just . . . lovely.'

'Mmmm.' Harriet sipped her tea and became thoughtful. 'She's already got a steady boyfriend, as you well know. All you could ever hope for is to be mates. Even then, I don't know that that would go down too well with Georgie.'

'I notice she doesn't wear an engagement ring.' Richard leaned back in the chair and smiled. 'She's not exactly promised to him.'

'That kind of talk'll get you a fat lip and broken ribs, my boy! She's all right with George. You keep your meddling for them nurses down at the 'ospital. Not promised to 'im?'

'I don't intend to come between them, Mrs Birchfield—'

'The name's Harriet.'

'I just meant that if it isn't as serious between them as you think it is, then I may just stand a chance.'

'Bollocks. That's not what you meant. I may be old but I'm no fool. I've lived eight decades to your two and a bit, don't forget. You can't flannel me. You're out to break them up and 'ave 'er for yerself. And then what? Once the contest's been won? You'll be away from 'ere like a bee who's picked up another scent.

'Well . . . I'm afraid you're in for a bit of a jolt, cock,' she drew breath and braced herself, checking his expression; the furrowed brow showed he had picked up the gravity in her voice.

'You,' she said, gently but firmly emphasizing the word, 'may never bed our Rosie.' She put up her hand to stop him interrupting with his declaration of good intentions. 'You and Rosie,' she said, 'are related. You're cousins. Second cousins it's true, but nevertheless . . . the same blood's running through your veins.' She looked sideways at him. 'It ain't just the name Birchfield that we share. My sister-in-law Mary Birchfield and your grandfather, Sir Robert Montague, spawned two babies . . . way back—when they were lovers.'

The room fell silent as Harriet waited for a response; welcomed one.

'It fits . . .' Richard murmured, looking earnestly into her face. 'It all fits into place.' He slowly shook his head. 'I *knew* she was different from the rest.'

Bewildered by his reaction, Harriet gaped at him. The last thing she had expected was this instant acceptance of cold facts. 'Won't this alter things a bit . . . ?' she asked, bemused by the way he was behaving.

'Oh no . . . no . . . it doesn't alter anything . . . it just strengthens what I already feel deep down. Fate works in mysterious ways. This is why I find myself in your territory. I've been drawn here. This family . . . Rosie . . . my destiny.'

182

'She's your second cousin. Mary and Sir Robert's illegitimate son ... is your father.' She watched as he gazed at the floor, shaking his head. 'Destiny?' She raised her eyebrows and sighed loudly. 'Ain't you even a *tiny* bit shocked, son?'

'Cousins can marry,' he murmured, speaking to himself more than to her. 'I can't wait to see her. Why didn't she tell me? Why keep something like this to herself?' He raised his glazed eyes to meet Harriet's. 'Where is Rosie? I must see her straight away.'

'You just slow yourself down a bit, young man. You slow down and tell me ... how come you're not thunderstruck at learning about your grandfather 'aving a mistress and your own father being a bastard?'

'Oh, Harriet ... we all knew he had a mistress ... but I never dreamed, not in a million years, that his sins would be my gain. I'm *already* a part of your family.' He slumped down on to a dining chair and covered his head with his hands. 'I can hardly believe it. It's wonderful.'

'I don't think that's the way your father and aunt'll see it,' Harriet said, wondering if the young man who sat before her was all there. 'In fact I know it's not,' she added, studying his eyes. 'This seedy side of the family was meant to stay in the cupboard. They're not gonna jump for joy.'

'I shan't tell them. It'll be good to turn the tables. Keep something from *them* for a change. Rosie can be my secret.'

'I think you're jumping the gun a bit, lad. Our Rosie's in love with George, not you. She only sees you as a mate.' Harriet was beginning to feel sorry for him. 'Mind you ... she's dead set on reopening

183

a fleapit of a music hall . . . and she's gonna need all friends on deck . . . perhaps you'd enjoy helping her with that? It's where she is now, with an army of helpers, scrubbing the place from top to bottom. If you take my advice you'll give her as much support with that venture as you can. Financial, if you're up to it. Put all your loving into the show— help her with it. She's gonna have a load on 'er plate once it gets under way. She'll be in it herself, dancing. Our Rosie's a smashing dancer. Always was. Takes after me.'

Harriet rose from her chair, still amazed by his lack of worldliness. 'I shall tell 'er you called round. Drop a note through the letter box next time you're thinking of popping in, though. Best she knows when you're coming. You never know when George'll be 'ere and you don't wanna upset him.'

'Right,' Richard nodded thoughtfully, 'I'll do that. And you needn't worry about my being too pushy . . . what will be, will be.'

His poetic display touched her. 'A kiss and a cuddle's not everything, cock. Settle for being good friends.

'Now then, my boy . . . before you go, one last thing. See if you can manage to get Rosie a dancing part in *My Fair Lady*. She's as good as any. And she won't let you down.'

'I doubt she'll have time for that, Harriet, what with her own show on top of everything else.'

'True . . . but if this crazy idea of hers falls flat, at least she'll 'ave something else to chuck herself into—other than the river.'

Fastening his duffel coat, Richard told Harriet that he could see the sense in what she was saying and that he would have a word with his aunt who had the contacts in the theatre.

'Best not tell 'er who the part's for though, eh?' said Harriet, showing him to the door.

'Don't worry—I intend to be as furtive as she's been. Thank you very much for the tea. It was kind of you.'

'It was a pleasure.' Closing the door behind him, she began to laugh. Of all the people that Rosie could have brought home from the Prospect, it had to be Mary's grandson ... and the image of Tommy; but without his strong character and sense of humour. Her past had not simply flashed before her in this, her eightieth year—it had arrived at her front door.

Once she had stoked the fire and got it blazing again, she made herself comfortable, content with just the sound of the clock ticking on the mantel-shelf. With her legs stretched out and resting on a footstool, she considered how many times in the past she had said 'it's a small world'. Now she really did know the meaning of the old saying.

Satisfied with her morning's socializing, she was ready for a doze, and looked forward to telling Rosie that Richard now knew they were cousins and was actually pleased to be part of the family, and not horrified by the revelation, as they would have expected.

*   *   *

Meanwhile, back at the Star, everyone was tired after a hard day's work. Dropping exhausted into one of the seats in a row behind her mother, Rosie closed her eyes, believing that Iris was alseep.

'You've made a good job of the floor, Rosie. It's

come up a treat,' said Iris, yawning. 'These seats are not as good as they look, you know. I've not been on this one five minutes and my bum's gone numb.'

'What do you expect? You've bin kipping for over an hour. You're bound to be stiff. That seat's down for repair, anyway. They're not all as bad.'

'An hour? Never! I dozed off for a few seconds, that's all.'

'No you didn't. Ask the others. At least we know the acoustics are good.'

Iris sat up straight and rubbed her eyes. 'I wasn't snoring, was I?'

'Not much you wasn't. Anyway, it's time to pack up. George'll be 'ere in ten minutes time. I can't wait for 'im to see the inside of this place.'

'Where 'ave the girls got to?' yawned Iris

'Look around yer. They're dotted around, worn out and waiting to go.'

Iris studied Rosie's face. 'You look all in as well.'

'I'll be all right, after a long soak in the bath. Look at the lino now—looks a bit different, don't it?'

'Amazing . . . it really is red. Who would 'ave believed it?' She gazed around and nodded thoughtfully. 'This place'll look a picture by the time we've done, Rosie. When's the next cleaning blitz gonna take place?'

'Tomorrow.'

'Sunday? Give us a rest, Rose, for God's sake.'

'You've got all night to sleep, ain't yer? What more do you want?'

'A lie-in tomorrow . . . a leisurely day . . .'

'You'll be lucky.'

Sighing, Iris gave her daughter a half-hearted

186

look of reproach. 'This had better be worth all our trouble.'

'It will—you'll see. Between us we'll bring a bit of life to this old place. That's gotta be worth giving up a couple of weekends, ain't it?'

'A couple? Half a dozen more like.'

Rosie gave her a cheeky wink. 'I knew you'd come round.'

CHAPTER TEN

From as far back as Rosie could remember, waking up in the morning had not been something she relished. Although it had been a very long time since she had ended her bedtime prayer with, 'and please let me sleep for ever . . .', waking moments had been veiled with despondency, until she realized that she was no longer a small child with nothing to look forward to. This morning signalled a very important change: Rosie had awoken without that fleeting sense of dread. It seemed as if the sun were radiating right through her, even though it was the beginning of a grey and dismal dawn. With a smile on her face, she closed her eyes and cherished the moment. Not only was she in love with George and he with her but since her chance meeting with Larry, life had taken on a new meaning.

Picturing the auditorium, the way it looked after just two weekends of the team giving it a good scrub, spit and polish, she felt sure that even better things were to come. She allowed her imagination to work overtime, visualizing freshly painted walls and ceilings, brass fittings gleaming bright, blue velvet drapes, deep-red floors and glass-shaded lights. She could almost smell the beeswax polish on the doors and wood panelling.

Going into Charrington's to work on a conveyor belt was something she now looked forward to. The girls were genuinely interested in her project, eager to know the latest developments and ever ready to be involved in some way. If she had let herself be carried away by their enthusiasm, she may well have found that there were too many Indians for the chief to instruct. Renovating the interior of the theatre could easily turn into a farce.

Gently, gently, Rosie, she told herself, throwing back the bedclothes and swinging her legs off the bed. There was much to do and a very long way to go before she could slacken the reins. With just two days to go before she and her workforce went into the Star for the third scrubbing session, she reasoned that it was now time for Iris to cough up some of Tommy's savings for paint, rollers and brushes. The men were on call, and a stack of old bed sheets for protecting the recently cleaned carpets was piled up in the passage, courtesy of Harriet, Iris and several neighbours. According to Harriet, one old girl along the turning had given her old laying-out sheets. Whether it was true or just her gran's strange sense of humour, she didn't care. Dust sheets were dust sheets, and they were going to need quite a few.

Glancing at her alarm clock, Rosie was surprised to see that it was only six-thirty. She felt as if she had slept round the clock instead of six hours. Wearing her warm candlewick dressing gown she crept downstairs to make herself a cup of tea, pleased that the radio had not been switched on and the house was quiet. It wasn't often that she was up before Iris and Harriet.

'If that's you, Iris, creeping about like Jesus, you can make that tea for two!' Harriet's voice drifted through the slightly open doorway. 'Now you've woke me up to the sound of creaking floorboards, you can wait on me.'

Pushing the door open with her foot, Rosie stood there, arms folded, unyielding. 'It's not Mum, and no I *won't* make you a cup of tea. I never woke you up. Look at yer! Reading a bloody book and wide awake. If the truth be known, *you* disturbed *me.*'

'And a chocolate Bourbon,' muttered Harriet, going back to her book. 'You're gonna need all the cash you can get your 'ands on. If I don't get a bit more service around 'ere, I'll spend me money on a world cruise, where I know I'll be abided by. Talks volumes, does money.'

'Yeah? Well ask it where it came from in the first place. Tommy? Put aside for my wedding day? He told me about it, Gran. I won't be 'aving one, so you're obliged to give it to me for my show.'

'Gonna die an old maid, are yer?'

'No. I'm gonna live in sin.'

'That's all right then. I'll let you 'ave the rest . . . when I think fit. Too much too soon and you'll think you're 'ome and dry. There'll be costs along the way you 'adn't even thought about. Get what you can out of the boys for now.'

With an eyebrow raised, Rosie sat on the edge of her gran's bed. 'No flies on you, are there? And thanks for telling Richard about my being his cousin. He took it really well. You worked wonders

189

there. He's in love with someone else now, can you believe?'

Looking over the top of her glasses, Harriet smiled and winked. 'I've been on the merry-go-round for a long time. Seen it all.' She placed her book on the bed and sighed. 'S'pose I've gotta make me own tea, then?'

'Listen, I want your honest opinion . . . about what I'm doing.'

'Getting cold feet already? I might 'ave known. Go on then . . . ask away.'

'You know what I'm gonna say, stop tormenting.'

Harriet sank back into her pillow and peered thoughtfully at her granddaughter. 'You'll still be 'ere next year, right. Well . . . you can either be 'ere, without 'aving put on a show, or 'aving put on one. Whatever you do, you'll still be trotting off to the brewery. Now then . . . will yer be pleased with yerself 'cos you did what you wanted and you did your best, even if it bombs? Or will you be annoyed with yourself for giving up and never knowing what might have been?'

Rosie gazed back at her, deadpan. 'We ain't got no Bourbons. I 'ad the last one.'

'Well fetch me a couple of tea fingers then.' She picked up her book and pretended to read. 'And you'd best not come 'ome from work without a packet of chocolate biscuits.'

'So you think I'm doing the right thing then?'

'Right thing? Ha! That'll be the day. I'll tell you what, though; if you don't tread carefully and slow down a bit, you might find Tommy's bedroom filled with an old man's things. If the authorities find out that Larry's living in that dump, he'll be ousted, no mistake. Put in an old people's 'ome or . . . in our

190

spare room.'

'He don't live in the Star, you silly cow. Spends a lot of time there, that's all.'

'He lives there. He wouldn't want us or anyone else to know. So keep your gob shut and don't treat 'im any different now that you *do* know. He's as sharp as a razor and too bloody proud for 'is own good. And before you ask, he's got his own reasons. It's none of our business. I'm just forewarning, that's all. Don't fetch too many snoops in too soon.'

Rosie stared pensively into space. 'It makes sense. That so-called reading room smells more like a place that's lived in. Poor sod.'

'Don't you believe it. He loves living there, especially now that you've pressed 'im into fetching a bit more life into the place. Tea?'

With doubts creeping into her head, Rosie went into the kitchen to fill the kettle. Why had she allowed a madcap idea to grow into a roller coaster? If she were to stop now and go back to her original plan of joining the classes, she would lose face, but that was nothing by comparison to what Larry stood to lose. Berating herself for not taking the time to sit down and ask him if he minded her closing in on his domain, she lit a cigarette, something she had not done in a long time.

Making a snap decision to go and see him straight after work, she felt a touch lighter inside. If he managed to remove her sense of guilt then she would continue, but mark her gran's advice. The last thing she wanted was to see him turned out on to the street. She half hoped he would tell her that he would rather she abandoned the idea now. Her thoughts switched to Tilly and the lovely curtains she had made. She and Iris had got on like a house

191

on fire, and in three short weeks had become friends, almost as if they had known each other for years, each making regular visits to the other. They had even been to the cinema, something which Iris had not done in years, and it was all thanks to the Grand Star which had become the focal point, bringing together people who would not otherwise have met.

If good things were coming out of this venture, why did she feel worried? Why did her mood swing from positive one day to gloom and doom the next?

'You're up early,' said Iris, yawning. 'Did the birds wake you as well?'

'Never 'eard 'em. Gran's been crowing, though. Wants room service.'

'Does she now? I dread to think what she's gonna be like when it dawns on 'er just how old she is. She'll pull every stroke in the book. Have us pushing her round in a wheelchair. I bet she can't wait.'

Rosie chuckled. 'Nor can I. You ready for toast yet?'

'No. Just a cup of tea for now. You'd best 'ave a cooked breakfast today. Won't get a chance to eat anything before eight, I shouldn't wonder.'

'Why eight? Gran off somewhere, then?'

'No. You are.' Iris caught Rosie's eye: her expression showed unease. 'Don't tell me you've forgot?'

'I ain't going anywhere tonight. George's coming round.'

'No . . . he's meeting you from work, and the pair of you are going to see a mate of his—who runs a pub . . . ?'

'It went right out of my mind! Sod it, I was

looking forward to putting me feet up and watching television. I wonder if he'll go without me?'

'Well it's up to you, but . . . if it was me, I'd want to be there. Find out what the profit is on drink. You might wanna stock and run the bar yourself. Or just get a bar manager in.'

'That's true. Left to George, he'd offload as much as he could. Thinks I'm taking on too much as it is. He wouldn't be able to run it—once he's got the tobacconist's up and running . . .'

She sipped her tea and sighed. 'Oh well . . . I'll watch television tomorrow night instead.'

'No . . . you've arranged to meet the carpet cleaner at the Star.' Iris picked up Harriet's cup of tea and backed out of the kitchen. 'I told you not to try to do it all at once.'

Alone in the kitchen, Rosie was both worried and angry with herself for giving her gran and mum good reason to find fault with the way she was doing things. It hadn't been her choice to become a one-man band. If an offer to take on any one of the arrangements came from anybody, she would be more than pleased. Everyone, it seemed, thought she was capable of making every decision, no matter how big.

Feeling worse by the minute, she remembered that she had also arranged to see another of George's contacts, an electrician, who had given a word of caution about not having the entire system checked out. Wincing against a sharp pain in her groin, she realized what time of the month it was and why her mood was swinging to and fro. She opened the cupboard and took out a bottle of aspirin, hoping they would work before the painful cramps began.

193

'Headache?' said Iris, returning from Harriet's room.

'No. I'm due for a period. I didn't check the calendar, otherwise I would 'ave taken these pills the minute I woke up. I'm not gonna go in today. I'm going back to bed.'

'I doubt if you'll get sick pay, Rosie.'

'I don't care. I feel lousy. Tell Gran to wake me around eleven. I'll see 'ow I feel then.'

She took her cup of tea and made her way back to bed, not feeling half as bad as she was making out. She knew that after a few more hours of sleep she would be ready to go and see Larry. She was in need of a pep talk and he, with his casual, relaxed manner, was the very person, if not the only one, who could reassure her. Besides which, she wanted to know if he had made any progress with his application to obtain a licence to reopen the theatre. If their request had been rejected and the project had to be dropped, it wouldn't be through any fault of hers. Once she was back in her bed with a hot-water bottle on her stomach, she drifted off into a light sleep.

*   *   *

The sound of the door knocker broke into Rosie's dreams but did not succeed in waking her. It wasn't until Harriet was by her bed and gently shaking her that she stirred. 'You've got a visitor,' she whispered. 'Larry's 'ere and looking a bit low. Won't tell me what's wrong. Shall I tell 'im to come in, or d'yer wanna get up and dressed?'

'No . . . tell 'im to come in,' yawned Rosie. 'I'm all right now. The pain's gone. You could fetch us

194

both a cup of milky coffee though . . . and a couple of fairy cakes.'

'Cheeky cow,' Harriet tut-tutted, and left the room. Lying there, Rosie wondered why Larry had called. There was no way he could know she was taking the day off. Maybe he and Harriet were having an affair? She smiled at the thought of it, and imagined them both in the living room, working out what he should say to ward off any suspicion. It was a nice thought.

'I told her not to wake you.' Larry stood in the doorway, a sad figure. His dated suit and well-worn polished shoes befitted an old theatre caretaker, but seeing him in different surroundings, she realized that to others he must appear a bit quaint, to say the least.

'What do *you* want?' She smiled fondly.

'To be a millionaire, but who's listening?'

'Ah . . . so that's it. You're after Harriet's money.'

He sat on the edge of her bed and rolled his eyes. 'And I thought it was her after me; after my body. Why are you in bed?'

'Periods. D'yer wanna hear the details?'

'Not particularly.'

'Right . . . come on then, out with it. What you doing calling on my gran in secret?'

'I came to leave a message for you to come and see me, this evening. It's time you had a phone put on. Bloody bus fares! I'll die a poor man at this rate.'

'What message?'

'We can get a licence to reopen,' he said, expressionless.

'Well don't look so pleased about it. It's good news, ain't it? You were ready to fight your corner;

195

now you won't have to.'

'That's right.' He stood up, keeping his back to her, and looked out of the window. 'It's good news.'

'So why the long face?'

'Concessions have to be made.' Still he wouldn't look at her.

'You mean they're gonna turn you out of your little bedsit?'

He nodded slowly and sighed. 'So your grandmother has a big mouth too.'

'I was getting cold feet anyway. I haven't 'ad a minute to myself since you started all this up.'

'*I* started it? That's news to me.'

'Shouldn't 'ave took me there in the first place. You knew what you was doing. Anyway . . . don't matter now, does it? I can please myself what I do in the evenings. Haven't been near a dance hall in ages.' She swallowed against the lump in her throat and murmured, 'Not since Tommy.'

Turning slowly to face her, Larry narrowed his watery brown eyes, 'You expect me to give in to those bastards? After all the effort I've put in, cleaning that place from top to bottom?'

'Excuse me . . . but I think that's my line. Bloody cheek! All you and Harriet 'ave done is inspect what we've done.'

'It shouldn't take long for the papers to come through . . . three months and you could well have a licence to put on your show. Do you think you'll have a show by then?'

'You're not listening, Larry. The Star can stay dark . . . and you can go on living there like a bloody hermit, if that's what you want. Is that what you want?'

'What I want and what I get are two different

things. The place has been fully inspected. They guessed I was living there. I've got my marching orders in any case. I haven't been paying rates since it was closed down. I'm lucky they believed me to be an ignorant old man. Now I've been told, I can't plead ignorance, can I?'

Filled with pity for the lonely figure at the window, Rosie felt the tears well up in her eyes. Taking a deep breath she said, 'You shouldn't be living like that anyway. You must get a pension? You can afford one pound ten a week … for lodgings?'

'That's what it has come to? I must live in some filthy, unfamiliar, poky room? And why? Because I refuse to see a fine music hall turned into a bingo hall or a supermarket, that's why. I would rather see it become its own tombstone. Let the bloody place fall down. I should care.'

'You should 'ave been an actor. Would 'ave been rich by now.' She got out of her bed and pulled on her dressing gown. 'I don't know about you, but I could murder some eggs and bacon. Come on— Gran loves to do a fry-up. You might as well try out her grub now, before you commit yourself to living 'ere.'

'Who said I would be living here?' he said, trailing behind her.

'Thirty bob a week ain't gonna break the bank … and for that you'll get your meals chucked in. You can 'ave Tommy's room.'

'Make it twenty-five shillings and maybe I'll take it. I don't eat bacon.'

'Twenty-seven and six.'

'Can't afford it.'

'All right, you tight sod, you win. But no fetching
197

girlfriends back late at night,' said Rosie as they arrived in the kitchen, knowing that her gran would hear.

'There's gonna 'ave to be more ground rules than that,' Harriet pointed a spatula at his face. 'The telly, for a start. I get to say what programmes we watch. I like *Beat the Clock* and I won't miss it for nothing. Wrestling, boxing, whatever.'

'You been earwigging again?' Rosie was hardly surprised.

'And I don't want you 'anging around like an old fart when you're not playing caretaker at the Royal. You can go out for walks if you've nothin' else to do . . . and when I stroll about in the morning in me housecoat, I don't want you ogling me legs.'

'With a face like that . . .' said Larry in his usual dry tone, 'who would want to look at your legs?'

'Go and show 'im 'is room, Rosie, while I chuck some bacon into the frying pan. Then you can get dressed. Walking about in your dressing gown at this time of the bloody day.'

'Is she always in this mood?'

'No. She's 'appy 'cos you've agreed to live 'ere. Come on.'

'So that's it? No long discussions? No checking with Iris?'

'If you want the room . . .' warned Harriet, 'best we don't ask 'er—otherwise there will be long-drawn-out ifs and buts. I know 'ow to handle Iris. She'll be pleased with the extra rent money.'

Once they had left what she now considered to be her kitchen, Harriet leaned against the sink and resisted shedding a tear of joy. To have a man about the place again would be heaven. She would have someone to play cards and dominoes with.

She closed her eyes and dabbed away the tear on her face: *Good boy, Tommy. I knew you was up there watching and guiding.*

Having enjoyed her breakfast, Rosie was ready to bathe, dress and make her way to the brewery. At least she had only lost half a day's pay, and she had saved herself a trip to the theatre to see Larry. While they ate, Larry had dispelled her doubts about the project and induced even more enthusiasm. As far as he was concerned, she had nothing to lose and everything to gain, adding that if she was going to change her mind, he would be only too pleased to stay in his theatre bedsit and defy the authorities. If the music hall was not reopened, as she had promised, he would have to fill his time with something else—chaining himself and his bed to a door handle. Even if it meant going to prison. What could she say?

*   *   *

Standing separate from the crowd of workers as they poured out of the brewery, Rosie, waiting for George, kept an eye out for her mother. When she did finally spot her, she was both pleased and surprised to see her chatting away to one of the men. She looked happier than Rosie had ever seen her. A smile on her face, she appeared a new woman. Once she and the man parted company, Iris looked around to see Rosie waiting.

'Not like George to be late, is it? He's usually here before we come out,' she said, wondering if she had got it wrong.

'He must 'ave got held up in the traffic. Anyway, I wanted to 'ave a quick word with you. Gran probably wants to tell you 'erself, but ... well ... since I was the one who instigated it ...'

'Instigated what?' Iris lowered her head to one side and waited.

'I thought the money would come in 'andy ... if we let Tommy's bedroom.'

'If that's meant to be a joke, it's not funny. In fact it's a very cruel thing to say, Rosie. I can't believe you said it.' She turned her face away and swallowed. 'You've still not forgiven me, have you? Still trying to get your own back.'

'That'd take years.' The words were out before she could stop them. 'Oh, don't pull that face; I never meant it. It's the things you say, at times. You get my back up. And I wasn't being funny ... I'd have a bloody strange sense of humour if I was joking.

'Larry's been turned out of his home. It's either our spare room or the doss 'ouse. He came round this morning to leave a message. We've got permission to open but there's a price to pay—that poor sod 'aving nowhere to live.'

'He didn't live in that place, surely to God?'

'Yes, he did. Try to imagine if it was Gran living all alone in a room in an old disused music hall.'

'I don't want to.' Iris sighed and shook her head. 'Why on earth didn't he say something before now ... and more to the point why has Tilly let it go on? She's got a spare room. She could 'ave taken him in.'

Rosie flicked back her long hair and chuckled. 'Can you really imagine Larry and Tilly living in the same 'ouse? You know she's houseproud. You could eat out of her lavatory. He wouldn't last five minutes—and anyway, he wouldn't want to go

200

there.'

'That's true, she does have a problem. The Star's benefited from it, I'll say that. Them old Victorian lavatories and washstands in the ladies—and the gents—were thick with lime scale. Now they're gleaming white as if they're brand new. So was it you who said he could stop for a while, or your gran?'

'Me. I couldn't 'elp it. I felt sorry for 'im. You would 'ave done as well—if you were there when he called round. Talk about dejected. Tommy would 'ave done the same if it was my bedroom going spare ... if it had been me who those bastards had—'

'Yeah, all right, Rosie. I take your point. So when does he want to move in with us, then?'

'I'm not sure. We didn't fix anything. Wanted to know what you thought about it first. It's your 'ouse, after all's said and done.'

'*Our* house Rosie; our *home*. I'll have a word with him. I s'pose he'll keep your gran off my back. She can play cards with him instead of nagging at me. I wouldn't mind if she played properly.'

'She can't help cheating, you know that. She don't know how to play straight.' Rosie looked around for George as the last of the workers drifted out of Charrington's.

'Perhaps I did get it wrong. Maybe he never said he'd meet you today.'

'He did. Definitely. You go on; I'll give him twenty minutes and then make my way home. No— on second thoughts, I'll go on to Shirley's if he don't come. Tell Gran to put me dinner on steam ... and Mum ... be nice to Larry, eh?'

''Course I will. Tilly's gonna get a mouthful,

though, when I see 'er. Fancy letting him stay in a place like that!' She gave Rosie a wave and strolled off towards home.

One round nicely scored, thought Rosie, *that'll take the wind out of Gran's sails*. She imagined Harriet looking forward to Iris's return, when she would play a little game of cat and mouse in trying to persuade her daughter into something she had already accepted. She wished she could be there to see it; *you don't know what you've let yourself in for, Larry*.

Checking her watch for the umpteenth time, she decided that fifteen minutes was long enough to wait and that if George was coming, she would see him on her way and flag him down. Strolling idly along, her mind back on the Star, she reached Whitehorse Lane before she knew it. Where her bloke had got to she had no idea; it wasn't like him to be late or to forget a date. The thought of him having had an accident made her feel sick inside— she couldn't imagine her life without him now.

'You're late, whore.' The familiar loathsome voice sent icy waves through her yet again and brought her up sharp. Bertie looked up at the clock above the pawnbroker's, 'Twenty minutes late. Been up against the wall, have you?' Smiling and cocksure, he sidestepped and sauntered off.

With anger rising from the pit of her stomach, she swore under her breath and strode forward, following in his footsteps and then overtaking him. Stopping, she turned to face him, blocking his way. 'That's the last time. I'm warning you, once more and I'll arrange for your nose to be put back the way it was.'

'My nose *is* the way it was—no thanks to you.'

202

'I don't think so,' she grinned back at him. 'Either your eyesight's not as good as you think it is or you can't face the truth. You're gonna have to live with that crooked nose . . . and you're gonna 'ave to live with the fact that you came off worse. Take it like a man.' She flicked her hair back and walked away, undaunted by his flow of abuse or his quickening footsteps.

'You won't know when I'm likely to pop up, which doorway I'll be lurking in on a dark night.' He was by her side and keeping in step. 'I can keep this up for months . . . years even. It adds a little colour to life.'

'Keep walking, otherwise I'll scream blue murder . . . and don't think I won't.'

He gave her a lopsided grin. 'What will you scream, pray? Rape?'

'No, you silly bastard—I wouldn't 'ave to go that far.' She stopped suddenly, took a deep breath and opened her mouth wide. Bertie was gone in a flash, marching away and disappearing into a side street. One more appearance and she would tell George what was happening; sod the consequences. At least this time he hadn't unnerved her: if anything, he had shown himself to be an idiot, educated or not.

Continuing on her way, having decided against going to her friend's house, she wondered why some people behaved so weirdly. Were lives so empty that they had to be filled with malice? She could understand the spite he first felt towards her but now, with all signs of genuine anger gone, there was no reason for him to continue playing his silly games. She shuddered and wiped his face from her mind. With other, more important things to think about she pulled her keys from her pocket, again wondering why George had not turned up. He was still showing off over Richard, but it wasn't in his nature to try and score points by standing her up. With the thought that he might be losing interest in her, she realized that she would have to pay him more attention. She had been neglecting him. So wrapped up in her thoughts over the musical, she had hardly given George the time of day, and she would rather risk everything than lose his love. The incredible attraction between them on that first date had developed into something far deeper than she imagined it ever could. She loved him through and through. Exactly when it had happened she didn't know. It was as if it had crept up and consumed her when she wasn't looking.

'The prodigal daughter returns,' Larry smiled as he rested back in a fireside chair, sipping a glass of stout. 'I hope you wiped your feet before you came in.'

'I might 'ave bloody known you'd 'ave your boots under the table already. No fetching women back after dark.'

'He's not in yet. Can't make up 'is blooming mind as to when he might kick his shoes off. You're gonna catch it from George, my girl. He waited till your mother got in and then went straight out to the brewery.' Harriet peered up at the clock. 'Another ten minutes and Richard the Lionheart'll be back as well. Fireworks'll go up if he gets 'ere before George is back.' She made no effort to hide her amusement.

'I *was* wrong, Rosie,' Iris said as she arrived with a casserole dish filled with piping-hot oxtail stew. 'He said he'd come round here after work. I said it
204

was me who'd got it wrong.' She placed the food in the centre of the table and nodded at Harriet. 'Show Larry to the table then.'

'Sod off, Iris. Show 'im to the table? Got eyes, ain' he?

'Such a charming woman.' Larry slowly shook his head. 'I don't know why someone hasn't snapped her up. It would be such a joy to wake in the mornings and see Harriet's face on the pillow.'

Rosie looked at Larry and rolled her eyes. 'Come on; get yourself up 'ere. It's oxtail by the smell of it—one of Gran's best. Make the most of it. You'll be paying for two days for it.' She made herself comfortable and dipped a slice of bread into the gravy. 'Count yourself lucky if you get away with only 'aving to say it a dozen times . . . how smashing this was.'

'I don't doubt it. So . . .' he looked at her with those half-asleep eyes, 'what's new?'

'I've found a writers' and actors' group.'

'You mean they were lost?'

Pandering to his humour, she ate her stew while explaining. 'No . . . they've been found, by me. I heard at work about a bunch of amateurs who are really good and I'm gonna find out if they *are* any good; if they can sing and dance . . . then, if they're interested in doing the show . . .' Her voice trailed off, a deliberate ploy to get a reaction. From the evening of their first meeting until this moment, she had got to know him very well. If she went silent he would get straight to the point. If she pandered to his quips, it would take twice as long.

'Fledglings,' he shook his head and smiled, 'some bloody show this will be.'

'This is lovely, Gran,' Rosie said quietly, trusting

that Larry would believe he'd hurt her feelings.

'Eileen from Accounts is part of that group,' offered Iris. 'They put on some really good shows from what I can hear. Did a panto last Christmas . . .'

'Where did it go on?' asked Larry, all-knowing.

'At the Stepney Jewish Club.'

'I thought as much. True-blue amateurs.'

'Better than true-blue snobs.'

Larry raised one eyebrow. 'I'm a snob?'

'What's the difference,' said Rosie, 'between an actor who gets paid for what they do and those who do it for love?'

'One's poorer than the other.'

'Exactly. But that don't make the poorer ones amateurs, do it?'

'I was referring to those who *get* paid. Those who can't afford *not* to. Those who must rely on *paid* work in the theatre.'

'Why do they 'ave to rely on it? Why can't they get a job like everyone else?'

'Because they are *actors*. Actors must be ready to drop anything at a moment's notice. They are constantly by the phone—in case it should ring.'

'You don't have to take that tone. I'm not thick.' Rosie could see she was irritating him, so judged that defence was her best tactic.

'You shouldn't knock what you don't know,' said Larry. 'A little knowledge can be dangerous.'

'Well, if this is the bleeding way you two are gonna go on we're in for a right old time of it. It's bad enough with 'er talkin' about the theatre all the time,' fumed Harriet.

'So you won't be 'appy if I use anyone from the group then, Larry?'

206

'Why use them when there are a thousand professionals looking for parts?'

'But what if one of 'em was exactly right for a part. Just what I was looking for? Really good, but hadn't taken up acting 'cos he'd had to get out there and earn a regular wage, to 'elp support the family? What then?'

'Give him the part . . .' said Larry, shrugging.

'At least we agree on that then.'

' . . . and risk getting yourself blacklisted by the union.'

'Blacklisted? You're talking out the back of your 'ead, Larry.'

'You think so? Do it and see. Professional actors won't come within a mile. They won't work with amateurs. It's why they're in the union.'

'Well I'll just 'ave to keep my mouth shut then, won't I . . . if I mix both.'

'That'll be the day,' he chuckled, 'you keeping your mouth shut.'

'We'll see.'

'Then of course there's the theatre union. You can't have any Tom, Dick or Harry helping you out the back. If your stage manager or assistant stage manager is not in the union, you'll get into trouble.'

Rosie placed her spoon in her half-empty bowl of stew, sat back and sighed. 'Anything else you'd like to tell me now that I'm in too deep to get out?'

'I'm not sure if there's a writer's union . . . you'd best check it.'

'You're not funny, y'know.'

'I wasn't trying to be. Do things properly, is all I'm saying.'

'I intend to—don't worry. But I don't see why nosy bastards should put their oar in when I'm paying to put the show on. I'm the one taking the risk, don't forget. It's our family money that's going into this.'

'That won't cut any ice with the unions.' He looked thoughtfully up at the ceiling. 'I wonder if there's a funding union, too? If there is they won't want you to use the theatre as a laundry for ill-gotten gains. I assume there will be some of those ... from your brother's friends' shady activities?'

'It's good honest money that's going into that show!' Harriet brought an end to that line of conversation. 'Don't pay too much attention to 'im, Rosie. He's got a warped sense of humour—always 'as 'ad.' She caught the expression of warning on Larry's face and then the questioning looks between Iris and Rosie. 'We go back a long way ...' she added quickly, 'didn't recognize 'im at first, but the minute we sat down in that café and he asked me to buy 'im a cheesecake, it all came flooding back.'

The brief explanation, a pack of half-truths, seemed to satisfy the women. 'He treated me to a bottle of pop, years back ... and then asked me to lend 'im 'is tram fare 'ome when I knew too bloody well he walked everywhere.'

'You've got a visitor.' The sound of the door knocker startled all three women but once again, Larry behaved as if he had expected it.

'How the hell did you know that was gonna 'appen?' said Harriet, impressed.

'Extrasensory perception. It's a pain at times. It's a pity it didn't work before you came back into my life. I would have locked the bloody door.'

Silenced by the happening Rosie left to answer

208

the door, fully expecting it to be George, but it was Richard's smiling face that greeted her. 'Harriet said it would be all right if I called back . . .'

''Course it's all right. Come on in.' Rosie brushed a kiss across his cheek and linked arms. 'You can meet Larry properly.'

Guiding him into the living room, she took his hand and held it tight. 'Larry . . . I want you to meet my cousin Richard. He's gonna direct my show . . . even though he's not in the union.'

'I'm pleased to meet you, Richard. I didn't realize that she had a cousin.' Smiling benignly, he looked from him to Iris. 'From your husband's side?' His voice was full of innocence.

'No, no . . .' said Richard heartily, 'it's quite a story really. Iris here is . . . um . . . my first cousin, and Rosie's my second. It's all very scandalous. My mother and Iris's father were brother and sister, who ended up on different sides of the track. But— tracks or no tracks—we're family and we've found each other.'

'Now that . . .' chuckled Larry, '*would* make a good play. Forget *Lavender Fields* . . . write this one.' He pulled his freshly laundered handkerchief from his pocket anticipating that he was about to cry with laughter. Harriet had filled him in on the story briefly, but seeing the son of Mary's snobby son standing in that small room, proud to be a relative, was too much. He coughed as much as he laughed and had to mop at the flow of tears.

With one hand on his face he used the other to point at the door, his long crooked finger trembling from his laughter. 'The door . . .' he managed to say between outbursts, 'someone is going to . . .' Once again he was right. The knocker went for the second time. It was George.

'Well . . .' said Larry, standing up, 'I promise to wash the dishes next time I come for supper, but for now . . . if you will excuse me, I must be going.'

'What d'yer mean, going? Going where?' Rosie said, while her mother went to let George in. 'I thought you was gonna—'

'Live here?' he chuckled. 'In this madhouse?'

'You mean you've changed your mind?' Rosie was genuinely disappointed.

'No, I haven't changed my mind. I need a bit more time, that's all. To get used to the idea. I love my room in the theatre. I'll keep it as long as I can. Another week or so. Besides . . .' he nodded to George who appeared in the doorway, 'I think two men are enough.' He grabbed his overcoat from a hook beside the door and made his escape. George looked far from happy.

Once Larry had gone and George and Richard were finally introduced, the atmosphere in the living room was sedate until Harriet began to chuckle. 'Two cockerels ruling one roost,' she said, enjoying the sight of both men trying not to look at each other.

'So . . .' George added quickly, before she could add another quip, 'Rosie tells me you're interested in helping her with the show.'

'I am, yes. I would love to direct it—if she'll let me.'

'She can't afford to pay you. You'll 'ave to do it for love.'

'Yes . . . I realize that. But it's . . . more for the experience than love. It's something I've always wanted to do. Besides which . . . we're family. If we can't pull together . . .'

'Oh yeah . . . she told me about that. Second cousins. I suppose you could say you were family. Long-lost cousins.'

'Yes, but now that we have found each other, we'll make up for lost time. Working together on something as exciting as this should bridge the gap. My parents should have told me. We could have spent some of our childhood together.'

'You've living in the land of make-believe if you think that,' said Harriet, a touch peeved by his casual statement. 'Your mother's a snob. She wouldn't have let you mix with latchkey kids.'

'My kids were *never* left to see themselves in!' snapped Iris. 'I was always there for 'em. As well you know. I might not 'ave been the best mother—'

'Oh, shut up Iris. Touchy cow. You're not on centre stage now.' Harriet turned to Richard. 'I think you are, though. George wants to make certain that you're not striving to pinch his girl.'

Abashed by her gran's straightforward manner, Rosie left the room and went to the kitchen to splash some cold water on to her burning cheeks, hoping that George might follow her out so that she could throw her arms around his neck and clear any doubts from his mind.

Richard lowered his eyes, avoiding George's formidable expression. 'I know I must appear naive, but from the very first day I came to this part of London I felt as if I were coming home. I really can't explain it. I just feel comfortable around here. I can only assume that it's because this is where part of my family roots are. Now that I've discovered . . .' he looked up, smiled and shrugged, 'Rosie, Harriet and Iris . . .'

'Yeah, well, as long as giving 'er a hand with the

211

show is all you've got in mind . . .'

'That *and* becoming part of this family. You have to understand . . . my family is not like this one. There isn't this kind of warmth.' He wiped perspiration from his brow with the back of his hand. 'I'm not criticizing my parents. It's just a different way of life, that's all. Very different. When I compare the way we conduct our lives to the way you seem to come and go . . . as if—'

'I think you're letting your emotions run away with you, son.' This time it was Iris who took command of the scene. 'I dare say if Rosie was to walk into your family scene she'd find fault with us once she started to compare. It's human nature to want what you haven't got. If truth be known, and if you had a choice between your upbringing and Rosie's, you'd want to be who you are and from wherever . . . you've spent your childhood. You're only visiting Wapping—you're not living 'ere. Not the way we have to live, anyway.' She looked into his earnest face and smiled. 'The grass is always greener.'

'No. You're wrong. You don't know what you've got here . . . this house . . . it's filled with love and care.' Twisting his handkerchief between his fingers, he slowly shook his head. 'Compared to this, our family home, as large and as palatial as it may be, is without . . .' he paused and tried to think of a word to describe what he was trying to say. 'There's no . . . well . . . no heart beating at the centre—if that makes sense. We're often there together, my parents, my sister . . . and I'm not suggesting that we don't love each other.' He looked back at Iris. 'We just don't show it in the same way. There's always a respectable distance

212

that has to be maintained,' he gestured with his hands, as if he were trying to find answers. 'We never seem to break through that invisible barrier . . . that small space between each of us.'

'You mean you don't cuddle each other?' said Harriet, making a real effort to show that she was trying to understand.

'We hug each other, of course we do. But that invisible gap is still there.'

'You're talking rubbish,' said George quietly. 'All that you've said is the same for families all over. Everyone needs to keep something to themselves. You sound as if you could do with a pint of strong ale, mate.' He looked at his watch. 'Rosie'll 'ave to wait in for me for a change. Come on. Half an hour down the pub is what we need. And I don't mean the Prospect.'

Taken aback by his friendly manner, Richard shrugged. 'Why not? Let's all go to the pub.'

'You joking, or what?' George raised an eyebrow. 'These two *and* Rosie, out for a drink? Bad enough I 'ave to put up with the three of 'em when I come round 'ere.' He stood up and stretched. 'Tell Fanny Adams that I'll be gone for half an hour. She can come with me to see the electrician when I get back.'

Standing next to Richard, George was clearly three or four inches taller—and broader. 'Come on. Hang around with women for too long and you'll turn into one. See you ladies.' He pushed his shoulders back and jerked his head towards the door. 'Move yerself, then.'

'Goodnight Richard, cock,' said Harriet, making it clear that he wasn't expected to return that night. 'Pop in whenever you like—during the day.' She

213

was pleased that, in his own straight way, George had welcomed Richard into their world.

Stepping forward, Iris tousled his hair. 'You can call round of an evening if you want. You'll always be welcome. Take us as you find us, though.'

'Richard!' Harriet suddenly called out. 'I knew your grandmother, you know. She was a lovely woman. You've got 'er eyes.' She too was embracing him into the family. Turning to face her, he obviously wanted to know more. 'You pop in and see me son, in the daytime, when this lot are at work, and I'll fill you in. Not all at once, mind; there's too much to tell,' she shook her head, chuckling, looking forward to telling her tale. 'Your grandmother and me go back to the late eighteen eighties. Your London Hospital was a bit different then, I can tell you.'

'I'll look forward to hearing about it.'

'You reckon?' Iris kept a straight face. 'Don't bank on it. She'll fabricate the truth and you won't know which bits are real and which bits she's made up. Driven me mad in the past, till I cottoned on.'

'Took her years to come to that conclusion,' laughed Harriet, 'and she still don't know what's what!' Harriet slapped her knee and enjoyed mocking Iris. She was such a pushover. Always ready to be knocked down off her pedestal. At least, that was the way Harriet saw it.

CHAPTER ELEVEN

Now that Larry had finally moved in with the family, the ambience had changed. His laid-back humour was very different from Tommy's, but it had nevertheless brought about a lighter atmosphere to the place.

'I think it's time we had a phone put on.' Studying her fashion journal while nibbling a slice of toast, Rosie spoke in a leisurely manner, as if she were talking to someone who wasn't actually there.

'Oh yeah? Who's gonna pay for that? Lucky bastard,' Harriet scoffed.

'Who's he, Gran, when he's at home?'

'Whoever came up on the pools last.' Harriet looked across the breakfast table and rolled her eyes at Larry. 'She lives with the fairies, most of the time.'

'It won't cost the earth. We could all chip in.'

'Well you can chip a bit in as well, then, 'cos I shan't use the contraption. A germ pit, that's what them things are. Disease'll spread through this country like lightning.' Peeved that Larry wasn't speaking up, she gave him one of her withering looks. 'It's worse than spitting in the street.'

'I shouldn't worry about germs, not with Iris around and Tilly as a friend,' chuckled Larry. 'The thing will reek of disinfectant. Do you want me to find out how much it will cost?'

'Yes,' said Rosie.

'No!' said Harriet.

'What what will cost?' Iris sat down at the table as if there wasn't a minute to spare.

'A mouthpiece. What's all the rush?'

'I'm going to the hairdresser's for a cut and set. What mouthpiece?'

'A telephone,' said Larry idly.

'Good idea. Save me running backwards and forwards all the time.'

'Backwards and forwards to where?' Harriet leaned forward and peered into her daughter's face.

'Hairdresser's, for a start. Be much easier to pick up the phone and book an appointment.' She mashed her Sugar Puffs into the milk in her cereal bowl. 'Do me a favour, Rose, make a fresh pot of tea, there's a good girl. I've only got five minutes.'

'We'll let Larry find out how much it'd cost, then?'

'Mmm ...' Iris nodded. 'We'll go three ways. Your gran shouldn't 'ave to pay—she won't use it. Too old-fashioned.'

'Right an' all,' Harriet murmured, thinking of the fun she could have, chatting to anyone and running up the bill for the hell of it, 'wouldn't catch me breathing into one of them things.'

'Good. Once you start yakking, you don't stop.' Iris looked at the clock and panicked. 'My watch must be slow!' She ran from the room, calling back after her, 'You'll 'ave to get your own bit of lunch! I'm goin' down the Waste to buy a new frock!'

'She's got a fancy man,' Harriet said, smiling. 'Someone from the brewery, is it?'

'Mind your own business.' Rosie had no intention of feeding her gran the slightest snippet of tittle-tattle. 'It was you who said she could do with a bit of the other.'

'Very nice I must say.' Larry pulled himself up

216

and stepped slowly to the fireside chair. 'Please God, George will come round this morning. I need a man to talk to.'

'Why don't you go round to the shop?' Rosie suggested. 'He's helping the old boy with his removals today so he can move in on Monday. You can yak to them for hours. Brighten up their day. I want the place to myself anyway. I've got a few people coming round and I don't want you two 'ere.'

'Bloody cheek. Where we s'posed to go?' Harriet was far from pleased.

'I don't care, Gran. Just go. I'll give you half a crown and you can treat Larry to a cup of tea in Joe Lyon's.'

With his bony hands clasped together, his long legs outstretched, Larry asked what time she would like them to vacate the premises. 'They're coming at eleven and I want to shift the furniture before they get 'ere. So the sooner you go the better.'

'And what time may we return?'

Rosie looked out of the window. 'Look at it. You'd think it was midsummer's day instead of late spring. You can go for a walk along Whitechapel, then over to Bethnal Green Gardens, the museum . . .'

'You think at eighty your grandmother should walk that far?' He wasn't just concerned over Harriet, he had his own problems to think about— angina.

'There ain't nothing wrong with my legs, thank you. I'll walk you out any day. Get your coat on and don't leave your change behind this time! Tight sod.' She held her hand out to Rosie. 'Half a note, if you please.'

'Ten bob? You must be joking.'

'Ten shillings or I stay. Suit yerself.'

Rosie went back to her magazine. 'I'll give it to you when you get back.'

'You'll give it to me now.' She waved her closed fingers in Rosie's face. 'Get your purse out.'

'Five bob now and five when you get back. In five hours' time.'

'It's a deal. Give.'

Larry's jaw dropped. 'I have to stay out half a day—with *her*?'

With two half-crowns clenched in her hand, Harriet tugged on Larry's sleeve. 'Come on—I wasn't gonna stay in anyway. We'll 'ave a little bet and then a cup of tea . . . pick up our winnings . . .'

Larry followed her out, shaking his head. 'You think she'll give you the other five shillings when you get back?'

''Course she won't. But a dollar's more'n half a crown, innit?' She went out laughing.

Once she heard the street door close behind them, Rosie sat back and enjoyed the silence of the house. Peace and quiet at last, and a chance to think about the impromptu meeting arranged in the canteen at work just two days ago with Vi, a woman in her early forties who managed the Stepney drama group. When she had first approached Rosie, asking about the show she was going to put on, Rosie's immediate reaction was to ward her off, saying that it was just pie in the sky, but when Vi's earnest expression changed and she broke into a warm smile, Rosie found the courage to admit that she did want to be involved in the theatre, but that it was a world she knew little, if anything, about.

218

'I know how you feel, darling,' Vi had said, squeezing her arm. 'Inspiration can be a bloody pain. It doesn't let you off the hook that easily, does it?'

Those few words had given Rosie what unknowingly, she had been looking for. This person knew what she was feeling and understood—had experienced those drawn-out hours of worry during the night when sleep seemed unattainable.

With just an hour to go before members from Vi's group were due to arrive, she began to rearrange the furniture to make space for more chairs, which she would bring in from the best room, rarely used now that Tommy and his mates no longer frequented it as a meeting place. It was also the room where her brother had been stabbed to death. She pictured his assailant's condescending sneer, awakening her anger yet again. She pushed him from her mind knowing that they would cross paths again: her gut feelings told her so. She would not have to seek him out . . . she could sense his presence in the locality, could almost smell him.

With armchairs pushed back to the wall and extra seating, the living room began to take on a different feel. The adrenaline was pumping, and she couldn't wait to be part of a group whose main interest in life was the theatre.

*   *   *

'The thing is Rosie,' Vi said, a serious expression on her face, 'you've got to be systematic. Pay attention to every detail and don't leave anything to chance. If you, or a trusted assistant, don't attend to the less important things, they won't get done, and that could be disastrous ... bring the end result to chaos.'

'You'll scare 'er off altogether if you're not careful,' said one of the other women, an actress.

'If that should be case, then so be it.' Vi looked from her to the rest of the group, four women of varying ages and two men, one in his sixties and one in his late teens. 'I was watching the builders the other day, over Cambridge Heath Road where another new tower block's going up. I'm sure they'll be lovely when they're finished, but all you can see now is cables, piles of bricks—'

'You're not going to apply for one are you, Vi?' asked Jim, the sixty-year-old. 'Those blocks look more like prisons than places to live.'

'No I'm not. I like my little back-to-back, thank you very much. The point I'm trying to make is this: if one of those labourers cut corners, couldn't be bothered with what he considered to be a minor detail, the whole lot could come a cropper later on. It's all very well 'aving lovely wallpaper and posh bathrooms and kitchens, but if the foundation ain't bang on ...'

'Don't build on sand ...' murmured one of the others.

'Exactly.' Vi raised her eyes to meet Rosie's. 'I've written a list of things you've got to think about. Do you want me to read 'em out?'

'You're gonna, anyway.'

'No, lovely. I've got better things to do than waste my time on deaf ears. Do you want to hear it or not?'

''Course I wanna hear it. Shall I make some more tea first?'

'No. Stop trying to put off the moment. Ready?'

'Oh get on with it, Vi. We'll be here all day at this rate,' Jim again.

'Right . . . I'll skip the actual preparation of the theatre 'cos you seem to've got that well under way. Just the show then. Now . . . publicity?' She looked at Rosie and waited.

'I don't think we 'ave to worry about that. Time my gran's finished everyone in the East End'll know it's on.'

'Not good enough. Knowing don't mean they'll come. If there's something good on the telly the night they thought they might come and see your show, they'll stop in. You've got to let people outside our area know what's 'appening. You'll need a team to hand out leaflets. Never assume you'll sell out, because you won't.'

'Where am I gonna get leaflets from?'

'Try the Whitechapel Art Gallery; tell them what you're doing. They'll put you on to someone.' Vi leaned forward, her face close to Rosie's. 'Get the leaflets, posters and programmes in the bag as soon as you can . . . and *delegate*. Don't try to do it all yourself.'

Leaning back in her chair, Rosie sighed and nodded. 'Fair enough.' She looked from one to the other. 'Anyone gonna volunteer?' The room went silent until the youngest member, David, smiled broadly. 'I know a few art students,' he said, scratching the side of his face.

'Good,' Rosie smiled back at him. 'You're on.'

'Come on then, Vi—next?'

'Musicians?'

'My bloke sometimes sings with a band at weddings and that, not often, but he's really

221

good—so is the band. I'll ask if he'll talk them into helping us out. I want George to sing in the show for me . . . so far he's fobbed me off, but I'll work on 'im.'

'Do you intend to write the songs yourself?'

''Course not. We're gonna use our favourites—from the hit parade.'

'You'll need to get permission and you'll have to pay royalties.' She pulled a sheet of paper from her folder, the address and telephone number of the Performing Rights Society. 'Ignore them and be damned,' Vi warned, and focused on Jim. 'You could take care of that for 'er, couldn't you?'

'Yeah—no problem.'

'Costumes?'

'We've got a wardrobe at the Star to go through.'

'Some things will have to be specially made. Would you like me to look after that side of things?'

'Yes please. Can I put the kettle on now, Vi?'

Laughing, Vi nodded. 'Go on then, but we've got a way to go yet. Make-up artist, hairdresser, set designer, choreographer—'

'Yeah all right—I've got the message.' Leaving the group to talk among themselves, Rosie went into the kitchen, leaned on the sink and willed herself to remain calm and collected. Her stomach felt as if it were somersaulting and her head crammed with things to do. More importantly, she was fired up: the buzz was back, the feeling of sheer excitement she had felt when she first set eyes on the dilapidated, wonderful Grand Star. With this new experienced team behind her, she was on the road, no longer half hoping she would land on a square where she had no choice but to slide down a very long snake back to the starting point, where she could change her mind and forget the whole thing. All she could see now were ladders, going up towards home and a win.

'The next step, of course,' said Vi, having read aloud her list of things to do, 'is to start auditioning your actors.'

'I wasn't gonna use all professionals . . .' said Rosie, handing out cups of coffee.

'I've been down that road and got myself into a lot of trouble. They have a very strict union. Hopefully that will change in time, but right now stick to those who have Equity cards.'

Feeling herself sink again, Rosie nodded. 'OK . . . when can I meet the professionals who are in your group?'

'They're sitting at your table, sweetheart. Why d'you think they came today?'

'If any of us are what you're looking for,' said Jim, 'we're prepared to work on a profit-share basis. We all think it's a great idea to get the Star up and running again. We can all belt out a song . . . but it's this young man who's got the voice.' He nodded towards David, the youngest member. 'Don't be put off by his shyness. Once he's on stage he's something else.'

'As it happens,' said Rosie, quickly filling the silence, 'there is a part for a younger bloke who has to sing a solo.'

'What song did you have in mind?'

'"I'm Sorry". It's a Platters' number.'

'Nice song. Do you want me to sing a few bars now?'

Rosie lowered her eyes and said quietly, 'No, that's OK. It brings back a time I don't want to

223

think about right now. I will, though. Soon. I'm nearly there.'

'Well, I must say this 'as been a useful meeting,' Vi said, sipping her drink. 'Very constructive. I hope you've got something out of it, Rosie. I certainly have. It's not often you find someone who listens and takes notice the way you do.'

'I've learned more than you can imagine. There's more to this than I thought. It's all very well thinking about the show and the audience. Getting to that point is something else.'

'Best you know it now though, eh? If you should find yourself alone and panicking, wondering what you've let yourself in for, give me or one of this lot a call. We'll talk you round.'

'I'll keep you to that. It shouldn't take long to get a phone put on. You've been great, all of you, for more reasons than one.' She tapped the side of her head. 'You're in there now, but the next time I see yer, you'll be down on paper—your peculiarities, sense of humour, the lot.'

'That's nice,' said Vi, 'she's been spying on us while we've been rattling on.'

'Would you 'ave rattled on in the same way if you knew I was clocking yer?'

'No. It'll be interesting anyway. Like looking in a mirror. Come on you lot, drink up and we'll leave her to it. She's got a show to write.'

With the others out of the room, Vi smiled at Rosie. 'Don't forget, we're actors—we can age up or down if needs be.' She winked at her and left.

Relieved now that they had gone, Rosie rushed up to her room and sat at the typewriter which was on loan from Charrington's. With no time to waste, she hit the keys faster than she had ever done

224

before, not worried about typing errors or spelling. Iris had offered to type it out properly for her on the electric typewriter in her office at the brewery.

It wasn't the play that Rosie was anxious to get down, it was her friends, the professional actors, who had left her inspired. She was writing a character piece on each of them, down to every detail she could recall . . . the way they drank their tea, sat, yawned, scratched a nose or rubbed an ear. Everything went down.

*   *   *

Three hours later and there was still no sight or sound of Iris, Harriet or Larry. Having written as much as she felt necessary, Rosie applied her make-up and brushed her hair, ready to meet Richard at a coffee bar close by the Drury Lane Theatre. He had made arrangements for her to have a tour and to speak with some of the staff at the theatre who had said they would happily give her advice about the running of things. Richard had also been trying to pin his aunt down too. With a bit of luck she would also be there with words of wisdom. In her heart, Rosie was hoping that the family secret would have been talked about and that she would be accepted by his family the way Richard had been by hers . . . and that bygones would be bygones.

Changing into her navy-blue two-piece costume, red blouse and shoes, she felt like a different person from the one who had been hunched over her kidney-shaped dressing table, writing about other people. Back in the real world, she collected her handbag and left the house, looking forward to the day when she might be able to take taxis whenever she wanted, instead of having to go everywhere by bus or train. Better still, she might, one day, be able to afford to buy herself a little car once she had learned to drive.

Arriving at the bus stop on the Commercial Road, she was pleased to see that there were only six other people waiting. Saturdays were a real problem at times, with more people waiting than the bus service could cope with. Oblivious to those around her, Rosie tried to imagine what the Drury Lane Theatre looked like inside, wondering if it was anything like the Star. Of course it would be much bigger, seating far more than the old music hall, but would it have that lovely old Victorian feel about it? She couldn't wait to be shown around, and to compare it with what, rightly or wrongly, she was beginning to consider her theatre. That was how it felt whenever she walked in there; it was almost like coming home. She loved the place, and could see why Larry had been content to live there.

Gazing idly at the cars as they slowly queued up from the traffic lights as far back as the bus stop, she played her game, Choosing. It helped pass the time in the same way as it had helped her get through school, when she would sit at the back of the class and study each of her classmates, *choosing* which one she might rather be. Even though her childhood had not been a happy one, she had never found anyone who she would really have preferred to be.

'Soddin' buses—wait all bloody day, you could,' one of the women standing close by nudged her. 'You know what we should do? Club together and all pile in a taxi. I bet it wouldn't cost no more.

226

Christ knows, there are enough of them about.' She tucked a few loose strands of hair under her headscarf. 'My brother's a cabbie. Pity he don't cover this patch.'

'Shouldn't be long now,' said Rosie quietly, wishing that people wouldn't push their way into her thoughts. She had just imagined herself at the wheel of an E-type Jaguar, a picture of which was plastered on a hoarding on the opposite side of the road advertising chewing gum.

'I wish I'd took the train now. I bet that sun goes in and the rain comes down.'

A negative voice was the last thing Rosie wanted to hear, especially since she was ready to embark on a journey that might well give her the biggest break of her life. She smiled politely and turned her attention to the road, to the cars, hoping the woman would pick on someone else. When the yellow Ford Zodiac drew slowly towards her, inching its way forward behind a blue van, she felt herself go icy-cold as it crept closer. With a mixture of dread and disbelief, as casually as she could, she leaned to one side and lowered her head to get a clear view of the driver's face. Alone and snarling, cursing traffic and people, sat the man she hated to the core. He was hunched over and gripping the steering wheel as if he were about to wrench it off, his sallow complexion flushed with fury.

Seeing him like that, instead of smarmy and cocksure, had a strange effect on her. He was someone who most would fear and steer clear of, but this chance sighting ignited a feeling of confidence in Rosie—a sense of equality. If a mere traffic jam could enrage him, what might *she* achieve? She leaned forward and smiled at him

227

smugly. He jerked his head up, suddenly aware that he was being watched, and looked back into her face, unable to hide his startled expression.

Seizing the brief opportunity to undermine him, she pointed a finger at his face and gave him a look of accusation and vengeance. Caught off guard and trapped in the traffic, he could not hide his humiliation. Trying to ignore her, he ran a finger around the inside of his shirt collar and then loosened his tie, showing his discomfort. Taking things a step further, Rosie walked slowly to the rear of his car and made it obvious that she was making a mental note of his licence number. As the Zodiac pulled slowly away, she stood watching it, resolute that she would bring him down and still her troubled spirit once and for all. It would not bring her brother back, but justice had to be done.

'What'd he do to upset you, then?' the woman asked, the whole queue wanting to know.

Rosie turned and shouted at the car, 'He murdered my brother!' With her first taste of retribution, she savoured a fleeting sense of release. She had, with that one outburst, inched her way towards liberty.

Leaving the woman and the rest of the queue silenced, she walked away, heading for the police station. She knew what she had to do. Since the time Reggie had advised her not to give evidence, she had felt as if something nasty had been trapped inside. She was more than ready to purge it from her being.

The sound of her stiletto heels tapping on the stone floor as she followed an officer into an interview room seemed to have a rhythm, as if rendering a message: *Tell them Ro-sie, tell them*

228

Ros-ie . . .

The young officer gestured for her to be seated and then sat down himself, a small table between them. 'How can I help?' There was a comforting, relaxed manner about him which she hadn't expected.

'My name is Rose Curtis.' There was no reaction, the name meant nothing to him. 'I live in Newman Street.' His patient, relaxed face was reassuring. 'My brother, Tommy Curtis, was attacked a few months back. He died from the wounds.'

The officer shifted in his seat and drew a breath. 'I'm going to have to ask a senior officer to come in—'

'No.'

He lowered his head thoughtfully and then raised his eyes to meet hers. 'You look as if you've got something important to say.'

'If you call anyone else in, I'll leave.'

He nodded slowly and pursed his lips. 'Do you wish to make a statement? Because if you do—'

'No.' She dropped her positive tone and sighed. 'Not yet. After we've talked a bit.'

He rubbed the side of his face. 'Go on then.'

'My brother was murdered and I know who did it. I was there. So was my mum and gran. Three Maltese kicked our back door in and then went for 'im. We weren't in the room. We were shoved out into the passage. They went in and knifed 'im.'

'Why didn't you say something at the time?' He used a tone of incredulity which angered her.

'That's my business.'

'No . . . it's police business.'

His serious tone and expression swept away her

229

self-confidence. She wished now that she hadn't been so impulsive; that she had heeded Reggie's words of warning. 'This ain't easy . . .'

'It could be, if you stop seeing the law as your enemy. We are here to help, you know.'

She looked away from his persuasive face and tried to calm an urgent impulse to leave. Her heart was pounding and her blood felt as if it would reach boiling point. She wiped the sweaty palms of her hands with her crumpled handkerchief. 'It's why I came . . .' she looked him straight in the face, 'I want you to help me. Help me go through with something that could put me in danger, not to mention my mum and gran.'

'This is nineteen fifty-nine,' he said, smiling, 'not the Thirties. We'll scoop those bastards up before they can even whisper the word grass—if that's what's worrying you.'

'Don't suppose I can 'ave that in writing, can I?'

'Sorry,' he shrugged and got up. 'If I don't call in the CID now, I'll get into trouble. Real trouble.'

'All right. I'll stay, and be the lamb to the slaughter.' She said this half-heartedly. He had put her at ease and she did feel safe. Walking out of there, into the small world where he might be waiting, was something else. Her mind began to work overtime. What if he had pulled in to a side road, ready to follow the bus to watch where she would get off? What if he had seen her stride past from his vantage point? What if he had seen her go into the police station? One quick stab is all it would take. After seeing to her, he would surely have to silence Iris and Harriet too. To him it would be as simple as killing a couple of rabbits for dinner.

Heavy with the burden of responsibility for her gran's and mum's welfare, she covered her face and asked Tommy to forgive her. *Don't be silly, babe*, his familiar voice which she missed so much drifted into her mind, *you're doing what I want, Rosie. Keep on keeping on, eh?*

Imagination running riot or not, she took comfort from the words and began to feel her confidence return. Of course she had done the right thing. It was unlikely that Tommy was the only person the mob had killed and, likely as not, left free the butchers would notch up a few more. The sound of the door opening frightened her. She had, after all, been brought up in a family that hadn't always been on the right side of the law, and she couldn't help being wary of the police. The familiar face in the doorway should have made her feel worse. It was one of the two inspectors who had badgered her in the first place to tell the truth about what had happened. But this time he was smiling kindly at her, thanking her with his eyes, expectant that she was going to help him in his daunting task of cleaning up the East End.

'Miss Curtis . . .' there was a note of compassion in his voice, 'I appreciate your coming in. I do realize how difficult the decision to come forward must have been.'

'No one else was involved, none of Tommy's friends . . .' she said, warning him not to ask her to mention other names.

He pulled up a chair and sat down. 'We know that. We know the gang who killed your brother . . . and we know why they did it.'

'He wasn't involved with prostitutes,' she said defiantly.

231

'No, but he did dip his toe in, Miss Curtis—into shark-infested waters. He needed the cash to pay his debts.'

'What debts? Tommy wasn't in debt. You've got it wrong.'

'Gambling debts. He owed money everywhere. Believe me, we've checked every avenue during this investigation. We have a documented file. It reads like a book and yet, without a statement from you, we can't make an arrest. The evidence wouldn't stand up in court, and those guilty of the crime know it.'

Rosie lowered her head, choked. 'I didn't know Tommy was in debt. He liked a bet on the horses, we all do, but no more than five bob . . . at least, that's what I thought.'

'It's a compulsion that can get to anyone—from any walk of life. Gambling and alcohol . . .' he slowly shook his head, 'good servants, bad masters. We knew that Tommy and his . . . mates, weren't into prostitution.' Seeing her tears, he lowered his voice. 'Like I said, your brother was only on the fringes of it . . . at the starting—'

'That's not why I'm upset,' she looked up at him. 'He paid for everything at home. Looked after us. From as far back as I can remember, he was the one who brought the money in. Our dad ran away before I was born. It was our fault he was in debt. If it wasn't for us, he wouldn't 'ave gambled in the first place.' She covered her face. 'He never saw me go short of anything and I still asked for more.' She was thinking about the day he died, when he had given her ten pounds to buy the dress.

Drying her eyes, she drew a breath. 'I think Tommy wants to see 'em in prison. Locked up—

232

away from us. If it goes wrong; if Mum or Gran come to any 'arm over this ... I'll break every window in this station ... *after* I've set the ball rolling: an East End bloodbath like you've never seen. And don't think I 'aven't got the contacts.'

'We know you have.'

'Well then, don't ignore what I'm saying, 'cos I will do it. I'll 'ave nothing to lose,' she pinched her lips together but failed to stop herself from crying.

'I think tea is in order ...'

'Yes, sir.' The duty officer nodded and left the room. 'Once tea arrives, if you're ready ... you can make a statement.'

'What if one of 'em saw me come in?'

'What makes you say that?' The Chief Inspector narrowed his eyes.

'I just saw the one who I reckon put the knife in. I was waiting for a bus ... he was in a car. A yellow Zodiac.'

'Did he see you?'

'Yeah. I made sure of it. I let him know I was clocking his licence number.' Her temper was back at the thought of his face. 'I *hate* him. I wanted to punch through the glass and stick a piece into 'is throat.'

He rubbed his forehead and sighed. 'I take it he recognized you?'

'Oh yeah ... this time he did—not the first, though.'

'The first?'

'I saw 'im once before ... I wasn't sure it was him, couldn't really believe it. I was walking 'ome from Charrington's, where I work. He was in the same car ... yeah, it was him all right. I know that now. He looked back at me through the window ...

233

showed me his tongue. He wouldn't 'ave done that if he'd recognized me. He probably thinks it's clever—see a woman, show her your tongue. He did it on the day Tommy was knifed.'

'I think it's time he went down, don't you?'

'Yeah . . .' she chuckled nervously, 'I'd rather it was six foot under, though.' She raised her worried eyes to his concerned face. 'Am I or my family in danger now that I've been in?'

'Don't worry. We won't take any chances. You'll be under close guard until we've brought them in. Your family too. *We* don't want any more trouble either.'

*   *   *

By the time Rosie arrived at the coffee bar with her police escort, a plain-clothes officer driving a grey Ford Anglia, she was two hours late and was not surprised that Richard was nowhere to be seen. In a way she was relieved. It had been quite an ordeal having to describe the three men and relate exactly what had happened from the time Tommy fell into the passage bleeding, until they found him slumped on the sofa, lifeless. Refusing to be taken anywhere in a police car, she had made it clear that if police protection was on offer, it would have to be carried out discreetly. She insisted that they were not to be recognized as the law. If Reggie discovered she had been talking before she had a chance to explain, it would cause a rift between them and she didn't want that. The Chief Inspector had listened to her excuses, that she would feel embarrassed in front of her neighbours being chauffeured by the law, but his knowing smile told her that he knew exactly

234

why she wanted to keep her liaison with them to herself. What she didn't know was that that was exactly what he wanted too. He just hoped that the gang member she had seen that day had not parked locally and witnessed her visit.

Sorry that she had let Richard down and not wishing to waste her journey, Rosie finished her coffee, paid her bill and left the French café, heading for the theatre in Drury Lane. It was a great comfort to see the plain-clothes officer acting as if he were an ordinary guy sitting in a car reading a newspaper. A day or so, and the cloak-and-dagger stuff would be over. It had been made clear to her that the force would act immediately to make an arrest.

Walking cautiously to the back door of the theatre, Rosie wondered what she would say and to whom, once she arrived. All she could hope for was that another Larry-type caretaker would be there; someone she could court sweetly in order to get inside the building. It was not to be. She was greeted by a lordly uniformed stage-door manager who was there to see off hopefuls and has-beens looking for walk-on parts. Had she said that she was a fan, after an autograph from one of the actors in the current production, she might have met with a better response. Lesson learned, Rosie, she told herself. If a doorman, director or tea boy has to have their vanity stroked, then so be it. She had learned long ago how to put her pride in her pocket.

Feeling like an old stray dog about to be seen off, she reproached herself for taking the wrong line. 'I've got an appointment with Mr Richard Montague,' she murmured, hoping the name would

235

mean something.

'There's no one here by that name.'

'He arranged for me to be shown round and to see some of the staff.'

'I would have been told,' he said coldly.

Miserable sod. Who did he think he was? 'If you made the effort to check, you might find that I'm expected!'

He waved her away with one finger and continued to read his paperback. 'Do the same as the rest of you lot. Write in.'

'Bloody dictator,' was her quiet reply. She threw back her hair and walked away, her head held high in an attempt to hide her humiliation. Where was Richard? Why hadn't he left a message at the stage door? Where was he?

'That was quick,' the plain-clothes officer folded his newspaper and nodded towards his car. 'Ready to go?'

'Yeah.'

'Stand you up, did he?'

'Something like that,' she didn't want to talk about it. 'Drop me off at the end of my turning.'

'Yes *ma'am*!'

Slipping into the front passenger seat, she smiled at him. 'Sorry.'

He sighed and shrugged. 'I'm thick-skinned.'

'Ain't we all,' she said, despising herself for treating him the way the doorman had just treated her. 'Do you smoke?'

'Only when I'm *really* fuming.'

'Very funny. D'yer mind if I 'ave one?'

'No . . . but if you could open your window . . .'

She stared straight ahead. 'I didn't want one anyway.'

'Suit yourself,' he said, pulling away.

Glancing at him, she admired his profile: he had a straight nose, pale complexion and lots of freckles. His hair was the colour of ginger biscuits. 'I don't s'pose this is much fun for you, is it?'

'I'm working—I don't expect it to be fun. Did he stand you up, then?'

She ran her fingers through her hair, pleased that he was showing interest. It lightened things. 'It wasn't a date. I was 'oping to get inside the theatre . . . to have a look round. My cousin who arranged it all was stood up, not me. I was two hours late, thanks to my act of bravery—or stupidity—depending which way you look at it.'

'That's a shame.' He was being sincere. 'Still . . . all in a good cause. I'm sure you'll get a second chance. Or is "your cousin" the type who sulks?'

He was still probing, wanting to know if he really was her relation. 'I don't think so. My boyfriend is, though. Make *him* jealous, and I know it.'

'Let's hope we don't cross him then. I don't fancy a black eye in the line of duty.'

Respecting his silence and appreciating it, she rested her head back and concentrated on her predicament and the best way to handle it. When she left the station she had felt confident that she and her family would be safe with the protection the police had promised. Her main concern was whether or not to tell either one or all of them at home what was happening.

'How long do you think it'll be before those murderers are pulled in?'

'Depends. Could have rounded them up already. Or they might wait for dawn . . .'

'As quick as that?'

237

'You might well have me and my colleague off your back by the time I check in at the station. If that's what's bothering you.'

'You're the least of my worries. A girl could get used to this, being chauffeured around by a good-looking plain-clothes. What colleague?'

'He'll take over from me once we've got you home. Then I'll relieve him in a different car after a few hours. Maybe this "plain-clothes" can chauffeur you around once this is all over?' he gave her a sidelong glance, hopeful.

'He definitely could if I wasn't already spoken for.' She began to laugh. 'I can just imagine George's mates . . . if I was to go out with you . . . a copper!'

'So you're engaged then?' he said, ignoring her remark.

'Sort of.'

As he turned into Turner Street, Rosie put up a hand. 'That's it! No further. I got so carried away with talking I didn't realize we was 'ere.'

Pulling in and stopping, his face turned serious. 'I hope you or your family are not planning to go out?'

Rosie looked at her watch. It was almost five o'clock. 'They should be back by now. None of us are going out . . .' she became thoughtful. 'Mind you . . . Mum bought herself a new frock today and went to the hairdresser's. She might 'ave a date.'

'Do you want to explain that she must stay in, or would you like me to—'

'I'll do it. If I 'ave to. If she's not goin' out I'll keep my mouth shut. George's coming round. I'll suggest we 'ave a night in and play Monopoly.' She pushed both hands through her hair and shook her

238

head. 'I daren't tell 'im what I've done. Not yet, anyway. Wait until you've got 'em under lock and key. He's gonna go mad.'

'Not if he loves you.'

'Love's got nothing to do with it. I've gone against—' She stopped herself just in time. He was the law, after all. 'It's difficult to explain the way things work.'

'I know the way things work. I was born in Wapping as well. One of my uncles spent time inside. If he hadn't have had a heart attack and passed away I would never have got into the force. Fortunately for me, he was the black sheep of the family. The rest of us are straight. Out you get, then.'

'Thanks for the ride and for . . . well, for looking after me. I'll put in a good word for you.'

'With?'

'God. See yer.' She got out of the car and strode towards her house as if she didn't have a care in the world. As if she were as free as a bird to come and go as she pleased. Inside, she was trembling; desperate to check her surroundings in case anyone was lurking in a doorway. She remembered the backyard and the back door. There would be a car watching the front of the house but what about the alley which ran along the back? She spun round ready to go back and tell the officer her fears, but he was already reversing out of the turning and another car was pulling in at the kerb and parking. She saw the two drivers look at each other and nod. The second shift had arrived. She turned around, leaving them to it. When she saw two other cars manoeuvring in the same way, at the other end of the street, she knew that there was a well-worked plan afoot. They were bound to be covering the back.

'What happened?' Larry's worried face peered at her as he stood at the street door. 'You didn't turn up for the appointment. I can't believe you forgot. Richard called—he's not very happy. He arranges something important for you and—'

'Larry . . . can I come in and get me coat off before you start?'

He shrugged and flapped a hand at her. 'Ah . . . it's your loss, not mine. Why should I worry?'

She closed the street door and shuddered, surprised at how relieved she was to be inside, safe and secure, without the feeling that someone was watching and waiting. 'Is Mum in?'

'She is. Looking very stylish too.' He pulled a face at her and rolled his eyes. 'A new hairdo. She's in the bathroom, trying out her new make-up. Love is in the air. So . . . where have you been?'

'That's my business. Where's Gran?'

'Having a lie-down.'

'Good. Let's hope she stops up there for hours. Could murder a cup of tea and a bit of fruit cake,' she said, going upstairs. How she was going to persuade Iris not to go out that evening she did not know. She tapped on the bathroom door and waited.

'Is that you, Rosie? I thought I heard the door.'

'Yeah. Can I come in?'

The bathroom door slowly opened. 'Desperate for the lav, are you?'

'No . . . no, I just wanted to see what they've done to you.' She pulled her head back and studied the new hairstyle. 'They've given you a tint, 'aven't they?'

240

'Yeah,' Iris blushed, 'dark auburn. What d'yer think?' She patted her hair and waited for the response.

'I like it. Yeah. Got rid of the grey streaks. Suits yer.'

'Honest?'

'I said so, didn't I? It looks nice. Should 'ave 'ad it done before now.' She sat on the edge of the bath, looking in the mirror at her mother's reflection as she teased strands of her hair around her face. 'You're not going out tonight, are you?'

'You know full well I am. Why else would I 'ave gone to all this trouble? Don't tell me that you three 'aven't been giggling behind my back?'

'You've got a date with Max.'

'So why ask if I'm going out then?'

'No reason. I thought it'd be nice if the six of us stopped in and played a board game . . . or cards. George can go out and get some beer and that, once he gets 'ere. He can buy us a nice box of chocolates as well. We can 'ave a Saturday-night nosh-in.'

Iris nodded thoughtfully, tweaked her hair again and then asked the real reason for the cosy night in. Fortunately for Rosie, the sound of the door knocker interrupted what might have been a tricky question to answer. She listened from the top of the stairs as once again Larry opened the door. This time it was George.

'You're early,' she said, pleased and much relieved to see him.

'D'yer want me to go away and come back—later when you can fit me in?'

'Don't be like that.' She kissed him on the mouth and asked him to hold her tight.

Lightly kissing the top of her head, he held her so close she could hardly breathe. 'What's up?'

'Nothing. I just love you, that's all. I'm pleased you're 'ere.'

'Oh yeah . . . ? Sounds to me like you need a good night out. Fancy spinning round the Palais? We 'aven't had a good jive for ages.'

'Not really . . . not tonight. We thought we'd all 'ave a night in. Play cards.'

'You might be,' said Iris, passing her and going down the stairs, 'but *I* am going to the pictures.' To his surprise, she kissed George on the cheek for the first time and steered him along the passage. 'What do you think of my new hairstyle then?'

Leaning on the banister, Rosie listened as they joked in the sitting room below her. She tapped her fingers on the handrail and began carefully choosing her words. There was no fooling any one of them down there and if she did try to pull the wool over their eyes, she would make matters worse. She was going to have to drop the bombshell, and the sooner the better.

*　　　*　　　*

'You've saved me a few bob, Harry girl. This braised beef is lovely. I was gonna take Madam to Ziggy's steakhouse later on.'

'Well you can leave what you was gonna spend as a tip for the cook. I wouldn't mind a new frock and hair set.' She eyed Iris and sniffed. 'Must be someone special. Going to all that trouble. Acting like a bloody schoolgirl, you are.'

'You'll find out for yourself soon. Max is coming round at half past seven.'

242

'Max . . .' Harriet quietly laughed, 'what sort of a name's that?'

'Don't you think it'd be nice for 'im to stop in and get to know us?' Rosie was still trying to avoid her confession.

'You want to scare him off?' said Larry, slow and sure. 'If you ask me—'

'Which we're not,' Harriet cut in, ever ready to goad him.

'If I were you, I would meet him on the doorstep and make a quick escape,' he continued, ignoring Harriet's wry smile. 'In other words, do *not* fetch him in to meet Mother.'

Checking their plates to be certain that they had all finished, apart from Larry who always took his time eating, Rosie said, 'So you won't stop in then?' She spoke in a hurt voice, hoping that might win Iris round.

'Certainly not.'

'What's the problem, babe?' George leaned back in his chair and looked her full in the face.

'I ain't got a problem. I just don't feel like going out. What's wrong with that?'

'So where did you get to this afternoon?' Harriet said, knowing full well that there was a motive in her granddaughter's persistence.

George narrowed his eyes and waited. They were all looking at her. Watching and waiting, and it took every bit of her will-power not to storm out of the room and go upstairs. What she really wanted to do was run. Get out of the house and run. But how could she? Feeling like a trapped bird waiting for the cats to strike, she got up, went to the sideboard and poured herself a drop of whisky, straight.

'We can't go out,' she said, a serious tone to her voice, 'none of us.' She shrugged and splayed her hands. 'We can't go out. Sorry.'

Sensing trouble in the air, Larry rose from his seat. If there was going to be a family row he was better off out of it, upstairs in his room, his sanctuary, away from the women. Mumbling an excuse about being tired after traipsing around with Harriet for most of the day, Larry tried to make his escape. He almost made it to the door when Rosie stopped him with her next statement. 'The house is being watched.'

'Why?' George, with that one word, brought a heavy silence to the room.

'The police are gonna arrest the gang responsible for Tommy's murder.'

'Tommy wasn't murdered, he was killed. There's a difference.'

'You might think so, George, but I don't. I've been to the police. Made a statement. This afternoon. After I saw the bastard who did it. You know, George . . . the one who was seen to by his own people and sent back to 'is own country? The one I've seen twice since the murder. The one who likes to show me his tongue. The one who don't 'ave a scratch on 'im. The one who I'm gonna see hanged if it's the last thing I do.'

'Tell me you're joking, Rosie.' There was a slight tremble to George's voice. His pinched expression and pursed lips showed fear and anger.

'I can't.'

'Yes you can. We won't 'old it against you. Cracking jokes which don't get laughs . . . we all do it at one time or another. You can't be amusing all the time.'

244

'Fuck *you*!' She threw her glass at the wall. 'Fuck the lot of you! You might be content to sit back and let that bastard roam free but I'm not! You want someone who amuses you, George? Well sod off and find someone like yourself. Someone who buries their 'ead in the sand when something serious 'appens! Something that's *not* funny!' She ran from the room and up the staircase to the top where she sat down and broke her heart. Cried louder than she had ever cried before, not caring who heard or who was upset by it. She cried for Tommy and she cried for herself—wishing she too had lost her life on that day. She wanted out. She hated and despised the world with all its weak and spineless people. 'Cowards!' she screamed, 'You're all fucking cowards! My brother might 'ave had his faults but he wasn't a coward! If it 'ad been you instead of 'im, George, he would 'ave made sure those bastards were seen to! You've let 'im down! All of you—you, Reggie, the whole fucking lot of you! You let him down!'

The house was silent and tense, as if it were waiting for the next move. Nothing stirred, no draughts from gaps under the front and back doors; even the old clock seemed silent.

'Come on, Rosie . . . there's no need for this.' George arrived and placed one foot on the bottom stair. 'Come back down. We need to know what's going on.'

She wiped her eyes with the back of her hand and shook her head. 'I 'ad to do it, George.'

'I know that.' He moved closer and held out his hand. 'Come on, silly. Come and tell us what you've been up to.'

Taking his hand and squeezing it, she limply

allowed him to pull her close and guide her back into the living room to three very worried and upset people. As she sat down, with George close by her side, she murmured her apologies. 'I'm sorry, Mum, but . . . I didn't know how to tell any of you . . .'

'I understand, love. Take your time.'

Very slowly, she unburdened herself, telling them everything in detail from the first time she spotted the killer to her journey, under escort, back from Drury Lane. Once she had finished her story, she looked at them, waiting for a response. There was none. She had left them speechless: even Harriet was lost for words. 'There are two cars out there. Out the front. I don't know whether they're covering the back alley or not. We could get a call any minute, telling us that they've rounded them up.'

'We'll 'ave to attend an ID,' said Harriet finally.

'No you won't . . . but I will. I've asked the police to leave you and Mum out of it for now . . . you'll 'ave to give evidence in court, though.'

'You can't take it all on by yourself Rosie . . .' Iris said, choking back her tears. 'You know what those men were like . . .'

'I've got to do it, Mum. I've gone this far . . .' she wrung her hands and sucked on her bottom lip. 'I'll be all right. Tommy'll be right by my side.' She tried to smile through her tears.

'What 'appens between now and then? We gonna be prisoners until they go down?' asked Harriet gravely.

'The police don't expect any trouble once the three of them have been pulled in.' She looked at George. 'They're not interested in you or Reggie or any of Tommy's mates.'

George nodded thoughtfully. 'We'll 'ave to let Reg know. He won't like it, but if the truth be known, he's been expecting it. He knew what you wanted, Rosie. What we all wanted. He'll be all right.'

'You're not wild with me, then?'

'No. I wish you'd told me what you was gonna do . . . but then, if you 'ad of done . . .'

'I didn't know myself, George, honest to God. I've thought about it, 'course I 'ave, ever since the time I first saw 'im after the . . . then when I saw 'im today for the second time—'

'You've *seen* him? *Twice?* Well then, why the fuck didn't you say something?'

'I wasn't sure the first time and today, well . . . I just went haywire.' She began to cry again. 'When I thought I saw 'im sitting in that car with not a mark on 'im, I thought about my Tommy and what he must look like now in that coffin—'

'All right, all right.' George pulled her close and stroked her hair. 'It's all right,' he said, unable to stop his own tears.

'I couldn't stop myself, George. I just kept walking towards that police station. It was as if someone else was inside me, driving me on.' She pulled away from him, wiped her eyes with the back of her hand and took a deep breath. 'I can't believe I did it,' she said, half laughing, half crying.

'You surprised yourself,' said Larry, smiling, 'and you shocked us.'

'Especially you.' She reached across the table and squeezed his hand. 'I'm sorry—poor bugger, you didn't know what you was letting yourself in for, did you? Moving in with us lot.'

247

'I wasn't born yesterday. If we're gonna play cards, make it Kaluki. Harriet doesn't know how to play it. She won't be able to cheat. Otherwise . . . we could always—' Three loud bangs on the door stopped him. He looked at Iris. 'Max?'

'Too early. He said he'd be here by eight.'

'I'll go.' George was out of the room in a flash.

'George!' Iris called after him. 'You're not gonna open it, surely?'

'Stop worrying! The police are out there, right?'

With bated breath, the four of them waited. 'He shouldn't—'

'Shush, Iris,' snapped Harriet, all senses quickened. They could hear muffled voices, and then the sound of the door closing and more than one set of footsteps approach. Following George into the room were two uniformed officers, half-smiling.

'You can relax,' said George, 'the pressure's off.' He looked at one of the officers and nodded towards Rosie. 'Tell her, for Christ's sake. She's scared stiff.'

'An arrest has been made. The suspects are in custody.'

'Thank God for that!' She relaxed back in her chair. 'That was quick work.'

'If you're ready, we'd like you to accompany us—'

'Now?'

'The ID parade, Rosie.' George squeezed her arm. 'I'll come with you. Get your jacket, babe. Come on . . . best get it over with. It shouldn't take long.'

'What will I 'ave to do?' The full implications of her actions were suddenly bearing down. 'I won't

248

'ave to get close to any of 'em, will I?'

George sucked his lip and sighed. 'You 'ave to pick out the three men from an assortment. When you see anyone you recognize, you put a hand on his shoulder. It'll be over in no time.'

'I 'ave to touch one of *them*?'

'Not necessarily,' said the DI, smiling. 'You can look at me and nod. How's that sound?'

'I feel sick at the thought of it.' She held out her hands. 'Look . . . I'm trembling already.'

'It'll be over before you know it. And they'll be out of sight for a very long time. You won't have to look at them again until the case comes up.' The assisting officer sounded less patient than the DI.

'I s'pose it can't wait till the morning?' Rosie pleaded, in a small voice.

'We may have the wrong men. We need you to identify them.'

'Do you want me to go for you, Rosie?' said Iris. She looked at the police officers. 'She's only twenty-two.'

'Nearly twenty-three . . .' murmured Rosie. She turned back to George and buried her face in his chest, murmuring, 'I don't want to go.'

'Come on babe, this ain't like you. Don't lose your spirit now . . . it's too important. Do it for your mum and gran . . . and for Tommy.'

'You will be there all the time, won't you?'

''Course I will . . .' He looked at the DI and raised an eyebrow, waiting for a nod of approval. It came. Reluctantly . . . but it was there. 'I'll stand in line with the others. How's that?'

Smiling again, Rosie thought he was joking. 'You mean you're gonna stand alongside those—'

'Not next to 'em. I won't go that far . . . unless

you really need me to?'

'No. Just be there. That'll make it a lot easier.'

'All right. But don't go tapping me on the shoulder, will you?'

With his arm around Rosie, George followed the policemen out of the room, calling back over his shoulder: 'We'll be back before you know it.'

'You needn't look so worried,' said Harriet to Iris, once George had slammed the street door behind them. 'She'll be all right.'

'I know she will. She's enjoying all the attention, don't you worry.' Iris's voice held little conviction. 'I wonder what Max's gonna think of all this? Fine bloody thing to 'appen on our first date!'

Rolling his eyes, Larry left the two women to themselves. Once in the kitchen, he gripped the back of a kitchen chair and struggled to control his breathing as he fumbled his heart pills from his waistcoat pocket. Popping one under his tongue, he lowered himself on to the chair and closed his eyes, waiting for the pain to ebb away.

'You all right, Larry?' It was Iris. 'You went as white as a sheet in there.'

He looked up at her, his listlessness giving him away. He could see the anxiety in her face but drained of energy, he could do nothing but signal with his eyes that he would be OK.

'Water?'

He shook his head and then raised a hand, a message for her to give him time. As the pain gradually subsided and his face relaxed, a little colour returned. Breathing more easily, he even managed a faint smile. He showed her the box of pills in his hand and shrugged.

Without reading the label, she popped them

back into his pocket and stroked his thin grey hair, and mopped the beads of perspiration from his brow with her apron. 'Can I get you something?'

'A glass of orange juice,' he whispered, closing his eyes. 'Cold orange juice.'

'What a thing to happen, eh? That Rosie! She's enough to give us all a turn.' She put the glass to his lips and waited until he'd sipped enough to satisfy him.

'I'm OK now.'

'I'm sure. Sit there for a bit longer. Max should be here any minute. He'll help me to get you tucked up in bed.'

'No need. I'll be as right as rain. Angina . . . it goes as fast as it comes . . . providing I take a pill or two. I want to play cards,' he said feebly.

Laughing at him, Iris put the kettle on. No doubt he would be asking for a cup of strong tea next. 'Make that a weak cup for me,' he said, reading her thoughts.

'You must be feeling bad.'

'Why must he?' Harriet arrived and peered at Larry. 'Got the gut ache, 'ave yer?'

'He didn't have time to eat in his usual slow way,' said Iris, covering for him. 'Indigestion.'

'Don't be tight with the sugar,' Harriet grumbled, leaving the kitchen for the living room. Both Iris and Larry knew why she had gone quietly. Her friend was poorly and she didn't want to see him like that. The tough old boot was as soft as butter underneath. No doubt, thought Iris, she would be shedding a tear in the other room and nursing her own anxieties. First Rosie, and now Larry.

The shrill ring of the doorbell made her jump.

251

'That'll be Max now,' she said. 'I hope you like him, Larry. He's a darling. Really thoughtful.' She left Larry to his own thoughts and went to let Max in. Into this crazy house where, it seemed, anything could happen, at any time. *Please God make him accept Harriet and her ways*, she prayed silently while opening the door.

Surprised to see no one there, she looked along the turning at a car speeding away and a familiar thought crossed her mind. Was it time to move away from the area to somewhere quieter? There was no doubt in her mind that changes were taking place in Wapping; it was no longer the place it used to be. Most of her old neighbours had moved out and on to new council estates in other parts of the East End. Some had gone from London altogether, to 'new towns' like Harlow. With the added worry of recent events, as far as she was concerned it was time to think seriously about leaving. Whether she could convince Harriet or Rosie was another matter.

She peered along the turning for signs of Max but there was no one about, which only fuelled her present mood. Once upon a time there would always be neighbours milling around, chatting at someone's front door, or youngsters grouped together outside one of the houses, laughing, talking and flirting with each other while the sound of music from a gramophone might drift out through an open window. She remembered when Tommy was twenty, when he and his mixed group of friends used to sit on the wall outside, listening and sometimes quietly singing along to Johnny Ray.

Seeing a figure turn into the end of the street,

she stepped forward to get a better view in case it was Max. Idly pushing something away with the toe of her shoe, she was too preoccupied to think about anything else at that moment other than her new friend, who she cared for more than she would dare to admit to anyone. When the soft bulk under her toe hardly moved, she used a bit more force and glanced downwards. What she saw startled her. The soft bulk was furry and ginger. She moved closer and lowered her head to get a better look. It was one of her neighbours' cats, Lord Marmalade, and his throat had been slit.

Shocked by the sight, she stepped back and covered her face with her hands. The knock on the door, the speeding car, the slit throat. This was a warning and no mistake. Panic swept over her. She had to hide the cat and fast. Grabbing her shopping bag from the hatstand just inside the front door, she acted automatically, pushing the bloody mess inside the strong plastic carrier and dropping it into her dustbin. Rushing back to the kitchen, she filled a bucket of water and added soda crystals, acting as if Larry were not there.

'What now?' he said, expecting the worst.

'A drunk. He's bloody well chucked 'is dinner up on the pavement. He's just been made a grandfather. At least one family in the street's happy.' She avoided his eyes and went outside, bucket in one hand, yard broom in the other, and came face to face with Max. She told him the same story, adding that Larry was in the kitchen and could do with a bit of male company. Luckily he had not noticed the bloodstained pavement.

Once she was satisfied that all trace of the horrific deed had been washed away into the gutter, she inhaled slowly and went back inside to join the men, smiling. 'I take it you've introduced yourselves,' she said, as chirpily as she could manage. 'Are you OK now, Larry?'

'Fine.' He pushed himself up from the kitchen chair and sniffed. 'Max . . . come and meet Harriet. It's quite an experience.'

With a bemused expression, Max stood in front of Harriet while she scrutinized him, looking from head to toe and back up again. 'What must you be . . . fifty-five . . . -six . . . ?'

'I'm sixty, and looking forward to sixty-five when I retire.'

'She's only fifty, you know. Sure she's not after your money?'

'She's out of luck if she is. I earn enough to live on . . . and put a bit by.'

'Well you must 'ave something she likes,' she sniffed, thoroughly enjoying the diversion from worry over Rosie. Plumping up a cushion on the sofa, she tapped it. 'Well, come and sit down, then. Tell us where you were born, who your mother is, what school she went to and what's 'appened to your missus.'

'I did warn you, Max. You can go now if you like, before she really gets going.'

'Wouldn't dream of it, Iris. I've been waiting for the day when I'd meet someone who's prepared to listen to me going on for hours. People usually back away politely.' He sat down next to Harriet. 'Right then, let's see . . . where I was born first, I think . . . it was a terrible birth by all accounts. My mother was in labour for—'

'Yeah all right, you clever dick, skip it. Bore someone else to death. Larry, for instance. Good

254

God . . .' She shook her head and sighed. 'The thought of you two going over old times . . .'

'Are we going to play cards or are you going out, Iris?' asked Larry, weighing his options. For him it was cards or bed.

'To be honest with you I would rather stop in, but . . .'

'Suits me,' said Max. 'Might as well give Harriet the chance to hear all about me.'

'No, that's all right, thanks. If you're playing cards you're playing cards. Rabbit on and you're out that door.'

Pleased that at least one thing had worked out that day, Iris cleared the table, pushing all thoughts of the macabre from her mind. She knew enough about the shady side of the East End to know the real significance of the dead cat. It was amateur, and the deed had been carried out by youngsters; probably members of the family who, with the adults arrested, had been quick to seize the opportunity to show what they could do. She would tell George what had happened and no one else. The arrest of three prominent men from Commercial Street had obviously caused a stir if not panic. The cleaning-up process had taken a big step forward, and she was pleased for more reasons than one. George had promised Iris that he had every intention of earning an honest living, running his tobacconist's and making a real success of it. That was his goal. That and raising a family, with Rosie as his wife.

Placing the dirty dishes into hot soapy water, Iris was suddenly overcome with pride for her daughter. She had shown real courage in going to the police. Especially when it was off her own bat, with no one to discuss it with. If Rosie had the guts for that, then surely putting on a full-length professional musical was not so far-fetched? Her doubts in Rosie's capability of achieving her ambitions for the Grand Star began to ebb away. The consequences of her daughter's actions were something else, however. That the family were under threat had to be taken seriously. They would, for a while, have to watch their step. Especially Rosie.

*   *   *

'I'll go round and see Reg tomorrow. Sooner he knows the better.' George spoke in a grave voice as he drove Rosie home from the police station. She had coped well with the gruelling process of identifying the three murderers, picking them without hesitation from the line-up. 'It's all very well 'aving those three banged up but word will've swept through by now.'

'So this ain't the end of it?'

'Hardly. I doubt they'll come anywhere near you. No . . . they'll get to you through us, guaranteed.'

'But only till the case comes up?'

'That's long enough,' he chuckled knowingly.

'Right . . . we'll go and see Reg now.'

'*We* won't go and see Reg at any time. *I'll* go. You've done enough.'

'That's why I wanna go!' She went quiet, waiting for him to reel off all the reasons why she should stay out of it. 'If you don't take me now I'll go first thing . . . or once you've gone 'ome tonight.'

George braked suddenly, his knuckles showing white as his hands clenched the steering wheel.

'You won't go round there! Stop acting like a *kid*!' He slapped his forehead. 'I'm up to 'ere with this, Rosie. Up to fucking 'ere with it!'

'Take me to see Reg.'

'*No!*'

'Please.'

'Don't even think about using that hurt-baby tone . . . just do as you're told for once.' He turned to face her. 'This ain't no game, babe. This is serious. If I 'ad my way I'd send you to Australia— as far away as possible—till it's over.'

'Take me there and I promise to do whatever you say after that. I've got to see 'im. I won't be able to sleep . . .'

George let out an exasperated sigh. 'You don't listen, do you?'

'I do, George. I know what you're saying but please . . . please, just this once . . .'

'You want to go *now*?' he said, unable to contain his anger.

'Yeah. It's really important. I feel like topping myself for what I've done. If anything 'appens to Reggie—' she swallowed and pinched her lips together. 'Tommy would never forgive me. You know how good he was to 'im—to all of us. Still is.'

He rapped his fingers on the steering wheel and shook his head. 'All right . . . 'ave it your way. We'll go and see 'im, but not a word on the way. I've got some thinking to do.'

'And I 'aven't?'

'Bit late for that. Should 'ave thought before you—'

'No talking, you said.'

'I meant *you*, not me.'

'So did I.' She looked at him and smiled wryly.

257

Quiet for the rest of the journey through the backstreets and into Bethnal Green, each of them really wanted the other to break the silence. It wasn't to be. By the time they reached Ravenscroft Buildings, not one word had passed between them. 'I s'pose you'd better come up,' said George, worried.

''Course I'm gonna come up. You don't think you're gonna leave me down 'ere in this dark turning by myself, do yer?'

'Reggie don't like too many people to know where he lives.'

'Oh, what . . . you think I don't know that? Silly bleeder. I'm more like family. I've been up there before. Used to run messages for Tommy.' Rosie peered out of her window, up to the third floor. 'His lights ain't on. He must be out.'

'He's in. Out you get.'

'The flat's in darkness!'

'The curtains are drawn. He's in. Probably on the bed 'aving a kip, or . . .' he looked at her and winked, 'something else.'

'Well this ain't gonna please him, is it? Us spoiling 'is fun,' said Rosie, opening the passenger door.

'Why should he be having a good time when my guts are working overtime?' He got out of the car, checked his surroundings and locked both doors. 'At least word 'asn't got to him yet,' he said, taking her arm. 'That's a good sign. The Maltese must have gone to ground, shaking in their shoes.'

'Or Reg has. He could well be in Dorset now, in his little hideaway.'

'Without his car?' He nodded towards a blue Mustang parked nearby.

'You should 'ave been a copper.'

'Don't go shooting your mouth off, OK? I'll break the news—*my* way.'

Knowing George well enough to realize that this was the time to hold her tongue, she followed him up the narrow stone staircase of the badly lit, Dickensian flats. 'About time they pulled this lot down,' he mumbled as they made their way up to the third floor. Using the knuckle of his third finger, he tapped lightly on the door and waited. There was no answer and no sound of movement from inside.

'I said he was out,' whispered Rosie.

George put his finger to his lips and knocked again, listening intently. 'Reggie, it's me, George.'

The sound of shuffling and a key turning in the lock brought a sigh from them both and a smile to George's face. 'I was right ... he's got a bird in there.'

When the door opened and Reggie stood there with a sawn-off shotgun in his hand, the cheeky grin drained from George's face. 'It's a good job you spoke when you did.' Reggie jerked his head to one side, an indication for them to get inside and quick. 'Shut the door and lock it,' he said, resuming his position in his chair, facing the door with his gun aimed at it. 'Sit over there, Rosie, out of the way. You as well, George.'

'What's goin' on?' George dragged a chair across the room and placed it next to Rosie. 'Who you expecting?'

'As if you didn't know.' He threw Rosie a look of misgiving. 'Keep well clear of that door.'

'You look frightened, Reg,' said Rosie, concerned.

'Frightened? I'm fucking terrified. Be quiet for five minutes.' He stretched one leg, brought his gun up and took aim, the centre of the door being his target. 'If they ain't followed you up we can relax.'

'There wasn't any sign of 'em, Reg.'

'They were out there. They're gonna come up any second and go for the three of us or turn back.' He flicked a finger to order silence and waited, creating a chilling stillness. After a few minutes had ticked slowly by, he drew a breath and sighed. 'Gone.' He stood up and stretched. 'You two 'ave just used up two of your lives and one of mine. Think yourself lucky they didn't jump you down there. Silly bastards. Put the kettle on, Rosie.'

'How'd you know they won't come now?' Rosie just managed to say, her face showing fear.

'That lot don't think things out. They're straight in.'

'So why didn't they—'

'Leave you for dead?' Reggie shrugged and chuckled quietly. 'Luck was on your side, babe. It would've bin the little boys trying to do a man's job.' He shook his head at the pair of them. 'Fancy goin' to the police.'

George narrowed his eyes, his expression serious. 'She had her reasons. One of the Maltese's been taking the piss. Kerb-crawling Rosie—been tormenting the life out of her.'

'You said they'd been seen to, Reg. There wasn't a mark on 'is face and he was smiling. Out there . . . free and smiling over it. I should think Tommy's body's crawling with maggots by now.'

'Yeah, all right, point taken. They're liberty-takers.' He dropped into an armchair and started to laugh. 'You're either hare-brained or gutsy,

260

Rosie. I ain't sure which.'

'The law's got the three of 'em you know,' George said, a touch proud of his girl. 'The ringleaders. They ain't gonna enjoy Christmas.' He sipped his tea. 'I think she did well, as it happens.'

'Luck was on 'er side, Georgie. If the Old Bill 'adn't picked 'em up straight away, all three of 'em . . . we'd be minced meat by now. You're gonna 'ave to go away for a while, Rosie. We'll 'ave to find you a little cottage in the country—miles from anywhere.'

'No you won't. I'm not going anywhere. I've got a show to put on.'

'Don't be silly. You can't stay round 'ere till the trial comes up—'

'Can't I?'

Reggie looked from her to George. 'Talk some sense into 'er, will you?'

'I've tried. She won't listen.'

'Take 'er to Scotland for a couple of months. She'll be all right up there. They won't make hide nor 'air of her accent.'

'S'cuse me,' Rosie said, straight-faced. 'I am 'ere. Could you talk to me instead of George?'

Reaching down to a small cupboard, Reggie pulled out a bottle of Scotch. 'Women. Why'd we bother with 'em?'

'Try existing without us.'

'I do, babe. Believe me . . . I do.'

'But you can't.'

'Get some glasses out of that cupboard over the sink,' he said, relieved that he had someone to drink with. Sitting alone, with death looking him in the face, had not been easy. 'I s'pose we're all gonna 'ave to keep an eye on you.'

261

'No you're not. I'm gonna go about my life as usual.' She grinned at him and winked. 'I've got the law on my side.'

Reggie shuddered and went cold. 'Tommy just turned in 'is grave.'

CHAPTER TWELVE

For three months Rosie had worked like a Trojan. Once the theatre was in fair shape, she left it to others to add the finishing touches. Larry had risen to foreman, not because he wanted the responsibility, but since Harriet had liked the title but not the work, he had had no choice. Not that he hadn't enjoyed spending time with the women: their earthy sense of humour appealed to him—he found their coarse jokes funnier than his own.

Having been released from that side of things, Rosie had thrown herself into rehearsals, working every hour that she was not at the brewery, and rewriting scenes into the early hours of the morning. Up until now she had rehearsed without a director, believing that she, knowing the play so well, could better instruct the actors what to do, but now it was time to bring Richard in—she was out of her depth and time was running out. The choreographer had come up trumps and worked out excellent dance routines, including a cameo solo for Rosie, who was to be in a dream sequence at the end of the first act and then at the close of the show. Things were going well, but it was clear that the actors were in need of a director. The man who usually directed the Stepney drama group in their amateur productions had offered to come in should they need him, but he had since had a heart attack and was on bedrest in the Bethnal Green Hospital. Richard had promised his time, but had been so busy with exams and his new girlfriend that he had been unable to comply. Now that it had become urgent, Rosie knew she would have to push him for an answer, or find someone else. Others had joined the show along the way, professional actors who had heard about the new project and were happy to come aboard, only too happy to support the cause. But they were used to real guidance, and they had become demanding.

With the murder trial coming up at the Old Bailey, Rosie did her utmost to try to push it from her mind by concentrating on her musical. Knowing that the killers were behind bars in Wandsworth Prison had helped, but as the time drew near for her to stand in the witness box, she was beginning to wish she had not gone to the police.

Her thoughts were invaded by scenes of herself in the High Court, as she strolled towards the Prospect hoping that Richard would be there. She hadn't seen him for quite a while. He had sent her a letter saying that the final exams were almost over, and that he felt confident he had done well, which was a relief for more reasons than one. He would not have to resit, which meant he would be free to help her. She had set a date for the show, now to be called *Love in Lavender*. They were to open on the eighth of September for a two-week trial run ... and that was just two months away! She had set herself a daunting task, and would have to focus all her time and energy to get it in shape on time, with the actors ready to give professional, well-rehearsed performances.

Going into the Prospect to meet Richard had become a routine, and the students had accepted her as one of the crowd—except Bertie, who kept his distance, sneering from afar. He had popped up twice since she had warned him off, and there had been no way of telling whether it was a coincidence or planned. She preferred to believe the former—it gave her one less problem to worry over.

'You've saved me a walk,' Richard said, taking her arm and leading her to a table outside, overlooking the river. 'I was about to call on you. Good news.' He smiled and winked at her, reminding her once again of her brother. 'Aunt Isobelle wants to meet you. She even apologized for not being able to get to the theatre that day when you were late and it all fell apart. I didn't tell her about that, naturally.'

'Why does she want to meet me?' Rosie asked, surprised by her own lack of interest. So much had happened since the beginning of the project, when she had wanted to meet other people in the business. Now all she was concerned with was getting on with it.

'She's happy to give you any advice she can, and ... is offering her help too.' He rubbed his finger and thumb together. 'She's loaded, darling ...' He looked more than pleased with himself.

'Richard, that's really good. Smashing news, but ... right now I'm more interested in *your* help.' Distracted and obviously happy now that the pressure of exams was off, he waved to a few friends who had just arrived in the pub.

'*Richard . . . ?*'

'Sorry. Sorry. Where was I, oh yes—Aunt Isobelle. I told her all about you, but not that we're related . . . and she can't wait to say hello.' He leaned forward and nudged her on the arm. 'She's never met a real cockney before, let alone listened to one. She asked me if you were a flower seller,' he chuckled. 'I think *My Fair Lady*'s gone to her brain.'

'Richard . . . what about *you*? You directing my show?' She was beginning to lose her patience with him.

'Oh that . . .' he smiled teasingly. 'I'm free from next Friday to help you with *Lavender Lady*—if that's still the title?'

She slumped back in her chair and closed her eyes, silently thanking God. 'The title's changed. It's *Love in Lavender*.'

The smile drained from his face. '*Love in Lavender*?'

'Yes. And it's final. I'm not going all through that again. Me and the cast 'ave already had a long-drawn-out discussion on what it should be. Anyway . . . the leaflets and posters are with the printer, so we can't change it. I don't *want* to change it.'

Laughing at her indignant expression, he reached out and stroked a young girl on the arm as she cleared the table next to them. 'Couldn't fetch us two g and t's could you, Linda?'

'I got ticked off last time I did that,' she said, mildly flirting with him. 'You're supposed to go to the bar like everyone else.'

'Please . . . ?'

She sighed hopelessly. 'Them bloody eyes of

265

yours.' She eyed Rosie and shrugged. "Ow can I refuse? If you ever get tired of him . . .'

'We're cousins.' Rosie reeled off the words with seasoned practice.

'*Second* cousins,' added Richard, looking into her face.

'We're still related.' She turned to the bar girl. 'He's all yours.'

Carrying her tray loaded with empty glasses, Linda winked and walked away smiling.

'So you do still want me to direct the show, then? Wouldn't prefer to get a professional in?'

'Don't talk daft. I thought it was you who was losing interest.'

'Have you spoken to anyone about designing the posters yet?'

'I just said, they're at the printer's. I'll make sure your name's in capital letters, don't worry.'

'I should hope so. I take it Bertie's been as good as his word?' he said, changing the subject.

'I don't know about that, but he 'asn't been bothering me. He's a drip, Richard. A pansy.'

'You could be right there,' he said, lighting a cigarette. 'I don't suppose you fancy a Chinese supper?'

'No. I 'ad me dinner before I came out. I'm full up. Anyway, I'm going to the Star. See how the old costumes cleaned up.'

'Can't keep away from the place, can you?'

'Nope. You can come if you want.'

'Nope. I'm bleedin' well starving,' he said, mimicking her.

Having finished her drink, Rosie stood up and placed one hand on Richard's shoulder. 'I'm glad you're coming on board. I need you. And thanks for putting a word in for me with your aunt. I won't let you down. I'll talk in me broadest cockney.'

He relaxed back in his chair and looked into her face. 'It is legal, you know. Second cousins—'

'I knew you'd check that out! Listen . . . if it wasn't for George, who I think the world of . . .' She flicked her hair back and returned his smile. 'Think of me as a sister.'

'Do you really love George?' he said, doing his utmost to sound astonished that she could choose him in preference to himself.

'Yes . . . and what's more, I intend to be his wife. Have his children. I'm spoken for, Richard. Get that into your daft head and we'll get on like a house on fire.'

'Fair enough.' He tried to sound hurt, but she had a feeling that his chase had all been a bit of a lark. It wouldn't have surprised her if he had placed a bet on her with his chums.

'I'm going to the Star. I'll be back 'ome by ten . . . if you're still around, pop in. You can finish off the shepherd's pie Gran made. You can take me to Chinatown another time . . . I don't wanna miss out.' She pinched his cheek affectionately and left, easing her way through the crowd of happy drinkers, knowing she had just delivered him a soft blow. She hadn't planned to tell him yet, or to tell him in quite that way: choosing the right words had been difficult but as it turned out, he had made it easier by pushing her into a corner, a spacious corner, but a corner no less.

With one worry off her mind, she stepped out of the crowded, smoky bar and braced herself for another testing walk through the backstreets. She had managed to convince everyone she was confident, but not a day had passed since Bertie assaulted her when she had not been wary, watching the shadows in case anyone stepped out. Forcing the fear from her, she brought the old costumes to mind.

When Larry had taken her into the walk-in wardrobe and given her the freedom to go through the boxes of well-wrapped cloaks, period gowns and a vast array of separates, she had experienced something unique. As luck would have it, there were eight matching light grey ankle-length cotton frocks which could be dyed lavender and were more than suitable for her flower-pickers. Other items, with a tuck and stitch, could be altered to suit other players. Tilly, ever enthusiastic, had volunteered to work alongside another of the women who had joined the troupe as costume designer.

Disappointment over two boxes which had not been fully protected from moths, had been redeemed by those which had survived intact. Shoes and boots had been wrapped in muslin bags together with cedarwood shavings. The clothes had been wrapped in the same fabric, with shavings of camphor wood and the seeds of the musk plant. Larry's mother, thankfully, had always shared his father's hope that one day the theatre would be used again and the costumes would see the light of day. Once Rosie had seen the collection of satin and lace period gowns, she had had to force herself to focus her mind on the play in hand and not get carried away with what she might do in the future, when she would make full use of the Victorian clothes.

Excited by the prospect of seeing those items

which had been dry-cleaned and those which had been dyed, she paid no attention to the old American car parked by the gasworks. So deep in thought was she that when three female medical students passed and said hello, Rosie was surprised to find herself five minutes away from the pub when it seemed as if only a few seconds had passed since she left the Prospect. Amused by the fact that she had been mumbling to herself when the girls had strolled by, she wondered what they might be saying about her. If she wasn't careful, she could easily be reputed as the crazy woman who talked to herself.

'You just can't keep away from the backstreets, can you?' From the shadows, Bertie's disparaging voice had a different effect on her than it had had on other occasions. It was a mixture of pity and repulsion.

'Ain't you got better things to do?' Her tone was a good match for his.

'Of course I have, whore. But I enjoy haunting you. It's light relief after a day of lectures and studies.'

'You do know that that lot . . .' she gestured back towards the Prospect, 'think you're a joke?'

He leaned forward and grinned at her. 'They think you're a whore . . . but whose keeping score?'

'Look . . . you don't frighten me any more. You're flogging a dead 'orse and . . . making yourself look like a prat. Forget it. You got what you deserved; I got what I didn't deserve; everyone's forgot, and can't be bothered . . .'

'I've not forgotten. That's the important thing. I'm—' The sudden slamming of a car door stopped him in his tracks. When the second and third door slammed shut, both his and Rosie's attention was riveted. *'Run!'* The word was out before she could think, and her body stiffened as if every muscle had locked. The one word of warning was not meant for him alone, but for both of them.

'Good grief,' he mused, 'three of them at once. You *are* industrious . . .' No sooner were his words out, than the three young thugs wearing smart suits and slicked-back hair were rushing across the narrow road, heading straight for them. The first to arrive grabbed Rosie's hair and pulled her head back. 'Who's he?'

Taken off guard, Bertie put up both hands and stepped back. 'She's all yours. I don't go in for sluts.'

'Someone's trying to be funny,' sneered one youth as he released the catch on his flick knife. With the point on the tip of Bertie's ear, he clenched his teeth and moved his face so close that they were almost touching. 'He asked who you were.'

Rosie, snared and unable to move her head, found her voice. 'Get help! Run!'

The point of the knife flashed from Bertie's ear to his throat. 'Move or say one word and you're dead.'

'We're not here to eliminate—*this* time,' said the third as he pushed a knuckleduster on to his right hand. 'It's a warning.' He turned to Rosie. 'Appear in court and your family will be pushing up blood-soaked daisies.'

'Look . . . I don't know what's going on, but she means nothing to me.' Bertie made the grave mistake of ignoring their request to hold his tongue.

'You were told not to talk.' The knife pressed against the fleshy part of his neck. Filled with panic, Bertie pulled back and tried to tear away, but two of them were on him in a flash. Having some advantage with his height, he grabbed each of them by the hair and banged their heads together, throwing them off balance. Releasing Rosie, the third lunged forward and kicked out with his boot, using a well-practised manoeuvre to send Bertie sprawling to the floor. Grabbing her chance to make her own escape, Rosie ran, screaming for help.

By the time she reached the Prospect, people were already coming out to see what the commotion was about. Falling into Richard's arms she began to tremble and cry, raising one arm and waving it towards the narrow road leading to the gasworks. 'Bertie . . . !'

'Bertie, *again*!' snapped Richard.

'Go! He needs *help*! You don't know what they're like!'

'What who are like, Rosie? Try to calm down.' Richard's passive tone and calm annoyed her beyond belief. Her eyes wide with anger and fear, she pushed him away, 'Just *go*!'

He gripped her shoulders, an attempt to still her, compose her. 'It's all right. The others are on their way.' And so they were. At least a dozen intent young men were running towards the trouble. 'Come and sit down, you're trembling.'

Allowing him to guide her into the pub and lower her into a seat, she covered her face with her hands and murmured over and over, 'What 'ave I done?'

'I don't know, Rosie,' said Richard as he sat

down opposite her and placed a glass of lemonade on the table. 'Drink this, it will help. Then maybe you can tell me what this is all about.'

'It's a long story.'

'Has Bertie been beaten up because he's been pestering you?'

'No ... I don't wanna talk about it. I—' The sound of police-car sirens stopped her. 'I've got to go.' She grabbed her handbag and stood, ready to leave, when an irate young student rushed into the bar, red-faced and out of breath.

'Bertie's been stabbed!' The pub went quiet as everyone stared at him, speechless. 'I think he's dead.'

Rosie squeezed Richard's arm and whispered in his ear, 'I'm going home. Send the police round when they arrive. I'd sooner talk to 'em in my own surroundings.'

Richard grabbed her arm. 'Did you hear what he said, Rosie? He thinks that Bertie is *dead*.'

'He saved my life,' she murmured, trance-like.

'Who *were* they?'

'Members of the underworld,' she shrugged, matter-of-factly. Then, smiling weakly, she said, '*This* is the real East End ... not the Hollywood version where all cockneys are the salt of the earth. Do yourself a favour and stay out of it.' She looked around the bar at all the people who now seemed like actors in a B-movie. 'Stay away from me till this blows over. I'll direct the show myself. You concentrate on your studies.' Pale and drawn, she hurried away.

*   *   *

272

'That was quick, wasn't it? You ain't been gone five minutes.' Harriet looked over the top of her reading glasses. 'What's, 'appening out there? Bloody police sirens . . .'

'You'll know soon enough.' Rosie slumped down on an armchair and kicked off her shoes, avoiding the questioning eyes of Larry and Iris. 'I was jumped by three Maltese. A student 'appened to be there. He stepped in and they knifed him. I ran . . . and I 'aven't got a scratch to prove it. Now can we forget it until I 'ave to go through everything in detail? Once the police get here.'

'What the fuck is it about you? Have you got a placard that you pin on to yourself the minute you walk out of 'ere—"Oi trouble! Try me!"'

'Something like that Gran, yeah. Make me a cup of tea—I've just escaped a flick knife. That sort of thing plays havoc with your nerves.'

'If this is meant to be a joke . . .' Larry let out a long sigh and brushed a piece of fluff from his shirtsleeve. 'I don't find it funny.' The sound of police and ambulance sirens invaded the room again. 'I take it you have bolted the front and back doors?' He addressed this question to Iris, who nodded nervously.

'Did they hurt you, Rosie?' Iris spoke with a trembling voice.

'No . . . well . . .' She massaged her head and neck. 'Not enough to make me cry. One of 'em yanked my hair back, that's all.'

'That's all?' Larry stood up, shaking his head slowly. 'Yobbos push a knife into a friend in front of her eyes and she says "that's all". Was there much blood?'

'I don't know, Larry. I didn't stop to look. They

273

killed him after I'd legged it.'

'They *what*?' Harriet sat bolt upright.

'Killed 'im . . . according to one of the students.'

All three of them stared at her, amazed at her lack of emotion. 'You can't be serious . . . ?' said Iris weakly. 'You wouldn't be sitting there . . .'

'What d'yer want me to do, Mum? What do you *expect* me to do?' Her eyes wide and glassy, she gazed at her mother. 'Fall apart? Say I've 'ad enough? Drift away into a dark hollow space? Or just sit 'ere till I stop feeling as if my stomach's gonna come up?'

'My God . . . you've gone as white as a sheet . . .' Iris lurched forward and grabbed her daughter's shoulders. 'Put your head between your knees!'

'No. I don't want to.' Rosie's voice was thin and vacant. 'All I want . . . is to be left alone. Just leave me be.' She clasped her hands together, stared into space and sat very still, as if she were in a trance, releasing herself from everything, feeling herself on the edge of one of the other worlds she had so often slipped into as a child.

'I think you should phone for the doctor, Iris,' Larry pursed his lips. 'Or do you want I should call him?'

'No, I'll do it. You and Mum stay here.' She spoke quietly, as if her daughter were not to be disturbed; as if she were sleeping. 'Try to get her to rest back in the armchair . . . in case she does faint.'

'Do you feel faint?' asked Harriet, once Iris had gone into the passage and dialled for the doctor. 'Stop messing about . . . there's a good girl. I'm too old in the tooth for tricks. Rosie . . . ?'

'Leave her be now. She's opted out, that's all.' Larry stepped forward, placed an arm around

274

Rosie and eased her backwards, pulling a cushion up to support her neck and make her comfortable. As he had expected, she showed no resistance. He was reminded of his late wife, when she had one of her bad turns, before she was admitted to St Clement's. Her withdrawal was part of her illness, whereas Rosie, he hoped, was suffering from shock and no more.

Turning to Harriet, he said, 'She needs some hot sweet tea.'

'I can't, Larry ...' Harriet dabbed her watery eyes. 'I can't ... I think I've had enough. I don't think I can take any more.'

'I must do *everything*? I have to watch she doesn't faint ... I have to make the tea ...' He handed her a clean handkerchief from a pile of neatly ironed laundry on the sideboard. 'And I must mop up your tears. I have three pairs of hands?'

'I'll make the tea ... just give me a couple of minutes.' Harriet inhaled slowly, an attempt to compose herself. 'I'll be OK. Stop looking at me like that! I ain't gonna go to pieces. The fuckers. I'll murder the bastards myself, so help me ...'

'Very nice language, I must say. In front of your granddaughter, too.'

'She can't hear me. She's fucked off into no-man's land.'

'Have you quite finished?'

'No I 'aven't. Go and make that tea before I start on you.'

Smiling to himself, Larry went into the kitchen. 'We all deal with it in our own way,' he murmured, massaging his chest to ease the gripping pain as Iris walked in.

'The doctor's on his way. He said not to worry,

she's bound to have a reaction. Let's hope he gets here before the police do.'

'Do you think . . .' said Larry, placing cups on saucers, 'that you could tell me what we might expect to happen next?' He looked at her pleadingly. 'I'm being serious. I'm not used to all of this.'

'You think we are? It's as if God's decided to punish us—non-stop.'

'You shouldn't blame God. It may seem as if He's hiding when you need Him most but in truth . . .' he shrugged, 'what can He do? It's human beings that cause all the trouble, not Him. Why should He punish you?'

'I should have tried to mend Tommy's ways, years back,' she said, tired, 'when he was a kid. But . . . then, how else was I supposed to put food on the table if he didn't go out and pinch off the market stalls and baker's van? Once my old man scarpered . . . I 'ad nothing to live on except the bit I earned cleaning from five in the morning till eight. Rosie was too small to leave with Tommy, and by the time she was five there wasn't any work . . . anywhere, not even in wartime. People moaned about coupons but in truth, Larry, they were a bloody godsend as far as we were concerned.'

'I take it that Tommy's . . .' he struggled to find the right word, 'death . . . was due to his way of living?'

She shook her head resolutely. 'It shouldn't 'ave been that way. His father's to blame and only his father. Tommy was a bright kid . . . had a quick brain . . . he could have made something of 'imself.' She poured boiling water into the teapot and

276

sighed. 'I expect there are plenty of mothers saying the same thing.'

'I'm sure. Look . . . I think you should sit with Rosie. I'll fetch the tea in.'

'Thanks.' She managed a faint smile. 'Sorry you came to live with us?'

'What do you think?' He looked at her sideways and raised an eyebrow before wiggling it to make her laugh.

'I think you love it 'ere.'

He shrugged. 'Never a dull moment. Now will you go, so I can stop worrying over the pest in there?'

'Thanks Larry. You've brought fun back into this house, you know that?'

'You want I should sing—"Don't Laugh At Me 'Cos I'm A Fool"?'

'I said *fun*. We don't laugh *at* you, we laugh *with* you.'

'I know that. I'm playing silly buggers to squeeze out a bit more praise. I milk what I can . . .'

'Well put plenty in my tea this time . . . you could stand a spoon up in your brew.'

*   *   *

'I'm not going to prescribe anything for you Rosie,' Dr Wilson spoke in a quiet, fatherly manner, 'but I do advise that you take a week off work and allow your mind *and* body to relax. From what you've told me, the past few months have taken their toll.' He placed a finger under her chin and lifted her face. 'Think of yourself as a vacuum cleaner that's been going non-stop.' He patted her head. 'This is like the dust bag, crammed full and ready to burst . . . and as for your motor, it's liable to seize up if you are not careful.'

'Yeah . . .' she closed her eyes and rested her head back on the cushion, 'I know. I just needed you to tell me to stop. I feel really tired. No energy.'

'We're waiting for the police, Doctor,' said Iris, worried. 'They'll want Rosie to go down to the station again, to make a statement, and if they've caught the gang, to identify them.'

'I see. Well please make certain she is given a lift back. After that, you should see that she goes to bed with a warm milky drink.'

Iris nodded, thoughtful. 'I'll take a week off work to—'

'*No.*' Rosie made it clear with one word that she did not want to be mollycoddled. 'It's bad enough one of us taking time off.'

Standing, the doctor picked up his trilby and smiled. 'I'll leave you to argue about that, ladies.' He turned to Harriet. 'I should think *you'll* be able to keep your granddaughter tied down?'

'With the 'elp of wild 'orses I might.'

'I'm sure that won't be necessary. I'll see myself out.' He looked back at Rosie. 'Don't forget— bedrest for one week. If you're no better by then, I'll book you into the London Hospital—see how you like that.'

Once the doctor had left the room, Harriet sat back in her chair and sniffed loudly. 'Good bloody job he didn't give me a check-up. I'd 'ave been sent straight to bed.'

'Shut up, Gran,' murmured Rosie, 'the doctor's talking to someone at the door.'

'It's the police,' said Larry, matter-of-factly. 'Go

and fetch them in, Harriet.'

Harriet drew her head back and glared at him. 'Above going yourself, are yer?'

Larry sniffed and crossed his outstretched legs. 'I'm not family.'

'Well I'm not going out there. I've 'ad enough of the law to last me a lifetime.'

'I'll go,' said Iris, sighing.

'It's like a soddin' railway station, in and out, in and out . . .' Harriet again.

'Do you think you could shut up for five minutes and *listen*! That does sound like the police.'

The room fell silent as they waited. Iris was the first to appear in the doorway. 'They've caught them already.'

That one line from Iris, plus the measured tone of the DI's voice, brought a sigh of relief. 'A superficial wound to the shoulder. But we'll still need Rosie to come down to the station. We caught them speeding out towards Whips Cross.'

'How do you know it's them?' asked Rosie.

'The youngest gave himself away. You ready?'

'No . . . but I don't s'pose I've got much choice, 'ave I?'

'You should be pleased. There won't be any more trouble now. Word'll spread like wildfire. The rest of the fraternity'll be scurrying back into the woodwork.'

'Soddin' foreigners,' said Harriet bitterly.

Ignoring her remark, he turned back to Rosie. 'Your courage in coming forward in the first place is getting results. The villains are nervous . . . *all* the villains. You should think about joining the force.'

'Don't push your luck.' Rosie lifted herself from the seltce. 'So dear old Bertie's gonna be all right then?'

'Hardly all right. He's bruised, shocked and stitched up.'

Only Rosie could raise a smile at the double meaning. Stitched up! 'At least he's a hero. My knight in shining armour! He came to my rescue.' This was one fabrication that would not be disputed. Bertie would hardly deny it, and the three thugs would be none the wiser. Word would spread, and Bertie would be appeased. She owed him that much for his trouble. After all was said and done, he had saved her from a beating, intentionally or otherwise.

'Come on then. Let's get it over with.'

'Do you want me to come with you, love?'

'No ... I'm an old 'and at this.' Rosie looked into the DI's face. 'You will fetch me back, won't you?'

'Of course we will.'

'The doctor said she's got to rest up for a week,' protested Iris. 'She's had another terrible shock. Must she go through all that bloody paraphernalia again?'

'We shouldn't be too long.' He nodded at the others and followed Rosie out.

'Do you remember ...' said Harriet pensively, 'when life was calm and peaceful around here?'

'Yeah,' said Iris, 'but we were just wallpapering over the cracks, weren't we?'

'You mean it's not always like this?' Larry tried to sound disappointed. 'What a pity. I mean ... who would want peace and quiet after a day running round a theatre after people bursting with creative energy and inflated egos?'

Amused by his dry sense of humour, Iris

280

squeezed Larry's arm. 'What would we do without you, eh?'

'It's funny you should say that. I was thinking the same thing myself, a second before you said it. Can we watch television now?'

Iris studied his face as if she were looking for some indication as to the way his mind worked. 'Do you really know what's going to happen before it does? Tell the truth now; don't mess about.'

'I did tell you . . . I have a sixth sense. We all do. Mine is sharper that most, that's all. Why? Does it worry you?' He was enjoying his sudden elevated position. 'It's not something I've learned to do. It's a gift. You either have it or you don't.'

'You just said we've *all* got a sixth sense,' said Harriet smugly.

'Sure. Some people are not bright enough to know it, though.'

'Well it's a pity you don't use your bloody gift and warn us when trouble's about to knock at the door.'

'You wouldn't pay any attention if I did. Besides . . . your troubles are almost over. One month, and you'll be looking back at all of this . . .'

'Another month of worry?' said Iris. 'God give me strength.'

'The trial begins next Monday, correct?'

'Yes Larry, it does . . . Saints preserve us. How we'll cope I don't know. The Old Bailey of all places! I've never stood in a witness box in my life.' Iris could feel herself going cold. 'Poor Rosie . . . she'll 'ave to go through it again, won't she . . . after tonight's shenanigans. I can't see her finding the courage to put on her show after all this. I think she's gonna have to cancel it. She'll never pull it together in time.'

'She doesn't have to cancel—she could postpone.' said Larry.

'Same bloody thing! Where my granddaughter's concerned, anyway. She'll see it as a failure. A weakness. She'll put it on when she said she would—out of sheer soddin' pride. She's as stubborn as 'er mother,' Harriet sighed.

'Here we go . . . I might 'ave guessed the blame would be laid at my door. If I'm stubborn—what are you?'

'Takes after 'er dad. My Arthur was an obstinate git at times. You remind me of 'im at times, Larry. 'Course . . . you go about it in a much quieter way. Crafty old bugger that you are.'

Larry splayed his hands. 'How come I'm drawn into this? I'm not family.'

'Yeah . . . Arthur was just the same. Would he give in? I should say not. He could keep a sulk up for days . . . weeks even. I don't know what I did to deserve any of this. Worry? I'm never free of it. When the day comes that I—'

'Is she all right?' Larry cut in, bewildered.

Iris motioned for him to pay no attention; her expression was one of concern. She placed a finger on her lips, implying that Harriet sometimes behaved this way when she was deeply worried or upset. In a world of her own, Harriet continued, 'All I ever asked for was to be left alone to get on with my life. That's all we asked for. Me and Arthur . . . and our little girl. He thought the world of his grandchildren. I'll say that for Iris and Bill . . . they gave us two lovely grandchildren. Thank God Arthur did go before our Tommy was murdered. It would 'ave broken his heart. Yeah . . .

282

broken-hearted he would 'ave been.

'Our little Tommy . . .' her lips curled under and her face distorted with grief. 'Our little grandson! Oh, we did love that boy . . . he was a good boy, Larry. You would 'ave loved him. Where did it all go wrong, eh? When did all of this start?' She looked across at Iris and blew her nose on her huge white handkerchief. 'You remember what it was like down Lilac Way, don't yer? You used to play out . . . skipping and that. 'Course, you was a pretty thing then. We 'ad a lovely little two-up, two-down, Larry. My Arthur grew flowers in the front bit and vegetables out the back. We used to 'ave a bit of a do with the neighbours now and then—a few drinks and a tune on the piano. It was a lovely life. We never 'ad much, but what we 'ad we appreciated.'

With a comforting hand on Harriet's shoulder, Iris put a small glass of brandy to her lips. 'Sip this, Mum . . . it'll help. Warm your insides,' she said, smiling, repeating another of her mother's favourite sayings.

'Ta, love,' Harriet whispered, grateful for the shot of medicine. 'You can be a thoughtful girl at times.'

'I think you've had enough for one day, don't you? Why don't I tuck you up under that big feather eiderdown of yours, eh?'

'Yeah . . . I think you're right. I'm ready for me old bed. Goodnight, Larry. Don't stop up too late,' she said, gripping Iris's arm and pulling herself up from the armchair. 'See you in the morning—bright and early.'

'Sure . . . night-night.' Larry could barely get the words out, he was so choked to see someone he thought was a tough old boot crumble before his

283

eyes within seconds. Arthur had been a good friend of his too. Jokes and banter aside, he realized that this family of females had wanted him to move in as much as he had needed to. Maybe Harriet had been right when she had told him that the spirits were responsible for everything that mortals did. He smiled at the thought of it—all those relatives up there, playing a hand in their lives.

'She'll be all right after a good night's sleep,' Iris told him on her return. She looked at the clock on the mantelshelf, worried. 'I hope they don't keep our Rosie too long.'

'Do you fancy a game of rummy?' Larry raised an eyebrow.

'Why not?' She knew he was trying to take her mind off things, and she was grateful for his thoughtful diversion. 'We'll play for jelly babies.'

'OK . . . winner takes all the orange ones.'

'It's a deal.'

Opening the drawer of the sideboard and taking out a pack of cards, Iris asked Larry if he had any regrets about moving out of the theatre and in with them. 'Privacy is precious after all,' she said, while spreading her green felt cloth across the table. 'Every mood is monitored in this house.'

Joining her at the table, Larry shrugged. 'Loneliness is worse, Iris, believe me.'

'Is it?' She asked, her sincerity undisguised.

'Yes.' He looked up, thoughtful, and narrowed his eyes, remembering. 'I suppose it's the long silences. You can fill the quiet by switching on the radio or the television, talking aloud to yourself, even . . . but having no one there, no one asking if you're OK . . . if you would like a cup of tea. No one to talk to when you go home. Long hours,

284

night after night of empty silences.' He cleared his throat and snapped himself out of his melancholy reverie. 'So, no, to answer your question, I have no regrets about moving in here.' He levelled his eyes with hers, 'I hope you don't either.'

She reached across and squeezed his hand. 'Of course not. We love you being here, Larry—that's the truth.'

'You would say if things got . . . well, if you felt it was a bit overcrowded . . . ?'

'That will never be the case but yes, if I do, I'll tell you. All right?'

'OK. Deal the cards.' He instinctively looked at his watch. 'She should be back in an hour or so. Maybe we'll have lifted our spirits by then. She'll need cheering up after this ordeal.'

As the two of them sat in the silent room, neither said a word in case they gave away what they were really feeling inside. The dark cloud which had been over the family during the past months seemed as if it would never go away. And they still had the murder trial to face.

CHAPTER THIRTEEN

When it was Rosie's turn to be cross-examined, her heart beat rapidly and she made fists of her hands in an attempt to stop herself shaking, where she stood separated from her family and friends in the courtroom of the Old Bailey. She had been briefed on procedure and up until the moment she was called by the usher, had remained fairly calm and resolute, but once she was in the witness box she lost her nerve. The intimidating atmosphere which emanated from the gathered authorities overpowered her from the second she stepped into the box. Feeling as if she were the criminal, she sipped a glass of water, hoping it would moisten her throat enough to enable her to speak.

With her eyes fixed on her white knuckles, she felt her entire body go rigid as the echoing voice of the court usher referred to the Bible and asked her to take the book in her right hand and read aloud from the card in front of her. The few seconds which ticked by before she finally managed to utter the words seemed like a lifetime.

'I swear by Almighty God that the evidence I shall give shall be the truth, the whole truth and nothing but the truth.'

The counsel for the prosecution opened with his first question: 'Will you please state your full name and address.'

Filled with panic, one thought rushed through her mind, over and over: *Tell them you've changed your mind . . . tell them you've changed your mind . . .* Opening her mouth ready to speak, she made the mistake of raising her eyes and looking towards the dock and into the unremorseful face of her brother's murderer, whose expression was one of defiance as he glared back at her, an icy stare which dared her to testify against him.

She withered inwardly, wanting to escape from the scene but Tommy's voice was back in her mind . . . *Keep on keeping on, darling. Do it for me.*

'My name is Rose Curtis . . .' she heard herself say, as if someone else was speaking for her; from her.

'Will you tell the court in your own words . . .'

She, the witness for the prosecution, was to tell the court in her own words? Tell them how her beloved brother met his violent death at the hands of the loathsome creature who stood with his head high, dressed like a tailor's dummy? *I can't do it . . . I can't . . . I can't . . .*

Yes you can, babe. Don't let the bastard get away with it.

'He killed my brother . . . him and two others kicked the yard door in . . . went into the front room . . . when they came out, my brother was bleeding to death . . .' Her sudden, piercing scream resounded through the courtroom, filling the churchlike silence as her fists thumped the wooden rail of the witness box. Pounding and screaming, she pointed a finger at the man who had been the cause of her worst nightmares: 'He killed my brother!'

*   *   *

After five long and arduous days in court, the defending counsel faced the jury and with a practised ploy, using a tone that suggested they were his allies, he began to sum up his case for acquittal of the charge of murder.

'It is time, ladies and gentlemen, that we brought a halt to the rising tide of crime in the Fifties. This is not America—this is England! To find these young men guilty of murder; to make an example of three wayward citizens who have been drawn into an evil, vicious circle, will simply add fuel to the fire of the atrocious underworld that corrupts this country. Are we to encourage another revenge attack? I think not. The three men you see before

287

you should be punished for their wrongdoing, of that there can be no doubt. Indeed . . . my clients have *asked* to be punished. For did they not admit their part in this tragic accident? Have they not pleaded guilty on the charge of manslaughter?'

The clever barrister had managed to convince the jury that the killing which, in his opinion, had been a revenge attack, had gone badly wrong for the defendants, who had visited the house on the day in question in order to give a warning, and not to kill. His closing, ceremonious speech about gang warfare in the East End had hit the mark: his stern oration was something that Rosie would remember for the rest of her life.

The three men, having been found guilty on three charges which were to run concurrently; one being manslaughter and not murder, were each given a fourteen-year sentence which, according to Reggie, meant that with good behaviour they could all be out of prison after serving just five years.

The worry over their release had to be shelved if Rosie and her family were to get on with their lives. George and Reggie had done their best to assure them that there would be no retribution once the gang were released. But, try as they might, their assurances held little conviction. The expression on the face of the one who Rosie felt sure had knifed Tommy was one of abomination. His characteristic sneer when he looked across at her, before leaving the court, spoke volumes—he was down but not out.

The local press had had a field day, running the story from the beginning of the ordeal until the verdict. Rosie had been photographed going into the Old Bailey and coming out of it. Not satisfied with that, a photographer had been waiting on the doorstep when she arrived home each afternoon. Everyone at the brewery wanted to know the details once she returned to work. She was a local hero—for all the wrong reasons. Publicity on this scale would have been wonderful had it come later on, after her show.

'It'll soon die down, love,' Iris told her as they came out of Charrington's at the end of a tiring day. 'This week's news is next week's fish-and-chip paper.'

'I hope so. I'm sick of telling people what happened. If I don't say anything, they'll turn on me in no time and I'll be sent to Coventry. I saw it 'appen to one of the women at the box factory after she'd been attacked and raped. She was too upset to talk about it . . . but could they see that? No . . . they're like vultures coming out to pick what's left on the bones. They accused her of asking for it in the end . . . just because she wouldn't reveal all.'

'Try not to think about it.'

'Some chance of that.' Rosie rubbed her eyes and pushed a hand through her hair. 'Listen . . . I'm not coming straight home, OK? I'm gonna make the most of what's left of the sun . . . take a stroll down Whitechapel . . . to the art gallery.'

'After a day like today you want to look at pictures?'

'Paintings. Don't ask me why. P'raps it's because they can't talk, eh? I'll see you later.' She showed a hand and strolled off along the Mile End Road heading towards the Waste, to Joe Lyon's tea rooms, where she had made arrangements to meet Larry, who had said that he wanted to see her away from what he now called the madhouse. She would

289

be fifteen minutes early, so could sit and drink coffee by herself with no one talking to her. Whenever she had felt the need to escape from everyone she knew, the small table for one in a corner by the window was perfect. She had been twice before by herself, and had found the solitude relaxing. Not that there hadn't been others there at the time—Lyon's was well frequented, but there was a certain quiet respect for people on their own.

Why Larry wanted to have a private word with her, she wasn't quite sure, but she did have a tiny hope that it would be something to do with the theatre. Maybe the owner had decided to sell it for a cheap price, and Larry had found joint buyers who were sympathetic to the cause? Or maybe the owner was an eccentric millionaire who was about to make a wonderful gesture?

Arriving at the London Hospital, on the opposite side of Whitechapel Road, Bertie came into Rosie's mind. Richard had given her a run-down of what people were saying and Bertie was clearly being seen as a local hero, which suited her down to the ground. There had been enough wrongdoing linked to her name, and she feared that any more might just tip the balance and she would be seen as someone who invited trouble.

As she passed the Whitechapel Art Gallery she smiled to herself. Iris had actually believed that she was going to go in there and spend time looking at pictures, when she was already behind schedule with her show. Spending a couple of hours wandering around a gallery was something she would have to shelve until her time was her own again. Life had delivered her blow after blow since she had had her first glimpse of the Grand Star,

290

and yet she could not bring herself to forget the idea and go for an easy life, even after all the trauma of criminals and courts. 'It's meant to be, Rosie . . . that's what it is—destiny.' Once again she found herself mumbling.

Aware that a young couple were eyeing her and giggling, she stepped up her pace, more than ready for a decent cup of tea. She wouldn't spend long in the tearooms, maybe half an hour or so. She and Larry could continue their private conversation when they walked home together. She had phone calls to make and work to catch up on, if she was to keep up the momentum and not lose the enthusiasm she had managed to instil in others. She knew that the cast had been more than relieved to hear that Richard was ready to step in and take over as director. Now that the trial was over she could concentrate all her efforts on her show. Too much time had been wasted already. *Thank God for Richard.*

When she arrived at the tearooms she was amused to see that Larry was already there, waiting for her. 'You're early,' she said, smiling. 'I thought I was gonna get a bit of time on my own before you arrived.'

'So did I,' he said in his usual droll fashion.

She pulled up a chair and joined him. It wasn't the table she would have chosen but it would have to do. 'What's all this about then?'

'Don't be in such a hurry,' said Larry, signalling to the waitress. 'It's not good news.'

'I hope that's a joke.'

'Well it's not, so prepare yourself.' He clasped his long fingers together and looked her in the eye. 'I'll come to the point if that's all right with you.'

'You usually do, Larry. Come on ... get it off your chest. I can see you're worried. Stop trying to act as if you're a tough old boot.'

'I'm going to have to sell the Star.'

'Oh yeah? Well you'd better buy it first, 'adn't yer.'

'I already own it.' His expression was certainly different. This was not his usual act—this was Larry being serious. 'My father left it to me, and it's been a bloody burden ever since. I could never bring myself to let it go but I couldn't afford to open it. The rates have gone up and I'm being forced to part with it. The bank won't allow me another penny. I already owe them.'

'If this is a joke, it's not very funny.' Rosie could feel herself sinking fast.

'Developers have been after that plot for years, but I've held out. I don't think I can any more.'

'Developers. Someone wants to turn it into a bingo hall?'

'I'm afraid so ... Bingo and roulette tables. I'm going to a meeting straight from here. They know about the show and it's ninety-nine per cent certain that they won't want to move in and start knocking it about until October.'

'Where does the other one per cent come in?'

'They won't write it into the contract ... that we are safe until October. It would be a promise and a handshake.'

'Great. Great news. You might 'ave said something before now!'

'I've been working like mad to get an arrangement with them. I hope to pin them down this evening. I didn't know any of this until after you'd made a hole in the cleaning of the place. I didn't have the heart to tell you. Now I have no choice. I've been searching around for another venue.'

'And?'

He shrugged. 'No luck.'

'And you really, really do have to sell it?'

'No. That's another reason I've been holding out. If we could be one hundred per cent sure that the show is going to be a success and that other companies will follow, the bank will wait and I have enough to tide me over. Enough to pay rent to your grandmother and pay for my food.'

Rosie sighed with relief and smiled broadly. 'Well, what you worrying about, then? You don't 'ave to pay rent and the show *will* be a success.'

'Never mind waiving the rent! It's the show that worries me. With all these other things that have been going on, you've not been able to give it enough attention. It's got to be a professional musical that will get good reviews if we are to get back the good name the Star once had. And I can't see that happening.'

'Well I can! Richard's coming in now. And my troubles are behind me. It's full steam ahead.' She clasped a hand over his. 'Don't agree to anything tonight Larry, please. Give me more time and I promise we'll make good progress. I'm due one week's holiday with pay and one without. I'll take it now and give my time to the show. Every minute, I promise. George as well. Once I tell him what's happening he'll do anything he can, you know he will.'

'What can George do? He knows nothing about the theatre.'

'Publicity. You've said yourself that's one of the

293

most important things. He knows loads of people . . . taxi drivers—'

'Taxi drivers . . .' Larry became thoughtful, 'that's not such a bad idea . . .'

'We could put a poster in all the black cabs in London—'

Larry put up his hand to stop her. 'How many cabbies does he know? Know well enough to call favours?'

'Dozens. His brother drives one, and 'is cousin. They're always round George's mum's drinking tea and playing cards.' She paused to draw breath. 'Look . . . give it a couple of days for the word to go out. Up until now I've not bothered George, 'cos I thought everything was OK. Come on Larry, you know what East Enders are like. We pull together. I'll ask George to take care of that side of things and me and Richard'll crack on with the show. I'll get the band involved now as well. We'll do it—I know we will!'

Larry pursed his lips, narrowed his eyes and nodded. 'OK . . . I'll slow things down a bit. I'll tell the developers this evening that I've had another offer and need time to think about things . . .'

'Honest?'

'I said I would.' He used a strict, fatherly tone which she hadn't heard before. 'But if I hear that you've been wasting time irritating boys in the Prospect or causing any more trouble with that impulsive tongue of yours . . .'

'You've got my word. I'll stop messing about and get cracking.'

'And you'll say nothing to anyone about this. When you speak to your chap about getting his support, tell him it's because you've not had your mind on the job and you need help. Use that bloody guile of yours to persuade and convince—it shouldn't be too difficult. You're well practised.'

'Thanks Larry. You can drink my cup of tea. I 'aven't got time.' She leaped up and gave him a quick wave of her hand. 'See you back at home. I'll be in my room—rewrites!'

Watching her flash out of the door and away, Larry leaned back in his chair and relaxed. He hadn't meant things to go that way. He had been determined to put her off the idea of continuing with the shambles of a show she was trying to get together. It had been true, all that he had conveyed to her and it was serious, but now, for some strange reason, he felt as if a worrying cloud had gone from him. Maybe it was possible? Maybe Rosie could pull off a first-class production and receive the publicity the Star needed if it was to have a successful future? One thing he did know—she had turned the tables on him. If she could do that within fifteen minutes, what else might she be capable of? His adrenaline began to stir and his hopes rise. He had fought long enough to keep his theatre out of the clutches of greedy investors. Why give in to them now?

By the time Rosie arrived home she was in no mood for idle chit-chat or long-drawn-out discussions about recent events. *Yesterday's fish-and-chip wrappings*, she told herself as she pushed her key into the front door.

'Ah . . . Madam's come home,' said Harriet while laying the table, 'and by the look on your face—'

'I'll take my dinner upstairs,' Rosie cut in. 'I've got some catching up to do. What we got?'

'Fish and chips. Larry's gone out to fetch it. Will

cod suit you?' Harriet put on her mock-subservient tone.

'Cod's fine. Where's Mum?'

'Just getting out of the bath—been washing away her sins. Max's coming round.'

'Once I'm in my room, apart from one of you fetching me my cod and chips, I don't wanna be disturbed unless Richard turns up—he can 'ave five minutes. That's all it'll take.'

'What about George . . . ? Shall I tell 'im he can come up and watch?'

Standing by the doorway, Rosie tried not to smile. 'George ain't coming round tonight. He's got enough to do at his shop.'

'It's a lovely thought, Rosie . . .' Richard's voice startled her, 'but I've got a headache.'

'Where'd *you* spring from?'

'He was in the kitchen, being a good boy and finding some glasses that matched. We're 'aving wine with our dinner tonight—courtesy of himself.'

'I thought it was time we celebrated your victory over the rogues.' He kissed her lightly on the cheek. 'Never dreamed you'd want to celebrate upstairs as well.'

'Fetch up two glasses of wine and an ashtray. I wanna talk to you about the show.'

'What about it?'

'I want to get everyone together tomorrow after work for a meeting. The band as well. At the Star. We'll throw the musicians and singers together, see what happens.'

'Rather sudden, isn't it? I doubt you'll get people at such short notice . . .'

'I'm taking the day off—going sick. Those I can't get on the phone I'll go and see. If they're not in I'll

296

put a note through letter boxes. I want you either to go through some notes with me tonight or first thing tomorrow.'

'Notes?'

'Yes Richard, notes. Have you even looked at your copy of the play yet?'

'You said it was just a rough draft and that there would be changes ... I thought I would wait for them.' Richard's tone changed in an instant; now he was being defensive. 'I'll read it in bed tonight, if it's important.'

''Course it's soddin' important! Why d'yer think I took the trouble to have copies made? Oh, don't look so guilty. Come on up and we'll go through it now.'

'Now? But I'm supposed to be meeting the crowd for a celebration drink. Exams have finished.'

'I don't care! I want to go through the script. You're supposed to be the director for Christ's sake. Are you in, or not? I'll soon get someone else, Richard. I can't be messed about; this show is gonna be a success whether you're part of it or not.'

He held up his hands for her to stop. 'All right ... all right. I'm in. Lead the way. Saturday too ... I won't even go on the Ban the Bomb march ...'

'Ban the Bomb?' she sighed and shook her head. 'It's not good enough. Your mind should have been on the show, not saving the world.' She turned her head away, worried. 'I don't think you're taking this seriously.'

'Well, to be honest ... I had a feeling you might have had a change of heart ... what with everything else ...'

'No! If I had, you would 'ave been the first to know. It's full steam ahead from now on, and I do mean full steam ahead. Every evening, every weekend . . . if we're not rehearsing with the actors, we'll be with the band and singers, right?'

'Every weekend *and* every evening? I'll have to go home, Rosie, to Berkshire, occasionally.'

'Fair enough. You can have a weekend off between now and when the show opens. Right?'

'You really mean it . . .' he smiled at her, impressed. 'You're going professional.'

'Too bloody right I mean it. It's gonna be a lot of hard work for everyone from now on. If you think I've got no right to ask you to do it for nothing other than a share of the door money, you'd best leave now.'

'I'll do it for more than that, Rosie. I'll do it for myself. I want to direct your show. I love directing . . . and now that you're taking it seriously . . .' He winked at her, his eyes shining, his cheeks flushed. 'Let's get this show on the road, cousin!'

She breathed a sigh of relief. 'Good. And don't you let me down, or else.'

'I'll end up where Bertie is?' he joshed.

'Maybe.' She punched him on the arm. 'Come on. We've go work to do.'

*   *   *

Three weeks later, sitting in the auditorium, Rosie watched as Caroline, the choreographer, demonstrated moves to three actors on the stage while the pianist played and sang 'Leaning On A Lamp-post'. When she arrived at the line '*She wouldn't leave him flat . . . she's not a girl like that'*, Caroline pushed her open legs together and got the reaction she wanted from the actors: laughter.

'Brilliant! Just right . . . a bit of humour before the emotional scene.' Rosie was more than pleased. 'OK girls, your turn. Start from the line "Oh he'll be there all right".'

Richard cleared his throat, quite deliberately, and then used his sing-song voice to get his message across. 'I think I should be the one to tell them that, Rosie dear.'

'Can we take a five-minute break, Rosie . . .' pleaded Caroline, 'we've been at it for three hours non-stop.'

Rosie picked up on Richard's message and glanced at her wristwatch, 'God, is that the time? That's flown by. I'll put the kettle on while Richard sorts you out. Keep 'em smiling, *cousin,*' she grinned, making her way to a corner of the theatre to a Formica-topped kitchen table which she had borrowed from the scullery at home. The makeshift kitchen was fully equipped with kettle, teapot, cups and a full biscuit tin. The auditorium filled with the sound of the pianist and the girls singing and dancing their way through a scene. *I can't believe this is really happening* . . . Rosie smiled to herself, as she rinsed the cups in a small enamel bowl. *It's working . . . it's actually working. We've got a show.*

Three weeks away from opening and things were looking good. The posters were about to be pasted on to walls and placed in shop windows, and leaflets had been given to libraries. All that was left was for a gang of volunteers to hand out more leaflets to the crowds as they poured in and out of the underground. One problem which did keep

Rosie awake at night was the bookings. The small switchboard at the theatre, manned by one or other of them, had not been busy. So far there had only been twelve bookings, and three of those were from pensioners on special rate. Disappointed that the advertisements which had been placed in five local newspapers around London had not attracted an audience, Rosie had racked her brain as to what she might do next in order to draw attention to the show.

'I've shut the switchboard down,' said Larry, arriving with his empty mug. 'No tea for me thanks—I'm going out.' He looked towards the stage and smiled. 'It must be in the blood. Look at Richard, the way he's got that lot's attention. They're all ears. He's a match for the directors I've seen at the Royal any day.'

'You're going out? What if anyone rings in to book a seat while you've gone?' Rosie said, disappointed and concerned.

'They'll call back ... if they call in the first place,' he looked at her and raised one eyebrow, sceptical. 'It's not looking good, Rosie.'

'I know.' She poured boiling water into the teapot. 'I don't know ... what else can we do? Maybe once the posters go up ...'

'Maybe isn't good enough. I have a couple of cards up my sleeve. Try not to worry.'

'So, where you off to then?'

'First to the newspapers ...'

'We've already put ads in, Larry. The money's running out.'

'That was where we made our mistake. We should have gone to editorial. Give them a story they may not be able to resist ... or have a duty to

300

print.'

'Like what?'

'Well, so far we've been trying to sell the *show*, correct?' Rosie nodded and waited. 'What we should have done was sell the story ... of the Grand Star. From when it first opened, to its closure when war broke out ... to its reopening now, and your saving it from becoming a bingo hall. That's what we should have done,' he shrugged. 'It's so bloody obvious, none of us saw it.'

'Do you want me to come with you?' she tried to sound hopeful.

'No. It's better that I spout on about you while you're not there ... tell them what a strong woman you are and how much you love the theatre ... etcetera, etcetera, etcetera.'

'What if they realize that I'm the same Rosie Curtis responsible for sending you-know-who to prison?'

'Would it worry you?'

'Not if it'll sell more seats. It might go the other way though. Bad publicity.'

'There is no such thing.' Smiling, he punched her arm fondly. 'I won't tell you about the other card up my sleeve. Not yet, anyway. Don't let them take too long over their break.' He turned away and walked slowly up the aisle towards the exit door, his head held higher than usual. He was obviously pleased with himself, and confident that his fresh ideas would bring results.

Pleased for him, Rosie wished that she too could shake off the feelings of despondency and impending failure. It was, after all, up to her to inspire optimism within the group. Busy with the production itself, she had overlooked a very important objective—attracting an audience that would fill the auditorium for one full month and give financial returns to cover expenditure. Funding apart, the humility she would feel if they played to an empty house filled her with dread.

Feeling blameworthy for setting everybody up to be knocked down, she was heavy with a burden of guilt. She should have listened to Larry in the first place when he advised her to forget her madcap ideas and settle for becoming a dancer. She wondered how she would face her friends if the project turned out to be disastrous. She couldn't run away because there was nowhere to run to—nowhere to hide.

'God, I'm ready for this,' said Caroline, reaching for her tea. 'It's going well though; I think this scene is really nice.' She eyed Rosie and waited for a response—a compliment, perhaps.

'It is going well, Caroline. You're brilliant.'

'So why the long face, then?' The choreographer sipped her refreshing drink. 'Problems?'

'Mmm.' She waited for the others to take their tea and drift away, chatting between themselves, before she invited Caroline to join her for a tête-à-tête. 'We're not 'aving much joy with bookings. Don't tell the others though, or they might lose heart.'

'I'm not being funny,' said Caroline, using one of her favourite lines, 'but don't you think we should get out there ourselves . . . give out leaflets and talk to people? Look at all the pubs around 'ere . . . the Blind Beggars, for instance. That gets packed every weekend.'

'Would the people who drink there want to come to a musical, though?'

302

''Course they would! Especially if it's us that tell them about it. I mean, we're not exactly old frumps, are we?'

'Sell it on our good looks, you mean?'

'No, Rosie. On our energy, enthusiasm ... and yeah, on what we are. If they see the sort of people who're involved, meet a few of the actors, and the author—*you*—it'll make them feel ... well, involved in something local. Something they can feel part of.'

'It's worth a try. I don't know what George would think of it ... me in a pub without him.'

'Tch. You're not going out to get a bloke!' She flicked back her long black hair. 'I'm not being funny, but you are a bit on the old-fashioned side. You're only a year older than me for Christ's sake. You act like a thirty-year-old at times. Loosen up a bit.'

'Well ... that's telling me.'

'Someone had to. You've got a young cast of actors—make the most of it. We should all go out on a Saturday night and do the parties.'

'What parties?'

'God, where have you *been*? Fridays, Saturdays and sometimes of a Sunday ... there are parties going on everywhere. All you 'ave to do is go to the Beggars, Kate Oder's, the Punchbowl, the Black Boy, the Sun. The fellas are always scouting for girls. Can't have a party without us, can they? Who they gonna dance with—each other?'

'I'll 'ave a word with George to see if it's—'

'Tell him you're having an early night. Get rid of him for a couple of weekends ... say you're with me, at my mum's, working out routines for the show.'

'It's not that easy, Caroline.'

'Tch. You've got yourself into a rut already. Twenty-two and you're trapped. It's all happening out there, Ro. It's up to you. You're in show business now ... the blokes'll be clamouring to know you. All work and no play makes a dull day ... and life.' She winked at her and walked away to join the others, giving the boss time to consider.

Breaking into a smile, Rosie suddenly felt elated. All that Caroline had said was true. She *had* forgotten about having fun. The past months since her world had been thrown into confusion she hadn't been out with her friends and she hadn't been to a dance hall. She looked across at the girls and noticed for the first time that they were all wearing up-to-the minute clothes, inexpensive but colourful and youthful. Pedal-pushers and knee-length full skirts. They were laughing and chatting, happy and carefree, young and enjoying life. She resolved there and then that she would no longer allow herself to be weighed down with the serious side of life—and that she would not step inside another courtroom. If the police wanted to nail the three flash boys, they would have to do it without her. Bertie could be the star in that particular drama. She had a feeling he would take to it like a duck to water.

She clapped her hands loudly, enjoying her status. 'Positions, please!' she shouted, smiling and mimicking the director she had seen in action at the Royal. Taken by surprise, the girls turned to her, bemused. At last their producer was lightening up.

'Music, Maestro!'

304

'Yes, ma'am!' came the reply, followed by the lively introduction to 'Leaning On A Lamp-post'.

*   *   *

'What you looking so pleased about?' said Rosie, kicking off her shoes. Larry was relaxing in an armchair, a smile of satisfaction on his face. 'I thought you would 'ave come back to the Star to let me know how you got on.'

'I'm here to tell you,' he said, splaying his hands, 'that it worked. Tomorrow a journalist will be at the theatre at three o'clock in the afternoon to interview you. Fame at last.'

'Tomorrow's Sunday. Newspapers don't work of a Sunday.'

'Journalists work any day providing there's a story. There'll be a photographer too, so have an early night and do something with your hair.'

She looked in the mirror over the mantelshelf. He certainly had a point. Her greasy hair was scraped back into a French pleat, with strands dangling. She had no make-up on and there were dark rings around her eyes. 'I'll do something right now, Larry. I'll take a bath, wash my hair and then have a doze. I wanna be fresh for when I go out tonight.'

Larry eyed the clock. 'It's already tonight— nearly seven o'clock.'

Iris flicked her newspaper down and studied her daughter. 'You all right?'

''Course I'm all right. Where's Gran?'

'In bed. She's got a summer cold. You sure you're all right?'

'Yes, Mum—I'm fine. I'll phone George and
305

then run the bath. I won't be seeing 'im . . . I'm going round Caroline's to go through a couple of the dance scenes with 'er. I might stay at her house. She said they've got a spare room now that her brother's joined the merchant navy. It'll save me walking back in the dark—or flagging a cab.' She surprised herself at how easy it was to spin them a yarn.

'So you're thrilled about the journalist, then?' Larry was, as usual, being his droll self.

''Course. You've done a great job. Get me as many interviews as you can. We'll get the lazy sods in to see our show hook or crook, eh Larry?' She flounced out of the room, singing 'Peggy Sue'.

'At last . . . her true personality emerges.' He turned to Iris. 'Is this the way she behaved before the tragedy . . . before Tommy?'

'Yeah . . . as it happens.' Iris became pensive. 'I'd almost forgotten what she was like. She's back to her old self again—God help us.'

'You're smiling too, Iris—it suits you.'

'Mmm. I think it's over, Larry. I can feel the dark cloud drifting away . . .'

'I'm very pleased to hear it.' He sank back in his chair, and Iris sank back in hers, each of them content to be quiet.

Caroline had, with her few honest words, done more for this family than she would ever know. 'We've got to be sold out before we open . . .' said Larry, thoughtfully. 'We're all going to have to pull our fingers out, even Harriet. We'll send her round to the mission hall. She can attend every meeting . . . I might even go with her. Between us we'll drum up interest. Old people will want cheap seats, it's true . . . but they all have families. We'll

306

talk non-stop about the wonderful new family show. You can do your bit at Charrington's. Go round and collect the bloody ticket money if you have to. Don't take no for an answer. Get Max to work on the men.'

'Pull out all the stops,' murmured Iris.

'Exactly. It wouldn't be a bad idea to begin right away. We'll stand outside the Empire and catch people as they go in. Then we'll go to the Forester's and catch people as they come out. Shove a leaflet in their hands. Why not, eh? Why not?' He looked at Iris and waited.

'I'm ready when you are.'

'Good! Let's go.' He stood up and stretched. 'I feel ten years younger—don't ask me why.'

'I know why,' she said, pulling on her mohair cardigan, knitted by Harriet. 'There's nothing like a challenge to get the pulse going.' She picked up a huge wad of leaflets from the sideboard and handed them to Larry. 'You get rid of those and I'll get rid of these.' She scooped another pile for herself. 'Let's show Rosie how to do it.'

'I hope she doesn't forget about tomorrow's interview,' said Larry, following her out.

'She won't. I saw the look in her eye. She can't wait.'

*   *   *

The journalist from the local newspaper, a man of thirty-seven with several years of experience behind him, induced a feeling of calm in Rosie. In this, he was very different from the reporters who had plagued her during the trial. Larry's room in the Star, as comfortable as ever, made the perfect

307

meeting place. Lighting a cigarette, the journalist, John Downing, asked Rosie to tell him about her upbringing, and life in the East End during and after the war.

'What's that got to do with the show?' Rosie tried not to sound impudent but she couldn't help feeling a touch suspicious that there might be another reason for this interview.

'I'm not here to talk about the show. I'll give it a mention, naturally. What intrigues me is that someone of your background has found a way through a . . .' he crossed his legs and gazed up at the ceiling, choosing his words, 'well, to put it bluntly, through a world which you know nothing about—unless I'm mistaken?'

'No. You're not mistaken. Mind you, 'aving come this far I know a lot more than I did when I started, and it's not really that much of a mystery, to be honest.'

'No?' He leaned forward, his interest taken by her casual, open manner. 'We'll forget your childhood for the moment then. Let's talk about this theatre. I understand it's your idea and your enthusiasm, not to mention hard work, that's brought it out of the doldrums and saved it from becoming a bingo hall. What inspired you . . . ?'

'If you don't know *that* . . .'

'I do know . . . at least I think I do. But my readers won't and they're what this interview's about. They don't buy their local paper simply to read snippets of scandal about people they might know . . . they have a genuine interest in what's happening in their neighbourhood.'

Chuckling to herself, Rosie was thinking of Harriet. 'My gran goes through it with a magnifying

308

glass, in case she misses something. I know what you mean though. We have your paper every week. It's a bit like, well, a family and friends link I s'pose.' She became thoughtful. 'Yeah . . . I suppose I'd want to know about someone who'd poked their nose into a world that most of us around 'ere feel we don't belong to.' She smiled at him, relaxing again. 'I've been so busy, what with one thing and another, that I hadn't really thought about it. I can just picture the faces of some of my old schoolmates—never mind the teachers. Rosie Curtis opening up an old music hall and putting on a show. That would be one in the eye for the 'eadmistress. She always used to say I was too lazy to get up in the mornings. Bored, more like. Them bloody lessons . . . geography? Who cares where tea and sugar come from? We buy 'em from Higgins's the corner shop.'

'Who was it who told you about this old Yiddish theatre?'

'Larry. I met 'im when I went to the Royal—'

'Here in Stratford?'

'Yeah. He's the part-time caretaker. Retired, but can't drag 'imself away. It's in the blood. Larry knows more about the theatre than anyone.'

'You're a theatregoer, then?'

'No. I went to see about joining a theatre workshop. I wanted to be a professional dancer. Still do. Larry was leaving just as I arrived . . . he was coming 'ere, so I came with 'im. I was curious. Once I saw the place from the inside—that was it.'

'You wanted to see it alive again and running?'

'Something like that. Wouldn't you? Now that you've seen it?'

'I'm sure lots of people would—but few have the

nerve to go about things the way you have.' He chewed the end of his pencil and gazed at her, his eyes showing his interest. 'Did you have any idea what you were taking on?'

''Course I did. Look ... it's no different from, say, opening a shop that's been closed down. You've still gotta find money to do it up and stock it ... and there wouldn't be any guarantee that people'd come in and buy what you had on the shelves.' She shrugged and leaned back in her chair. 'Nothing'd get done if we all went for an easy, quiet, safe life ... would it?'

'True.'

'It's not gonna kill me ... and as my gran said, I'll still be here in twelve months from now, and it's up to me whether I'll be here with or without 'aving done what I'm doing. If I die somewhere in between I'll be even more annoyed that I didn't do what I wanted ... what I really wanted.'

'That's a philosophy shared by—'

Rosie leaned forward and interrupted him. 'Look ... I don't know anything about philosophy or famous playwrights or poets or ...' she opened her palms, 'or any of that stuff. Someone once asked me if I was well read. I didn't 'ave a clue what he meant till I asked him to explain. He thought that was hilarious ... me opening this place and directing a show I wrote myself ... but then he's at the medical college, so what can you expect? It's books, books and more books with that lot.'

'You don't think education's necessary then?'

'For some it is ... but not me. I'll learn what I need to know as I go along. Why waste time memorizing stuff for the sake of it? Had enough of

310

that at school when we had to read something over and over, just so we knew the answers to ten questions at the end of the week. Ten questions about things that didn't matter a jot.'

'So when you left school you were ... semi-literate?'

'If you say so.'

'Did that make life difficult when it came to employment?'

'I got a job straight away—at the box factory in Assembly Passage, Mile End. Not brilliant pay, but it was all right. I work for Charrington's now ... 'ave to,' she shrugged, 'more money.'

'Ah ... so you're working longer hours to help finance the Star?'

'No. To put a bit of beef in the pot. When my brother was killed it was down to me and Mum to bring in the money.'

'I see ...' he averted his eyes and became pensive.

'Well, go on then, get on with it. Ask me about the murder—get it out of the way.' She broke into a smile. 'I wasn't born yesterday. I know that's why you've come out on a Sunday.'

'You're wrong, actually, although ... I had hoped you might tell me something about it, but I've no intention of pushing you. As a matter of fact, now that I'm here I would rather we talked about you, Rosie. My newspaper's already covered the story—'

'You don't 'ave to tell me that.'

'But if you could just give me one or two quotes ... nothing heavy. The readers will expect it.'

'I know. Go on then, fire away.'

He checked his notepad and turned the page. 'Where did the money come from ... for all of this?' he swept a hand through the air. 'The rent must be sky-high.'

'I'm not paying rent. The owner's not charging ... well, not for the first twelve months anyway. Don't ask me who the owner is 'cos he doesn't want anyone to know. He's shy.' She raised her eyebrows. 'I've shocked you?'

'Well, it does seem incredible ...'

'And as for the cleaning, paint and polish ... compliments of my friends and neighbours. Gran coughed up the money for fuel for the boiler and small repairs. It was meant to be for my wedding ... she had it tucked under the mattress. I've not had to spend a penny, which is just as well 'cos I haven't got money to chuck around. Some well-wishers 'ave put their cash up. Angels I think they're called, according to Larry.' She began to laugh. 'Angels from hell were 'is exact words.'

'Ill-gotten gains?'

She tapped her fingernails on the table as she casually looked around her. 'This room is used by "intellectuals", for play-readings. Done it up nice, ain't they?'

'What about costumes?' he said, smiling.

'Ah ... now they are a sight for sore eyes. I'll show you our wardrobe if you like.'

'I would like, but first ... tell me about the show. It's a collection of songs from the hit parade, with some dancing ... correct?'

'Don't you want to know about the story?'

'What story?'

'*Love in Lavender!*'

'Oh ... it's not a variety show, then?'

'No. It's a play . . . a musical. The characters talk to each other as well as sing. It's a tragic love story,' she added, haughtily.

'You mean you've taken a published play and added published songs . . . ?'

'I *mean* . . . I've written a play and added songs. I'll show you a script if you like.'

'A script?' He was looking more impressed by the second. 'A proper script . . . with characters and dialogue?'

'Yeah . . . and all neatly typed up with holes punched in the corners . . . and treasury tags to secure the fifty pages . . . of dialogue.'

'You're a playwright,' he said, incredulously, 'a playwright and an impresario.'

'What's an impresario?' she asked, slightly exasperated at his using long words to impress her.

'I don't suppose there's a chance of another cup of coffee, is there? I need to rethink this interview.'

'There is time, yeah. I'm expecting our lead singer, as it happens. I'll put the kettle on and you can sit here and think about what you're going to write while I go and see if he's here. That sound OK?'

'That sounds fine,' said the journalist. 'Maybe I could have a word with him too . . . and with some of the actors?'

'I'll ask the director. He's a bit of a slave-driver—a perfectionist. He might let them take five—depends how well rehearsals have gone.' She left the room, closing the door behind her and smiling. *A piece of cake, Rosie . . . a piece of cake.*

*   *   *

'What you looking so chuffed about?' George was in his usual seat, at the back of the auditorium. 'You look like the cat who got the cream.'

Slipping into the seat next to him, she squeezed his arm. 'I feel like the cat who got the cream. I can't stop long ... I'm being interviewed by the press,' she said, using a theatrical tone.

'So where'd you go last night then?' he said, looking at her sideways.

'Tell you in a minute. I've just remembered something I forgot to tell Caroline. Won't be a sec.' She backed away, giving him and wink, and headed for her friend.

Placing her mouth close to Caroline's ear, she whispered, 'George wants to know where I was last night ... I don't know what to say.'

'Tell him we worked late and then got through half a bottle of sherry between us. Richard wants me to change the bedroom romp scene. I'm not sure if he's right though ... I could do with your support, Ro. I want to keep the—'

'You're out of order, Caroline. Take your orders from Richard ... he's the director. I don't want a war on my 'ands.'

Moving away, Rosie hunched her shoulders. 'That's show business ...'

'What is?' said George, blocking her way.

Spinning around to face him, she winked and clicked her tongue. 'You wouldn't understand darling,' she said, humouring him. 'Do me a favour and pour us both a drink, yeah? The bar's open and there's a bottle of vodka and some orange juice as well. I'll get back to the journalist and be straight down.'

'So why didn't you go home last night?' George

314

was obviously not going to let her off the hook so easily.

'Me and Caroline worked our socks off and then got into a bottle of sherry . . . I collapsed on the spare bed and didn't wake up till ten o'clock this morning. Did you go out drinking?' She held her breath, hoping he would say no. She, Caroline and a couple of the dancers had covered quite a lot of ground on their pub crawl, and although she had sent one of them in ahead of her each time, to check that George wasn't there, she couldn't be certain she had got away with her secret night out with the girls.

'Too busy stocktaking. I could have done with some help, as it happens.'

'Could you? Tch. You should 'ave said.' She kissed him lightly on the lips. 'Soon as I'm finished giving the interview and we've had a drink, I'll leave this lot to it and come with you to the shop. How's that?'

'It's about time, Rosie. You've not seen the flat since I first took you to have a look. Mum and Aunt Josie's scrubbed it from top to bottom. It looks like a different place now that the old boy's junk is out of there. It's bigger than we thought.'

She expressed her apologies with a look. 'I don't suppose they think much of me, then? Not proving to be a promising wife, am I? Wrapped up in all of this instead of making the flat nice.'

'The flat is nice. I slept there last night. It was a great feeling . . . could 'ave been better, mind,' he gave her a cheeky wink.

'You know why I've not been able to get there before now. My time's 'ardly been my own, has it?'

'Your time's always your own, Rosie. It's up to

315

you what you do with it.' It was obvious from his tone that he was feeling neglected. 'If this show means more to you than me . . .' he shrugged, 'that's that. I'll have to find myself another woman to take back to my flat.'

She punched his arm. 'Just you try. Go and wait in the bar . . .'

'Fifteen minutes and I'm out of here, right?'

'And I'll be right by your side.' She kissed him on the lips and playfully pushed him away towards the exit door leading to the bar.

Watching him leave, she knew that his pride had been bruised by her giving instructions when that was the role he liked to take. *You've got some making up to do, Rosie, if you're to save this romance*. 'George!'

He turned his head slowly, looking over his shoulder at her. 'What?'

'Don't go without me, will yer?' She knew he had no intention of doing so, but it was all she could think of to say in order to stroke his ruffled feathers. He responded well, tut-tutting as if she was a silly girl.

*   *   *

'How did the interview go?' asked Larry as he collected a few empty glasses from the bar.

'Great. He was all right. You did a good job there, Larry. We might even make the front page. He lapped it up . . . Poor Girl from the East End Heads for the Big Time,' she grinned as she backed away. 'Listen, I'm gonna 'ave to run. George's waiting for me in the car. Richard, Caroline and the girls are still on stage.'

'Go. I'll catch up with you later . . . back at the house.'

'I might not come home tonight, Larry. I'm helping George to get the shop ready. He's opening it tomorrow. We'll be working right through the night by the sound of things.'

Smiling, he shrugged. 'I'll tell that to Harriet for you . . . she won't believe it, but there you are.'

She blew him a kiss and rushed down the stairs to join George at the side door. 'Sorry. Larry started to yak on. You know what he's like.'

Nodding, George unlocked the car door, hesitating before getting in. 'There'll always be someone who wants your time . . .' He stopped short when he felt Rosie's hand on his neck, squeezing it seductively. Slowly turning to face her, he sighed. 'I've missed you, Ro. Where've you been, eh?'

'I haven't been anywhere.'

He stroked her hair. 'You know what I mean, babe.'

'Yeah . . . my mind's been all over the place lately. I'm here now though, and things *are* sorting themselves out. The show's nearly ready . . . the court case is behind us . . . and I love you very much.'

'Good.' He drew her close and kissed her on the mouth. 'I don't suppose you fancy trying out the makeshift bed tonight?'

'I thought you'd never ask. The trouble is, once I stop over you might not get rid of me.'

'Which leads me to the big question,' he ran a finger down her cheek, 'let's get married soon, Ro. Why wait now that we've got a flat?'

'It would 'ave to be a poor-man's wedding.'

He creased his brow and drew a breath. 'Is that a yes?'

'As soon as the show's over we'll make arrangements ... if that's what you want?' She waited for his reaction, unsure if she had been too quick with her response and change of heart. So far she had said she would prefer to wait a couple of years.

'If it's what I want?' he spoke as if he had not heard right. 'What *I* want?'

'Yeah. I know it's a bit sudden, but ... I hardly ever see you and, well, I miss you. When I'm in bed at night I put a pillow next to me and pretend it's you.'

'Rosie ... if this is meant to be a joke, it's not funny.'

'It's not a joke. Look, before we get in the car, I'll tell you. Last night, well, I wasn't working. I went out with the girls on a pub crawl. It was Caroline's idea and a good one. We were publicizing the show and it worked but ... I don't want to be out there, George. Chatting to blokes I don't want to have to chat to. It made me realize how much I love you. I'm sorry I lied to you but—'

'Rosie—shut up.' His face alive with happiness he clenched his fists, punched the air and grabbed her by the waist, lifting her in the air. 'Will you marry me?'

Laughing, she told him to put her down. 'Not until you answer my question—is it really what you want?'

'You're supposed to get down on your knee, you silly sod—not chuck me about.'

'Will you marry me this year? Answer yes or no.'

'Yes!'

CHAPTER FOURTEEN

Just two days before the musical was due to open, Rosie had gathered the cast for a dress rehearsal which had proved disastrous. Tilly had done her job well; every alteration was perfect and there were no problems in that quarter but when it came to actors having to make quick costume changes, backstage it was chaos. Tempers were fraught to say the least. No one seemed to know where their costumes were and there was not enough time between scenes to remove one set of clothes and put on another.

'Who is your stage manager?' asked Larry in his usual placid way.

'What?' Rosie was uncharacteristically impatient with him. 'What are you talking about now? Stage manager? We've all been getting on with it. Me, Richard, Caroline, the cast . . .'

'I see. You didn't stop to think that the cast would be engaged in their acting and that Richard had more than enough to cope with? That they would need one or two people out the back, under the guidance of a stage manager, to help them change and make sure they had their personal stage props?' Now it was his turn to show her another facet—he was frustrated by her incompetence. Frustrated and annoyed.

'Where's Tilly?'

'I don't know! Scrubbing her kitchen floor. Bleaching the bath. Why?'

'Why? You ask me why? Why the seamstress is not here for a full dress rehearsal? And what about

319

the costume designer? Has she gone missing too? Or didn't you think it was necessary for her to be here either?'

Rosie slumped down into the seat next to him and gazed up at the stage, reflecting on the chaos. 'It's falling to pieces.'

'It isn't falling to pieces, you are. You should have thought things through. I'll phone Tilly and ask her to come over and fetch a friend. She's bound to know someone who has a tidy mind.' Lifting himself from his seat he told Rosie to instruct everyone to take a break. 'Take half an hour for coffee and give them all time to calm down. It's like a bloody circus up there.'

'You're right, Larry, I should 'ave listened to Richard. He kept asking about stage management. I thought he was trying to take over.' She looked at him and shrugged. 'Thanks for pointing it out. How's things with the bank and all that jazz?'

'Fine . . . for now. God help me if the show flops.'

'It won't Larry—I won't let you down. That's a promise.'

Once Larry had left, Rosie followed his advice and within ten minutes each of them were suitably pacified. 'It's my fault,' she told them, 'I overlooked the fact that we would need support back there. Larry's making a phone call and two helpers will be here soon. It's just as well we found out now instead of on the night.'

'It's just as well,' said Caroline, 'that we did go for a dress rehearsal today and not tomorrow when the set-builders arrive.'

'I know. You were right to insist on it.' Pouring milk into a large white jug, she told everyone to

320

help themselves to tea or coffee and then resumed her position in the front row with a cup of tea in one hand and a cigarette in the other. 'Don't worry folks—it'll be all right on the night!'

'When did you say the band would be arriving, Ro?' one of the actresses asked. 'This afternoon?'

'No. They're all at work. They won't get 'ere till about seven o'clock.'

'You mean we're going to be here all day and evening too?' Vi, who had a main part in the musical, looked far from pleased.

'You can go home at two and come back at seven if you want,' Rosie was too tired to argue. 'Take a taxi and I'll give it you out of expenses.'

'Have you looked at your watch recently?' asked Vi, a touch sarcastic. 'It's half past twelve already. By the time we do a proper dress rehearsal it will be gone four. If we're to be back by seven it won't be worth going.'

'That's true,' she sighed, wishing to God she hadn't got herself into this situation. 'You can always 'ave an afternoon nap in Larry's room. There are two armchairs up there and a settee that pulls down into a double bed.'

'That's more like it.' Vi looked at her wristwatch. 'Right . . . If anyone else wants to join me now for one hour's sleep they're welcome. The next shift will be at a quarter to two. Then at three o'clock . . . four-fifteen . . . and five-thirty. I suggest we all put our heads down at some time whether we go off to sleep or not. It's going to be a long day, and tomorrow will be the same if we're going to be properly rehearsed. We don't want to look like a bunch of bloody amateurs on stage. People will be paying good money to come in to see a

321

professional show. Get Richard to take a break as well. Poor devil's not stopped. Lecture over.' She made her way towards the stairs, heading for what would now be referred to as the green room.

'Hang on, Vi—I'll come with you,' said another actress. 'Had a late night last night and one too many drinks.'

'And that's another thing!' Vi called back. 'From now on, no socializing and no alcohol. Once you leave this theatre it's home and to bed! We don't want another fiasco on opening night!'

Feeling like a complete and utter failure, Rosie lowered her head, ashamed; hoping the others would ignore her. It seemed that everyone was beginning to lose confidence in her, and for good reason. Up until now everything had gone well, but that did not compensate for the last-minute shambles.

'Take no notice of Vi,' said Caroline, 'she's nervous, that's all. Putting on a professional show in a proper theatre's a bit different from what her group have been doing. Not that I don't admire 'em. They know their limitations and their audience. They don't 'ave to worry about the crits, either. The am dram circuit have a lot of fun ... and I'm not being funny, but things are getting a bit heavy around 'ere. Vi's probably worrying about the vultures as well.'

'The what?'

'Theatre critics ... journalists.' She waved her arms. 'This is a bona fide theatre and you'll be getting people in who are paying bona fide prices. They're bound to turn up ready to knock you down. You knew that, surely?'

'Yeah ... 'course I did. I just didn't quite catch

the word ... I thought you said gits,' she lied, saving herself from more humiliation.

Laughing loudly, Caroline called to the others. 'Did you hear that? Rosie thought I said that the gits are bound to turn up! Crits—gits, get it?' The others saw the joke and their welcome contagious laughter brought a smile to Rosie's face.

'Watch out, everyone! The gits 'ave arrived!' said Caroline again, thoroughly enjoying the quip, not caring that she was breaking the rule, about not *laughing at your own jokes*. Whether she had meant to or not, within seconds she had changed the mood from one of despair to plain relief. Rosie had a feeling that Caroline knew exactly what she was doing, and silently thanked her.

Taking some time out was an excellent idea—everyone was now relaxed and laughing amid the pandemonium backstage, and the air was a lot clearer than it had been ten minutes previously. Once Tilly arrived and took on the role of backstage manager, things would fall into place. Tilly was a born organizer, and no doubt any friend she brought with her would be out of the same mould.

'Caroline ... I'm not really gonna be needed, am I, not until Tilly sorts things out with the costumes and that?'

Caroline gave Rosie a sympathetic pat on the back. 'Yes you are. I want you up on that stage for another run-through.'

'You said I was great earlier on. Flawless.'

'I know, but that dream sequence is really important. We're closing the show with it. I want to make sure I've not missed anything. You're a brilliant dancer, Ro, I'm not questioning that. It's my choreography I want to be sure of. And you know what they say: something good is worth doing well.'

'Yeah ... all right then. One more time, and then I've got to put my head down.'

'Just what I was about to say. I'm not being funny, but it's beginning to show. You look dog-tired.'

'Once I do go up there I might not come back down. Knock on Larry's door if I'm gone longer than half an hour.'

'Will do. Go on then—get up on that stage.'

*   *   *

Having given another of her best performances and satisfying Caroline, Rosie dragged herself up to Larry's room to find Vi had flopped out in an armchair and was sound asleep. She tiptoed over to the settee and very quietly eased it open to make a bed. Lying down, she reached out for a cushion from a second armchair and arranged it under her head. Seconds later she was drifting off ...

*   *   *

'Don't you think it's time I woke those two, Caroline? They've been up there for over an hour.'

'Do us all a favour, Larry, and leave 'em be. Everyone knows their part and I'll fill in for Vi. It was the costume changes that were giving us problems, not the run-through. Tilly and her friend are doing a smashing job out the back; I think we should leave things as they are.'

324

'You're a very shrewd young lady,' he smiled. 'You'll go far.'

'I intend to.'

'I'm sure. What would you like me to do? If I can help . . .'

'Be our critic. Sit in the back row. That way you'll be able to tell us if anyone needs to raise their voice . . . or if anyone's shouting above the rest. If anything's not working as well as it could do, let me know and I'll 'ave a quiet word.' She drew on her cigarette. 'What do you think of it so far? The dance routines?'

'I think it's wonderful. But don't get too big-headed. Now that I'm a critic I may have something else to say that you *won't* like.' He assumed a posture of importance and made his way sedately to the back of the auditorium.

'OK, everyone!' Are we ready to run through it again?' Richard had also taken a nap: fifteen minutes and he was ready to go again. Clapping his hands authoritatively, he called them to order.

Tilly was the first to speak as she appeared on the stage, calm and serene. 'They're ready when you are, dear.'

'Good. From the beginning, then! I'll read Vi's part from down here, OK?' Richard waited a few moments and then yelled, 'Quiet please!'

Dressed in clothes of the Thirties and carrying a suitcase, the lead actress playing the part of Sarah made her entrance, looked around as if she had found herself in another world and then called out to one of the lavender pickers, 'Excuse me . . . could you tell me the way to Fairweather Hall?'

One by one the women turned their heads to gaze at her. 'Follow the yellow brick road,' one of them said, jesting. A chorus of laughter followed. 'Or go back to London now before the lord of the manor turns you into a slave as well!' said another.

'Pay no attention my dear,' said Caroline, filling in for Vi. 'They're pulling your leg. You just keep on walking to the end of the lane ... you can't miss it.'

'Thank you,' murmured Sarah, 'thank you very much.' With her head lowered she carried on walking and make her exit.

'Looks a bit green if you ask me! Pretty green mind ...'

'No one is asking you. Get back to work!'

'Green now—blue later,' chuckled another picker. Then very quietly they began to sing, a touch mischievous ...

'Lavender's blue, dilly-dilly, lavender's green,
She'll meet the king, dilly-dilly, she shall be queen ...'

'Don't the costumes look good,' whispered Rosie, slipping into the seat next to Larry, her voice still husky from sleep.

'Shhh ... I'm concentrating,' he whispered back, taking his role very seriously indeed.

'I've had a lovely rest ...'

'Good. Now can we be quiet? You want a good show, or don't you?'

'Good? It's gonna be great, Larry. Providing we get an audience we—'

'Shhh ...'

'It was a good article, wasn't it?'

'I told you—it was excellent.'

'Front page.'

'Mmm.'

'But only eleven phone calls inquiring . . .'

'That's better than no phone calls.'

'We will get an audience, won't we?'

'Wait and see. Most people just turn up and buy their tickets on the night.' Had Rosie paid attention to the tone in his voice, she would have realized that he had been up to something . . . arranging things here and there.

Closing her eyes she prayed silently, *Please God, let these seats be full—if only for the opening night.*

*   *   *

At five-thirty the following afternoon, on the eve of the big day, Rosie was curled up on an armchair at home, fast asleep. The sound of the clock on the mantelshelf striking the half-hour did not bring her from her deep slumber. 'Look at 'er,' said Harriet, 'out to the world.'

'I'll have to wake her,' said Richard, worriedly. 'We're meant to be there by seven. She'll want to wash and change.'

'The show don't start till half past, do it?'

'No, but it's better to be early.'

'Rosie!' Harriet suddenly called out. 'Wake up, mog! We're going out!'

'Eh . . . ? What . . . ?' she lifted her eyelids a fraction and peered at her gran. 'Who's going out?'

'We are. Your mother's putting on a bit of make-up and doin' 'er 'air. Fancies she might meet a rich bloke, no doubt.'

Stretching, Rosie asked Harriet what she was talking about. 'Nothing to do with me. Blame 'is lordship 'ere. I said you wouldn't wanna go out the

327

night before your own show, but no one listens to an old woman who knows her granddaughter better than anyone.'

Rosie looked from her to Richard. 'What's she talking about?'

'It's a surprise.' He held up a hand and showed her four tickets. 'Compliments of Aunt Belle. Get your skates on.'

'What for?'

'We're going to see *My Fair Lady*,' he said, hardly able to contain his excitement. 'It's a surprise.'

'Richard ... our show opens tomorrow. You don't really think we can go out on the town when I'm sick with worry? I've been awake for twenty-four hours. I spent the entire night rehearsing my solo scene. If I had the energy, I'd be dancing now as well.'

'It's why I asked for tickets for tonight's performance. To take your mind off *Lavender Lady*. We both need to distance ourselves from it ... if only for a few hours.'

'*Love in Lavender*,' she corrected. 'Remember?'

'How could I forget?' He had been arguing against it since she told him of the change.

'You just did.' She slumped her shoulders, yawned and uncurled her legs. 'I'm deadbeat, Richard. You go. Give Larry my ticket. Where is he, anyway?'

'Gone out ... again. I reckon he's got a fancy woman,' said Harriet.

'Splash some water on your face, Rosie, and put on your red dress. You'll feel like going then.' The plea in his voice got to her. Any other time and she would have jumped for joy at the chance of seeing this particular musical.

'Make us a cup of tea then . . . and I'll move myself.' She peered at her gran. 'You've 'ad your curlers in. You knew about this, didn't yer?'

'I did,' she said proudly. 'I've bin looking forward to it. So don't you go and put the damper on things.'

'How we gonna get there?'

'Taxi,' said Richard. 'We're doing this in style.'

'Right . . . I'll go up and get washed then.' She stood up and cupped Richard's face in her hands. 'Thanks, cousin . . . this is just what I need. I'll do a tap-dance in the foyer, shall I?'

'I . . . don't think so . . .'

'I'm kidding, Richard, I'm kidding.'

Laughing at him, she left the room, feeling suddenly awake and excited, all worries about the following evening were drifting away. Remembering what Caroline had said, *Loosen up a bit*, she rapped on the bathroom door. 'Got any scent, Mum? I've run out of mine.'

'You'll find a small bottle of Evening in Paris on my dressing table!'

'Oh . . . no, that's all right thanks. I'll splash on a drop of Gran's rose water instead. Don't be long in there!'

While Rosie rushed around upstairs, washing, dressing and arranging her hair, Richard kept Harriet company in the living room. 'I should have asked for five tickets . . .' he said, regretfully. 'I never thought—'

'George wouldn't 'ave wanted to go anyway. He's rehearsing with the band. I can't believe how seriously he's taking it. Calls himself the MD now . . . musical director,' she smiled. 'Who would have thought it?

'He's got a lovely voice, and that band is smashing,' Harriet went on. 'I thought I'd walked into the wrong theatre the other day when I went in to do a bit of hoovering. They were practising.' She smiled and shook her head. 'Sounded more like a polished performance to me.'

'I wasn't thinking of George,' said Richard, 'I was talking about Larry.'

'Whoops,' smiled Harriet, catching the look of remonstration on Richard's face. 'Beg your pardon.'

'Granted,' came the curt reply.

'Larry's wrapped up in his own business in any case. I shouldn't fret about 'im. Will there be any grub at this theatre? None of us 'ave 'ad our tea.'

'I think we should eat something after the show.'

'Me and Arthur always used to have a sausage in bread when we came out of the old music halls. Old man Wilkins used to be there with 'is brazier full of red-hot coals with a grid over the top. You can't get sausages like that nowadays. They were lovely. We was gonna 'ave sausages for tea, as it 'appens . . . Yeah, that's what I'll do! Soon as we get back I'll chuck 'em in the frying pan and we can have 'ot sausage sandwiches, with sauce.'

'Sounds wonderful.'

A glazed look in her eyes, Harriet shook her head slowly. 'I 'aven't been to a theatre in donkey's years. I don't s'pose it's changed much, eh?'

'No . . . I shouldn't think so. Although the West End is a little different from—'

'The penny gaffs me and Arthur used to go to?'

'Well . . . yes.'

'You can stop worrying. When we was eighteen or so we went to classier places—still in the East

330

End, it's true, but proper music halls—where we saw some very good acts, I might tell you.' She rubbed an eyebrow and grimaced. 'Bloody foundation cream of Iris's. I knew I shouldn't 'ave put it on. Bit of powder does me. Bit of powder and a spot of lipstick.'

'Well?' Looking glamorous, Rosie appeared in the doorway. 'Didn't take long, did it? Where's my cup of tea then?'

'Sorry . . . got carried away listening to Harriet,' said Richard as he went into the kitchen.

'What's wrong with you putting the kettle on, Iris?'

'You know he likes doing things . . . makes him feel like one of the family. So . . . it's a cup of tea and off we go?'

'Look at yer . . . anyone'd think you was goin' to a grand ball.'

'That's what it feels like. Just think, Gran—tomorrow night I'll be up there on stage in the Grand Star dancing to a packed theatre, fulfilling a dream . . . and our Tommy's spirit'll be there willing me on, proud as Punch. Proud of 'is little sister. Your little cockney granddaughter.'

'Head in the clouds again,' Harriet murmured, closing her eyes and ending it. There was a strange feeling in the old woman's stomach. A feeling that the evening was not going to go quite the way Rosie imagined. There was a touch of trouble in the air—she could sense it. 'Go and put some biscuits on a plate. We'd best get something inside us before we go.'

In a dream-world of her own Rosie murmured, 'Head in the clouds, feet on the ground . . .'

'You must 'ave a bloody long neck then,'

chuckled Harriet.

*   *   *

Arriving at the top of Drury Lane, the taxi driver pulled up and spoke through the partition. 'You can always tell when a show's a hit,' he said, 'look at the crowd. I would normally drive right up to the entrance . . .'

'This will be fine. Thank you.' Richard got out of the cab and paid the driver. 'We'll look out for you when we come out.'

The cabbie laughed sarcastically. 'You'll be lucky. It'll be like Piccadilly Circus shoved on one pavement. You'll 'ave to be out of there like a shot if you wanna grab a cab, sir.'

'Right,' said Richard, straightening his shoulders. 'Let's go into the foyer.'

Talking excitedly among themselves, the women followed him into the theatre. 'Wasn't that cabbie a nice man,' said Harriet, a little daunted by her surroundings and all the people milling around, dressed up to the nines and acting as if they were royalty.

'We'll go straight to the bar,' said Richard, preoccupied and looking, Rosie thought, a little nervous.

'I 'ope they serve stout in 'ere,' mumbled Harriet.

'They might well do . . .' smiled Richard, 'but tonight we'll be drinking something a little more special.'

'Oh yeah . . . ? Like what?'

'Champagne.'

'Are we now? Who's gonna cough up for that,

then?'

'My father.'

Harriet threw him a look of alarm. 'Is that meant to be a joke?'

He took her arm and coaxed her towards the bar. 'It's all right . . . I haven't broken my promise. The champagne's in honour of your granddaughter.' Turning to smile at Rosie, he saw that she had stopped in her tracks. Putting his mouth to her ear he whispered, 'He's just relieved that I'm not like Oscar Wilde.'

Rosie peered at him. 'Who?'

'I've never taken a girl home.' He shrugged. 'I haven't had what you would call . . . a steady. My father was beginning to get worried. If you could just pretend to like me . . .'

'I *do* like you, Richard; don't talk stupid. What you mean is that you want me to look as if I adore you . . . that we're . . . sweethearts?'

'It would help to keep him off my back. He does rather drone on a bit about a man being a man and all that.'

Chuckling quietly, it was Iris's turn to jest. 'And you think he's gonna be thrilled when he meets her family . . .' She nodded towards Harriet and waited for a retort from her mother, but there was none. 'What's up with you? You're quiet for a change, and . . .' Her words trailed off when she saw the look in her mother's eyes. 'You OK?'

'I want to go home,' murmured Harriet. 'Take me home.'

'Richard! Richard my boy! Over here!'

Clearly it was too late for a quick exit. Placing one arm around her mother's shoulder, Iris squeezed her. 'They're only people, Mum. Flesh and blood ... like us. Just mind your language though, eh?'

Harriet, turning pale and suddenly looking her age, was lost for words. Her eyes reflected the fear and misery of the past as memories came flooding back. 'They won't even recognize you,' said Iris, trying to reassure her, 'it was years ago.'

Nodding, unconvinced, Harriet put up a shaky hand. 'I'll be all right,' was all she could manage to say as Richard's father, mother and Aunt Isobelle eased their way through the packed bar towards them.

Shaking his father's hand, Richard smiled nervously and attempted to begin the introductions, but Harriet and Isobelle's eyes had met, instantly dissolving the welcoming smile. 'It's been a long time ...' Harriet said, her confidence returning when she saw the expression of disparagement on her old enemy's face.

Her eyes narrowing, Isobelle drew breath and instinctively stepped back as she turned on her nephew. 'If this is meant to be a joke, Richard, it is not amusing!'

'Ah ...' said Richard feebly, 'you've recognized your aunt Harriet.'

'*She* is no relative of mine!' Glaring at his red face she said, 'How dare you pull such a trick on your parents and me?'

'There was no trick intended, Aunt, I assure you. Harriet *is* a relative ... she was your late uncle's wife and her daughter Iris is your cousin,' answered Richard, defiantly.

Harriet could contain her anger no longer. She raised her voice in order to be heard above the loud conversations going on around her. 'Don't

334

take it to heart, Richard . . . it's obvious that your aunt Isobelle is in a state of shock. Her shabby behaviour will never change. She's as bad-mannered now as she was back then, when her mother was a high-class whore.'

Grasping Isobelle's arm to prevent her retreat, Iris stepped in to deliver a stream of home truths. 'You accused my parents of incest when they weren't related. I wonder where you got such a disgusting idea from?' She looked from Isobelle to Richard's father. 'Don't judge people by your own standards.' She tightened her grip and pushed her face close to Isobelle's. 'We've got papers to prove that your mother took my mother in when she was ten years old and living on the streets. *She* had compassion. We also have papers to prove that my father was your mother's only living relative, once they were orphaned. It's a pity that Mary didn't pass her good nature on to her children.'

Having said her piece, Iris tossed back her head and released Isobelle, allowing her to be led hastily away by Richard's distraught mother.

'Get these people out of here,' Richard's father spoke, in a low, angry voice, desperate not to attract any more attention.

'We've got tickets,' Rosie scowled, 'you can't have us thrown out.'

'Oh yes I can, my girl. Those tickets are complimentary.' He held out his hand to Richard. 'Give them to me.'

'Why are you doing this, Father? These people are relations, part of our family . . . our family history—'

'Sentimental rubbish! The tickets, please!'

Withdrawing the tickets from his inside pocket

335

Richard tore them in half, tossing them at his father's feet. Then, turning his back on him, he ushered the three women towards the exit.

With renewed composure, Harriet squeezed Richard's arm and signalled that she wanted a quiet word, allowing Rosie and Iris to walk ahead of them. 'You've made a mistake, son. This wasn't the way to go about it. Now listen and listen well. Don't go against your father. Let him think you've seen the light. Tell 'im you won't mix with our kind ever again. Then come and see us whenever you want, without 'im knowing. Whatever you do now will mark you for the rest of your life. Put your principles in your pocket. You made a mistake— now put it right.' She gave him a look to convey her message: if he did not do as she advised, he would not be welcome in their home again.

Gently pushing him in the direction of his father, Harriet was suddenly aware of the sea of faces in the bar, watching. 'The show you've just seen and the one you're about to see,' she said, turning her back on Richard, 'is nothing compared to the one that'll be opening tomorrow night at the old Star in Stratford, E15. I shouldn't miss it for anything!'

*   *   *

'I don't ever want to go through something like that again,' said Harriet as the three of them stood on the pavement once again. 'That young man has a lot to learn about tact and diplomacy. You wait till he turns up again—I'll annihilate!'

'Don't be too hard, Mum. He was only trying to bring his family together. What a bitch that woman is.'

Warmed by her daughter's continuing forthright manner and her loyalty, Harriet raised an eyebrow. 'She managed to get to you as well, then. Now you know. Can you imagine what it was like back then—me and your dad as youngsters, living with them two?'

'Don't give me all that, Gran . . .' said Rosie, looking out for a cab. 'You must have given as good as you got.'

'True,' she smiled at the memory. 'It was when me and your grandfather took to being sweethearts that the worms turned, but—' She stopped mid-sentence, narrowed her eyes and peered across the road. 'My eyes deceiving me, or what?' She nodded towards a tall, lean, bent figure handing out leaflets to people as they made their way to the theatre. 'Would you credit it?'

'That's Larry! What's he doing up here?'

'What do you think he's doing, Iris? He's drumming up business.' Laughing, she shook her head. 'What a lovely sight for sore eyes, eh? Come on . . . if he can do it, so can we.'

Catching sight of them as they approached him, Larry looked like a child who had been caught with his hand in the biscuit tin. 'Give us a bundle then,' said Harriet on arrival.

'Have you been following me around *all* day?'

'No, cock . . . we've just come out of there,' she nodded towards the theatre. She eyed the thin wedge of leaflets in his hand. 'Is that all you've got left?'

'Yes—thank God. I've got rid of hundreds. What's going on?'

'We'll tell you on the way 'ome,' said Rosie, taking his arm. 'I think you've done enough for one

337

day.'

As they rode back to Wapping, the women related the scenario with gusto, sometimes amused and sometimes indignant. 'Poor Richard ...' said Iris, 'I did feel sorry for him.'

'A bit of humility never hurt anyone. He'll learn from it,' said Larry, sitting back and appreciating the comfort of the taxi. 'Bang goes your chances of dancing in that particular show,' he murmured, preoccupied.

'So what?' said Rosie, stubbornly. 'I've got my own show now. Anyway ... I don't reckon Richard's aunt's as influential as he thinks. I bet she's just one of the hangers-on who like to pretend they're part of management.'

'You're wrong there. Madam is one of the investors. An *angel*. She has more influence, and power, to have blacked you than if she had been the director. Thank God *we* don't need people like her to finance us.'

Intrigued by his confident tone, Rosie peered into his face. 'I think you know something that I don't ...'

'That's right. And that's the way it will stay ... for the time being.'

'You've had good news?' She tried her best to contain her excitement.

'Mind your own business.' Enjoying his moment in the sun, Larry winked at her. Yes, he had had some good news, and it had not been from lack of effort on his part. He had finally managed to get the bank to see that there was great potential as far as the Grand Star was concerned, and they were looking into a proposal he had put forward that would give him part ownership.

338

'I wish you'd met that bloody woman, Larry . . .' said Harriet, miles away in a world of her own. Clearly, she had not got over the way they had been treated that evening. 'She's turned out exactly the way you'd expect. I wish I'd 'ave given 'er a few good hidings years back. Knock the snobbery out of 'er. Poor Mary . . . I bet she suffered as well once me and Arthur had gone. God knows how those brats treated her once they had gone from precocious little snots to grown adults. Poor cow.'

'Mary was a strong woman. She would have been able to handle them.'

'You knew her well, then, Larry?' asked Iris curiously.

'So so.' He was in a mischievous mood; he longed to reveal just how far he and Harriet went back and just what good friends he and Arthur, her father, had been. But to open his mouth now might anger the ever-tempestuous Rosie. If she discovered too soon that her old grandmother had been to see him at the Royal to ask a favour for her granddaughter, sparks might fly. He would save that for later—when the show was up and running and madam Rosie needed to be brought down a peg or two.

'Bangers and mash,' said Harriet, changing the subject. 'That's what we'll 'ave. With fried onions and processed peas.'

'Good. I'm bloody starving,' added Larry, closing his eyes to show that he was switching off. 'I think we should all have an early night tonight. Ready for the big day. I take it the sausages are beef?'

*   *   *

When the most important time of Rosie's life arrived, just two hours before the musical was to begin, she was in a fluster backstage, checking that everyone knew their cues, that Tilly and her assistant had the wardrobe organized and that all personal props were in their right boxes for when they were needed.

'Rosie . . .' Caroline lit a cigarette and blew the smoke over her shoulder. 'Don't get me wrong, but shouldn't you be out the front? There's bound to be people out there that know you. They'll be looking out for you. The crits even. You should be out there using your charm to put everyone in the right mood. The atmosphere the audience creates makes a big difference.'

'I can't do that. What if I'm needed?'

'What for? There are enough of us back here to cover for you . . . and I'm not being funny, but shouldn't you 'ave changed and put your make-up on by now?'

'What's the point of changing? I'll only 'ave to strip off again when I'm due on. It takes me a good fifteen minutes to get myself into that costume, you know it does.'

'Eight minutes . . . don't exaggerate. I timed you. And you could get it down to six minutes, no trouble.'

'Yeah . . . if you were there to help me.'

'I *will* be there. Now please . . . do us all a favour and go away. You shouldn't be backstage.' She drew on her cigarette. 'You're making everyone feel nervous.'

'Am I?'

'Yes.'

'Oh, right . . . I'll go upstairs then, and smarten

up . . .' She looked Caroline in the eye. 'You're sure about this? The cast won't think I've jumped ship?'

'To be honest, I think they'd rather you did. Your job's done. It's their turn now. You're making 'em feel as if you can't rely on 'em. Richard's great. He's calm and in control.'

Rosie put up her hands. 'Enough said. I'm going.' She turned away, relieved to be told that she had become a spare part backstage. 'I'll just check out front to see how many people—'

'No! Go upstairs and do something with yourself. Put some make-up on . . . brush your hair.'

'My sentiments entirely,' said Larry, arriving. 'Leave my job alone. I'm the sales manager, thank you. Go and make yourself look like a successful impresario. Then go and meet your public.'

Watching her stride off, Caroline said, 'I thought we'd never get rid of 'er.'

'She can be a pain at times . . .'

'What's it looking like out there, Larry?'

'There are a dozen or so in the bar, mostly friends . . . it's early yet. Like I've said before, most people don't turn up until the last minute.'

Closing her eyes, she slowly shook her head. 'I hope you're right, Larry. I hope you're right.'

*   *   *

Leaning against the closed door in Larry's room, doing his utmost to calm Rosie when he knew he should be in the pit with the band, George said, 'You look lovely, babe. Now stop admiring yourself and come and have a drink.'

'I'm not admiring myself. I just wanna know if

I'm overdressed! I'm not a famous actress, after all.'

'Just as well, 'cos you don't look like one. You look like a woman who's wearing a lovely pink frock and red shoes to show her guests that she thinks her musical is worth getting dressed up for.'

'That's not why I'm wearing it. Tommy treated me to this. He'd want me to wear it tonight.'

'Great. Best reason. Now . . .' He looked at his watch. 'There's just twenty minutes to go before curtain-up. Come and have a *drink*.'

'I can't. I'm terrified.' She held out her hands. 'Look . . . I can't stop trembling.'

George grabbed her arm and pulled her towards the door. 'Enough of this. You're coming down *now*!'

She jerked herself free. 'Just one more question and then I'll come.'

'Go on then,' he said, trying to be patient.

'Tell me the truth. Are there many down there?'

'Enough to fill half the seats. OK?'

'Half fill?'

'Yeah . . . almost. But that was ten minutes ago. They were pouring in when I left the bar to come up here.'

'I s'pose if we half fill it, that's not so bad.'

'It's a bloody miracle. Now come *on*!'

Half supporting, half dragging, he managed to get her as far as the foyer where they came face to face with Larry, who sported an expression of triumph. 'The coaches are arriving now.'

'Coaches?'

'That's right, Rosie, coaches.' He tapped the side of his nose. 'Publicans. They're the ones. It came to me a fortnight ago. I've done a deal with the busiest pubs in London. Where do you think I've been going every evening?' He chuckled in his usual fashion. 'I've been busy on the blower too. Long-distance. I knew there had to be a place somewhere that grew lavender in fields . . . and that it was somewhere in Norfolk.'

'I could 'ave told you that, Larry.'

'I like to find these things out for myself, thank you. Two coachloads of employees from the lavender growers and other local people are on their way.' He winked at Rosie. 'They have pubs up in Norfolk, too.'

The rising noise of people talking and laughing as they piled into the entrance commanded their attention. 'I can't believe it,' she said, choked and watery-eyed. 'Larry . . . I don't know what to say.'

'Go and get me a large whisky—that will do for now. You can pay my expenses later. I have them written down.'

She turned to George, her lips pressed together. 'Did you know about this?'

'No . . . but I'm really not that surprised. Larry's a dark horse. Now can we *please* go and get a drink?' He loosened his tie a fraction. 'I'm meant to be somewhere else.'

Preoccupied with her own worries, Rosie had stopped listening. 'It's curtain-up in about an hour.'

'I don't reckon your audience'll be that upset if we're a bit behind time. Everyone likes a drink before they go in.'

'My sentiments entirely,' said Larry. 'I'll go backstage and tell them they can have a thirty-minute reprieve should we need it.' His cheeks flushed, his brown eyes sparkled. 'I could get drunk on this kind of success . . .'

343

Seeing a familiar figure laughing and talking with other students from the Prospect of Whitby, Rosie was surprised to see that Bertie was there. So too were most of the other medical students. Gazing at him, she caught his eye. He shrugged and held up his hands, as if gesturing for a truce, and put up a thumb to wish her luck.

'You don't have to worry about him sabotaging the show,' George said. 'I wormed all I needed to know out of Richard.'

'You didn't—'

'I did. Without bruises. Words speak louder than fists sometimes. I bided my time and then went to have a little chat with 'im. He's all right. He stopped you from getting a hiding from the Maltese, so . . .' he shrugged ' . . . I let him off lightly.'

'What else has been going on behind my back?' Rosie was very pleased and relieved.

'Well . . .' smiled George, 'take a look over there. Richard's just rushed in.'

Moving her head to one side, Rosie could just see her cousin talking and smiling into the face of a very pretty student with long fair hair.

'He should be out the back!' As soon as her words were out, Richard was backing away from the girl, flushed and smiling, on his way backstage.

'Well?' said George, guiding Rosie through the packed foyer. 'Happy now?'

'I'm too scared to be happy.' She withdrew her hand from his and took a deep breath. 'What if I freeze when I'm up on that stage?'

'You won't freeze. Don't be silly.'

'George . . . I've never danced in front of an audience before. You lot, yeah . . . but . . . look

344

around you. This is the real thing. These people have bought tickets. They expect a first-class production.'

'Yeah . . . well? That's what we're gonna give them, isn't it?' A look of concern swept across his face. 'You're not telling me that the cast are not properly rehearsed?'

'*I'm* not properly rehearsed. And anyway . . . my solo scene . . .' she shrugged. 'I don't think we need it.'

'Rosie . . .' George lowered his voice and put his mouth to her ear. 'Go backstage. I'll bring you a drink through. Carry on like this and others'll pick up on it. This place'll empty in a flash if they think the show's gonna fall apart. No one likes to be embarrassed.' He looked her straight in the eye. 'I'm serious. Slip away now before anyone sees how nervous you are. Go and get changed into your costume and *think* yourself into the part you're gonna be playing.'

'I'm not playing a part. That's what I'm trying to tell you. We could cut my scene and it wouldn't spoil the show.' Her quivering voice added to George's determination to get her away from the buoyant crowd of theatre-goers. He took her firmly by the arm and, smiling, walked her out of the foyer.

'You should have stopped me when I first came up with this stupid idea! Why didn't you tell me not to do it?' Rosie was almost in tears as he dragged her through to backstage. 'I've never been on a stage in my life! It's all right for *you*. You're used to performing at weddings!'

'Come on, Rosie. You want to be up there and you know it. This is not the time to have a tantrum.'

345

Pulling her arm from his grip, she cursed him and her family for letting her be a lamb to the slaughter. As they drew close to the dressing rooms she could hear laughter and excitement coming from the cast. 'I'm not having a tantrum, George. I'm sick with nerves and my throat feels as if it's closing up.' She spun around and looked into his face, 'Be honest with me, babe . . . tell me the truth . . . *is* it a good show?'

'You know it's a winner, Rosie. Come on—be honest. Today's rehearsal was fabulous and you enjoyed every minute of it. Once you were up on that stage and the band was playing . . . you lit up. It was as if someone had switched on the Christmas tree lights in a dark room.' He stroked the side of her face, 'I was really proud of you, I didn't know you could dance like that, babe . . . straight up. I nearly cried . . . yeah . . . tough old George shedding a tear and the band saw and they didn't take the piss. You know why? Because they was just as choked as me.'

'All right,' Rosie murmured, dabbing her watery eyes, 'all right. I'll dance . . . but it'll be my first and last time up there. I'll get someone else to cover me tomorrow night.'

'I'm sure.' George couldn't help laughing at her. 'Go on. Go and get ready. And don't forget—I'll be in the pit . . . playing just for you. They're gonna love the show, Rosie. It's a winner.'

'Yeah . . . but only because of the company. They've pulled this off, not me.' She blew her nose, inhaled slowly and managed a smile. 'How's your singing voice?'

'Terrible.'

'Is that right? The band's expecting you to open

346

the show with my favourite song—"Heartbeat".'

'Are they now . . . I suppose I'll have to oblige then, won't I?' He grinned knowingly.

'You crafty sod—you knew all along!'

''Course I did. You think the band was gonna let me sing that number unrehearsed?'

He took her arm and squeezed it. 'Don't think we're not all as nervous as you, babe; this is our big night too. It's a big jump from playing at weddings to this.'

'You'll be terrific,' she said, her old confidence returning.

'Thanks, babe . . . that's just what I needed to hear.'

'I'll tell you what though, George,' she said as he backed away, 'never again. I'd rather deliver six babies than produce another show.'

'Till the next time,' he said light-heartedly, until the words sank in. '*Six babies?*'

'Yeah . . . didn't I tell you? I want a big family.'

'No, Rosie . . . you never mentioned that little detail. But then, nothing you decide would shock me. Nothing.'

Once she was inside the ladies' dressing room with the cast, Rosie immediately perked up. The fervour inside that room swept away her fears and brought a smile to her face. A genuine smile of happiness. All that she had ever dreamed of had become reality. Seeing everyone in their costumes was the best tonic she could have asked for.

'About time as well!' Caroline slipped Rosie's emerald green satin and net dress off a hanger and laid it across her arm. 'Move yourself then! Get this on. We've got a show to run.'

Laughing, Rosie asked if they had all been

347

drinking. 'You bet we 'ave. Champagne at that—courtesy of a bloke called Reggie. Get this gown on and we'll let you 'ave a glass. Two if you're—'

'They're coming in!' Vi, flushed and glassy-eyed, rushed into the room. 'Is everyone ready? Five minutes and you're on! Where's Sarah?'

'Behind yer! And my name's Polly.' The actress playing the lead role of Sarah was reclining on an old sofa with a glass of champagne in her hand. 'Mind you . . . I've never really liked Polly—'

'How much has she had to drink?' Vi looked far from pleased.

'Two glasses . . .' said Polly, smiling and shrugging. 'They said that was all I could have so I'm making it last.' She pointed a finger at Vi, 'I bet you've 'ad more than two?'

'*Where's Richard?*' Vi, it seemed, was the only one who was in a panic. Vi, the usually composed, unflappable stage manager, was in a spin. 'I've never known anything like it! The first night of a big show . . . nine minutes to curtain-up . . . and the bloody director's in the sodding bar!'

Slipping into her soft silky gown, Rosie felt like a queen and couldn't wait to get into her matching shoes. 'We've got a full house, Caroline,' she whispered, 'the bar was packed.'

'What did you expect?'

'I don't know. I was frightened to expect anything.'

Kneeling in front of Rosie, Caroline withdrew a green satin dance shoe from the white tissue paper inside the cardboard box and slipped it on to Rosie's stockinged foot. 'There we are—the slipper fits. She *shall* go on stage!'

The sound of the band warming up brought a

chorus of shrieks. 'Oh my *God*!' yelled Polly—'this is it girls! This is *it*!'

'Positions please! Glasses down! Fags out! Get in line and *no* talking or giggling!' Vi was back in control. Within seconds the actors who were in the opening scene were standing in line outside the dressing-room door, silent and ready,

No one said a word as Richard appeared and, in his usual fashion, raised one finger and then motioned for those playing the parts of the lavender pickers to enter the stage.

Hearing the applause from the audience, Rosie sipped from her glass of champagne and sighed with relief. It was the beginning, yet she felt as if it were the end of all her worries. The night had arrived and she couldn't wait to go on.

When the moment came and Rosie, alone on the stage, looked out towards the dimly lit auditorium, she felt fit to burst as she began to dance as if she were the only one in the building. Consumed by the music as the band played 'Fever', she whirled and spun as she danced around the stage with one thought going through her head—*I'm dancing, Tommy, I'm dancing.* Stretching herself to the limits she was almost disappointed when the music came to a close; she wanted to dance until midnight. Taking her bow, the thunderous applause from the uplifted audience sent waves of ecstasy through her entire being. Glancing and smiling at the band as they clapped enthusiastically, she winked at George and mouthed the words— 'love you'.

*   *   *

349

As the clock in the bar of the Star struck midnight, George popped the cork of a bottle of champagne, one of several courtesy of himself and Reggie. The reception from the critics had been ecstatic and everyone, Harriet included, was buzzing with excitement. Even Larry could not contain himself: his usual droll act was overcome with joy as he wove his way through the crowded bar, singing lines from 'Summertime Blues'—and getting them wrong.

Holding up his glass of champagne, George called for attention. 'No long-drawn-out speeches,' he said, his voice full of laughter. 'All I want to ask is that we raise our glasses to the girl who, with her unyielding enthusiasm, has given every one of us a night to remember!' A loud cheer went up. 'So I ask you, ladies and gentlemen, to remain upstanding as we drink a toast to the very successful and lovely . . . Rosie!'

'To Rosie!' The chorus of happy voices filled not only the bar but the entire theatre. This was followed by a very loud rendition from one and all of 'There's No Business Like Show Business'. Rosie was the only one not singing, but her tears were most definitely from joy and not sorrow. She had come a very long way, and weathered the storm. The end result was more rewarding than any of them could have imagined—even Rosie. Looking around the room at all the happy faces as they belted out the song, she murmured . . . 'I'm dancing, Tommy . . . I'm dancing.'

EVENING STAR
THEATRE REVIEW by William Drake.

Love in Lavender is a musical which has more content than its title would have us believe. Set in the late-forties during a hot summer, the lavender-pickers discover that there is more to the lord of the manor than they had realized! The author, Rosie Curtis, makes no speeches but raises issues through the skilful dramatization of events. Curtis's unsentimental musical is peppered with great songs from the hit parade, which give the show an original slant much needed in the theatre. Her choice of songs cannot be faulted. The amazingly talented Rosie Curtis surprises her audience when she unexpectedly performs a mesmerizing dance routine in a cameo scene. She is obviously a woman of many talents with a sparkling future.

LOVE IN LAVENDER

Showing for four weeks only
The Grand Star, Stratford, E15.
Running time: 1 hr 50 mins